Annie O'Neil spent most of her childhood with her leg draped over the family rocking chair and a book in her hand. Novels, baking, and writing too much teenage angst poetry ate up most of her youth. Now Annie splits her time between corralling her husband into helping her with their cows, baking, reading, barrel racing (not really!) and spending some very happy hours at her computer, writing.

Karin Baine lives in Northern Ireland with her husband, two sons and her out-of-control notebook collection. Her mother and her grandmother's vast collection of books inspired her love of reading and her dream of becoming a Mills & Boon author. Now she can tell people she has a *proper* job! You can follow Karin on Twitter, @karinbaine1, or visit her website for the latest news—karinbaine.com.

Also by Annie O'Neil

The Princess and the Paediatrician
Hawaiian Medic to Rescue His Heart
New Year Kiss with His Cinderella
In Bali with the Single Dad

Also by Karin Baine

The Surgeon and the Princess
The Nurse's Christmas Hero
Wed for Their One Night Baby
A GP to Steal His Heart

Discover more at millsandboon.co.uk.

CHRISTMAS WITH THE SINGLE DAD DOC

ANNIE O'NEIL

FESTIVE FLING TO FOREVER

KARIN BAINE

MILLS & BOON

First published in Great Britain 2022
by Mills & Boon, an imprint of HarperCollins*Publishers* Ltd,
1 London Bridge Street, London, SE1 9GF

www.harpercollins.co.uk

HarperCollins*Publishers*
1st Floor, Watermarque Building,
Ringsend Road, Dublin 4, Ireland

Special thanks and acknowledgement are given to Annie O'Neil for her contribution to the Carey Cove Midwives miniseries.

Special thanks and acknowledgement are given to Karin Baine for her contribution to the Carey Cove Midwives miniseries.

ISBN: 978-0-263-30140-3

10/22

This book is produced from independently certified FSC™ paper to ensure responsible forest management.
For more information visit www.harpercollins.co.uk/green.

Printed and Bound in Spain using 100% Renewable Electricity at CPI Black Print, Barcelona

CHRISTMAS WITH THE SINGLE DAD DOC

ANNIE O'NEIL

MILLS & BOON

To Nettybean, who has been with me
from the beginning…may it long continue!

CHAPTER ONE

'DASHING THROUGH THE...' Kiara stood back from the snowflake stencil she'd taped to the window, then gave the aerosol can a good spray. 'Snow!'

She carried on humming the Christmas song as she filled in the dozen or so other gaily shaped stencils, until her windows were transformed into magical snow crystal portals. Seeing actual drifts of snow outside her house would've made the effect even more enchanting, but the one thing Kiara wasn't in charge of in her new life here in Cornwall was the weather.

Unless...

She could dip into her Christmas Decorations Fund just a teensy bit more than she already had and buy some fake snow. Or— Ooh! A rush of excitement swept through her. A snow machine! After all, she quickly justified, any expenditure would be worth it, considering she was doing all of this mad over-the-top decorating for charity.

As a midwife, she knew just how important funding for specialised equipment was, and First Steps, her chosen charity, was renowned for helping families in need to furnish their homes with the specialised equipment they needed to give their newborn the very best chance to live a happy, healthy life. Ventilators, specialist cots, apnoea monitors… They all made the world of difference to an infant…just like being at home did.

As such, she pulled out her phone and on her increasingly long 'Christmas Decorations' list tapped in *snow machine.*

With a grin, she perched atop the armrest of her new sofa and admired her handiwork. Inside, it already looked like the day before Christmas. Stockings? Check! Chimney. Check! Tree, plate of biscuits, nativity scene, miniature glittery reindeer and unicorns? Check!

Sure, it was only the beginning of November. And, yes, she was aware of the handful of side-eyes she'd already received from some villagers, clearly wondering whether the new kid in town was a bit bonkers. She wasn't bonkers. Just new, and a bit lonely. And making the cottage feel all cosy and set for the festive season was her way of settling in. Especially as the view outside her window was no longer the familiar bustling London high street.

She twizzled round so she could look out of her new front window. Through the prisms of faux flakes she could see that outside the clear blue sky shone brightly over a crisp and increasingly autumnal Carey Cove. The leaves had turned and, courtesy of the warm afternoon sunshine, were glowing in multicoloured hues of red, orange and yellow as they floated down in colourful drifts. Not so much that the trees lay bare, but just enough to ensure there were always plenty of leaves for her to skip through if no one was around, as she went on her daily trip into the village to explore the smattering of shops along the solitary high street. Which was blissfully far away from London.

London.

The word hardened like a shard of ice in her chest. This would be the first year ever she would miss the Christmas lights being switched on. There would be no bustling into a pub after, to raise a glass of festive cheer with friends and family. No walking around the twinkling streets of London arm in arm with her boyfriend as all the shops decked their halls with boughs of—

Stop!

She didn't live there any more. Or have that life. She lived here, in the picture-postcard village of Carey Cove. A glorious seaside village that didn't have a patch on big, old, overcrowded London, where it was far too easy to fall in love with dazzlingly talented surgeons. Surgeons who, along with having piercing blue eyes and flax-coloured hair, were *liars, liars, pants on fire.*

As if sensing the vein of discord threatening to break into her happy but still fragile new existence, her phone rang with her mum's tell-tale ringtone: a Bollywood song her mother regularly sang in an off-key, happy voice similar to Kiara's.

'Hey, Mum. Perfect timing as ever.'

'Hello, darling…' Her mum's voice instantly thickened with concern. 'Everything all right? This isn't a bad time, is it?'

'No, not at all. I meant it's just nice to hear your voice.'

And it was. Even though she was twenty-eight, and had lived on her own for years now, she was an only child, and she and her parents were very close. Her mum had stuffed countless tissues into Kiara's hands over the past ten months. Nor had she been shy about voicing her concern when Kiara had announced that moving to a different hospital in London wasn't the solution to her post-breakup blues. But a new home was.

A new home in a new village in a new county. Far, far away from London. Even her father, a poster boy for Britain's renowned stiff upper lip, had expressed concern that moving a five-hour train ride away from her family in London might not be the wisest of decisions.

'Are you all right?' her mother asked, not even pausing for breath as she added, 'It's not too late to back out, you know.'

'What?' Even the idea of leaving made her blood run cold. 'No, Mum. Honestly. I love it here. Not to mention the fact I've already signed my contract for Carey House.'

Her eyes flicked up the hill and along the treetops where, courtesy of some bare branches, she could just make out the golden stone chimney tops of the transfigured cottage hospital that commanded an arresting view of the harbour village. This was a new thing for her. Working somewhere small enough to actually learn everyone's name.

After her life had imploded last year, Kiara had felt cornered into leaving the enormous inner-city hospital where she'd worked for five years. Shame and regret had been powerful motivators. Anger, too. She'd begun what had become a long string of short-term posts in maternity wards across London, hoping to find something—*somewhere*—that would make her feel as if she was starting her life afresh. A life reboot.

She'd finally found it. Here in Carey Cove. And that

was why she couldn't wait to start her new permanent midwife post at Carey House.

'I'm not backing out before I've even begun.' Kiara charged her voice with the confidence she knew her mum would be hoping to hear. 'The last thing Carey House needs is to be short-handed when all those Valentine's babies arrive.'

Her mother made a confused noise. 'I'm sorry, love. I'm not making the connection.'

Kiara grinned, perfectly able to envisage her mother's bewildered expression. 'C'mon, Mum. You know how to add. A night out on February the fourteenth with wine and flowers and romance leads to what to remember late in the month of November...?

'A baby!' Her mum laughed, but before it descended into silence she carefully began again. 'I just want to make sure you're feeling strong enough, after things with—'

Kiara cut in before her mum could bring up The Ex Who Should Not Be Named. 'All good! I love it here. And, hey...remember that charity thing I told you I set up with First Steps?'

'Oh, yes...?' Her mother said, her tone indicating that she clearly didn't remember.

Rather than mention her front garden, which was already bursting with Christmas decorations, Kiara proudly announced, 'I've got a window's worth of snowflakes.'

'Is it that cold down there?'

Kiara laughed and told her mother it wasn't. After they'd nattered a bit more, she hung up the phone, then tugged the ever-present scrunchie off her wrist and made her practised move of pulling her long hair into a swishy ebony ponytail.

She'd inherited her Indian-born, English-raised mother's jet-black hair and her British father's golden-brown eyes. Of course she missed her parents, especially near Christmas, but last year, having the carpet ripped out from underneath what she'd thought was her reality, had been quite the eye-opener. Making this change was the best thing she'd ever done.

She'd only been here in Carey Cove a fortnight, but it had been love at first scone. She looked down at her tummy and gave it a poke. Yup. Definitely a wee bit bigger than it had been. It was little wonder the Cornish were proud of their baked goods. She'd never enjoyed so many fluffy, jam-filled, clotted-cream-dolloped treats in her life. It was a good thing she was starting work tomorrow, otherwise she'd be looking a lot more like a roly-poly Mrs Claus than the too-thin version of herself who'd skulked out of London under the shadow of romantic humiliation.

She gave herself a short, sharp shake and made herself resume her off-key singing. Sure, she was single, eight weeks before her favourite time of year. And, no, it wasn't snowing…yet. But everything else in her life was firmly under her control.

As if to prove her point, she sprayed one more snowflake into place. A level of snowflake excess her ex would definitely have rolled his eyes about. So wasn't it lucky she didn't have a boyfriend to be judgemental over everything she did any more?

She put her things away and then, after tugging on her favourite bright red gilet, went out onto the small thatched-roofed porch at the front of the cottage. The estate agent had promised that in the spring it would be bedecked with graceful strands of wisteria blooms, but right now it was swathed in garlands of pine and fir and wrapped in whorls of red ribbon and fairy lights.

Unlike Carey House, which was built of large butter-coloured stones, her cottage had been painted white, with beautiful green window frames and, of course, the traditional thatched roof. It was almost impossible to believe that selling her small one-bedroomed flat in London, perched above a busy sandwich shop, had bought her this amazing picture-perfect cottage.

Memories of her ex's flat—the one she'd thought was his home—flashed through her mind's eye. Glass. Steel beams. A preponderance of grey. Barely a personal item in sight. It was so obvious to her now why she'd been buffeted with frequent refusals to let her soften the place up with some cushions and a bit of bric-a-brac.

Anyway…

That was then and *this* was the build-up to Christmas. Kiara-style.

She stepped out onto the pavement in front of the house, which stood at the end of a lane about two streets up from the harbour. One of the many things that had attracted her to both Carey Cove and Mistletoe Cottage was the fact that all the homes had a front garden. Perfect for her ever-increasing display of Christmas delights.

She scanned the decor outside her new home with an exacting gaze.

Cuckoo for Christmas…but classy?

She pulled a *Who are you kidding?* face at the nutcracker figure standing guard at her front door. Classy only because it was for charity. This was pure unabashed devotion to decorations.

So far, she had three fairy-lit deer grazing outside the small porch. She hadn't yet decided on which sleigh she wanted to harness them to…or if she wanted to get a Rudolph to attach to it. Her first instinct had been to put a sleigh on the lawn, but… One on the roof would totally be better. Maybe if she met someone at work who was taller than her—which wouldn't be hard—she could get them to help her.

Her current favourites of all the decorations were the three penguins she'd bought with her loyal customer discount at an online Christmas store. Should she get more? Or plump for the snowman who did a little jig when you pressed his button nose? Decisions, decisions!

Perhaps a little sing-song would help.

She patted the pockets of her gilet and tugged out the remote control. After a surreptitious look around—although heaven knew why she was being shy about it…she didn't exactly know anyone here—she pressed the power button.

Her insides went all tingly with childlike glee. Who didn't love a singing and dancing penguin? If there were any Scrooges around she was determined to win them over with her pure, unadulterated love of Christmas. Which reminded her… She had some huge fake candy canes she wanted to attach to the little white fence that ran along the front of her garden, leading people to the miniature Santa's Workshop donation box she'd affixed to her front gate. And those snowflake baubles. And the first of three living Christmas trees she wanted to decorate—all before she started work tomorrow.

She kept the penguins switched on while she ran into the house to get the other decorations. They would keep her company while she worked. Who knew? Tomorrow at work she might even start to make some friends who could actually talk back to her.

'Harry! Remember what I said about going too far ahead on your scooter.'

Lucas's daredevil three-year-old slowed down for about two seconds, and then…because little boys would be little boys…began to speed up again. Uphill.

Despite his concerns, Lucas laughed. He knew exactly what he'd fed his son for breakfast, and it certainly hadn't been rocket fuel. 'Harry! What's the name of the game?'

His son stopped abruptly and, with one foot on his scooter, one foot on the ground, turned round. His blond hair fell in soft curls beneath his bright red helmet. The same helmet Harry had spent the morning begging his father to refashion into a Santa's hat, even though they'd only just had Halloween.

His son's grey eyes, a reflection of his own, glittered with fun. Then he unleashed an arrestingly warm smile that could only have come from his mother, gave his father a stately salute, and pronounced, 'Safety first, Daddy.'

He smiled back, despite the sting of emotion tugging at the back of his throat as he remembered Lily's long list of things he wasn't to do once she was gone. No smothering. No over-coddling. No imposing his awareness of how fragile life could be on this little bundle of energy whose only perspective on life was that it was endless.

And, of course, the kicker: no more wearing his wedding ring after the first year.

He'd cheated. A bit. And by 'a bit' he meant an extra year and a half.

He'd taken it off when he'd been greasing up Lucas's scooter and seen that the ring was loose because he still hadn't got around to taking that Cooking Healthy Meals for your Child class the ladies at the Women's Institute kept tempting him with. The moment it had left his finger he'd realised it wasn't what connected him to his wife. His heart was. And that would be with him wherever he went, so the ring had finally gone into the keepsake box. The one his wife had started when they'd first met at uni. First cinema tickets. First airline tickets. And now first and very likely only wedding ring.

Lucas jogged up, his arms weighted with his son's all-weather coat, his backpack, his lunch, and pulled his little boy in for a hug. 'That's right, son. Safety first.'

He gave the top of Harry's helmet a loving pat and then, after giving him one more reminder about speed and distance, they set off again towards the nursery—which was, conveniently, only a hop, skip and a scooter ride from work.

Lucas stemmed another cautionary call when Harry added leaf-catching to his repertoire.

For the billionth time, man! Life isn't full of assurances. Plasters exist for a reason. Knee patches. Helmets. And doctors.

He, of all people should know that. Not just as a doctor, but as a husband. How could he forget the cancer he and his wife had convinced themselves would go into remission—

'Harry! Not too far.'

'I'm not too far, Daddy! I can still see the whiskers on your chinny-chin-chin!'

'Hey! I shaved this morning!'

Hadn't he? He put a hand up to double-check that he hadn't missed anywhere. *Struth...* He hadn't shaved. So much for being on the top of his game again. At least stubble was considered trendy. Not that his looks were a priority. His son was. Their routine. Getting their lives on a forward trajectory. And, of course, his job. The one thing besides his son that brought a smile to his face.

Since they'd relocated here to Carey Cove from Penzance, where there were far too many memories, he'd finally cracked getting their lives up and running. Morning story and cuddle in bed with his son. A shower for him while Harry played. Nursery 'uniform', such as it was, ready to be stepped into one leg at a time, then arms up overhead for the logoed sweatshirt, collar out. Hair semi-tamed into submission. Check. Check. Check.

Why had things gone wrong this morning?

Socks.

That was it.

They had a massive pile of socks and yet somehow, against the odds, there hadn't been a pair amongst them.

Note to self: buy more socks.

He had to laugh. So much for having their lives back on track. If something as simple as locating a pair of matching socks threw a spanner into their entire morning routine—

Be kind to yourself.

Another one of his wife's reminders. And, to be fair, he hadn't forgotten to shave in well over a year. Nor, as he'd done two and half years ago, had he completely given up, using what energy he had to try and soothe a crying baby whose mother would never hold him in her arms again.

'Daddy, look!' Harry pointed towards the end of the lane where…yes…there it was. Mistletoe Cottage.

And that was when the lightbulb went on. This house—a homage to Christmas—was yet another reason his so-called 'game' was off-track right now.

The cottage all but screamed a daily reminder of the countdown to Christmas, and it was a time of year he found impossible to enjoy. Not because it had been Lily's favourite, or because it had been when they'd lost her. No. She'd lost her life in the throes of the most beautiful spring either of them had ever witnessed. It was more that Christmas was about *family.* And the most important member of their family wasn't there any more. Never would be.

And even though he'd promised himself he would make this a Christmas to remember for Harry—who, to all intents and purposes, was finally old enough to truly understand and fall head over heels in love with Christmas—he simply couldn't light that same flame of enthusiasm burning inside Harry in himself.

Thank goodness there was someone else in the seaside village who was feeling it as much as Harry. Not that they'd seen the new owner of Mistletoe Cottage yet… The 'For Sale' sign had come down a few weeks back, but it had been two weeks ago when the decorations had begun appearing. First a little Santa's house. Then a few evergreen swags. Then wreaths and baubles and a preponderance of fairy lights. Every day there was something new. Including today when… Were those *dancing penguins*?

'Penguins!' Harry crowed.

Okay. Now there were penguins. What next? Waltzing polar bears?

If Lucas had thought Harry was hot-rodding before, he'd been wrong. One sighting of the bum-wiggling penguins and his son took off, one foot madly pressing the pavement behind him, as if his life depended on it.

Lucas quickened his pace, eyes trained on his son, until something in the corner of his eye caught his attention. A woman was coming out of the front door of Mistletoe Cottage holding a box of decorations in her arms. Petite. Dark-haired. He was too far away to make out anything else.

'Aah-ow!'

Lucas's blood instantly roared in his ears. One second with his eyes off Harry and, as he'd feared, boy and scooter had parted ways.

His speed-walk turned into a run. With the low hedge in the way, he'd lost sight of Harry. But he could see the woman's head snap back as she dropped her box of decorations on the porch and raced towards his son.

By the time he reached the cottage there were no yowls of pain. There were voices. The woman's and his son's. And then…there were *giggles*.

Harry was still on the ground, and although he'd definitely grazed his knee, he somehow seemed entirely unfazed by it. Normally there would be howling by now. But the woman crouching down, face hidden by a sheet of glossy black hair, was somehow engaged in a greeting ritual with his son.

'How do you do, Harry?' She shook his hand in a warm, but formal style. 'It's such a pleasure to meet someone who loves Christmas as much as I do.'

If she was expecting Lucas to join in the I Love Christmas Every Day of the Year Club she was obviously recruiting for, she had another think coming. It was only November. He had enough trouble mustering up excitement for the day of December the twenty-fifth.

Clearly unperturbed by his lack of response, she smiled at Harry and pointed at his grazed knee. 'Now… Important decision to make. Do you think you'd like a plaster with Santa on it? Or elves?'

'Elves!' Harry clapped his hands in delight.

The woman laughed and said she would run into the house and get some, as well as a cloth to clear away the small grass stains Lucas could see were colouring his son's little-boy knees.

Her voice had a mischievous twist to it, and underneath the bright, child-friendly exchange was a gentle kindness that softened his heart.

'I'm ever so sorry. Harry is just mad for—' Lucas began, but when she looked up and met his gaze anything else he'd planned on saying faded into nothing.

Though he knew beyond a shadow of a doubt that they'd never met, his body felt as if it had been jolted into a reality he'd always been waiting to step into. Every cell in his body was supercharged with a deep, visceral connection as their eyes caught and held. Hers were a warm brown…edging on a jewel-like amber.

Her skin was beautiful, with an almost pearlescent hue. Glowing… Cheeks pink. Lips a deep red, as if they'd just received a rush of emotion.

Perhaps it was the unexpected excitement of a three-year-old boy careering into her front garden. Perhaps it was the fresh autumnal weather. Or maybe…just maybe…she was feeling the same thing he was. A strange but electric feeling, surging through him in a way he'd never experienced before.

She blinked once. Then twice. Then, as if the moment had been entirely a fiction of his own creating, realigned her focus so that it was only on Harry. Pulling him up, dusting off some invisible specks of dust, she walked him over to the steps of her small, elaborately decorated porch and sat him down, asking if he could count how many seconds she'd be away while she ran into the house to get a plaster, and starting him off with a steady, 'One…two…three…'

She was back as Harry began to stumble over his elevens and twelves, and without so much as a glance at Lucas she turned her back and knelt down in front of his little boy. She began to clean his knee in preparation for the plaster.

Feeling weirdly blind-sided, Lucas made a lame attempt at conversation. 'Quite a display you've got here. I'm guessing you like Christmas?'

'It's for charity,' she said. 'First Steps. Do you know it?'

'I like Christmas,' Harry said.

Though Lucas couldn't see her smile, he could hear it in her voice as she answered his son. 'It's a pretty special time of year, isn't it?'

'It's when Santa comes!' Harry said.

'And who doesn't like Santa?' Lucas tacked on, feeling stupidly left out, but also completely out of his element. He wasn't into Christmas. Not at all. He wanted to make it fabulous for his boy, but…

He forced a limp smile onto his lips. The woman gave him a quick glance. It was dismissive, in the way someone might try to figure out where a fly was buzzing and then decide the fly wasn't worth her attention. Or maybe she'd seen right through him. Knew he was more *bah-humbug* than *ho-ho-ho.*

Either way, he'd definitely imagined whatever it was he thought had passed between them. It might have been electricity, but it certainly wasn't the type that led to candlelit dinners and—

Whoa!

He clearly hadn't screwed his head on straight this morning. His life was about his son and himself and making sure they were healthy and happy. End of story.

'Daddy?'

Lucas's son's expression was all the confirmation he needed that he'd definitely woken up on a side of the bed he'd never woken up on before. The cuckoo side.

'Right!' The woman stood up and briskly zipped her rather professional-looking first aid kit. 'That's you sorted, young man.'

'Say thank you to the nice…erm…' Lucas left a blank space, so that the woman could fill in her name, but no luck.

'Thank you!' Harry beamed up at her and received a warm smile and a miniature candy cane 'for later' in return.

'Have fun today,' she said, her eyes on Harry, and

then, without so much as a glance at Lucas, she disappeared into her house, leaving nothing but air and mystery between them.

CHAPTER TWO

AFTER APPLYING A couple of coats of 'first day at the new job' mascara to her lashes, Kiara tugged the maroon scrunchie off her wrist and swept her hair up into a high ponytail. Her hands went through the motions intuitively, but as she got to the part when she grabbed two fistfuls of hair to cinch the ponytail tight her brain immediately flashed back to yesterday morning, when that poor little boy had crash-landed in her garden.

Though everything had happened super-quickly, she had felt as though she'd crammed an entire new relationship—highs and lows and finished—all in a matter of seconds. Somehow, when she'd come out of the house with the decorations, her scrunchie had caught on a one of the pine branches, yanking her head back, pulling her hair out of her ponytail, before she'd lurched forward to help the boy—only to look up and see that the gorgeous little boy belonged to the hottest dad in the whole world.

Deliciously chestnut-coloured hair that, despite a clean, short cut, held hints of moving round his ears and collar in the same soft curls his little boy had if he were to let it grow. Amazing grey eyes. The perfect amount of tall. She was guessing he was spot-on six foot. Anything else would require her to have a step-stool for kissing him. There had been dark shadows under those dark-lashed eyes of his. Shadows that hinted at something that might be troubling him.

But he was a dad—meaning he very likely had a wife or partner somewhere. Which, of course, made him totally off-limits for ogling, wondering how tall she'd have to be to kiss him, or imagining him wearing absolutely nothing but a Santa hat and a sprig of coyly placed mistletoe.

She'd learnt that lesson the hard way. So she'd shut down faster than Santa could put someone on the naughty list for kicking a puppy.

You'd think after what she'd been through, she would have been able to put two and two together a lot more quickly than she had. Little boy plus father equals married man.

The fact that the man was seriously hot and had a haunted little-boy-lost lost look that made her want to make him warming winter stews set off alarm bells she couldn't ignore.

She knew exactly how things would pan out if she succumbed to one solitary, forlorn *woe is me* smile. Because she'd travelled down that path before.

I'm so lonely. All I do is pour myself into work, saving children with my incredible surgical skills, and there's no one there for me at the end of the day. Just an empty flat...with an empty bed...

Pfft. She gave herself an eye-roll, then forced herself to realign her focus on the fact that she'd both physically and emotionally moved on from the hurt and shame and, yes, the heartbreak she'd endured, and that today was the first day of the rest of her new professional life. And no matter what, it was going to be a good one.

A walk up the hill in the crisp autumn air was all Kiara needed to get those endorphins flowing again. The leaves were colourful heralds of a happy, shiny, fresh start. And why shouldn't they be? She was heading to her new job in a new village in a new nook of England, and one solitary spotting of a gorgeous dad whose adorable son clearly loved Christmas as much as she did wasn't going to throw her off her stride. No way!

When she finally reached the top of the gravelled front drive, and could soak in the full glory of her new workplace, her heart did a little jig right there in her ribcage.

Carey House could not have been a more perfect place to start her life over. There was a small general practice there, but the bulk of the hospital's business was delivering happy, healthy babies.

Helping women bring babies into the world in a cottage hospital overlooking the sea, with a gorgeous, picture-postcard village below…

Perfection.

All but skipping up to the front door, she was virtually bursting at the seams with excitement to get started.

Cheerfully wondering when—or if—the powers-that-be at Carey House would decorate the place for Christmas, she pulled open the door and saw Hazel, the warm-hearted receptionist, chatting to someone tucked just out of her line of vision in the GP's waiting room.

At the sound of the door opening Hazel turned and smiled. 'You'll be needing Nya. Hang on a minute, love, I'll fetch her for you.' She gave Kiara a wiggly-fingered wave, then held a solitary finger up to indicate she'd be over in just a moment.

Kiara grinned. She'd met Hazel Collins when she'd come down for her interview, and she was every bit as warm and welcoming as Kiara remembered. The sixty-something woman could have been a stunt double for Mrs Claus any day of the week. She had a beautiful billow of white hair, done up in thick plaits and pinned atop her head, pink cheeks, and a smile that would warm the coldest of hearts.

Hazel claimed she had worked in the building since it had been built. This, of course, was patently untrue. What might be true was the fact that her ancestors had worked here. Formerly a large family home, Carey House had been put together, stone by beautiful stone, at least two hundred years ago…if not more. It had been converted into a cottage hospital in 1900, to help improve maternity services in the area.

At that time, pregnant women who lived here, or in the more remote islands off the Cornish coast, had often struggled to find quality medical care. These days they had St Isolde's Hospital over in Falmouth to take on any high-risk pregnancies or oversee unexpected complications, but with Head Midwife Nya Ademi in charge here at Carey Cove, suffice it to say, they delivered a lot of babies there. The vast picture wall of beautiful little faces was testament to that.

Kiara allowed herself to get lost in the myriad of tiny little button noses and tightly clenched eyes and teensy fingers clutching pastel-coloured swaddling until she heard Hazel approach.

'Gorgeous, aren't they?' said Kiara.

'They certainly are,' said a very male voice. One that spilled down her spine like warm caramel. One that certainly wasn't Hazel's.

Kiara whipped round and found herself nose to chest with Extremely Hot Dad.

A short, sharp intake of breath only made it worse. He smelled *delicious*. Like molten butter on a loaf of bread fresh out of the oven. Fresh air and—*mmm*—nutmeg.

Sweet mother of God. The man smelled like French toast in the Alps.

Her knees threatened to buckle. Her tongue turned leaden. Which was probably just as well, because the first words that popped into her head were highly inappropriate: *I'd like to climb you like a tree.*

Whatever that meant.

As it dawned on her that she was leaning in to inhale more of him she jerked back, her heart somersaulting and then lurching up into her throat. Because looking up into his face from this proximity was even better than smelling him.

He was clean-shaven today. She wasn't even sure she'd realised he'd been all rough chestnut stubble yesterday until now, when he wasn't. Would it feel good to run her fingertips along the softness of that stubble? Or would it be abrasive?

Come to think of it, how had this stranger managed to imprint himself so thoroughly on her subconscious that she was desperately trying to memorise even more of him now?

She made the mistake of looking up.

His eyes were a mesmeric grey. Like multilayered storm clouds. Each tiny sector was a different shade, demanding and receiving her full attention. Dark lashes gave them added punch. If he had been evil they would've been like little Venus flytraps, waiting to snap and snare her into his power. But something told her he wasn't evil. The tumult she saw in his eyes wasn't of his own making…it was life. And that was something she could definitely relate to.

Her gaze slipped away from his eyes, down along his nose, and landed soundly on his mouth. One of his front teeth was caught on his bottom lip—as if he, too, was struggling to figure out how to make his brain and body work together again.

Where her heart had once been, a glitter bomb had detonated. One filled with gold and starlight and warm bursts of response in her erogenous zones. Which instantly filled her with horror.

She had made a solemn promise to herself that there would be no glitter bombs detonating anywhere near her for at least a year—and *definitely* not for an insanely attractive man who was already taken.

A burning hot rage replaced the glitter bomb. This was *her* place. *Her* new sanctuary. *Her* new job. *Her* new colleagues, populating *her* new world, and despite all the precautions she'd taken to stitch her heart back together, after such an ignominious and insulting end to the love affair she had thought was real, she was keenly aware of how loose that stitching had been.

A physical ache clawed at her chest as she stepped away from him and demanded, 'What are *you* doing here?'

Lucas almost laughed. Not because Miss Mistletoe's face was full of delight or warmth or joy. More because he'd never met someone so free with their distaste of him. He couldn't exactly say he liked it, but…

Her nose crinkled in frustration as she waited for him to answer.

Crikey.

He rubbed at his jaw, perplexed to find himself in such a peculiar scenario.

He'd never seen anyone so openly repulsed at the sight of him before. And on two separate occasions. Perhaps he had a doppelgänger out there? Someone who'd caused this poor woman pain? He hoped not, for her sake, but he did kind of hope it was true for *his* sake. Because… Dammit, he didn't know why. But he wanted to get to know this woman. And the reasons were slightly too potent to explain. Particularly in this scenario.

If he were to tell her he'd had one of the most erotic dreams of his entire life last night—starring her—he imagined he would win himself a slap on the face. Deservedly so. He didn't even know her name, let alone just how soft the curves of her breasts were, or whether or not she would groan his name when he licked them and then drew her nipples into his mouth as his hands teased and…

'I'm sorry,' he began. 'I think you might be mistaking me for someone—'

'No. There's no mistake. You're you. I mean—'

She pulled her hair out of her ponytail and then swiftly re-did it, splitting her dark hair into two thick shanks and tugging it tightly into place, so that it swung from shoulder to shoulder after she'd freed it from her grasp.

His awareness of her hair, how it would feel if he

ran his hands through it, was so visceral he could almost have sworn he'd done it before. Surely he must be imagining it?

His body was telling him otherwise. His fingers were twitching, as if they hungered to touch. He almost physically felt the silky strands sweep against his skin, even though she was nowhere near him. It was like a memory freshly resurfacing after having long been buried. He closed his eyes and an image passed behind his lids that should have made him blush.

She'd found her voice again, and in a crisp, clear tone he imagined would be fitting for a Victorian schoolmarm, chastising a naughty young boy who'd been pulling faces, asked, 'I meant who are you and why are you at Carey House?'

Her eyes flicked away from his before he could answer. He pounced on the free moment to scan her features—an unguarded instant to try and find something, *anything*, to divine where this open hostility had come from. But before he could find much they were back on him like golden-brown searchlights.

Even so, she had looked away long enough for him to see that her charged tone was actually fuelled by insecurity. And…worse…by fear. It made his heart clench tight for her. Never, ever would he want anyone to be frightened of him. Had it been Harry's crash? Had she— His breath caught in his throat. He hoped to God she hadn't lost a child. Losing his wife had been like being eviscerated, but losing his son… He couldn't even begin to imagine the horror.

'I'm sorry.' He held out his hand. 'I'm Lucas Wilde. The GP here at Carey House.' He pointed towards the room Hazel was just coming out of, her hands full with two plates of biscuits. 'That's the surgery in there.'

She stood there and blinked uncomprehendingly at him, as if his offering a hand to shake was the most peculiar thing she'd ever seen. What was he meant to have done? Gone in for a cheek-kiss?

'Ah! Kiara!' Hazel cut in. 'I see you've met our Dr Wilde.'

'Er…' Kiara managed.

'Oh, deary me, Dr Wilde,' Hazel chastised him warmly. 'Did you not introduce yourself to our newest midwife? This is Kiara Baxter. Kiara—this is Dr Wilde. He's our main GP here at Carey Cove.'

She carried on talking about locums, visiting GPs and the specialist doctors who sometimes came in from St Isolde's, but it all became a low buzz to Lucas, who was still trying to separate his wickedly sensual dream about a version of this woman—Kiara—from the woman who was staring at him as if she were a bull preparing to charge.

'I've just put a fresh plate of biscuits in your surgery…' He heard Hazel's voice come back into focus. 'Kiara, you're welcome to grab one from there if you like or—' She stopped herself. 'Better yet, why don't you take this plate? You're going up to the lounge, are you not? Where the lockers are? That's where you store your handbag and personal items.'

Kiara's eyes darted between the two of them as if she was trying to figure out whether or not this was some sort of joke, but then, looking down at her hands, she moved forward to accept a plate of what Lucas knew to be Hazel's secret recipe ginger biscuits.

'You'll definitely love getting your teeth into one

of those,' he said, giving the side of his nose a tap and unleashing a cheesy grin.

Now Hazel was looking at him as if he had sprouted antlers as well. If he could, he'd roll his eyes. Going back to sleep and starting this day over again would be an ideal option if only the idea of going to sleep and having another one of *those* dreams was something he had any sort of control over.

They all stopped short when a cry came from just outside the building. Plates of biscuits were quickly deposited on the reception desk, and the sound of running footsteps began echoing through the corridor as Kiara raced out through the front door with Lucas quick on her heels.

A woman was virtually doubled over on the driveway, with her arms wrapped round her large, very pregnant belly.

This wasn't an infrequent occurrence on the drive of Carey House. Often Lucas found there was an ashen-faced father racing up holding a jumble of the expectant mother's handbag and overnight bag and anything else she'd demanded he bring. The staff here encouraged all expectant women to make the birth experience as personalised as they wanted. Down in his surgery he sometimes heard drifts of music coming from what he privately called 'the contractions playlists'.

Kiara had reached the woman and helped ease her back up to stand, but their conversation was too low and too far away for him to grasp.

Wait a minute.

Though he couldn't see her face, Lucas recognised the petite figure. Her stylishly cut blonde bob was masking her features, but he was sure of it now.

The woman clearly in the throes of a contraction was Marnie Richards, one of the hospital's own midwives. Lucas ran across to join them.

'Hello, love. I'm a midwife here. My name's Kiara. I'm guessing you're in labour?'

'Good guess!'

Kiara laughed good-naturedly. She'd clearly been through a fair few of these tightrope walks before, Lucas thought. The kind where the expectant mother was thrilled to be having a baby but experiencing feelings she'd never had before, so was lacking her usual charm and warmth—characteristics Lucas knew Marnie had in spades, despite her reputation as the hospital's most fastidious midwife.

'I've texted Nya—she's my midwife. Hopefully she'll figure out that I haven't quite made it indoors yet.'

'I can run in and fetch her if you like,' Lucas volunteered. 'I'm sure Kiara here would be more than happy to— Oh! Oh, dear… Another contraction?'

As Marnie let out a growl of pain Lucas took one of her hands in his and made swift introductions. And as Kiara coached her through her breathing techniques, he gave Marnie an impressed smile.

'You've got quite a grip, Marnie. I'll be picking you to be on my tug-of-war team at next year's summer party.'

Marnie laughed and said, 'Just you wait until the contractions start—oh! Coming—oof! Faster!'

'I think we might've hit that moment.' Lucas threw Kiara a pained look he hoped she'd know was for comedic effect.

She gave him a shy smile, cheeks lightly pinkened, then looked away.

As he and Kiara gently escorted Marnie, step by careful step, towards the door, Marnie huffed out her answers to Kiara's questions in short, sharp, staccatos.

Lucas caught, 'Waters broken…' 'Contractions…' and something along the lines of 'Time for this baby to enter the world now'. But perhaps not put quite as politely.

'Marnie!'

Lucas looked up to see where the new voice had come from.

Nya Ademi, the head midwife, was rushing out through the door towards them. With an apologetic smile, she nudged Lucas out of the way. 'I'm pretty sure you've got patients waiting, Dr Wilde?'

Lucas knew it wasn't a chastisement. It was Nya doing what she did best—exemplifying the Six Cs the staff at Carey House embodied. Compassion, care, competence, communication, courage and commitment.

She gave Marnie's arm a squeeze and took over the hand-holding without so much as a wince. Nya's hands must be made of steel. 'Hello, love. We didn't expect you so soon. Why didn't you ring? We don't want you having the baby out here on the drive, now, do we?'

'Ow!' howled Marnie, stopping in her tracks, trying and failing to breathe through a fresh contraction. When it had passed she gave Nya a look already tinged with fatigue. 'To be honest with you, I don't care where I have it. If I was up a tree right now, I'd have it there!'

Kiara's eyes flicked to Lucas. He shot her a questioning look. Her cheeks flushed with streaks of red. She swiftly returned her attention to Marnie.

What was that about?

A mad thought occurred to Lucas. Had she had a naughty dream about *him*? Now, that would be an interesting turn of events…

Surprise darts of heat arrowed below his belt line. The idea that she had spent some of her nocturnal hours dreaming of being tangled up in the sheets with him held appeal. Too much appeal.

He forced his concerned doctor face back into place and, spying a duffel bag a few metres back, jogged to get it.

'Up a tree? You don't want to copy that nursery rhyme, do you?' Kiara lightly teased Marnie. 'Someone's already rocked their baby on a treetop and it didn't end well. I think the Carey House birthing centre is a far more comfortable option.' Kiara counted through the breaths with her until Marnie's contraction had finished, then pointed towards the building, now only a handful of metres away. 'Let's get you inside, where we can get some monitors on you and the baby out.'

'Dr Wilde?' Hazel called from the front door. 'I'm ever so sorry, but your nine o'clock appointment is here and looking a bit anxious.'

'Be right there, Hazel. Just ensuring our number one pregnant midwife is all tickety-boo.'

'I'm perfectly all right, Lucas. Go in and see your— Sweet crumbs and empty biscuit tins!' wailed Marnie. 'No one said it would hurt like *this*!'

Kiara laughed again—a warm, inclusive laugh that

said, *I hear you.* Lucas liked it. He was beginning to like a lot of things about this woman.

He opened the front door, placed Marnie's bag inside, then called to a colleague to find a wheelchair, half listening while Kiara gave Marnie some more cues on her breathing as another contraction struck when they were only a few footsteps away from the entrance.

While Marnie trained her focus on blowing slow, steadying breaths, Kiara playfully lectured her. 'As you're a midwife yourself, I'm pretty sure somewhere along the line you were warned about the pain. In fact...' she flashed Marnie a cheeky grin '...I would lay money on the fact you were.'

Kiara looked up again as Lucas ushered them in, and, for an instant he was caught in the flare of one of those genuine smiles of hers. It felt like being bathed in sunlight. Then, as if it had been an accident, and her brain had suddenly told her who she was smiling at, her attention was quickly rediverted to Marnie. Which, he sternly reminded himself, was where it belonged.

A volley of questions ensued.

How long had Marnie been having contractions?

How many minutes in between the contractions?

Was there anyone they should ring?

'Just get me inside! I don't want to miss the window for getting an epidural.'

Kiara shot a look at Nya, who had run inside to steer the wheelchair to the door, and then to Lucas. The look spoke volumes. The window for that kind of painkiller had opened and shut a while ago.

Again, his eyes caught hers, and this time something entirely different passed between them. Trust. A shared understanding that what was happening was well within Kiara's toolbox. Not that he'd doubted it, of course—Carey House only hired the best. But in his experience everyone began their first day at work in a new hospital in a completely personalised way. Some people—like Kiara—were clearly the 'in at the deep end' type. Others liked to observe. Some insisted on leading, to prove right off the bat that they knew their stuff. He liked where Kiara sat on the spectrum. She was comfortable with her skills and neither needed to showboat nor defer to anyone.

'Dr Wilde?' Hazel called him again, this time tapping her watch.

He ducked his head so that Marnie could see him. 'Are you three going to survive without my alpha male cheerleading?'

Marnie huffed out a laugh. 'I don't know. If it comes without painkillers maybe not!'

CHAPTER THREE

KIARA LAUGHED AS Lucas accepted Marnie's insistence that she was fine, and that he really should go and tend to his own patients now.

As schoolgirlish as she knew it was, she had to look back as he disappeared into the GP surgery. And, to her surprise, she was rewarded with another one of those soft smiles of his as he glanced back too. The kind of smile that ribboned round her heart and freed a chorus of invisible birds, singing as if it were the first day of spring and not the beginning of November.

Sweet crumbs and empty biscuit tins, indeed!

It wasn't a saying she'd heard before—and maybe Marnie had made it up, to prevent herself from swearing too much, as many mothers in labour did—but it actually suited what she was feeling. The two encounters she'd had with Lucas—her new colleague, no less—had been like delicious crumbs, strewn on a path that only led to danger. For her anyway.

Yes, he was gorgeous. And, yes, it was a bonus that he worked in the health profession—she'd learned early on in her dating 'career' that not many people understood the strange demands of a midwife's role. It wasn't as if babies worked to a schedule when they decided to appear. But those alarm bells had rung for a reason when their paths had all but literally collided yesterday. Lucas Wilde was a father. And where there were fathers there were usually mothers. And mothers very rightly didn't like it when their husbands wove them a tale of deception in order to woo a twenty-something midwife who thought she might be starting a family of her own one day…

Nya's steady voice pulled her attention back to where it needed to be. On Marnie.

'That's right, love. Let's get you in here and pull off some of these layers before— Oh! Easy, there, darling… Kiara, do you think you could help Marnie get her things off while I run and let the desk know we're here and ready for action?'

'Absolutely,' Kiara said, guiding Marnie over to the bed. 'Why don't we get your coat off? Then you can have a seat and I'll help you with everything else.'

'None of it's gone according to plan!' Marnie panted. 'I have lists. I have charts. I do this for a *living*! I thought I was the one in control.'

We all think we're the one in control.

Kiara stemmed the quip. It wasn't what Marnie needed or wanted to hear. It also referred to a dark mark on her own past that she wanted to leave behind. Which was exactly why she needed to remember to give Lucas the cold shoulder whenever their paths crossed again. But smiling at him was so easy! She hadn't noticed yesterday that there was a twinkle in his eyes when he tried to be funny. How he could make dad jokes sexy was beyond her. Dad jokes should never be sexy. Especially to her.

She knelt down and got to work on Marnie's winter footwear. 'That's right…just sit back against that big, snowy mound of pillows while I get these boots off for you.'

'Sorry about all the laces,' Marnie apologised. 'Again—not part of the plan.'

Kiara smiled up at her before putting both the boots in a small cupboard ready for the expectant mother's personal items. 'It'd be great if babies listened when we told them the plan, wouldn't it?'

Marnie laughed appreciatively. She gave her belly an affectionate rub. 'I was out for a walk. I thought it'd be good for the baby and my swollen ankles if I had some gentle exercise. I had my first contraction when I was out on the beach, but I thought it was a Braxton Hicks so decided to ignore it. If I'd known it was the real thing I would've worn some slip-ons.'

Marnie gave a self-deprecating chuckle, then sighed.

'Heaven knows why I thought I'd be the one in charge of all this.' She pointed at her stomach, and for just a moment her smile shadowed as she said, 'I guess it's because I'm the one who organised this whole scenario. Her,' she corrected herself, her smile warming again. 'She's not a scenario. She's a her.'

'Oh?' Kiara said, keeping her tone light, but neutral.

She'd learnt hundreds of babies ago that it was always best to leave the baby's origin story to the mum to tell. Not every family came pre-packaged with a fairy tale romance, a diamond ring and a baby nine months after the honeymoon.

Another contraction hit before Marnie could explain, but once it had passed, and Kiara had got Marnie out of her clothes and into one of the soft hospital gowns, she glanced at the empty chair usually occupied by the birth partner and thought it was safe to ask, 'You didn't say before, but is there anyone you'd like me to ring?'

Marnie's cheeks coloured. 'No,' she answered curtly, and then, her forehead creasing apologetically, added, 'Sorry. Sorry… I'm pregnant on my own through IVF treatment—which most people already know. I haven't had to explain how I got to look like a beached whale without having a boyfriend in a while.'

'You just let me know what I can do to help, okay?'

Kiara meant it, too. Having a baby was a big step. Having it on your own was even bigger. It took courage to do what Marnie was doing and she definitely wasn't judging. Everyone's path was of their own making, and Marnie's voice was rock-solid. She wanted a baby and now she was having one. Exactly the same way Kiara wanted to celebrate this Christmas with complete and utter abandon.

Okay, fine… It was a little bit different. But the endgame was the same. She and Marnie were living their lives by their own rulebooks. And she respected that.

Kiara silently began hooking Marnie up to the relevant monitors, making it clear that it was up to Marnie how much she did or didn't say.

'Do you mind if I take a little look,' she asked eventually. 'See how far along you are?'

'Please,' Marnie said. 'I'd do it myself, but…' she pointed at her large belly '…this is in the way.'

Kiara glanced at the door, certain that Nya would be reappearing any minute. 'I know you work here, but I think that if there was a day of all days when Nya would be happy for you to sit back and let someone else do the work, today would definitely be the day.'

The women shared a warm smile. And Kiara thought she'd look forward to working with Marnie when her maternity leave was finished.

'Nya's probably got stuck at the desk answering four million questions. If you want to take over for her, please feel free.'

'Are you sure? If she's your midwife—'

Marnie gave a combination of a laugh and a moan. 'When you work as a midwife *everyone's* your midwife.' Her smile softened. 'Nya has been the one to do all the exams, but it's shift-change time, so honestly… Oh!' Her hands flew to her belly. 'You can go ahead. Please.'

'Right you are, then. But if you want me to step aside for Nya, just say.'

Kiara gloved up, put some gel on her hand and pulled a stool over so she could do a quick examination.

Rather than flinch, as many patients did at the first touch, Marnie suddenly beamed a big, huge, beautiful smile. 'I'm going to be the mother of a little baby girl!'

'You are!' Kiara beamed back. 'And…' she finished her examination '…by the looks of things, you'll be holding her in your arms and picking out the perfect name any minute now.'

'Sorry…sorry!' Nya appeared at the door, her smile mischievous as she briskly walked to the wall-mounted glove dispenser. 'A woman having twins cornered me on the way here, but I knew I'd left you in capable hands.' She gave Marnie a discerning look. 'You're choosing names already, are you?'

Marnie nodded and then, as a contraction hit again, somehow managed to get out, 'I know—I haven't—

physically experienced—this—before—but I'm pretty sure—'

'You're crowning!' Nya and Kiara chorused in tandem.

At Marnie's request, Nya took on the hand-holding role. Then, after two, possibly three minutes of encouragement, some deep guttural cries and some concentrated pushing later, Kiara was holding Marnie's baby girl in her arms.

'She's a beauty!' Kiara held her up so Marnie could see, and as if on cue the little girl uttered a loud cry, announcing her arrival in the world.

They all laughed and, exhausted, Marnie fell back against her pillows.

Nya and Kiara cleaned and dried the baby, then placed her in Marnie's outstretched arms so that they could share that all-important skin-to-skin contact both mother and baby craved organically.

Kiara was relieved at how easy it had been to fall into a rhythm with Nya who, despite being her boss, was treating her as an equal, only taking the lead when it came to finding things—which, to be fair, was something Kiara did need guidance with.

'Nothing like starting your first day with a baby born in the first ten minutes,' she said, and grinned.

Nya shared a complicit smile with her. 'It's the best way to start a new post, isn't it? One perfect baby on a beautiful day.'

Nya prepared a Vitamin K injection and Marnie reluctantly handed her little girl over to Kiara for weighing and measuring. They dealt swiftly with the umbilical cord and the placenta, offering Marnie a local anaesthetic for the inevitable pain she felt, and finally moved the new mother and her freshly swaddled daughter to a bright, clean bed.

'I can see why new mums sometimes get teary at this part,' Marnie said, blinking back her own tears.

Kiara gave her a warm smile. 'There are a billion hormones running rampant in your body right now,' she told her. And she was also alone. There was no one special to share this life-changing moment with.

She pictured this moment for herself. Her brain summoned the images and she was shocked to see that Lucas was the one standing in the room next to her—not her ex, Peter. It wasn't so much a clear image of Lucas as a doting father, but more his presence she imagined. That calm, warm, humour-filled aura that had surrounded him from the moment they'd discovered Marnie on the driveway.

'I know…' Marnie sniffed, already holding out her arms for her baby again. 'I've known all that professionally for years, but now I feel like I truly *know* it. In here.' She tapped her heart. 'I don't know how she's done it, but this little girl has made me complete. I feel like I've just become the person I was always meant to be.'

Kiara smiled, but said nothing, knowing that her voice would squeak up into the higher registers if she did. She knew the feeling of knowing there was something missing in her life…not yet having it. She also knew that the sense of wholeness had to come from within. That more than likely whatever had led Marnie to go through IVF and have this baby alone had been a step in the process of recognising and owning the type of woman she wanted to be.

Kiara wanted to be a woman who could trust and

love a man again. She wasn't going to tar all men with the same brush her ex had been lavished with, but…

Again, an image of Lucas flashed up in her mind's eye.

She tried to bat it away but it wouldn't go.

This was insane. She'd barely met the man. And yet just a few moments in his presence and she'd known instinctively that he was someone she could rely on. Professionally. Obviously. Just because looking at him set butterflies loose in her tummy, it didn't mean she couldn't take a step back and acknowledge that, at her place of work, he was a good man to know.

The thought snagged.

Having a doctor's respect meant a lot to her. Perhaps that was why she'd been so smitten by her surgeon boyfriend. A surgeon dating a midwife… It was so clichéd. But that first time Peter had asked her opinion about something and nodded along, as if she'd just offered him the most valuable insight ever, had thrilled her. The 'respect' had turned out to be just for show, of course. Peter had only ever valued Peter's opinion.

But with Lucas the respect had seemed genuine. The man had surely delivered a few babies over the course of his training, if not during his career as a GP, and he had seemed completely at ease leaving Marnie's care to Kiara. She hadn't got the impression from him—even for a nano-second—that he considered her less than capable of looking after her patient. She respected him for that.

And it spoke of the self-confidence he possessed that he hadn't felt the need to micro-manage her—a stranger whose skills were completely unknown to him. A stranger who had kind of been a little bit rude to him, now that she thought of it. She'd been warm and kind to his son, but she'd been crisp and dismissive of him…right up until they'd shared *that* look. The one that had turned her insides into a warm cupcake.

'Are you all right, Kiara?' asked Marnie.

Kiara shook her head, as if that would shake away the image of Lucas now firmly embossed in her brain. 'I'm just really delighted that your baby was the first one I helped to deliver,' she said.

'You and Lucas saved me from having her outside!' Marnie laughed, then gave a sigh that was difficult to read. 'Have you had a chance to chat with him yet?'

Kiara shook her head, even though it wasn't strictly true. He had tried to chat, but she'd shut it down.

'He's such a good man,' Marnie continued. 'Not everyone would be as kind and thoughtful as he is, given his situation.'

Kiara's eyebrows drew together. 'What situation?'

Marnie's eyes darted to the open door, then back to Kiara. 'It's not really my place to say, but a good man like that deserves to meet someone really special.'

Like me?

Marnie was making poor work of stifling a yawn.

'Why don't you have a rest?' Kiara helped Marnie arrange her covers and pillows just so, unable to stop her smile twitching into something broad, as if she'd just received the best Christmas present ever.

Lucas Wilde wasn't married!

She tried to pull her smile into some sort of control. Boyfriend-shopping was not on her list of things to achieve here. Delivering babies and decorating her house to collect money for charity were. And looking after herself. That was it.

Even so…just a handful of minutes with Lucas today had shown her a side of him that she really liked. Beyond the sexy hair, the beautiful grey eyes and those lips that really did look inviting enough to kiss…

A good man like that deserves to meet someone really special.

An image of her wearing a sexy elf costume, one leg wrapped seductively round a giant candy cane, popped into her head. And Lucas was wearing nothing more than a Santa hat…

Kiara! Stop it. He's a single father, not a boy toy.

She wrapped things up with Marnie, who looked more than ready for a sleep, especially now that her daughter had nodded off, and headed down to the central desk to do her notes.

'Well, that's a new way to approach the desk!' Nya smiled as she approached. 'It's not often someone skips to come and do their notes.'

'Was I skipping?' Kiara hadn't even noticed. The Lucas Effect? 'It was a great delivery,' she said. 'Always gives me a boost.'

'You're certainly in the right job if delivering babies gives you added pep!' Nya gave her arm a squeeze, then showed her where to do her notes, telling her the two of them would soon sit down to discuss her future patients.

Kiara started filling out her forms, but she couldn't stop her mind from wandering just a bit. Had Lucas Wilde really made her *skip*?

Sure, he was great. But finding out he was single couldn't be the main reason she was so happy. She'd already had a three-year run at having a man as the centre of her universe. It had blown up in her face in spectacular style. And that was the thing she needed to remember. Along with the fact that perhaps she didn't need to be quite as cool a customer when it came to a certain Dr Wilde...

Lucas scanned his patient's test results, together with the symptoms she'd described, and gave her the information he knew she didn't want to hear. 'I'm afraid you have entered the phase of life known as perimenopause, Mrs Braxton.'

'Oh, please...' The forty-seven-year-old woman batted away his formal address, reaching for one of the tissues out of the box Lucas had extended to her. 'Call me Becky. Everyone else does, and it's the one thing that still makes me feel young. Well...that and my thirty-something boyfriend.' She threw him a watery smile, dabbed away a few tears, then blew her nose, sitting back in her chair with a sigh. 'It was a bit mad thinking I still might be...you know...'

Lucas did know, but he thought it best to let Becky say the words herself.

'Able to have a baby. At my age.'

He held out the tissue box again. 'It isn't an impossibility, but I will caution you—'

'That pregnancy at my age comes with added risk.' She threw her hands up and gave a tearful laugh. 'I know. Down's. High blood pressure. Gestational diabetes.'

'There are risks for both you and the baby, so if you are sexually active and still trying for a child it's worth remembering the possible risks that could arise from a geriatric pregnancy—'

'Oh, God! Let me stop you there.' She repeated the

words *geriatric pregnancy* with a tone of pure horror. 'It just sounds so…so…*old*.'

'Eighty-eight is old,' Lucas said with a gentle smile. 'A hundred and three is old. And, for the record, I have seen patients of both ages earlier this morning—both of whom, I am happy to report, are fit and well despite their additional life experience.'

Lucas hoped his smile would say what propriety wouldn't allow him to. Becky Braxton was an attractive, intelligent woman, who was clearly in a happy, healthy sexual relationship with a younger partner who adored her, seeing as he'd texted three times already during her visit.

Children might not be on the cards for her, but that didn't mean she had to buy herself a wheelchair and consider her life over and done with.

He tapped the test results he'd just printed out. 'You are healthy and fit. Those are valuable assets.'

He was about to say she would have decades of other experiences ahead of her, but he knew first hand that life didn't always work out like that. So he gave her a couple of pamphlets and said he was more than happy to talk through some of the physical changes she could expect over the coming years, or offer a referral if she preferred to discuss it with a woman doctor.

'Heavens, no!' Becky pooh-poohed the idea. 'You're ever so kind, but I suppose… Oh, I do hate to be personal, but when I heard about your situation, and saw you were getting on with your life, I thought, *If young, handsome Dr Wilde can take one of life's more serious blows on the chin and pick himself and get on with it… so can I*.' She pressed her fingers to her mouth, then let them drop into her lap, her expression anxious. 'I hope that isn't too intrusive? It's just—you know—it's a small village, and people know things about people here. In a friendly way.'

'I know,' he said. 'It's a very welcoming place.'

More than enough stews and casseroles had been left on his front porch when he'd first moved in, to make it clear that life in Carey Cove was about being part of a community. Not hiding away and licking his wounds as he had back in Penzance, when he'd been not even thirty, the father of a six-month-old son and newly widowed.

He'd learnt the hard way that life after a bereavement was not about forgetting—because how could you forget someone you'd promised to love till death parted you? You couldn't. Nor could you stop loving them. Especially when you woke up to a three-year-old version of that person every single morning.

'How do you do it?' Becky asked. 'Get on with life when it's not going to be remotely like the one you thought you'd be living?'

'Good question,' he said, doing his best to lean into the question rather than avoid it. People came to their GP when they were feeling vulnerable. Frightened. He knew he couldn't give her a perfect answer, but he could explain what he'd done. 'For me and Harry—my little lad—it was finding a way to live with our new reality. It was less difficult for him, of course, but—'

'I'm sorry,' Becky cut in. 'That was extremely personal of me. I suspect I need to go home, have a bit of sulk and a think, and then just get on with it. That's what we British do, isn't it?'

'As long as you're not letting anything fester,' Lucas said, meaning it.

He'd known that if he'd stayed in the house he and Lily had thought was to be their 'for ever' home he'd have been tending wounds that would never heal. The move here had felt like a physical necessity.

'If you need a referral to talk to someone, or would like some phone numbers of charities, I'm happy to pass them on.'

A thought caught and snagged his attention. He didn't know what it was, but something told him Kiara's move to Carey Cove had been for exactly the same reason his had. To give herself a clean slate. A fresh start.

Losing his wife had been a gut-wrenching loss, but he'd at least been able to pour his love into their son, ensuring that Harry felt as safe, happy and secure as they had wanted all their children to feel—*their child*, he silently corrected. Because there wouldn't be more children, would there? Not without falling in love again, trusting his heart again. Taking the risk of stepping off the edge of a cliff and believing, once again, that this time he would actually get to spend the rest of his life loving and caring for someone who felt the same way about him.

He stemmed the thought.

Once in a lifetime had been a blessing.

Harry was a blessing.

Kiara was just—

Wait. What? Kiara wasn't mean to have entered that particular thought process. Particularly when he was thinking about falling in love again.

He realigned his focus to where it should be. On his patient. 'Have you considered adoption? Fostering?'

She shook her head. 'No, not really.' She grabbed another tissue, dabbed her eyes clear of mascara, and popped on her usual bright smile. 'Anyway, it's simply too embarrassing, sobbing my heart out in front of you. I'll figure something out.' She gave his hand a pat, as if their roles had suddenly been reversed and she was the one consoling him. 'Thank you, Dr Wilde. No disrespect, but I hope our paths don't cross again too soon. Unless—' her smile genuinely brightened this time '—it's down at the harbour? They're turning on the Christmas lights tomorrow night. Your little one might like that. It's always such a lovely evening. Mulled wine, mince pies, and of course all the lights.'

'That sounds wonderful.'

Lucas saw her out of the surgery and as it was now lunchtime thought he'd pop upstairs to the room Nya had told him Marnie was in. He'd rung earlier, to see how the labour had gone, and had been delighted to hear she'd delivered her healthy little girl in record time.

A few minutes later, he was just about to enter the room when Kiara came out, chart in hand. Her eyes brightened at the sight of him. It was a nice change from the cool reception he'd been given the first couple of times their paths had crossed. Perhaps he'd surprised her, or caught her out… Who knew? There were a million reasons why someone's initial encounters with another person might not be perfect.

'I take it she's sleeping?' Lucas said in a low voice.

Kiara's dark brown eyes flicked back towards the bed. She nodded, and gently pulled the door shut behind her. 'Like a baby,' she said. '*With* her baby,' she added with a soft laugh, her gaze dipping and then lifting to meet his.

Something hot and bright flared between them,

causing them both to look away. There was something both of them were shy of, Lucas thought. Was it something neither of them had expected or wanted?

It was a question he couldn't answer.

'How are you getting on?' He gave a teasing glance at his watch. 'What's it been? Four hours? Delivered any more babies?'

Kiara shot him a shy grin. 'Not yet. Although there have been a couple more December babies added to my roster, so I'll definitely be looking forward to swaddling them in seasonal blankets.'

Lucas threw her a questioning look.

Kiara led him over to the supplies cupboard and pointed to a couple of fresh stacks of swaddling blankets with a variety of patterns: Santas, elves, holly and ivy, even bright red reindeers in a Nordic design.

'I didn't even realise we had seasonal swaddling,' Lucas said.

Kiara flushed and admitted, 'That would be my fault.'

'How?'

'Back in the hospital where I used to work, we would sometimes get samples from companies wanting to sell these. When I knew I'd be moving here at Christmas time I contacted one of the suppliers to see if there were any samples available, and they sent this huge box full. They're last year's designs, so…'

'So Carey House is the lucky recipient?' Lucas said. 'I'm impressed. You're not just a fan of Christmas at home, you spread the joy.'

Again, her gaze dropped, then lifted to meet his. The compliment—however generic—had obviously touched her. Her response, lightly pinkened cheeks and a tooth snagging on her lower lip, made his heart skip a beat.

Something—or more likely someone—had hurt this woman. Made her feel less valued than she should be.

'Well…' Kiara finally broke the silence. 'I wanted to do something to show how appreciative I am of being taken on as part of the team here.'

'Christmas swaddling blankets was a nice choice,' Lucas said, and then, because he couldn't help himself, asked, 'You worked in London before, right?'

Kiara let out a low whistle. 'Word travels fast in these parts.'

Lucas gave her a knowing grin. 'Tell me about it. When I moved here—'

He stopped himself. He wasn't ready to bring up the cancer, the months of praying that this time, this check-up, his wife would get the all-clear.

He began again. 'When I moved here, I received a very warm welcome. There are fewer folk to spread the news to, I guess. Fewer than up in London, anyway.'

The expression on Kiara's face suggested to him that she'd seen the dark shadows flit through his eyes when he referenced his move. Or perhaps she'd read him like a book the moment she'd met him. Seen the light blue shadows that had taken up residence under his eyes in those last heartbreaking days of Lily's life and refused to leave. Sensed the void in his life he didn't know how to fill or what or who to fill it with.

But instead of trying to prise more information out of him, Kiara volunteered, 'I worked at London Central.'

Lucas looked impressed. 'You'd certainly get your daily steps in at that place. I mean—' He stopped, smacking himself on the forehead with the heel of his hand. 'Not that you need to count steps. Midwives are some of the most active people I've ever met, and you're obviously very fit and slender and—' He was about to say *beautiful*, but something stopped him, so he faked a cough and asked, 'Did you enjoy your time there?'

Kiara quite happily pretended she hadn't noticed his weird gaffe. She was obviously private, too, but she did volunteer, 'It was amazing. I started there straight out of university, and it was trial by fire, really. But the care there is much more doctor-led. Not to diminish what you do—obviously it's super-important. But I guess before I did the job I had imagined that being a midwife would be more like it has been here from the moment I arrived.'

Lucas felt himself caught in her enthusiasm. The warm glow of her smile. 'You mean pregnant women appearing on the driveway about to give birth?'

Kiara shot him a cheeky grin. 'If she'd been riding a donkey and had a man in hessian robes alongside her it would've been even better.'

He gave her a disbelieving look.

'No!' She was laughing as she waved the nativity image away. 'I was obviously delighted we got to Marnie in time, and that we didn't have to worry about there being no room at the inn. It was more... Well, you, for example. You saw that the midwives had things under control and honoured the fact that it's our area of expertise.'

'But it *is* your area of expertise.' Lucas felt he was missing something here. 'That's the point of midwifery.'

'I know!' Kiara laughed and clapped her hands. 'Exactly. It's just…lots of times in the London hospital there were incidents when male obstetricians would elbow us aside although we were perfectly capable of handling the situation. Women helping women, you know?'

Lucas scanned her expression, looking for something that might signal that she disliked or mistrusted men in general, but found nothing. Maybe there'd been a bully in her department? Or perhaps it was simpler than that? Perhaps she was referencing the traditional customs of childbirth that went back much further than modern medicine did?

Kiara must've sensed that she needed to explain herself a bit more, so she continued, 'I like being a woman's wingman. And her partner's—if there is one,' she added hastily, with a quick glance towards Marnie's room. 'Being with her almost from the beginning as she rides the world's most exhilarating and terrifying rollercoaster of all. Bringing someone new into the world…'

Her passion spoke to him. It was akin to his love of being a GP. Helping people throughout the various stages of their lives.

'You look like someone who loves her job very much,' he said.

'I do. I love it. Absolutely. And I just know I'm going to love it here too.'

Her eyes shone bright. To the point where Lucas knew he'd be caught in their brilliance for longer than was appropriate. So again he resorted to the fake cough manoeuvre and excused himself.

He was responding to Kiara in ways he'd never thought he'd experience with a woman again. Curious to know more. Wanting to be around her. Hyper-aware of himself when he was. And that wasn't even counting the starring role she'd had in the erotic dream he'd had last night.

It scared him. He and Harry had only just got themselves into a steady, workable routine. He wasn't sure he had it in his emotional toolbox to change things yet again. Not in this way.

He could feel her eyes on him as he left the ward… and for the first time in years he liked knowing that someone was looking.

He kept his pace slow and steady—and then, when he hit the stairs, surprised himself by hoisting his bum cheek up onto the banister and sliding all the way down.

When he got to the bottom, he was smiling.

And so was Nya, who'd seen the entire thing.

CHAPTER FOUR

JUST AS SHE was about to do her first lash, Kiara gave her mascara wand the side-eye and then, after one long hard stare, set it back down. She wasn't going to dress up for her second day at work, and she definitely wasn't dressing up for Dr Lucas Wilde. Even if he did make her skip along the corridor at work and think surprisingly saucy thoughts as she slipped into bed.

Even so, when she went out to her front garden—coat on, backpack loaded and ready to go to work—she found herself accidentally on purpose dawdling. Changing the angle of the dancing penguins by a smidge. Realigning a couple of waist-high candy canes that were listing ever so slightly in the crisp breeze coming in straight off the sea.

She had all the lights on already. With the mornings dark for so long, she thought it might be fun for the hardworking fishermen to look back to the coast and be able to spot her home, shining bright like a Christmas lighthouse, welcoming them back to the beautiful little harbour below when they brought in the morning's catch.

She turned and looked out to sea, just making out the skidding movement of white horses atop the waves. When she turned back around, the twinkling delights of her decorated cottage hit her afresh. It looked like a real-life gingerbread house. One that was hosting visitors from all over the North Pole. She tapped the black nose of the polar bear she'd set up last night after work. He was standing guard over a pile of 'presents'—colourfully decorated weatherproof boxes, arranged in an artful tumble and coming out of a huge Santa sack.

She'd checked with the neighbours first, assuring them that she wouldn't have the house flashing and blinking like a Vegas casino, and had been thrilled to discover they were all collectively delighted with her efforts. They'd even pledged to donate to First Steps in the name of Mistletoe Cottage.

It wasn't the glory she was after…it was knowing that something she'd done would be bringing care and solace to families unable to afford medical equipment for their poorly newborns. Life was hard enough when you brought a child into the world. Having medical problems to take on board when your finances were tight was even worse.

She shouldered her backpack, locked the front door, and gave her home an appraising look. It looked spectacular. If you loved Christmas, that was.

Her gaze drifted down the lane to where she had first seen Lucas and Harry, but it was completely devoid of human life. Just a few leaves scudding across the pavement.

A strange feeling of emptiness threatened to nibble away at the glow of anticipation she'd woken up with. She'd practically bounded out of bed. And it wasn't just the joy of going to work at Carey House she'd been looking forward to. It was the giddy sense of excitement about who she was going to see at Carey House. Today, she'd vowed silently, she would be less wary of Lucas Wilde and more…

Hmm… She'd have to work on that part, because obviously pouncing on the man and kissing him was out of the question. No. That sort of 'staff Christmas party' behaviour was not going to be a part of her strategy. As if she were as calculated as that. She wasn't. Not in the slightest. What she really needed here in her new home was a friend. Independent of her attraction to him, Lucas Wilde seemed like excellent friend material. And also a very, *very* sexy dad.

A sound at the end of the lane caught her attention. As if thinking about his father had magicked him into appearing, a familiar looking blond boy, kitted out in a red woolly hat and a matching puffer jacket, came careering round the corner, one foot madly pushing away at the pavement that stood between him and her increasingly over-the-top Christmas display.

Her heart softened.

Harry.

With or without the sexy dad he was a darling little boy. Precocious. Full of beans. And clearly as in love with Christmas as she was.

'Morning, Harry! Remember to slow down for the corner— Oops! There you are. Nice one. You're getting better at stopping, aren't you?'

'Penguins!' he cried, as the timer she'd set clicked into action.

She gave him a complicit grin and readjusted his knitted hat as he leant his scooter against the fence. 'Want to take a closer look?'

Wide-eyed with a combination of disbelief and pleasure, he looked up at her, his big grey eyes a carbon copy of his father's. 'Yes, please.'

'Well, go on, then. They were asking for you this morning.'

'They were?' Harry's eyes grew even bigger.

'Absolutely.' She put on a funny voice she hoped sounded like a penguin. '"When's Harry coming over for a dance?"'

Harry needed no further encouragement.

'Good morning, Kiara.'

Lucas's butter-rich voice all but physically pulled her up to stand. When she met his gaze, she was delighted to see it was matched with a smile. Less dubious than it had been yesterday at Carey House. There was warmth in it. Comfort. And, if she wasn't mistaken, a hint of that same fizz of anticipation she knew was glittering in her own eyes. They held one another's gazes for a moment, the atmosphere between them teetering on the precipice of too nice for Kiara to be able to resist and...*uh-oh*...blushing.

'Morning.' She feigned a crucial readjustment to her bobble hat and pointed to the lane. 'Off to work?'

Of course he is, you idiot! He's not heading to the zoo.

Lucas nodded, his eyes skidding from one decorative tableau to the next. 'And to the childminder's. Harry insisted we left early enough to visit The Christmas Lady.'

His face became less easy to read. Though he was obviously trying to fulfil his son's wishes, something about her or Christmas wasn't letting his smile reach his eyes.

'Are you not a fan of Christmas?' she blurted, instantly regretting it when he winced.

'Is it that obvious?' He waved the words away. 'That's not exactly the case. It's more—' His phone beeped and he pulled it out. The wince turned into a frown. 'Sorry. We've got to get going.' He took in her hat, the bag on her shoulder and the winter coat as if seeing her for the first time. 'Want to join us?'

Yes. Absolutely, she did. But if this was precious father-son time she didn't want to intrude. 'If you're sure…?'

Lucas's smile was genuine now. 'I am. Sorry. It's just—' He did a quick scan of her house and called Harry over with a loving, 'Time to go now, son.' Then, 'I don't have the best relationship with Christmas, and as this is the first one this little monkey is going to properly remember I'm trying to plumb some of the Christmas spirit by proxy.'

Kiara took this as her cue. 'You want Christmas spirit by proxy? I can do that. In spades.' She gave him a little salute. 'Christmas spirit by proxy, at your service!'

Lucas gave a good-natured laugh and then, to her surprise, reached out and gave her candy-cane-striped scarf a little tug. 'If it's anything like your midwifery I'm sure you'll be an excellent guide.'

Her blush deepened. 'You hardly saw me do anything.'

'I saw enough to know that you're good at your job. And, perhaps more importantly, that you love it. Have you had any updates on your patient?'

She pulled out her phone and thumbed up the photo she'd asked one of the night nurses to send her. Marnie and her baby nuzzling one another's noses. It was a really sweet photo, and unexpectedly tugged at a longing she didn't dare give voice to. She was around babies every single day and had never before had this response to a mother-baby moment. Not even with her ex. What had changed?

'Hold it up a bit?' Lucas was asking, putting his hand under hers to bring it to his eyeline.

Again, that twist of longing swept through her, but this time it came with glittery sparks of delight whooshing through her bloodstream. Sparks that had absolutely nothing to do with the tall, dark and handsome doctor with a snowman backpack hanging from his arm, leaning into her personal space to look at the photo.

God, he smelled good.

This morning he was more like vanilla latte with hints of cornflakes and berries than the sexy woodcutter aroma he'd left in his wake yesterday. Not that she'd be smelling him every time their paths crossed. Much. But that was hardly her fault. He was like the scented version of a kaleidoscope.

When he pulled back, she instantly missed his proximity. She'd never known lust at first sight to be so potent.

'They look well. I'll have to check in on them today,' Lucas said, mercifully having missed the twist of her features as she took a final look at the photo and then closed it down.

She wasn't jealous of Marnie. She was happy for her. Though she hadn't yet heard her whole story, Marnie seemed a picture of contentment…just her and her baby.

Kiara had always pictured something different for

herself. Something like what her parents shared. A happy, solid friendship that had led to a loving marriage. They'd had their ups and downs through the years—she was beginning to learn there weren't many couples who enjoyed entirely smooth sailing once they vowed to spend a lifetime together—but they had always dealt with their problems together. As a family. She admired them for that, and knew that her ideal relationship would contain those core principles of love and respect.

'So…' Lucas began after they'd walked in silence for a bit. 'Do you always decorate for Christmas like this?'

She barked a laugh. 'No. This is new. I don't think the rest of the tenants in my building in London would have taken to me turning their homes into a great big flashing Christmas orgasm. Oh, God!' She clapped her hands over her mouth. 'I'm sorry. I don't know what made me describe it that way. Especially in front of your son—' She squeezed her eyes tight in humiliation. 'I'm making this worse. Much, much worse. The more I talk, the worse it gets. Please save me from myself!'

Lucas, to her relief, was laughing rather than looking horrified. He lowered his voice and, as if they were sharing a secret, leant in and intoned, 'Maybe in future you could use the phrase "festive wonderland" when Harry's within earshot?'

Her cheeks burnt with embarrassment. 'I am so sorry. I'm not really getting off on the right foot as your number one Christmas spirit guide, am I?'

He shook his head, but didn't look annoyed or even put off by her series of verbal gaffes. 'This is the childminder's.'

She stood back as the carer came out of her lovely

rambling home, tucking a well-loved cardigan around herself as she greeted them with the news that the children would be having a biscuit-making party after lunch today.

Harry cheered, then waved to Kiara. 'I'll make you a Santa biscuit!'

She grinned, and pressed her hands to her heart in thanks. She looked across at Lucas, whose expression had suddenly gone blank. Unreadable. He seemed to be actively avoiding eye contact with her.

Had she done something wrong?

He knelt down in front of Harry and gave him loving but stern reminders to wear his coat when he was playing outdoors and to listen to the childminder—especially when she said it was time for a nap. He gave him a kiss on the forehead and tugged one of the little blond curls peeking out from under his hat. And then, as if it had suddenly become physically painful for him to leave his little boy, he briskly rose, turned, and walked back out to the pavement, where he instantly set off at a clip.

Kiara wasn't sure what had just happened. Was that sort of a goodbye normal for them? Maybe it had been a bit stiff because she'd been watching. Or was it because Harry had offered to make a biscuit for her?

This and a thousand other questions clamoured for supremacy as she jogged up to him and, in as light a tone as possible, asked, 'Are you upset that you're not going to get to go to the biscuit-making party? I get it. I love making and decorating biscuits—all those hundreds and thousands…'

He stopped and threw her a look saturated with sadness. His grief was so pure, so undiluted, it tore her own heart open with compassion. Whatever was haunting this man was big. Well beyond anything she'd endured. And that wasn't slighting what she'd been through at all.

It had been life-changing. And not in a good way.

But it had led her here…

'I really want to give Harry a special Christmas this year,' Lucas said finally, his brow furrowing tight. Not really the expression someone should wear when announcing they wanted to spread cheer and joy for Christmas.

'Like I said, I'm completely happy to be your Christmas elf.'

Lucas shot her a sharp glance, slowing his pace as if he was genuinely absorbing her offer. To her surprise, he pointed towards the village below them. 'They're turning the Christmas lights on down at the harbour tonight. Harry's never experienced anything like that, and you're new here in Carey Cove… You wouldn't, by any chance, possibly—'

'Yes,' Kiara interjected, hoping she was putting him out of his misery. 'I would love to go.'

He looked horrified.

Oh, no. She hadn't put him *out* of his misery—she'd thrown him straight into a pit of despair. She was clearly meant to have said no.

She tried to backtrack. 'I mean… I'll go as a friend. Because I'm friendly. But not overly friendly. I don't even have to stand with you, if you don't want. Like a date would. Because it wouldn't be a date.'

Lucas was now looking both horrified and confused.

She soldiered on. 'Unless you mean would I go as Harry's friend? In which case I'm totally on board with— I'll stop there. This talking thing always gets me into trouble at moments like this.' She laughed nervously. 'A *date*!' She feigned disbelief that the word had even been on the table. 'We wouldn't want to start any undue gossip at Carey House, now, would we?' Again, she popped her hands over her mouth, then muttered, 'Please stop talking…please stop talking.'

He looked at her, seriously for a moment, as if actually considering her question, then nodded. 'Good. Grand. Harry will love that. Right!'

He clapped his hands together, as if to bring an end to all the awkwardness, and to the clear relief of both of them they arrived at Carey House, where a shift-change meant there was enough hustle and bustle for her to wave him a quick goodbye and pretend she hadn't just humiliated herself as much as she thought she had.

Lucas closed the door to his surgery and silently banged his head against the wall—one, two, three times—before leaving it there as a low moan escaped his throat.

She didn't think it was a date, did she?

Did he?

No. He wasn't a dater. Not now, anyway. Not even when their chemistry was—

Hang on. Did he *want* it to be a date?

No. Absolutely not. She was a colleague. He was a widower. He had a son to look after.

He thought of the way his body had responded when their hands had inadvertently brushed as they'd both reached to pull shut the small gate at the childminder's. It had been an electric connection. Through *gloves*. Well… In her case mittens. Bright red things, with tiny white reindeer and Christmas trees knitted into the pattern. Not that he'd been staring at her hand and wondering what it would be like to reach out and weave his fingers through hers.

Another low moan emptied out of his chest.

His wife had been right. He was horrendous with women. Terrible at asking them out. Making them feel at ease. In fact, if memory served, he was fairly certain it was Lily who had asked *him* out first back in time. Not that he'd meant to ask Kiara out. This was for Harry. For Christmas. For Harry and Christmas.

He rubbed his hands over his face and shook his head.

The fact he'd managed to woo and win his wife's hand in marriage was a miracle. One miracle in a lifetime was more than enough. Unless you counted Harry, and then that gave him two. Falling in love again was one miracle too many to wish for.

Right?

'Let yourself love again. Don't be afraid to let someone else into your and Harry's lives. And remember to give her flowers.'

His wife's words came to him unbidden. A reminder that he was in charge of his heart. He'd barely registered them at the time. She'd been so very ill, and devoting himself to anything other than their infant son and her care had seemed an impossibility. He'd felt so helpless. So lost. Umpteen years of medical training hadn't prepared him to endure witnessing the woman he'd begun a family with waste away to nothing. So how on earth could he absorb dating advice from that same woman? It had seemed impossible at the time.

So he'd done what he'd imagined any grieving husband might. Closed down the option of ever loving again. And yet here he was, almost three years after losing her, remembering her wish that he and Harry would find room in their hearts for someone else.

Was Kiara that someone?

Eight hours later, as he pulled on his coat and walked to the new mothers' ward, he was still asking himself the same question. Usually a full roster of patients enabled him to push uncomfortable thoughts out of his mind—but not today. Then again, he didn't usually have a date—*not* a date!—waiting for him at the end of the day.

He popped his head into Marnie's room, pleased to see the tell-tale glow of motherhood lighting up the room as Marnie took her daughter into her arms for a feed. Not wanting to interfere with this private moment, he left them to it and headed to the central desk, where he saw Kiara doing a handover with Nya and another midwife—Sophie French. All three of them were wearing multicoloured reindeer antlers. Kiara's were flashing. She leant in and said something in a low voice to the women and they all gave a knowing laugh.

In-jokes already? Only two days on the job and she seemed completely at ease. The fact that she was a good midwife was not in doubt. It was more… Her aura embodied something less tangible. There was a heightened sense of presence about her behaviour that spoke of a feeling of gratitude. He didn't know why, but he got the impression she needed a place like this. Not just Carey House, but Carey Cove.

When he'd moved here with Harry he had been feeling lost, overwhelmed, bereaved. Then he'd driven in along the coastline, seen the beautiful village laid out in lanes that worked their way up the hillside to where, on top, was the golden stone former manor house that was now the cottage hospital. He'd instantly felt as though he'd entered a place of solace. Warmth. Not necessarily a place to forget his past, but a place to heal and then, one day, move forward.

The second Kiara laid eyes on him her expression changed from smiling and bright to purposeful. For reasons he couldn't pinpoint, the shift in mood put him at ease. It was as if she'd read and processed this morning's gaffe over the date/not date invitation and repurposed their outing into what he had intended it to be: for his son.

She shared a quick look with the other women and he didn't miss the mischievous expression Nya sent his way when Kiara disappeared into the midwives' lounge to get her things. He was guessing her humour-filled smile was largely fuelled by his out-of-character slide down the banister yesterday.

'I'm guessing both you and Harry will be hungry,' Kiara said through the muffle of her thrice-wrapped scarf as they left Carey House and headed towards the childminder's. 'If you like, I can meet you down at the Harbour at six. That's when the lights are going on, apparently.'

Her smile was soft and warm. There was no expectation in it and for that he was grateful.

'He's usually had some sort of afternoon snack at the childminder's that tides him over. It's the days at nursery when he needs immediate feeding. I can assure you…a hungry Harry is not a beautiful sight to behold.' He pulled a monster face as evidence.

Kiara put on a shocked expression. 'What? A three-year-old not being beautifully behaved at all times? I refuse to believe it.'

They shared a companionable laugh and carried on walking, the question of when and where to meet still unresolved.

It struck him that she was leaving it up to him. Not in a helpless way. More in the kind of way that meant she wasn't going to push for something that wasn't there. Had her heart been broken, too? Surely not in the way his had. But he sensed a vulnerability in her…a spirited type. One that wasn't going to allow anyone to take command of her heart and treat it without due care.

'Maybe…' he began, just as she started to say something.

A ridiculous politeness pile-on ensued.

'You go…'

'No, you go…'

'Really…'

'Please…'

'You first. I insist.'

Eventually they got to the point where they both stopped talking—although, if he wasn't mistaken, Kiara had succumbed to a case of the giggles behind that extra-long scarf of hers.

Crikey. He was making a right hash of this. He steeled himself and asked the question that had been poised on the tip of his tongue. 'Would you like to join us for supper? Nothing fancy. Or homemade.' He grimaced apologetically. His cooking still had plenty of room for improvement. 'We could have fish and chips down by the harbour?'

Kiara shot him a look, clearly trying to ascertain

if she needed to read anything into the invitation. He smiled and held out his hands, as if that was an indicator that he really meant it.

He must have made a convincing show because her smile brightened. 'I do love a hot packet of fish and chips all wrapped up in paper.'

Lucas's smile matched hers in enthusiasm. 'It's great, isn't it? Shame it's not newspaper any more. Sometimes the traditional way of doing things is the best.'

Her smile faltered, then regained purchase so quickly he wouldn't have noticed it if he hadn't been looking. 'Right. That's settled, then. Fish and chips down by the harbour followed by some festive lights.'

She let out a whistle. 'Look at you, getting into the Christmas spirit.'

'It helps having you guide me on the way,' he said, pointing at her antlers. 'Both literally and figuratively.' And he meant it, too.

They collected Harry, who had made and decorated not one, but several gingerbread biscuits. He was instantly bewitched with the blinking antlers. Without a moment's hesitation Kiara switched them from her head to his, sending an *Is this all right?* glance back at Lucas as she did so.

Of course it was. And it also made him want to kick himself. It was magical flourishes like this that his little boy was missing out on by having *him* as his only parent.

After stopping to admire Kiara's dazzling display of Christmas delights, they dropped the biscuits and Harry's backpack off at his house—which Lucas suddenly felt a bit ashamed of. Not because of the house itself. It was a beautiful stone cottage, in keeping with the rest of the village's solid but welcoming aesthetic. It was because it was entirely bereft of Christmas decor. When Harry asked why their house wasn't more like Kiara's, he muttered some excuse about things being lost in the post, but it was, of course, a fiction. The simple truth was that he didn't know how to celebrate Christmas any more.

Kiara didn't comment on it, but he could see that she'd clocked the absence of decorative Christmas cheer and his awkward way of explaining it away.

No wonder his little boy adored her. She embodied the spirit of the season. Warm, generous, kind.

Beautiful.

The thought pulled him up short. She didn't look a thing like Lily—which, if he were psychoanalysing himself, made his attraction to Kiara feel less like a betrayal and more a biological reality.

He buried his head in his hands, grateful that Kiara and Harry were walking ahead of him.

What a Casanova!

If, by some extraordinary turn of events, whatever was happening with Kiara evolved into something romantic, he would have to find a way to express his admiration for her with better word-choices. 'Biological reality' wasn't really a turn of phrase that made a woman swoon. Besides, his response to her was more than biological. It was… It was that same ethereal thing that drew any two strangers together. Kismet? The stars? The spirit of Christmas? He didn't know. All he knew was that it was too strong to ignore. For Harry's sake, obviously. Kiara was the key to making this Christmas a truly memorable one for his little boy.

To his relief, Kiara and Harry commandeered the evening and, mittened hand in mittened hand, led the way down to the harbour, where there was already a small crowd gathering, many with fish and chips.

'Guess we aren't as original as we thought,' Lucas said as they joined the queue.

Kiara's mood only seemed further delighted by his observation. 'It's wonderful being part of something bigger than yourself, isn't it?'

He looked around the harbour area and suddenly saw it through her eyes. She was a stranger here, and yet the atmosphere was anything but exclusive. As people milled in the cobblestoned square, he saw a sea of smiles lifted by a soundscape of laughter and excited chatter. It was a happy place, made cheerier with each new arrival.

One of the retired sailors who was often seen propping up the bar in the local pub was roasting chestnuts in a large metal drum on the harbour's edge. The publicans had set up a stall outside The Dolphin Inn—aka The Dolph—for mulled wine, and from the looks of the number of families in the queue something for the little ones as well. Cornish apple juice with a bit of cinnamon, he guessed from the waft of aroma coming his way.

'You know, you're right.' He smiled down at her as he drew his son in for a hug. 'It feels infectious. In a good way,' he hastily tacked on.

She laughed. 'I would hate the Christmas spirit to be infectious in a bad way.' She threw him a look that was equal measures delight and caution. 'I meant what I said this morning. I'm happy to help.' She lowered her voice so Harry wouldn't hear. 'If you want me to take

Harry to anything that's not appealing to you…' She rattled off a list of events happening around the area, including a Christmas train ride, a nearby Christmas fair and a Christmas-decoration-making afternoon at the weekend.

Lucas laughed. 'You really do love Christmas, don't you?'

She smiled brightly, but her voice was serious and her dark eyes shadowed when she said, 'I love being able to celebrate it as wildly and with as much joy as I want.'

There was a story there. One she clearly felt happy to allude to, but not offer specifics on. He got it. He had his story, too. Moving here hadn't just been about getting out of the house where he'd nursed his wife through to her final moments. It had been about being able to go to the village shop and not have people stare at The Widower. Or having all his patients offer their condolences when he was the one who was meant to be caring for them. He knew, as well, that his son had to be allowed to be Harry Wilde, the energetic little blond boy with curls and a smile to soften even the steeliest of hearts. Not Harry Wilde, the poor little boy who'd lost his mum when he was only a baby. It was a fact. Yes. Just as it was a fact that Lucas was a widower. But he had known they couldn't continue having their loss be the defining factor of who they were and who they might one day become.

'These are amazing!' Kiara beamed when they'd finally got to the front of the queue and were each holding warm bundles of freshly fried fish and deliciously moreish chips doused in salt and vinegar. 'Harry…' Kiara dropped Lucas a complicit wink. 'If you hold on to my hand, I bet I can take you to the best spot to watch the Christmas lights being turned on.'

Harry looked from Kiara to his father, then back again. 'Can we?' he asked his father.

'By all means,' Lucas said, bewildered as to how Kiara managed, after little more than a fortnight in the village, to know already the best place to sit—especially with just about the entire population of Carey Cove being present.

She led them out to the small stone quay where a smattering of sailing and fishing boats were moored. After a quick word with a young man sitting on the back of a mid-sized fishing trawler that was alight with multicoloured lights spanning across its rigging, she stood back, pointed up to the Navigation Bridge, which was strewn with unlit fairy lights, and with a swirl of her free hand announced, 'Ta-da! Your viewing platform, gentlemen.'

Harry looked wide-eyed with disbelief. Lucas realised he probably did, too. 'How on earth—'

She explained as they climbed aboard. 'The captain's wife had a baby yesterday.'

'And you delivered it?' Lucas finished.

She smiled and nodded. 'Her regular midwife had been held up with a more problematic birth, and she kindly agreed to let me step in and help.'

'And somehow, in between teaching her breathing techniques and delivering the baby, you managed to find out that her husband had the best spot to see the Christmas lights.'

She smiled up at him, and yet again Lucas felt that warm glow of connection light up his chest—one that went beyond the parameters of friendship.

'I call it The Distraction Technique,' she quipped, then added, 'She said her husband had decorated the boat specially for her. However, the one scent she hadn't been able to stomach ever since falling pregnant was…' She looked down at what remained of her meal and then grinned at him.

'Fish?' Lucas finished for her, popping the last piece of his battered cod into his mouth with a smile. 'Well, lucky us.'

'Yes…'

Kiara's smile softened and then, as a light flush caught the apples of her cheeks, she looked back to the village just as a swell of music filled the air. A hush spread across the crowd all the way out to where Lucas, his son and Kiara were perched in the trawler. Lucas hoisted Harry up on to the captain's bench so that he could see the magic of the lights as they came on in their full festive glory.

His fingers twitched with an instinct to take her mittened hand in his. As if sensing the impulse, she glanced over at him and then, clearly feeling the same reticence he was, looked back to the lights, glittering away with nothing but promises of the season yet to come.

CHAPTER FIVE

'HERE YOU ARE, BETHANY.' Kiara lifted one tiny swaddled bundle and handed it to the new mum, then once she was settled asked, 'Are you ready for your second son?'

Bethany threw her an anxious smile, tears suddenly blooming in her eyes. 'I guess…' She gave a watery laugh. 'I think I might be missing Graham.'

Kiara smiled warmly and said, 'It's perfectly normal to feel overwhelmed. It's such a shame this is his busy season, but the way your phone keeps pinging to check on you is proof that he wishes he was here instead. And remember…' she tapped the side of her nose '…you can blame hormones for all sorts of things for a while yet.' She handed her a tissue.

Bethany laughed and wiped at her eyes, then held her free arm out to accept her son's twin brother. 'I suppose I'm going to have to get used holding both of them with Graham at work so much.'

'It has only been a day,' Kiara said gently. 'There's no need to be hard on yourself. Motherhood is one of the steepest learning curves there is.'

Kiara caught Bethany's quick glance at her bare

ring finger and felt the absence of the natural follow-up question: *Do you have little ones yourself?*

The question had never stung before, when it had felt like such a future certainty. But for the last year it hadn't felt certain—and, although she never begrudged new mums their children, she was beginning to feel the sting of being a singleton.

Kiara stayed close until she was certain Bethany had good purchase on both of her children and then pulled two tiny little elf hats out of her pocket. 'Ready?'

In a sudden about-face, Bethany giggled. 'This is so silly. I mean, they're not even going to remember their first Christmas.'

'But you are! And so is your husband. They're memories for you to share with the boys as they get older.' A thought pricked and lodged in her mind. She had no idea what had happened in Lucas's past, but she was curious as to why Lucas was trying to make Christmas so special for his son but not for himself. Was the fact he hadn't had a spouse or a partner to share his son's earlier Christmases what made it so difficult?

She knew why *she* was marching all guns blazing into the Christmas season. Her ex hadn't just been a married liar. He had been a bit of a control freak—and a snob too. Apparently highly successful surgeons didn't drink cranberry-flavoured cocktails with glittery salt round the edges of the glass, or dance around Christmas trees in Covent Garden for the sheer joy of it.

'Is this okay?' Bethany asked, slipping her own elf hat over her head at a rakish angle.

'Perfect!' Kiara beamed, grateful for the reminder that her life was here in Carey Cove now.

She took a few shots, all at different angles, then, just as she was popping the phone on Bethany's bedside table, heard a soft knock on the doorframe.

Lucas.

Her insides went warm and sparkly.

'Those will be nice additions to the family album,' Lucas said.

Bethany beamed. 'You think?'

'Absolutely.' He indicated the twins, who Kiara was now gently easing back into their shared bassinet. 'It's a nice starter pack of elves you have there.'

Against the odds, Bethany's smile grew even brighter. Kiara gathered up her tablet and a couple of other items and wished Bethany a good night, along with giving her a reminder that her husband would be calling in for a visit in an hour's time.

'Nice day?' asked Lucas.

'Very.' Kiara beamed. 'We have a dozen new November babies and it's only a few days into the month!' She laughed and gave him a wink that halfway through took on a flirtatious flare she'd never known she possessed. 'Valentine's Day has got a lot to answer for.'

Lucas smiled, then slowed his pace. 'Speaking of Valentine's…'

Kiara's eyes shot to his. Was he going to ask her out for next February? That was forward planning on a whole new level. However, they did say good things came to those who waited, so…

Lucas must have seen the confused look in her eyes, because he pulled a face of his own and rubbed his hand along his jaw—clean-shaven again today—and then dropped it. 'That was a terrible segue. I wasn't meaning to talk about Valentine's at all.'

Her heart surprised her by plummeting. Of course he wasn't. She was stupid to have even gone there in her mind. Stupid winking…turning everything ridiculously flirty. She made a silent vow never to wink again.

He paused, and then clawed one of his hands through his hair as he started and stopped talking a couple of more times.

Kiara gave him a sidelong look. 'I'm not so scary that you can't just ask me something outright, am I?'

'No, I—'

Kiara bit down on her lip as her heart skipped a beat. He was going to ask her out on another date/not a date!

'I was wondering if—'

'Yes!' she blurted. 'I mean…if it's more Christmas stuff with Harry, I'm in. Like I said the other day… I'm your Ghost of Christmas Present.'

The instant she said the words she regretted them. There was very clearly a Ghost of Christmas Past in Lucas's life…just as there was in hers…only his seemed more ingrained in him.

'I mean… Sorry… I…' She pulled a face, then said, 'Should we start this whole conversation again? My mum calls them do-over moments.'

Lucas's lips twitched into a grateful smile. 'Your mother sounds like a very wise woman.'

To Kiara's delight, his eyes grew bright as he lifted his eyebrows and cupped his chin with his hand, a finger tapping away on his cheek, as if he was in thoughtful consideration of how one commenced a 'do-over', then abruptly turned and walked away.

'Hey!' she called after him. 'Where are you going?'

Quick as a flash, he whirled around and with a

warm, confident smile said, 'Oh, hi, Kiara. I'm glad I caught you here. Harry and I were thinking of heading over to the Christmas market and fair a bit further down the coast tonight. We were wondering if you'd care to join us.'

Happiness bubbled from Kiara's toes all the way up to the sparkly Santa hat she was wearing. She felt as if Lucas had dropped a bath bomb in her insides. 'Excellent do-over,' she said, impressed.

'You think?' He doffed an invisible cap. 'I aim to please.'

Their eyes caught and held. For a precious moment Kiara felt linked to him in a way she hadn't imagined ever feeling with a man again. Not after last year. The energy between them had built into something almost tangible. A magnetic force connecting them in a way that surely had to make their trip to a Christmas market and fair more date-like than not.

And then Nya appeared.

'Hello, you two.' She looked much more amused than bemused as she asked, 'May I ask if you plan to hold your little staring contest here in the corridor for the foreseeable future? Or is it just a temporary thing?'

Kiara, who heard the teasing tone in her voice, turned to her and pointedly blinked her eyes. 'That's us done.'

'We're heading off to the Christmas fair just outside Mousehole,' Lucas said. 'For Harry.'

'Yes,' Kiara pounced on the much less date-sounding description. 'Harry does love his Christmas bling.'

Nya gave an approving nod, then shooed them out of the corridor towards the stairs, her voice taking on the tone of a concerned mother. 'Two nights out in the same week? That little boy's going to be over the moon. You'd best get a move on. Here's your coat, Kiara. Lucas, make sure you wear a hat. Set a good example for your son. On you go, now, and make sure you get Harry home early. It's a school night!'

When Nya had finally headed back to her desk, Kiara and Lucas shared a giggle. 'Well, that's us told, then,' said Kiara.

They laughed again, and expressed their mutual admiration for Nya. Kiara felt no compunction about enthusing about her being a good boss. The best she'd had, actually. Warm, but exacting. Generous and humane. It made working here really feel like being part of team rather than the cog in a huge machine that she'd sometimes felt like back in London.

Exchanging information about their days at work, they briskly made their way down the hill, collected Harry and, at Kiara's suggestion, enjoyed some cheese on toast at her house, with the added bonus of Harry being allowed to help Kiara select which box of decorations to put out next. Then they set off down the road towards Mousehole.

Before they'd even rounded the corner to the next cove they could see the lights. Harry, who seemed to be filled with jumping beans tonight, was clapping his hands in anticipation.

When they got out of the car they walked to the central green, where the Christmas market was being held, they all held their breath as one.

In the very centre of the square were three enormous ice sculptures—a snowman, a reindeer and, tallest of all, a huge, jolly Santa Claus with an enormous bag of presents slung over his shoulder. Kiara had no idea how they'd done it, but frozen into the 'bag' were actual toys. A nutcracker, a teddy bear, a doll, and a dozen or so other old-fashioned toys that made the visual display all the more remarkable. The sculptures were illuminated, so that they sparkled like diamonds.

Harry's eyes were so wide, Kiara could actually see the sculptures reflected in them. She knelt down so that she was at eye level with Harry. 'Which one's your favourite?

'The reindeer,' he said after a moment's hesitation. And then, 'The snowman.' He threw her a panicked look. 'Can't I love all of them just the same?'

'Of course you can!' Kiara laughed pulling him in for a cosy hug. 'You've got a huge heart, haven't you, Harry? Such a big, huge heart.'

She let herself fall into the moment. Enjoy the little boy arms around her neck. His energy. His scent. A little boy elixir made up of crisp cheese, earth and soap. She looked up and realised Lucas was watching the pair of them with an intensity the moment didn't necessarily warrant. But…who knew? Maybe it did.

A memory of her reaction to seeing Lucas that very first time he'd loomed above her sprang to mind. It had been visceral, her response to him. Core-deep. As if somehow she'd been waiting to meet him for her entire life.

She felt a shift then. Something in her gave way. Something that hadn't managed to move since her relationship had come to such an explosive end. It felt as if light was pouring into the little cracks and crevices inside her. Fissures she'd thought she'd blocked, so that she wouldn't ever allow herself to feel so hurt again. But this feeling was different. There was a vulnerability to it, yes. But there was also hope and possibility infused with the warmth that she knew came from meeting Lucas.

He held out a hand and helped her to stand up, and although they didn't continue to hold hands as they walked around the fair, with Harry running from stall to stall, intent on sampling all the Christmas treats, she still felt the strength of his hand as it had wrapped round hers for those few seconds. And something deep inside her told her she would miss that touch for evermore.

'You all set, mate?'

Harry wobbled uncertainly in Lucas's hands for a moment, and then, when one of the teenaged girls hired as a coach for the special pre-schoolers' skate session held out both of hers for Harry to join the rest of the little ones on the ice, Harry took them without so much as a backward glance.

Despite the hit of loss, Lucas had to smile. His son's first moment on skates…

'It's amazing how they take to it, isn't it?' Kiara appeared beside him, holding two steaming mugs. 'Hot chocolate to keep you warm?'

He took the mug gratefully. 'They've really done this whole event up to the nines, haven't they?'

It was truly magical. But rather than agree, Kiara let out a contented sigh and took a big sip of her hot chocolate, which left an impressive dollop of whipped cream on her nose.

'Here. You've got some…' He dug into his pocket and pulled out a clean handkerchief. Their eyes locked as he held it just above her nose, poised for action, and asked mischievously, 'Unless you were keeping it for later?'

'Hmm...' she began, as if considering the option. 'I do like a bit of whipped cream before bed, but...' Her tongue swept across her bottom lip just before her upper teeth caught it tight. Her cheeks pinkened, as if she'd admitted something slightly too intimate for the occasion.

He took a step back and offered her the handkerchief instead of wiping the cream off himself, as he had planned to, suddenly aware of how many of their interchanges bore the hue of flirtation about them. Interchanges neither of them had pushed beyond a glance or a flush of acknowledgement.

He felt an abrupt and urgent need to explain where he was in life. How meeting her had opened up a rush of feelings and...yes...he'd admit it...an attraction he hadn't thought he'd ever experience again.

Before he could stop himself, he said, 'Harry's mother would've loved to see a moment like this.'

He nodded out to the ice rink, where Harry was now holding hands with a little girl, her hair in near identical blonde curls to his peeking out from underneath a knitted cap with snowflakes woven into the design. The two of them looked like a Christmas card.

He tried to say more, but the words caught in his throat. Because if his wife had lived, he wouldn't be here with Kiara—he'd be here watching Harry, and one of them would most likely have a baby strapped to their chest. Perhaps a little girl. Or another boy. It wouldn't matter. They'd said they wanted children, not boys or girls. Because it hadn't mattered if they'd be picking up mud-splattered jeans or tutus. What had mattered was family. Having babies, then toddlers, then school kids, then teens, to nurture and love until one day they had children of their own. He'd seen it all so clearly back then, but now the future…it was a blank slate. One that, courtesy of a Christmas-mad midwife who'd just happened to move to the same tiny village in the same nook of Cornwall as he had, was now bathed in possibility.

He looked into Kiara's eyes and saw nothing but compassion there. And a thousand questions he realised he was going to have to answer.

'She passed away,' he said simply. 'Cancer,' he added by means of explanation. It had been one that had crept up on them a matter of weeks after they'd found out Lily was pregnant. The malignant cells had attacked and reformed into tumours with such ferocity it had completely blindsided them. 'Gestational trophoblastic disease.'

Kiara gasped. It was clear from the expression on her face—and the fact she was a midwife, so probably had encountered similar cases—that there was no need to explain about this particular, quite rare form of cancer.

He gave a few details. The discovery of the cancer. His wife's refusal to have chemotherapy, terrified that the treatment had the potential to compromise their son's welfare. Their disagreement. Their ultimate compromise… She would get treatment as soon as Harry was born. And then, to their horror, the realisation it was far too late.

Lucas knew that his normal voice had been replaced by the strange, automated version of it that had come to him in the days and weeks following the funeral, but he wasn't sure what would happen if he allowed even an ounce of the emotion he was feeling to sneak to the surface.

A little voice rose loud and clear in his subconscious. *You'll bend or break, Lucas. And I know which way I think you'll go.*

His wife had believed he had the power to bend and bounce back. He'd tearfully told her she had more faith in him than he had in himself. That there would be no regrouping from a loss like the one he and Harry were about to endure. The day she'd died he'd felt as if his entire body had been filled with darkness. It would have consumed him if he hadn't had his son. This tiny creature, only a few months old, wholly dependent upon him.

Throughout his explanation Kiara stood solidly, her eyes glued to him as he spoke, her attention unwavering, her hot chocolate untouched. He knew she was there for him. One hundred percent. And, as if her strength of character was physically supporting him, for the first time since he'd lost his wife he spoke freely about what he'd gone through.

He hadn't bounced back. He'd felt as if he'd been cleft in two…one half of him with his wife and the life they were meant to have led, and the other half desperately trying to gain purchase on the life Harry deserved to be living. One in the here and now.

'Truth be told,' he said to Kiara, 'I just never imagined doing anything but breaking into a thousand pieces if a scenario like this one ever arose.'

'What do you mean?' Her brow furrowed in confusion.

'I—' he began, and then backtracked. 'Being out

with a woman,' he said. Then, when her response was one difficult-to-read blink, he added, 'You know… Not on a date, but in a situation where people who didn't know we weren't on a date might think we were together.'

'Oh…' Kiara's voice drew the sound out as if the thought had never occurred to her. She let her gaze drift out to the rink, where Harry was, once again, picking himself up off the ice.

Her reaction threw him. It *was* mutual, wasn't it? The attraction they shared? And, to be honest, to him this felt like a date.

A swift, icy-cold spear of panic lanced through him. Had he read this situation entirely incorrectly? Had she genuinely meant that she wanted to give Harry the best Christmas ever and that was where it ended? Perhaps he was the one desperate for a connection and had been dotting 'i's and crossing 't's where there hadn't been any.

Or maybe…

He looked at her. Really looked at her. And saw what he hadn't before. A desire to listen and be there for him but a wariness not to overstep. A nervousness about crossing that line.

To be fair, it was a big ask. To pour his heart out about losing the love of his life to someone with whom he shared a physical and increasingly emotional attraction and expect her to say, *Oh, that's sad...do you want to kiss me?*

Not that Kiara would ever do anything as crass as that, and not that he was even close to ready to be stripping off and jumping in the hay with her except in his dreams, but he'd dreamt a very erotic dream about her.

And each time they'd met he'd felt a magnetic energy shift between them on more than one occasion. Including tonight, when he'd pulled her up to stand and been so tempted to keep her mittened hand in his.

And now he was throwing a bucket of ice on what should, by all counts, be a romantic evening.

Was he self-sabotaging?

Or testing himself?

He hadn't cracked into a million tiny shards of glass. Or lost himself in a sea of misery and grief. He hadn't run. Or broken down. Or lashed out at the world around him for the cruelty that was cancer.

Quite the opposite. He was standing in front of a woman he shared an undeniable attraction with. His feet were solidly on the ground. He was, to his astonishment, offering Kiara what he hoped was a smile. It was the least and the most he could offer her at this moment. And he hoped to heaven she could see that.

When she returned his cautious smile, his heart bloomed and began pounding out large, approving thumps against his ribcage.

Maybe he was doing it right. Maybe, after a loss like his, you just took it step by step. One sip of hot chocolate after the next. One walk home under a starry sky with her mittened hand tucked in his.

One first kiss?

He almost stumbled back a step at the thought, then forced himself to regroup. Life was precious. He of all people should know that. It wouldn't just be stupid to crumble at this, the first and probably most important hurdle of his friendship with Kiara. It would be a form of self-sabotage that would serve no purpose.

If he was being truly honest with himself, he knew

Lily would've liked her. They weren't peas in a pod. Not by a long shot. But Kiara championed everything he valued and was everything he had sought in a woman when he'd been a young singleton back in med school. Honest. Kind. Infused with strong family values.

Kiara brought a smile to his lips more often than not. His son thought she was on another level. She was incredible at her job. She'd brought more Christmas cheer to her home than he'd seen anywhere in a lifetime of celebrating Christmas.

'And that,' he said, with a weird half-bow he hoped would break the awkwardness of his confession, 'is our origin story. What brought us here to Carey Cove, anyway.'

Kiara pressed her free hand to her mouth, her red-mittened fingers pushing the colour out of her lips. Her cheeks, so recently flushed with pleasure, were now pale. 'I'm so sorry, Lucas. I didn't know.'

He shook his head. 'You're possibly the only one in a ten-mile radius who doesn't.'

'Did you want it to be a secret?'

Her question was a genuine one.

'No,' he answered truthfully. 'It was more that we put ourselves on a path that led forward, you know?'

Kiara shook her head. Unsurprisingly, she was clearly unable to understand his feeble attempt to explain what he'd wanted from the move. He realised this was actually the first time he'd tried to put it into words. He took a sip of his hot chocolate and gave her a smile before refocusing his gaze on his son—the reason behind the move.

'Everyone knew Lily where we were. I guess, rather

than having Harry live in the shadow of someone he was never going to meet, I wanted him to live in the light. I thought moving would help us both focus on what we did have. Not on what we didn't.'

He tried to keep his tone light, but it was impossible to keep the rough edges of emotion at bay.

'You two sound as if you were very much in love.'

Tears glistened in Kiara's eyes, and it surprised him to realise his instinct was to dab them away for her. To care for her. And not just as a friend. He wanted something more. He simply didn't know how to make that shift.

He nodded. 'Yes. We were.'

He took the handkerchief which Kiara had balled up in her hand and folded it into a neat triangle with the bit of whipped cream tucked on the inside. He handed it back to her and pointed to her eyes.

'I suppose the main thing I have is that I've known true happiness. So should it ever cross my path again…'

He left the sentence hanging, but when the atmosphere between them threatened to shift into something that felt more intimate than any other silence they'd shared, Kiara asked, 'Did Harry…? I mean, how has he dealt with things?'

Lucas shook his head and gave his jaw a rub. 'He was only a few months old when Lily died, so he doesn't have any memories of her apart from what I've told him.'

His eyes scanned the rink until he found Harry who, in a moment of bravery, had broken away from the chain of youngsters only to end up falling on his bum.

Lucas gave a little laugh. 'That's roughly what it's been like for the pair of us. Falling down. Getting up. Falling down again. Finding a new way to get up. Well…' He shot her a self-effacing smile. 'That's mostly been me. Harry grabs on to all of the happy things in life and runs with them. I'm still learning from him, to be honest.'

'I can't even imagine…'

He could tell from the depth of emotion in her voice that she was feeling his pain as if it was her own. 'Thank you,' he said, meaning it. 'I dare say there are a few things I could learn from you, too.'

Their eyes caught and held. He felt as if he could see straight into her heart then. And what he saw was pure and kind.

'Has moving here helped?' Kiara asked, and her question was weighted with something else. Something personal.

'Yes,' he answered simply, hoping his straightforward answer would help with her unasked question.

Will it help me, too?

'The people at Carey Cove are so kind,' he continued, returning his gaze to his son. 'And, of course, so are the folk up at the cottage hospital. I only worked in one GP surgery before—before we lost Lily—and I feel like I've really landed on my feet here.'

'I'm so glad. I can't even imagine… Especially with Harry being so young.' She made a quick correction. 'I can't imagine going through what you have at any phase of life. Losing someone you clearly loved so very much. I'm guessing that might be why you find celebrations hard? Christmas, anyway…' She gave an awkward laugh. 'Seeing as it's the only time of celebration I've known you.'

He was gripped with an unexpectedly intense desire

not only to see Christmas through her eyes, but all celebrations. New Year's Eve, Easter, Valentine's Day…

That last one caught him up short. Was he really feeling this? Attraction and interest in a woman to whom he was explaining about his deceased wife?

'Don't be afraid to let someone else into yours and Harry's lives. And remember to give her flowers.'

Lucas stared at his son for a few concentrated moments, allowing himself to absorb just how easily his son had taken to Kiara in their handful of outings. He leant in close, letting their shoulders brush against one another's, and said, 'Thank you for showing me how special it can be.'

'Pleasure,' she whispered back.

It's all mine, he thought.

Acting on an impulse, he put his arm around her shoulders and pulled her close to him for a hug as they both watched Harry fall once again and then, with an ear-to-ear grin, get back up again and wave to the pair of them as if he'd been doing it all his life.

CHAPTER SIX

'ARE YOU SURE this is all right?' Kiara winced, not wanting to overstep. She held out the flyers so Hazel could take a proper look. Not that they were hard to read even from a distance. She'd made them bright and cheery—Christmas colours, of course—and the font was extra-large.

Mince Pies at Mistletoe Cottage!

She realised it was short notice, but last night, when she hadn't been able to sleep and had been decorating inside her home, she'd decided a mini gala in the form of mulled wine, mince pies and, of course, a huge swag of mistletoe would give the fund she'd been accruing for First Steps an added boost.

'Of course, love.' Hazel dug around in the reception desk drawer for a moment, obviously looking for a couple of drawing pins so that Kiara could put her flyers up on the noticeboard. 'Who doesn't love a mini gala?' Then she gave Kiara a slightly confused look. 'Although, come to think of it, I don't think I know what a mini gala is, so I'll have to go just to satisfy my curiosity. Ah! Here we are.'

Kiara beamed as Hazel handed across a small clear plastic box of pins. They were tiny little Christmas trees! 'Aw… Thank you. And you do know it's for charity? This definitely isn't for personal gain.'

'I do, love, and let me assure you the enjoyment the villagers are getting from your incredible decorations is—well, it's like nothing Carey Cove has ever experienced before. You're a wonder.'

Kiara flushed and, to her embarrassment, felt the opening prickle of a rush of emotion tease the back of her nose. She swallowed it back, but felt it lodge somewhere between her heart and her throat.

Taking the pins, Kiara quickly turned away and, with a fastidiousness the task didn't really warrant, began to display her flyers.

She was just feeling sensitive this morning. Perhaps a bit *too* sensitive after her night out with Lucas and Harry.

It had been lovely, of course, but finding out about Lucas's wife and seeing first-hand how much he'd loved her had stuck a pin in the elation she usually felt whenever their eyes met. She was positive she hadn't been imagining it—that electric connection she felt each time they looked into one another's eyes—but there was no chance she would be able to find herself any room in a heart that was clearly filled to the brim with love for another woman.

And no chance she would even try.

Elbowing out Harry's mother to make room for herself?

Not a chance.

She'd unwittingly already played that game, and had definitely not come out the winner. She'd spent the past year re-inflating her crushed hopes, dreams, ego… you name it. All of them had been smashed beyond all recognition. The woman she'd rebuilt herself into was someone she liked. But no matter how brave a face she put on she was still fragile. And she certainly didn't want to experience heartache like that ever again. So from here on out she'd wear the firmest of emotional armour when she was around Lucas. She'd keep her heart safe…like Rapunzel in her turret.

As if to prove it to herself, she took a hold of her ponytail and twirled it into a very self-contained bun. *There.* No princes would be climbing up her hair. Not tonight. Not ever.

'Mince pies at Mistletoe Cottage, eh? Sounds like a dream evening. Are father and son duos invited?'

Lucas's warm voice wound its way round her spine like molten caramel. She steadied the wobble in her knees and smiled brightly, hoping her face didn't betray how she was really feeling. 'Yes. Everyone's welcome.'

Lucas's smile stayed put, but he frowned at her comment, the creases in his forehead actively registering the statement she was really making: *You're not a special guest.*

'Ooh! Mince pies at Mistletoe Cottage?' Sophie, her fellow midwife, joined them at the noticeboard. 'Is this for everyone?'

'Absolutely! The more the merrier,' chirped Kiara, and then, remembering how cool she'd just been with Lucas added, 'All for charity.'

Cringe!

'Hey, Lucas…' Sophie's bright blue eyes suddenly

widened. 'Are you going to see Santa tonight? You and Harry?'

Lucas looked at Kiara first, as if to double-check that he hadn't forgotten any plans they'd made, then shook his head. 'I hadn't heard Santa Claus was coming to town. I'd better watch out!'

'Ha-ha. Very funny.'

Sophie rolled her eyes and Kiara choked on a genuine laugh. The joke was silly, but funny. To her, anyway. She'd always imagined having a boyfriend who told goofy jokes. Dad jokes, really. And that the boyfriend would become her husband and a father one day.

Despite her best efforts to keep the image at bay, a mental list of the ways in which Lucas was absolutely perfect for her unfurled in her mind like a list of Christmas wishes.

'What about you, Kiara? A bunch of us are going to be there. Want to come?'

'Oh, I…' She looked at Lucas. His expression was quizzical, as if he was looking to her for a read on the situation. She didn't blame him for being confused. Yesterday Kiara would have pounced on the invitation and insisted Harry and Lucas join her. How on earth was he to understand why today Kiara was hesitating?

But, as if reading her mind, Lucas said, 'Harry has had quite a few nights out this week. Perhaps a night off—'

'But it's Santa!'

The words were out before Kiara could stop them. It appeared giving Harry the world's best Christmas experience trumped her own discomfort.

Lucas's smile brightened, the light returning to those grey eyes of his. 'You sure? He might get cranky.'

She pursed her lips. 'Cranky-schmanky. If I can handle women giving birth on a near daily basis, I can handle an overtired little boy. Besides…' she looked to Sophie '…if it's for the little ones, it isn't going to be late, is it?'

Sophie said no, and filled them in on the time and place. A village green about five miles further down the coast. 'So, see you there?' she asked.

'Yes, definitely,' Kiara answered, with a confidence she was trying to get the rest of her body to feel.

Sophie said she was off early, so would meet them there, then went off to the birthing wing where a patient was waiting. Which left Kiara and Lucas standing there on their own.

'You sure you're okay with this?' Lucas asked. 'I don't want to strong-arm you into anything.'

'Yes, of course.' She couldn't let Harry down just because his sexy dad was off-limits. It wasn't fair. And if she'd learnt anything over the past year, it was that happiness came in the smallest of moments. 'I can't wait to see his little face light up when Santa arrives. I wonder how he'll do it. There isn't any snow forecast, so…will he arrive by boat?'

Lucas shrugged, his smile now more relaxed. 'Who knows? We'll all have to wait and see. I'll pick you up after your shift?'

Her resident butterflies lifted and did a few gentle laps of her tummy. 'Sure. Sounds good.' Then, as if to prove to herself he was only a friend, she added, 'See you then, mate.'

If Lucas thought her turn of phrase was peculiar—

which it was—he didn't let her see it. Instead, he gave her a little salute and disappeared into the GP surgery.

At which point, she finally let her knees wobble.

It was going to be a long day…and an even longer night.

'Ooh!' Harry was all eyes, and his mouth was a big round O as they took in the scene.

It seemed every village form Carey Cove to Land's End and back again was doing its utmost to celebrate the arrival of Christmas. Even Lucas, who was now happy to admit he'd been Christmas resistant, was feeling a buzz of excitement as more and more children's excited chatter filled the air.

'Daddy. I can't see.'

'Would he like to ride on my shoulders?' Kiara asked, a hint of shyness tinging her voice.

Lucas bent down to pick up his son, hoping to hide his reaction to the walls that seemed to have appeared between them since he'd told Kiara about Lily. He hated it that she felt awkward around him, and wondered if this was what it would be like if he were to proactively go out and start dating.

He checked the thought, and with it felt a new understanding take purchase in his chest. He didn't want to proactively start dating. Downloading apps. Letting the kindly women at the bakery who'd been all but begging him to let them set him up with their daughters organise a few 'chance meetings'.

But he did want to see Kiara. And not as a colleague. Or even as a friend. More as…a possibility.

But he found it impossible to say as much.

'How about we take turns?' he suggested. 'I'll do round one.'

He dipped his head to see if he'd hit the right note and was rewarded with one of those soft smiles of hers. The kind where her teeth skimmed along her bottom lip as if she wasn't going to allow herself a full grin. Feeling as though he was at least heading in the right direction, he popped Harry onto his shoulders so his son could properly ogle the huge throne where Santa would be sitting when he arrived.

Kiara shot him another one of those shy smiles, then shifted her gaze towards the huge tree at the edge of the green, its thick evergreen boughs expertly swirled with festive lights and topped with a sparkling star.

'Have you two got your tree up yet?' she asked.

Lucas's smile turned guilty. 'Not strictly speaking.'

'Are there plans to put one up?'

Again, out of Harry's earshot, he had to confess, 'It's not exactly on my "To Do" list.'

A purposeful look wiped away any shyness she'd been carrying in her features. 'I am afraid I'm going to have to stage an intervention. Three-year-old boys who love Christmas as much as your son does should have a Christmas tree.'

'Oh, no. You've already done so much for—' He stopped himself. 'That would be great. We'd really like that.'

She beamed and gave Harry's foot a tap. 'You all right up there? Not too cold?'

Harry bounced his feet up and down, clapping his hands and singing, 'Happy! Happy!'

Kiara laughed as well, her smile softening into

something so pure Lucas felt as though its warmth was physically touching his heart.

He had to admit, Christmas fan or not, he was moved by the way Kiara behaved with his son. Her heart was completely open with him. When Harry laughed about something she joined in completely organically. When he was hurt—as he had been that first day, after their literal run-in—her immediate instinct was to wipe away his tears and bring a smile to his face. To care for him.

The ache in his heart doubled.

He'd never imagined another woman caring for his son as a parent, but here was proof it could be done. With both ease and grace. And perhaps, one day, with love…?

Kiara must've felt his gaze, because she turned to him and said, almost apologetically, 'I'm so grateful that you and Harry are letting me tag along on your Christmas adventures.'

'What?' Her comment was seriously out of left field. 'Not at all! It's us who should be thanking you.'

She scrunched her nose up, clearly unconvinced.

He was about to ask her where all this was coming from, but he thought he knew the answer.

It had come from him.

Even thinking it brought a thousand emotions to the surface. His body felt as if it was being torn in two directions.

This was it. The turning point he'd heard other widowers describe.

The moment when he could choose to devote himself to a familiar but heartbreaking past—or look, at long last, towards a new future.

'You're the one who's making this season special for Harry,' he said. 'For both of us,' he added, a second too late.

She blinked, and her gaze shifted from him to Harry, then back to the hum of human life around them. Families, mostly. He watched an invisible cloak of loneliness wrap around her as she took it all in. Mothers dabbing bits of food off their children's faces or clothes. Fathers doing the same as he was, hoisting their children up onto their shoulders or giving them a piggyback. Older children helping little ones with their mittens or hats.

He knew in that moment that whatever it was that had happened to her in London had stolen this from her. Being part of a family. And, worse, she'd been made to feel ashamed for wanting it. His heart ached for her. He might not have his wife, but he had his son, and the power of that was incalculable.

Could he offer her a cobbled-together version of a family?

The thought all but knocked him sideways.

He *really* liked her, and it wasn't just as a new friend and colleague. But he was still brand-new to navigating the world as a single dad. His flirting skills were properly rusty—and there was also the fact that he had no idea what he could promise.

Listen to your heart, you idiot! Life's full of risks.

An epiphany struck. Loving Lily had been one of those risks.

Aren't you happy you loved her when you had the chance? If you hadn't, you wouldn't have Harry.

The voice in his head had a point. But on the flipside... His number one responsibility was Harry. What if he got attached to Kiara? Too attached? And what if things didn't work out? Kiara was obviously trying for a fresh start in life and who knew? Maybe Carey Cove was all well and good for her right now...but would it be always?

Not everything's an 'always'. That doesn't mean it's wise to run away from life. Run to *it. You've only got this one chance to be you.*

Rather than ignore the voice in his head, Lucas reached out and did what he should have done the other night. What he should be doing right now. He took her hand in his, then gave it a light squeeze. 'I appreciate everything you're doing for me. It's not easy bringing Christmas cheer to a bah-humbugger like me.'

She looked at him, startled, but then, as his words registered, her lips began to twitch with hints of a smile. 'Anyone would be happy to do it,' she countered.

'Rubbish. Harry deserves the best and we got the best.' He saw her smile flicker with pride. 'We wouldn't be having nearly as much fun if you weren't our festive Christmas guide. Would we buddy?'

He looked up at his son, who had been distracted by a loud hum overhead. One that was growing louder by the second.

When he looked back at Kiara, she too was looking up at the sky, but he could feel her fingers lightly pressing into his palm. A calmness came over him. A peace he hadn't expected to feel when he touched another woman in this way.

Suddenly it was as plain as day: Kiara felt the same way about him as he felt about her. There was a shared attraction. But they had both been hurt. Possibly in very different ways. So they'd have to tread carefully. Respectfully.

He returned the gentle squeeze, half tempted to put his arm round her and pull her in close, when all of the sudden a huge searchlight appeared from the ground, illuminating the tell-tale red and white of one of the local Search and Rescue helicopters. The door swung open as the helicopter expertly hovered overhead.

To the crowd's delight, Santa Claus appeared, one foot already stepping onto the guard rail as he hooked himself onto a winch, and then slung an enormous red bag over his shoulder.

'Oh, my *days*! I can't look!'

Lucas and Kiara dropped their linked hands as their colleague Sophie's voice cut into the warm bubble of calm surrounding them. He wasn't sure who had let go of the other first, but it was clear neither of them wanted the rumour mill to include the two of them.

'Everything all right, Sophie?' Kiara put an arm around the other woman's shoulders, the concern in her voice taking the lead.

'No. Seriously…no.' Sophie shaded her eyes and looked down at the ground as the crowd cheered. 'How can they all watch?'

Lucas looked up to see what could be causing her such distress. Santa was being winched down…no surprise there…

'Ooh, I can't look!' Sophie repeated, looking down at the ground and stamping her feet, as if willing herself into another time and place.

'Are you afraid of heights?' Kiara asked, dipping her head so her colleague could see her face.

'Big-time. That Santa's either insane or more intent on spreading good cheer than any other Santa I've ever seen in my life. I mean—' She threw a panicked look at

Harry, who had just looked down at her. 'Not that I've met any different Santas. That's Santa. Obviously.' She winced. 'Are you sure you're all right up there, Harry?'

Harry clapped his hands, then pointed up to the sky. 'I want to be up *there*!'

Sophie gave a low moan.

Lucas gave her back a gentle rub. 'You're looking a bit pale, Sophie. Can we get you something?'

'I can take you somewhere to sit down and get you some water if you like,' Kiara offered, throwing Lucas an *Is that all right?* look.

Of course it was. Anything Sophie needed. Poor woman. He had the opposite situation going on. A three-year-old boy bouncing on his shoulders with sheer delight, begging to climb up and meet Santa.

Kiara put a hand on his arm and in a low voice said, 'I'm going to take Sophie away from the crowd for a bit. If we don't catch up at the end of the event, I'll figure out a way to get back to the village on my own.'

'Don't be silly. We wouldn't leave you here.'

Her eyes snapped to his as if he'd said something much more personal. More intimate. And he wondered again what on earth had happened to her back in London to make her so grateful for simple kindnesses.

But maybe they weren't simple. Perhaps those were the moments that should be cherished the most. Fingers brushing. Eyes locking. Heartbeats pounding out the beats as a reminder that you were alive. After all, those few precious moments when their fingers had been interlocked were still buzzing through his bloodstream like a brand-new life force.

Later, after Santa had handed out small gifts to all the children and heard their wishes, then been winched back up to the helicopter to the cheers of the crowd, Kiara found her way to them. She said she'd walked Sophie to her car in the end and, after ensuring she felt well enough to drive, had left her to go home.

Harry fell asleep almost the instant he was buckled into his car seat, the brand-new teddy bear from Santa clutched in his arms.

They drove home in relative silence, and when they stopped at her house—a beacon of Christmas cheer that now instantly brought a smile to his lips because he knew who was behind it—Lucas decided to tell Kiara just how much having her in their lives meant to him.

Just as he began to stumble through some words, Kiara unbuckled her seatbelt and quietly eased herself out of the car with her finger to her lips. She pointed to Harry with a whispered, 'See you in the morning.'

He waited until she got to her front door, and when she waved goodbye and disappeared behind it an emptiness filled him he hadn't expected to feel.

When he got home, and was tucking Harry into bed after their usual night-time story, Harry curled up to him and asked, 'Can Kiara stay here sometimes? I think she'd be good at telling stories, too.'

The question knocked the air out of him. It was an innocent enough question for a child. His little boy could hardly know about Lucas's very adult dream and nor would he. Harry was simply stating a fact: He liked it when they were all together.

He wasn't trying to replace Lily. To be fair to his son, he didn't even remember her enough to miss her. He'd only ever known life with the two of them, and yet he seemed instinctively to know there was something missing in their lives. One more piece to the puzzle they had yet to complete.

Instead of answering—because he simply didn't know how—Lucas kissed his son's head, wished him sweet dreams and told him to sleep well so they'd be on time to pick Kiara up in the morning.

'But that's hours away!' Harry whined through a yawn. And then, as exhaustion took over, he fell asleep, his new teddy tucked beneath his hand.

A restless sensation took hold of Lucas. He wandered through the house picking things up and putting them down somewhere else, then returning them to their original position. He turned on all the lights. He turned them off. Pulled the curtains shut. Opened the curtains. Rather than seeing the things he had done, he saw all the things he hadn't. There were beds, and sofas, and even a throw cushion or two. But it didn't feel like his childhood home had done, with designated places for all the furniture to be rearranged to make room for the Christmas tree. The presents. The space where he and his siblings would play with their toys for days after, until his mother, fed up with tripping over train tracks or dolls' houses, finally made them take their shiny new possessions up to their rooms.

It didn't feel like a home at all.

And, although he'd managed to pick up the pieces after Lily's death—raise his son, find a new job, find a new house—he still seemed to be missing one elemental part of himself.

The next morning was a disaster. He and Harry had both slept poorly—to the point when Harry had left his own bed and crawled in with Lucas…something he hadn't done for months. Once sleep had finally come, they'd both slept through the alarm.

Getting themselves together had been chaos. And now Harry was overtired and cranky. Irritable to the point where Lucas wondered if he was coming down with something. At least he was with the childminder today and not at nursery. The calm atmosphere there would do him good.

When they reached Kiara's house, Harry dropped his scooter and ran to the door, demanding that Lucas pick him up so he could reach the bell. After several unanswered ding-dongs they were forced to accept that she wasn't at home, and Harry had a proper meltdown.

There were tears. Wailing. Tiny fists pummelling the artificial snow blanket laid out beneath the dancing penguins. If he hadn't been so tired himself, Lucas might've tried to console his son more than he did. Instead, he knelt down in the 'snow' beside him, rubbing his back and saying on a loop, 'I know, son. I know…'

He wished she was here, too.

After he'd finally managed to soothe Harry, he dropped him off at the childminder, who assured him she'd dole out some extra TLC, and possibly an extra nap today. She also suggested a quiet night at home to counterbalance the excitement of the season. She said it kindly enough, but Lucas knew what she was really saying: *Are you sure you're prioritising your son?*

By the time he'd greeted Hazel at the hospital, taken off his jacket and made himself a cup of tea he thought he had regrouped enough to be as present for his patients as he needed to be. The childminder was right. He'd leapt too far, too soon, with this whole Christmas thing with Kiara. His son was only three. He didn't need all the bells and whistles. Especially when there was confusion. He'd dial it back…maybe get Harry a snow globe or something to tide him over until the big day. And then, one day when Harry was older, they'd set about figuring out how to do Christmas their way. Whatever that was.

But when he opened the door to his surgery, his resolve to face the season on his own disintegrated instantly.

There, on the table, was a tiny living Christmas tree, all decorated, with a small handwritten note that said simply:

A starter tree for the two Wilde men in my life.
K x

CHAPTER SEVEN

KIARA SHOWED HER patient the blood pressure gauge. 'We can do it again if you like, but I think it might stress you out more.' She released the cuff and untagged the Velcro from around the woman's arm. 'It is worth bearing in mind that one fifty-nine over one ten is edging on severely high.'

Audrey Keene gave her arm a rub where the cuff had been and blew out a breath that clearly didn't calm her in the slightest. The poor woman was all nerves.

'Would you like to call your husband?' asked Kiara.

'Can't.' She said briskly. 'He's away until Crimbo.'

'And he's out of touch until then?'

'Oil rigs. His is way out. He can send texts sometimes, but I don't want to tell him this in a text.' She pretended to type on her phone. *'Hey, babe. Your wife and child might be dead by the time you get back. Merry Christmas!'*

'Hey...' Kiara soothed. 'No. We've got this.'

She took the phone out of her patient's hand, put it on the desk, and then took both of Audrey's hands in hers. She looked her straight in the eye. This was her first child, and she was only young. Twenty-three. Having a husband who worked out on the oil rigs most of the year didn't help either.

'There are risks with any pregnancy but being aware of what's happening with you and the baby is half the battle. You're at the best midwifery centre in the area. And there's a hospital nearby if—'

'Hospital!'

Audrey paled further, and Kiara could actually see her pulse pounding in her throat. Oh, crumbs… Were they were heading for a panic attack?

'We're here now. Look at me, Audrey. Focus on my eyes. Breathe in and out. Nice and slow. That's it. Now, is there anyone else we can ring for you?'

Audrey pressed her lips together, then pushed them out, her face contorting as if she were about to cry. 'I'd really feel happier if my GP was aware of this.'

'Not a problem.' Kiara's heart went out to Audrey. She picked up a pen. 'Just give me the number and I'll give them a ring as soon as we're done.

'I mean…' Audrey squeaked. 'Right now. I think we should tell them right now.'

Kiara and Audrey stared at the blood pressure machine. It was telling both of them the same thing. Audrey's blood pressure was way too high and she was potentially staring down the barrel of pre-eclampsia—something definitely worth avoiding. Professionally, Kiara knew she was spot-on with her diagnosis. And years of experience had taught her that trying to talk a frightened pregnant woman out of something when she was feeling alone and vulnerable was a bad idea.

'Not a problem,' she said again. 'Shall we get a urine sample and take a blood test first?' she suggested. 'That way we can give her a fuller picture of what's going on and—'

Audrey cut her off. 'My GP's a he—not a she.'

'Sorry.' Kiara pressed a hand to her chest. 'My bad. I shouldn't have assumed.'

Her thoughts instantly pinged to Lucas. She wondered, if he had become her GP, would she have wanted to stay with him because he was a good GP, or run for the hills. Because how on earth could she tell him if she had…um…warts, for example? She didn't, but…

Her frown tipped into a smile as it occurred to her that Lucas was a man she could probably say anything to, no matter how embarrassing. He had a way about him. A calmness that assured her she wasn't being judged. Or dismissed. Or being kept in a tiny corner of his life so that he had plenty of room left to lead his real life.

In inviting her to help him steer through Christmas with Harry, he had invited her into the heart of his life, and she knew it had taken a lot of trust for him to do as much. Being with them brought her so much joy… Although maybe leaving the Christmas tree on his desk had been a step too far. There was hanging out together and there was inserting yourself into someone's life far more than they wanted.

Which was how Peter's wife had found out she existed. Kiara had made him a playlist and sent it to his phone. His wife had found it when she'd been going through his messages… The thought mortified her. If she'd been suspicious enough to be going through his phone messages, there was no chance Kiara had been his first affair. It was just too humiliating to think about.

She pushed the thoughts way back into the recesses of her mind and reminded herself that she'd only done the Christmas tree thing as her way of drawing a line in the sand. Or should that be putting a piece of tinsel on the snow?

Either way, whatever she thought had been buzzing between them hadn't been real.

She refocused on the situation at hand. Audrey and her high blood pressure. Pre-eclampsia was no joke, and they needed to get to the bottom of this.

Kiara softened her tone even further and, putting away the blood pressure equipment, said, 'Right, my dear. Are you happy to do bloods today? See if we can get a better picture of what's going on?'

'Um…' Audrey fretted her fingers into a weave, then shook them out as if they had ants on them and began tapping her index fingers against her chin as she spoke. 'Please don't think I'm only second-guessing you. I'm second-guessing everyone. You can't even begin to imagine what I'm putting my husband through. He was just home, and I'm pretty sure I'm the one who drove him back out to the rig. The poor man didn't know whether to buy me pickles or peanut butter or ice cream. No wonder he left!' Tears bloomed in her eyes and her voice lurched up an octave into a wail. 'I'm *impossible* to live with! How is he going to want to live with me when I have the baby?'

'Hey…' Kiara soothed, handing her a tissue as the tears began to fall. 'You're a mass of hormones. Don't give too much weight to the micro-moments. It's the big picture you need to keep in mind.'

It was advice she could do with listening to herself. Whenever she was near Lucas, she, too, was 'a mass of hormones'. A *mess*, more like. Especially as she had to keep reminding herself, *He's not available. His heart is already full and there's no room at the inn for you!*

As a result, teasing reality apart from fantasy after they'd spent the evening together had become her number one pastime. And the number one thing she'd tried not to think about at work.

Even so…

She curled one of her hands into the other, feeling her body instinctively pulling up the memory of Lucas taking her hand in his and giving it the lightest of squeezes. It could have meant nothing. It could have been an accident. It could have just been a friendly thank-you. Or it could have meant he was feeling that same electric connection she was every time they were together.

She looked from her hands to Audrey's and realised her patient's hands were trembling. 'Audrey, I'm here for you. I am your midwife and we've got this. We're going to do the tests and sort everything out—all right?'

'No!' Audrey snapped. 'No. It's *not* all right. *Nothing's* going to be all right.' A look came over her face that was almost frightening. 'I can't do this on my own. I never even have the right food in the house. How on earth am I going to grow this baby properly, let alone *have* the baby. What if I die? I might die!'

Audrey was definitely having a panic attack. Kiara wondered if she'd had more than one—hence the high blood pressure.

She got down on her knees in front of Audrey and covered her hands with her own. 'Audrey? Can you look at me please?'

Audrey began to shake her head back and forth, muttering something she couldn't quite make out. Her breathing was coming in short, sharp huffs now.

'Audrey? Audrey… I need you to look at me. We're going to slow down your breathing, otherwise you might get dizzy.'

Audrey kept murmuring the same thing. The words had a familiarity Kiara couldn't quite work out, until all of the sudden she heard it loud and clear: *'Dr Wilde.'*

'Is Dr Wilde your GP? Dr Lucas Wilde?' She had to keep repeating his name, all the while reminding herself that she shouldn't let it taste so sweet on her tongue.

Eventually she got a nod of affirmation out of her patient.

'Would you like to see him?' Kiara asked.

'Yes!' Audrey was all but pleading.

Kiara's body flooded with an energy that didn't know what to do with itself. She had a patient who needed help. From Lucas. The one man in the world Kiara loved to be with but also didn't. Because whenever she was with him her emotions took on a life of their own. One minute they were demanding she give him a Christmas tree. The next they were regretting it because of the ample opportunity to misread the gesture.

Was it friendly? Or over-friendly? An invitation to throw caution to the wind and see what all the crazy frissons buzzing between them were about? Or the total opposite? Which, of course, made a whole other set of feelings burst to the fore. Because whenever she looked into Lucas's eyes she felt something so much more powerful than anything she'd ever felt when she was with Peter. It terrified her—because how would she ever survive another broken heart?

She wouldn't. Not to mention the fact that there wasn't a storage unit large enough for all her Christmas things, let alone the decorations she had yet to buy. And, of course, she'd have to find a new place to live and a new job—which she didn't want because she completely loved it here. And Harry! She couldn't even get started on how she felt about Lucas's son, because just when she thought she'd tapped into the bottom of her emotional well, it became insanely apparent that there were fathoms of emotions yet to go.

'Kiara?' Audrey's expression was a mix of concern and confusion as she continued to fight for breath. 'Do you not like Dr Wilde?'

'No! I mean yes. Of course. Why would you ask that?'

'Your face has gone all funny.'

Kiara's cheeks burned with embarrassment, and she made a heroic effort to refashion her expression into something vaguely approaching professionalism—because her focus shouldn't ever have veered from Audrey.

See? This is why you don't get all gooey over colleagues who aren't available. You take your eyes off the ball and go into a tailspin whenever their names are mentioned.

She gave her spine a sharp wriggle and took hold of Audrey's hand again, all the while lobbing her swirling mass of mixed emotions into the ether. And hopefully beyond.

'Let's call him right now. He's only downstairs.'

She took the phone and coached Audrey through some more steadying breaths as she rang down to Reception.

'Hi, Hazel? Is there any chance you could put me through to Dr Wilde?'

Hazel said she'd just seen him heading to the break room—most likely for a cup of tea. 'Would you like me to fetch him for you, love?'

'Yes, please. And can you tell him it's quite urgent? It's about one of his patients.'

Right. Excellent. That was more like it. Patients first. Totally uncontrollable emotions squished. Job done.

Lucas flew up the stairs, skipping every other one. He had seen enough of Kiara at work to know she would only call for help if she really needed it. But if it was extremely urgent, there were people closer to hand than him.

Hazel hadn't mentioned who the patient was, and he could only guess that the omission meant Kiara was honouring patient confidentiality. Whoever it was, she must be one of his.

The door to her room opened just as he was about to knock.

Kiara's expression was focused and in control. Before she stepped aside, she quickly explained. 'I've got Audrey Keene with me. A discussion about her high blood pressure has escalated. I've been trying to steady her breathing, but she kept requesting you, so I thought I had better defer to the patient's wishes.'

He walked into the room with a nod of thanks as Kiara closed the door behind him.

Seeing her like this, charged with energy and drive, reminded him anew of just how fundamental a response he had to her. It wasn't just Christmas trees and dancing penguins that had drawn them together. It was more visceral than that. They were a match. In good times and, if her expression was anything to go by, in bad.

Before Kiara could say anything else, Audrey began wheezing. Lucas took two long-legged strides and was soon squatting down so that he was at eye level with her. 'Audrey? It's me. Dr Wilde.' To Kiara he said, 'Can you find me a small paper bag?'

She nodded and went straight to the supplies cupboard, returning seconds later with a plain white bag. After she'd handed him the bag, she scribbled something on a bit of paper and held it up out of Audrey's eye line.

Panic attack?

He nodded. Audrey had been prone to them even before she fell pregnant. He was surprised Kiara hadn't noticed the mention of them in her notes. He had definitely made a record of them. Then again, Kiara was new here. Perhaps Audrey had staggered in this way, already mid-flow. Or, more likely, they'd been going through her notes together as Kiara got up to speed and, unfortunately for Audrey, a case of the nerves had leapt to the fore.

'Audrey?' Lucas put a hand on her shoulder, 'It's Dr Wilde,' he repeated. 'Kiara and I are both here to help you. Did you come in this way? Feeling anxious?'

Audrey reached out a hand and gripped his, as if

trying to physically channel some of his easy, steady breathing into her own lungs.

In a low, steady voice, Kiara said, 'Audrey came in to see Marnie, not realising she was on maternity leave. She and I came in here to go through her notes and I thought her blood pressure was a bit high.'

'What were the numbers?'

She told him, and in that same, low, steady voice went on, 'Her husband's away working and it doesn't sound like there's anyone else to ring. Do you think it might be something else? Should we run an ECG?'

He shook his head. 'Not just yet. But you're right. We should definitely do some tests before she leaves.' He added some sunshine to his voice and said to Audrey, 'Sometimes we take a little walk when things get too intense—don't we, Audrey?'

She was staring at him, wide-eyed with fear, one hand on her belly, one holding the paper bag to her mouth.

'That's right… Slow and steady… One…two… three…four… And hold for one…two… Excellent.' He sat back on his heels, listening as Audrey's breaths started to come in short staccato bursts again. 'Audrey? Kiara and I are concerned about you and the baby. We're going to breathe with you, okay? All three of us breathing together… One, two, three…'

After a few moments, Kiara shot him a look. It wasn't helping. Their eyes locked, and in the few seconds their gazes held they exchanged a raft of information. These short, sharp exhalations of hers were pushing all the CO2 out of her body. The absence of CO2 would make her blood more alkaloid, which would then kick off a domino effect on the metabolism of calcium, which she would feel in her hands, then her feet, and then, unless she could regain control, her heart.

'Shall we see if we can get you up and walking?'

Lucas took one of Audrey's hands in his and wrapped an arm around her shoulders as she pushed herself up and out of the chair with the other hand. He signalled with his eyes that Kiara should take Audrey's other hand, which she did, wrapping an arm around the back of her waist as she did so. Which was just as well, because the moment she rose out of the chair Audrey gave a precarious wobble.

They steadied her as if they were one, exchanging glances and unspoken thoughts as organically as if they'd worked together for years.

'Thank you for the Christmas tree,' he whispered as Audrey regrouped for a moment.

Kiara's eyes lit up in surprise and then softened with pleasure. She gave him a smiley nod but said nothing, pressing her lips tight together as if she was holding his thanks inside herself like a present.

Audrey began to pull at her collar, as if she were trying to get fresh air on herself. Beads of sweat began to present on her forehead.

'Audrey?' Lucas turned his full attention back on to their patient, an idea growing from seeing the gesture. 'Let's get outside in the sunshine, shall we?'

Audrey managed a nod, which was good. It was progress. It meant she was breathing slowly enough to be able to listen.

Lucas began to guide them towards the stairs, anxious that taking the lift might trigger more panic. Their progress was slow. From the looks some of their colleagues were throwing them, Lucas was beginning to wonder if he'd made the right call, but the first thing Audrey did when they finally were outside in the beautifully manicured gardens, lit golden by the winter light, was take a huge, relieved breath. As if it was being indoors that had been the source of her anxiety and nothing more.

Relief flooded through Kiara's features. She wore an expression which no doubt matched his own. It was always a tenuous call—leaving behind the myriad of machines they could hook her up to and the medicines they could give her to calm her down. But he knew Audrey well enough to go with his gut, and it had paid dividends.

He and Kiara pointed out various things in the garden: bright yellow winter jasmine, the colourful cyclamen beds, a low hedge made of orange and red dogwood boughs, glowing with the same colours. There were holly trees weighted with berries. And, of course, a huge evergreen, circled from bottom to top with fairy lights.

'Are you looking forward to Christmas, Audrey?'

Kiara's own excitement shone through, instantly bringing a smile to Lucas's face.

'I love the simplicity of this tree…' she pointed to the towering evergreen '…but I think Dr Wilde can confirm that my love of Christmas is…erm…'

'Not exactly subtle?' Lucas supplied, when Kiara failed to find a description of her glittering love of the festive season.

'Oh. My. Gawd.' Audrey stopped in her tracks, as if the entire panic attack had never happened at all, then threw up her hands and clapped them together as if she'd just discovered Kiara was a rock star. 'Do you live in that adorable cottage that looks as if it's straight out of the North Pole?' she asked.

'Guilty.'

'Why guilty?' Audrey looked at Lucas, as if trying to garner support. 'That place is pure magic! Right? I mean, I'm totally right. Magic,' she reiterated, with a stern look at Lucas as if daring him to contest her.

How could he? Kiara's love of Christmas was what had first put them in one another's path, and he had to admit this Christmas season so far had been his best in years—if not ever.

Lucas and Kiara shared a smile as Audrey began a long, detailed explanation of how much she adored Mistletoe Cottage, and how she'd been making sure to walk past it every day since the first set of decorations had gone up. It reminded her of her love of Christmas as a young girl, and she'd been hoping that whoever lived there would decorate it that way for ever, so she could walk her baby past, and then her toddler, and then hopefully, because of Mistletoe Cottage, her baby would love Christmas as much as she did.

Suddenly aware that she'd been gabbling on, she clapped her fingers to her mouth, pressing a giggle into submission. 'I'm sorry. I didn't— Hey!' She widened her hands and grinned at the pair of them. 'The panic attack is gone! Your Christmas cottage cured me!'

Laughing, the three of them headed back into the warmth of the hospital. Lucas noted that a swag of mistletoe had appeared in the doorway to the staff lounge as they made their way to Kiara's room.

'I'm happy to stay while Kiara takes your bloods and other stats,' Lucas began, but Audrey stopped him.

'I'm good. Kiara and I need to discuss the merits of seasonal glitter balls.'

'And you'll make sure to ring one of us if you ever feel panicky again?' he asked.

'Better than that!' Audrey beamed. 'I'm going to take myself on a walk to Mistletoe Cottage next time. How could I not relax, looking at all of that joy?'

Kiara grinned at him as she pumped up the blood pressure gauge, and to their collective delight he saw that it was significantly lower than it had been the first-time round.

Lucas headed to the door, but before leaving he ducked his head back in and asked Kiara, 'Hot chocolate later?'

She scrunched her nose. 'I can't.' She threw a look at Audrey, then explained, 'I'm having an open house tomorrow night.'

'Oh, yes. Of course. Harry ensured I put that on the calendar.' He was about to offer to help, but as Audrey was there decided now wasn't the time.

He gave her a wave goodbye just as Kiara was explaining to Audrey about the charity she was collecting money for, and then he heard Audrey's squeals of delight as Kiara started telling her about her festive cushion collection.

He hadn't realised how broadly he was smiling until he passed the main desk, where once again Nya was giving him that mischievous smile of hers. Rather than look bewildered, as he had before, this time he gave her a jaunty salute and danced what he hoped looked like a small but carefree Christmas jig.

CHAPTER EIGHT

MINCE PIES?

There were scores of the star-topped, sugar-dusted beauties, fresh out of the oven, covering every platter and plate Kiara owned.

Mulled wine?

Gallons of it. The warm, enticing scent of cinnamon, cloves and allspice was almost literally wrapping her house in an extra layer of magic.

She had even warmed up some apple juice as well, and lightly spiced it with cinnamon. And she'd made gingerbread men and put out bowls of nibbles just in case anyone happened to stay into the early evening.

She'd also put up countless more baubles, but…

She went outside to look at her cottage with fresh eyes. It was all there. The dancing penguins. The snowman and his pals. Stars. Candy canes. Huge gingerbread men. Even Santa was up there on her roof now, courtesy of the man who'd come to adjust her television aerial the other day. And a few elves.

The decorative trees in her front garden had twirls of lights on them, as did all of the super-sized candy canes and the wicker reindeer. There were moving light displays too, that made it look as if the house was being softly blanketed by huge, decorative snowflakes. And there were fairy light angels who, when a button was pressed, sang Christmas carols. There were super-sized 'presents' and glittery bell baubles.

Every single Christmas decoration she could think of.

She had set up several fake gingerbread houses, which were actually coin collectors, at the front gate, by her front door and on the kitchen counter, all with pamphlets explaining about First Steps and why it was such a great charity. She'd already managed to collect an impressive amount of money in her little Santa's workshop donation box, and was hoping today would put her at her target goal.

But still there was something missing. And she didn't have a clue what it was.

Night fell early this time of year…in the afternoon, actually. And she had taken the day off especially to make sure her open house was truly open to the public by the time schools let out. She knew Harry and Lucas wouldn't be coming until later, but from the moment people started arriving—first in trickles, then in a steady flow—she simply couldn't stop scanning the crowd, looking for that tidily cropped head of brown hair attached to a man she knew she really shouldn't be falling for but, against her better judgement, had already fallen for.

'Kiara!'

Before she could register who had said her name, Kiara was being wrapped in the arms of a definitely pregnant woman. She realised it was Audrey, her patient from yesterday. She looked an entirely changed woman. Her dark hair was twisted up underneath an adorable knitted cap in green and white stripes with a line of reindeer knitted along the base and a huge gold bauble on top. Her cheeks glowed with health and her eyes were sparkling bright. But it was her smile that was the best thing to see.

Still holding on to one another's arms, they pulled back and grinned at one another. 'You look amazing,' they both said at the same time, then laughed.

More seriously, Kiara asked, 'Are you feeling all right?'

'Much better.' Audrey's voice was ripe with gratitude, and once again she pulled Kiara in for a hug. 'I can't thank you enough for everything you and Dr Wilde did for me.'

'Uh-oh! What have I done now?'

Lucas's buttery voice swept with warm caramelly magic down Kiara's spine, swirling and dreamily pooling in her tummy, where… Yes, there they were…the Christmas butterflies had taken flight.

Their eyes connected and that increasingly familiar buzz swept through her, as if a thousand fireflies were heralding the arrival of her soulmate.

Which, of course, was completely ridiculous.

He'd loved his wife. Who he couldn't be with any more. So he would not love another woman. No matter how right it felt when they were together.

Lucas's lips parted, his expression soft, as if he, too, was going through a similar internal checklist.

I like her, but I don't love her. I can't *love her.*

Before he could say anything, Lucas was being wrapped in one of Audrey's heartfelt bear hugs.

'Kiara!' Harry appeared from around the other side of the picket fence and dropped his scooter, running and jumping up into her arms as if he'd done it a thousand times. He was wearing a knitted beanie that looked like a gingerbread man, his blond curls peeking out from beneath the hat and a bright red yarn bobble topping it all off. He looked adorable. And so, so lovable. She hugged him close, cherishing his little boy scent. She didn't care what the nursery rhymes said. This little boy smelt of sugar and spice and everything nice.

'Daddy!'

Kiara looked up to see that Lucas was standing in front of them, holding out his arms for his little boy.

'Here. I'll take him.' He was smiling, and his expression was kind, but there was something about the gesture that cut her to the quick. It was as if he was reminding her that Harry wasn't hers to love. Not in the way a mother would. Just like her ex's wife had.

'You think you can have what we have? A family? You'll never have a family. You'll never know this kind of love.'

Lucas's brow crinkled and he stepped in closer. 'He's a bit heavy for you, isn't he?' He angled his head to try and meet her gaze. 'Kiara…?'

The movement, his proximity and the scent of him—juniper and pine—jarred her into action. 'Yes. Of course. You're right. I tell everyone I need to build up my upper body strength. Ha-ha! You'd think carrying babies around all day would do the trick, but nope!' She handed Harry over and gave her bicep a little squeeze. 'Nothing there but flimsy noodles! Protein…' She tapped the side of her nose in an attempt at a wise gesture. 'I have it on good authority that I should eat more protein.'

Oh, God. If the earth could open up and swallow her whole right now, she'd be nothing but grateful.

Lucas shifted Harry onto his hip and gave one of his little boy's hands a kiss before giving her a slightly perplexed smile. 'You don't need to change a thing, Kiara.' Lucas seemed genuinely confused by her peculiar monologue. 'You're perfect as you are.'

What? He thought she was perfect? No one in the history of her entire life had ever called her anything close to perfect. Did that mean—

Lucas made his voice bright and childish as he gave Harry's hand a jiggle. 'Isn't she Harry? We wouldn't want our new friend any other way.'

'Happy…happy!' sing-songed Harry.

Of course. Perfect as a friend. Well, that was her solidly placed in the Friend Zone.

A sinkhole clearly wasn't going to help her out here. Panic began to grip her chest in the same way she'd seen it take hold of Audrey yesterday. But this was not the time or place to have any sort of meltdown.

Having her emotions split into a kaleidoscope of conflicting emotions by a man who had unwittingly swept into her heart and made her feel whole again was a brand-new level of heartache she wished she didn't know existed.

'Um… Mince pies.' She pointed randomly over her shoulder and then said, 'Apple juice,' before quickly excusing herself, refusing to register the bewildered expression playing across Lucas's face as she turned away and quickly absorbed herself into the crowd.

An hour later, as the crowd began to clear, Lucas appeared in front of her with a broom and dustpan and a very sleepy Harry at his side. 'I thought maybe we could help you clean up.' Harry unleashed a huge, unprotected yawn. Lucas gave him a fond look. 'And by "we" I mean me. Any chance I could put this guy in the spare room for a nap?'

'Oh, gosh…' She pulled a face. 'You don't have to stay and help. That's ever so kind—'

Lucas held up a hand. 'It's the least we can do after all the joy you've brought us.'

Harry leant against his father's leg and wrapped his arms around it, looking as if he might fall asleep on the spot. The complication of emotions she'd felt earlier suddenly lost their relevance. How could they be relevant when Harry so clearly needed to be sleeping? Besides… Even though adrenaline was still running through her from an evening spent mostly trying to avoid Lucas, she had to admit an extra set of hands to help with the clearing up would be genuinely useful.

They cleaned the place as if they had been doing it together for years. Intuitively knowing when the other person needed a hand or when it would be all right to head off to another room and tidy up there.

'Gosh!' Kiara looked around her living room with a smile. 'It looks as good as new.'

She smiled at Lucas, who was standing by her wood basket. He was so handsome. So kind. It tore at her heart that she had found someone so perfect to love and yet her love was so destined to be unrequited. A loneliness crept into her bones. She didn't want to give it space, but despite her best efforts to push it away she shivered.

'Shall I pop a couple of logs on the fire?' Lucas asked.

'That'd be nice. Kiara smiled in gratitude and then,

suddenly wanting more than anything not to have this moment end, blurted, 'You wouldn't want to stay for a quiet glass of wine and a final mince pie, would you? Something to fortify you before carrying that son of yours home.'

What the *hell*? Had she gone *mad*?

The good fairy on her shoulder—the responsible one—was looking at her as if she'd just grown an extra head. Women who'd had their hearts crushed by one married man did not invite emotionally unavailable sexy dads to stay and drink wine on their sofa with them.

That naughty fairy—the one who was greedy and wanted to spend just a few quiet moments with Lucas before she officially called the evening to a close—didn't think there'd be much harm in just one more glass of mulled wine by the fire, with only the twinkling lights of the tree lighting up the room…

The good fairy prepared herself to stage an intervention.

'That sounds like a great idea.'

Lucas was already putting logs on the fire, and from this angle she had a really good view of his very pinchable bum.

He turned back and smiled at her. 'Thoughtful of you to give Harry some extra sleeping time.'

Ha! Yes. Totally *not* what she'd been thinking. But she made a vague noise, indicating that that had definitely been her intention.

She was going to make a joke about trying to lift a sleeping Harry and failing, but thought better of it. Rehashing her more humiliating moments in front of the man she wished she could love was an exercise in self-defeatism she didn't need to subject herself to.

She bustled around a bit, until finally presenting Lucas with a plate laden with mince pies, some cheese and crackers, as well as the promised glass of wine.

He noticed she was now empty-handed. 'You're not having anything?' he asked.

Unlike the first time her ex, Peter, had taken her to the pub, and she'd agreed not only to a second but a third glass of wine, this evening the imaginary good fairy had proactively taken her by the shoulders and shaken her when she'd pulled a second glass from the cupboard just now. Tipsy and besotted were not a good combination. Not for her. Not at any time of year. But especially not at Christmas. And super-especially not with Lucas Wilde sitting on her sofa looking like the Christmas card of her dreams.

She shook her head. 'I have enough Christmas cheer running though me already.' She pointed back at the kitchen, where the kettle was coming to a boil. 'I'm on the herbal tea now. Christmas spice.'

She waggled her hands and Lucas laughed.

'Leave it to you to find Christmas tea. What is it? Gingerbread-flavoured?'

'Close!' Her voice matched his playful tone, and despite her effort to keep herself in the Friend Zone she heard herself walking a fine line between fun and flirtation. 'Spiced apple.'

'Sounds good.' He rubbed his tummy.

And, as ridiculous as it was, she loved the homeliness of the gesture. It was so Papa Bear.

To stop herself from throwing herself at him, ripping his shirt off and begging him to tell her if his emotional landscape was as tumultuous and horny as hers, she went back to the kitchen and stuffed her head in the freezer for a count of ten deep breaths.

But even that didn't work. As she prepared her tea, and a small plate of snacks, she let an image of the two of them as a couple slip into her mind. Right here in Mistletoe Cottage. It was still decorated for Christmas, but maybe not quite to the level she'd done it this year. They'd have just had a dinner party, maybe. Or, like tonight, a neighbourhood open house, ripe with laughter and community spirit. They'd be keeping their voices low as Harry slept, aware of his building excitement for Christmas. Come Christmas Eve they'd be hanging three stockings by the chimney with care. Laying out surprise Christmas presents. Curling up on the sofa together…

She balled her hands into fists and mentally tried to knock some sense back into her head. Being with Lucas wasn't her reality, and it definitely wouldn't be her future.

'You're the one who invited him to stay, but it isn't your fault he said yes and then looked all sexy and desirable,' said the naughty fairy.

'You're the one who will sit at the opposite end of the sofa and eat mince pies with him and talk about the joys of getting urine samples...then stand as far away as possible as you wave him off when he and his son go back to their own home. Their real home,' said the sensible fairy.

'That plan is stupid,' said the naughty fairy, pouting.

'Everything all right?'

Lucas was at the doorway, concern creasing his features as he took in the mad vision of Kiara clutching her head. And very possibly talking to herself.

'Good! Fine! I—' she began, and then, hoping her parents wouldn't mind, she covered the moment with a half-truth. 'Just missing my family, that's all.'

Lucas pressed one of his hands to his chest in a gesture of undiluted empathy. 'I hear you… It can really hit you out of the blue this time of year, can't it?'

She nodded, grateful that he understood. And doubly grateful that they now had a sort of neutral topic to discuss. One that wasn't about the two of them, anyway.

Lucas crossed over to her and picked up her plate, the gentle waft of his man scent obliterating anything the sensible fairy had suggested from what was left of her brain.

'C'mon. Grab your tea and let's get you settled on the sofa for a well-deserved break.'

When he turned his back to lead the way into the living room, Kiara feigned a swoon. How could someone so perfect be so far out of reach?

Because he's not meant to be yours. So suck it up and eat a mince pie.

Kiara settled on the sofa, popping a Santa face cushion on her lap to stand in as a table. When she looked up to find him looking at her, a rush of shyness swept through her. They'd never sat like this before and just… talked. There was always some sort of festive buzz happening around them. Or work things. It didn't surprise her, though, to realise that it felt as natural as if they'd been doing it for years.

'Does your family do a big Christmas?' she asked, after a few moments of contented munching.

Lucas shook his head. 'Not so much these days.'

Kiara nodded, more interested in what he wasn't saying than what he was. 'Is that recent?'

He gave a forlorn huff of a laugh. 'If you mean is it since Lily died? No. It was before that. I guess the Wilde family were never really wild about Christmas.' He quirked an eyebrow at her. 'See what I did there?' He waved off his silly pun, then explained more seriously, 'My parents retired to France a few years ago, and my sisters go there for Christmas. Lily's parents took to going on cruises once the children had flown the coop, and I was usually working right up until "the big day", so I never made too much of an effort to get down to France. And once the little guy was born… I guess it was just another excuse to stay put. Sort things out as best we could.'

Kiara frowned. 'Do you all get on? Your families?' She shook her head. 'Sorry… That's quite a personal question.'

'Oh, yes we do.' His response was genuine. 'Seriously, I didn't mean to give you any "crazy family" vibes. I suppose we're more significant birthday types than Christmas types, that's all.' He leant forward to give her knee a tap and his smile warmed. 'I think this is the first year I can genuinely say I have been properly infused with the Christmas spirit.'

Despite her silent warning to herself that this was just a friendly chat, she blushed, flattered to the core by the compliment. And then the rush of feelings she'd been trying to keep at bay swept in and filled her body with a warm glow she never wanted to shake.

And why should she?

Here she was, on the sofa with a man she admired

and was stupidly attracted to. His son was sleeping peacefully in the spare room. A fire was crackling away. There was wine and herbal tea and snacks, and the energy of a genuinely gorgeous evening all around them, but…

Sensible fairy piped up. *'Your heart will be broken in the end, Kiara. Pull the plug now.'*

'Are you happy here?' Lucas asked.

He'd thought she must be, but there was something that was suddenly missing in that soft smile of hers. *Her eyes*, it occurred to him. *The light hasn't reached her eyes.*

She thought for a moment before she answered, and when she did her voice was steady, but it bore an undercurrent of emotion that lifted and rose into her cheeks. 'I love my house.' She grinned and put her hands out, as if she were a model in a showroom. 'I also love my job and my colleagues,' she said in a more heartfelt manner, and then, as if realising he was one of her colleagues, she looked away and sighed.

'What?'

He tipped his head to one side and looked at her. Really looked at her. She was such a beautiful woman. Sitting here in the glow of the firelight, with the lights from outside the window providing a soft fairy lit warmth around her. It was a reflection on her overall aura. She was a kind woman whose personality instantly drew people to her. She'd lived here less than a month and already she had the entire village eating out of her hand. In contrast, he'd come into town under the radar. On purpose.

Everyone loved Mistletoe Cottage and its dazzling

decor. And the fact that she was doing it all for charity. They loved *her.* But he could see now, in this moment of vulnerability, that she wasn't as brave as she seemed. Nor as happy. And that cut him to the quick. This was a woman whose heart was so generous, so empathetic. She deserved all the happiness she desired, and yet something was keeping her from attaining it.

A need gripped him to do anything he could to help. 'There's something missing, though, isn't there?' he asked. 'Is it your family? The distance from London?'

She shook her head, her smile tinged with melancholy. 'No. I love my parents, but I moved out of their house years ago, so we're used to living our independent lives. Although we talk all the time. No, it's more…' She picked at the tufty white beard sown onto her Santa cushion and then gave an embarrassed smile. 'It's more they thought I'd be married by now. Having children. Setting up house. The whole nine yards, as they say.'

'And you? Is that what you thought?'

She met his gaze. 'I thought so as well.'

There was something about the way she said it that suggested she'd been on track for exactly that, but it had been stolen from her. 'Was there someone specific you thought you'd be married to?' he asked.

She turned crimson.

He was feeling the heat of the question as well. It wasn't his business, and he wasn't even certain he wanted to know the answer. The idea of Kiara, dressed as a bride, walking down the aisle towards someone who—well, someone else, tugged at a part of him that hadn't seen oxygen in years.

She took a sip of her tea and then, as if having made

a decision, set it down and looked him square in the eye. 'I did have a boyfriend. We were together for three years.'

'Sounds serious…' Lucas took a sip of wine and then put it to one side. He didn't want to get tipsy listening to this story. He wanted to be as present for her as she had been for him when he'd told her about Lily.

She nodded in acknowledgement of his comment, then continued in a way that suggested she hadn't talked about this in a while—if ever. As if she needed to get it out quickly…as if letting the words loiter in her body for a moment longer than necessary would cause her physical pain.

'He worked at the same hospital as me. He was—is—a surgeon.'

Her brow crinkled, as if remembering caused her pain. Lucas wanted to reach out to her, comfort her, but he knew this was a story she needed to tell from the safe nook of her sofa, with her cushion taking the blows as her fingers clenched and unclenched against it.

'We flirted at work, and that led to drinks afterwards, which led to…other things. And soon enough we were an item. Our schedules were always busy, so it was a bit haphazard as far as a traditional courtship goes. I'm sure you can imagine…'

Her eyes flicked to him, as if hoping for an acknowledgement but not a judgement, so he nodded. He understood. Surgeons worked mad hours, as did midwives. Babies didn't keep to a nine-to-five schedule.

'Anyway…' she continued. 'We did some of the normal boyfriend-girlfriend stuff. Dinner dates. He met my friends. He met my parents. They thought he was brilliant. My mother kept saying things like, "Our daughter…marrying a surgeon!'" She pulled a face, as if to say they'd been as deluded as she had.

Lucas felt ire raise in him. Whoever the hell this guy was, he certainly hadn't deserved Kiara. And no way did she deserve to hold this amount of pain and, if he wasn't mistaken, shame.

'We had weekends away and so on. But we never spent Christmas together. Last Christmas I asked him—*again*—if maybe this year we'd be spending Christmas together, and again he put off making a final decision. Later that night my phone rang.' Saying the words seemed physically painful for her. 'It was his wife.'

She paused for effect, but he could see tears bloom in her eyes. He ached to go to her. Move in close and wipe them away and curse this creep of a man who'd led her on. It was cruel, what he'd done to her.

Kiara's face was pure anguish as a solitary tear trickled down her cheek. 'I had no idea. If I'd had even the slightest of clues that he was married…'

She couldn't finish the sentence, succumbing to long-held-off sobs.

Lucas no longer checked his instincts. He moved across the sofa and held her close to him. He didn't offer trite words of consolation that wouldn't mean anything. Instead he just let her cry, expel the grief that she'd so clearly held inside.

Eventually, when the tears had gone, she pulled back and said, 'The worst part is, my parents don't even know.'

'What? Why not?'

'I was too ashamed.' She buried her head in her hands, then peeked out between her fingers. 'I was too humiliated to tell them that the man I'd been so cock-a-hoop for was a liar. Not to mention his poor family. I mean—he has *children*!' Her eyes flicked to the corridor which led to the room where Harry was sleeping.

Lucas's heart slammed against his ribcage. He felt humbled and moved that she should be thinking of others before herself when she had been so very wronged.

'He was a con man,' Lucas said indignantly. 'He took advantage of you. He was only thinking of himself. No one else. You can't possibly blame yourself for his selfish, heartless inconsideration.'

Kiara dropped her hands from her face, tears still glittering in her eyes. 'I just feel so stupid, you know...? Those first few months after we broke up I went over and over everything, trying to figure out if there had been signs. Things I should have noticed. Like him not ever wanting to share Christmas with me.' She huffed out a laugh that—incredibly—wasn't embittered.

His heart went out to her. 'A man like that—' he began, and then stopped himself. Slandering someone he didn't know wasn't the point. Ensuring Kiara knew that this wasn't her fault and that she should not carry one ounce of the burden of guilt was. 'You are not to blame. He presented himself as a man who was available.'

Kiara cringed. 'But seriously... After three Christmases, when he knew how much I loved Christmas, why wasn't I able to figure it out?'

Lucas thought of the last two years, when he hadn't been able to see the joy in the festive season no matter how much he had tried to talk himself into a bit of Christmas cheer. In little more than the blink of an eye Kiara had effortlessly all but transformed it for both him and Harry. She'd made this season that he found so troubling a time of generosity and joy. It was fun! She was a woman who should be made to feel amazing for the happiness she brought to people. And, of course, at work she brought calm. She was a rare breed of woman, and it killed him that someone had made her feel otherwise.

'You're a good person, Kiara. You didn't deserve to be treated like that.'

She blinked up at him, her lashes stained pitch-black with spilt tears. 'Thank you for not judging me.'

'Of course not,' he whispered. 'It wasn't even an option. Listen…' He took her hands in his and rubbed his thumbs along the back of them. 'You're one of the most extraordinary women I have ever met. If it were two hundred years ago I would definitely be threatening a duel with this scoundrel!'

His bravura won a smile and a hiccoughing laugh from her, which melted his heart even more. He liked being the man who'd brought that smile to her lips. His eyes dropped to her mouth and remained on it. She looked down, then back up at him. The atmosphere between them shifted in that instant. Energy surged from the pair of them and met in the ever-decreasing space between them.

He became acutely aware of her presence in his arms. The fabric of her Christmas jumper…the curve of her arm beneath it. The shift of her shoulder blades. The cadence of her pulse. He felt her as she presented to him: as a woman.

He'd often wondered about this moment. The one where he'd take a step away from his past and towards a different future. One he had never entirely been able to imagine. But maybe that was what life would be like with Kiara. One welcome surprise after the other.

Though his pulse had quickened, and his body had begun to feel heat travelling in darts of approbation to areas that hadn't been lit up for a long time, the moment also felt perfectly natural. It was as if she had belonged here in his arms all along, but that they'd each needed to follow the paths life had put them on to eventually guide them to one another.

Sweeping aside a few strands of hair that had stuck to her tear-streaked face, Lucas closed the space between them, feeling their shared energy come to fruition in an explosion of heat as their lips connected in a long-awaited kiss.

CHAPTER NINE

KIARA DIDN'T KNOW if she was in heaven, on earth, or in some magical place in between. Wherever it was, she didn't want to leave.

This was the stuff of fantasy.

A glittering Christmas tree. A heartfelt, meaningful talk with a man she was not only attracted to, but whom she respected. A man who not only refused to pass judgement, but who openly wanted to champion her. To kiss her!

The moment his lips touched hers she felt as if the final piece of the year-long puzzle she'd been piecing together had been completed. Cornwall plus Carey Cove plus Lucas was everything she'd ever wanted.

'You all right?' Lucas whispered against her lips.

'Mmm…' was all she managed.

Kissing Lucas was like finding herself anew. There was no comparing him to any other. Nor being drawn back to a time and place where she'd been in another man's arms. A man who had made her feel the very worst kind of humiliation. She'd thought she would panic if a man ever tried to kiss her again, but Lucas's kind words had served as a balm to the thoughts that had kept her up more nights than she cared to acknowledge.

The pain of discovery and subsequent fall-out had taken a physical toll on her. She hadn't realised how fragile she'd felt, starting this new existence. How much courage it had taken to sell up, find a new job, move across the country and start again…and not in a mild, self-recriminating way. In a way that announced who she was and how she wanted to live her life. And, against the odds, it had led her to Lucas. A man who had borne his own heartache and, if his tender touch was anything to go by, who was also looking for a foot-hold on a new future.

A shiver of delight whispered down her neck when Lucas traced his finger-pads along her cheeks as if he had mandated himself with a mission: to explore her, inch by careful inch.

'You're so beautiful,' he murmured as he ducked his head to the soft crook between her ear and her chin, dropping velvety kisses along her neck.

Her body absorbed his attention like sunlight. His fingertips traced her jawline, the backs of his palms brushed the fine hairs of her cheek and his soft stubble grazed her delicate skin as his lips touched, explored, tasted…

But each time she tried to take the reins, return the exquisitely detailed attentions he was giving her, he'd murmur, 'No. Me first. I want to know everything about you.'

It was a level of care she hadn't realised she'd hungered for. As if being cherished was an essential nutrient she'd not known she'd been missing all along. Vitamin Lucas.

No. Not even that was right.

He didn't complete her. He made her life better. And that was the key difference. Another person didn't make you whole...they admired you for everything you were and didn't hold you to ransom for the things you weren't.

The nanosecond of dark thought she'd permitted to enter her system must have translated into hesitation to him. He pulled back, his expression wreathed in concern. 'Are you sure this is all right?'

It was more than all right. It was soul-quenchingly delicious.

'Yes,' she said, cupping his cheeks in her hands and looking him straight in the eye. 'More than.'

'Good.' He pulled her to him and drew a long, luxurious kiss from her. The kind that made time irrelevant.

'And you're okay?' she asked, when a natural pause introduced itself.

It was important to her to check. This was as much a first for Lucas as it was for her. Just as importantly, Lucas didn't just have himself to think about. He also had to consider his son, sound asleep in her guest room.

'I'm okay,' Lucas assured her, running his fingers through her hair and down her back.

The sensation was both new and familiar all at once. As if he'd been doing it for years and might for years yet to come.

'Better than okay.' His smile was warm. Genuine. 'Best Christmas party I've ever been to.'

This time his smile was wicked. The lights reflected in those grey eyes of his glimmered with something more heated than she'd seen there before.

If someone had told her she was made of starlight and fairy dust right now she would have believed them.

Her response to Lucas went beyond the elemental aspects of their very obvious chemistry. He *appreciated* her. And, more importantly, he wanted to make sure she knew it. Not to make her feel lucky that she'd been graced with his presence, as her ex had. She refused to allow herself to feel that shame again, even as she recalled how desperate she'd been for his attention. How grateful she'd felt when he'd deigned to shine his light on her. She saw it clear as day now. Her ex had been an arrogant, self-serving, egocentric jerk. His pleasure hadn't been to make her happy. His pleasure had been to hold power over her and his wife. Doling out his attentions as if they were fine gifts.

She felt a shift in her body chemistry as Lucas pulled her closer into his arms. *This* was genuine affection. This was what being cared for felt like. This was what she had wanted all along.

She untangled her limbs from his and, when he protested, put her index finger on his lips and said, 'My turn.'

She was smaller than him, so arranging herself on his lap so that her legs wrapped around him was not a problem. When she wriggled her hips and bottom into place her lips twitched with delight as Lucas gave a low moan of satisfaction. She reached for the top button of his shirt, desperate to feel her skin on his. He caught her hand in his, giving the back of it a kiss as his eyes darted to the corridor.

'Is there somewhere more private?' he asked.

The implication of his question exploded in her like lava. He wanted more.

She rose from the sofa and held her hand out to him. 'Follow me.'

Lucas felt more alive than he had in years. As if he could pinpoint each cell in his body and tell it where to direct its focus. His energy levels were soaring, as if they were absorbing the hyper-real sensations coursing through his bloodstream.

It was, he realised, the power of two.

Two hearts. Two minds. Two people attracted to one another on multiple levels.

Sight. Sound. Touch. All his sensory capabilities were focused on one thing: Kiara.

Holding her in his arms without a stitch of fabric between them was on another level. As if he'd never touched warm, soft skin before.

Being with her was nothing like what he'd thought making love to someone who wasn't Lily would feel. Truth be told, he'd not let himself consciously consider being intimate with another woman. But, courtesy of his deeply erotic dream, being with Kiara felt more natural than he could have imagined. As if the dream had somehow prepared him for this different realm of pleasure with a woman.

There was no point in comparing, he'd realised, as slowly and purposefully they had taken one another's clothes off. They were both adults. People with pasts. With experience. And yet…this felt brand-new. As if the slate hadn't been washed clean, exactly—their histories would always be a part of them—but more as if one chapter had ended and another had begun.

He groaned in equal measures of loss and pleasure as Kiara pulled away from him, then made it clear it wouldn't be for long. She twirled her finger, indicating he should lie on his back, then slowly walked to the end of the bed where she stood, her brown eyes scanning the length of him as if he were a Christmas present she'd never imagined receiving.

She climbed onto the mattress on all fours, hovering over his legs and then, tantalisingly, his midsection. He was leaving her in no doubt that he desired her. She bent at the elbows, her breasts brushing the length of his chest as she swept her body along his, eventually lowering her lips to his for a hot, succulent kiss that magnetically arched their bodies against one another.

If the beginning of this chapter was anything to go by, he never wanted it to end.

Kiara pulled back a little...just enough so that the feather-soft warmth between her legs slid along the length of his erection. She was ready for him. If she wanted him.

Her eyes met his, as if asking him the same question, and there was only one answer. Yes. A thousand times yes. He wanted her as much as she seemed to want him.

She pushed herself up, her hands reaching for his. Their fingers wove together as the tip of his shaft met the heat of her feminine essence. The contact shot flames through him. It wasn't the length of time between now and the last time he'd made love...it was the intensity of the sensation, incinerating everything he'd used to be and rebuilding him into this new version of himself. He felt desired in a way he'd never known before. Cared-for. Appreciated fully for the man he was today.

It was an extraordinary feeling. Knowing he was made of so many elements different from the person he'd once been awed him. And that he was sharing it with this woman—this beautiful, kind, incredible woman—was as humbling as it was empowering. He came with baggage. A lot of it. But today he felt as if he could handle it all. The past, the present and, more importantly, the future.

Time took on an otherworldly type of energy. The air around them was charged with more than oxygen. There was hunger…and need. And yet there wasn't any urgency about it. No voraciousness. There was a softness to their movements. A smouldering, slow burn shared between two people who wanted one another but felt no crush of pressure to do everything all at once. As if hurrying things would take away from the intensity of each touch and caress they shared.

After a delectation of time, they seamlessly moved and shifted into place, teasing and pleasuring each other to the point that he had a physical need to feel himself inside her. He confessed to not having any protection. She whispered that she was on the pill.

They exchanged a look. One charged with purpose and intent. Heated by desire. But their decision to go forward was a deliberate one, and that made the emotional impact of it even larger. He wanted her in a way he'd never wanted a woman before, and with her nod of consent he let the rest of the world fade away into nothing so that it was just the two of them.

He placed his hands on her hips and, after checking

once again that she was happy to be with him like this, guided her down the length of himself.

His body was bombarded with sensations. Heat. Liquid pleasure. Movement undulating like the sea. It was a rhythm he realised he was participating in as Kiara rocked her hips in sync with his, their fingers woven together, their eyes locked on each other's, until at last he sat up and pulled her close to him, her taut nipples grazing his bare chest as he said, 'Wrap your legs around me.'

He didn't need to repeat himself. With a reserve of strength he hadn't realised he possessed, he picked her up and reversed their positions, so that he was on top. With her legs still around his waist he began to slowly recapture the rhythm, as if it had become a part of him. A part of them both.

Neither of them spoke again. It didn't seem necessary. All the time he'd spent with Kiara seemed to have built to this—a pure, unadulterated connection. He felt the intensity grow in him, and with it a shift in Kiara's energy, as if she felt it, too.

They clung to one another as their bodies took over. Movement overpowered thought as they merged into one beautiful, shared sensation of pleasure which built moment by moment until it did, finally, become urgent. The swell of accumulated potency finally reached its pinnacle and waves of pleasure washed through them both. The strength of their shared orgasm seemed inevitable and yet also to take them by surprise.

After a few moments Lucas lay down beside her and held her close, her heartbeat translating through to his until, after some long, lingering kisses, the pair of them fell asleep.

* * *

Before Kiara even opened her eyes she knew something was different about her bedroom. It wasn't that Lucas was there—because there was no way the evening they'd just shared wasn't going to be imprinted on her mind for ever. It was that he wasn't.

An icy slick of fear shot through her, holding her heart's ability to beat properly in its arctic hold. She forced herself to be still. To listen. Perhaps it wasn't that at all. Perhaps…

Again a glacial wave of panic swept through her as flashbacks to all the mornings she'd woken up alone came back to her. Mornings alone that she now knew hadn't been due to her ex's calls to the surgery ward, but to his family home.

No. Stop it. Lucas isn't like that. He let his son stay here, for heaven's sake.

She forced herself to take a slow breath, calming her hammering heart enough to let her listen to any sounds that might be coming from beyond her closed door.

Perhaps he'd thought a nice cup of tea in bed would be a lovely way to cap off a magic night. Or coffee? A mince pie? She sniffed the air for hints of any or all three. Listened for the tell-tale rumble of the kettle. The clink of spoons on the big chunky mugs she'd bought. The ones with Christmas trees and Santa faces and—her and Harry's favourite—the one with Rudolph the Red-Nosed Reindeer.

There was one sound. But it wasn't from the kitchen. It was the sound of a little boy, still drowsy and confused.

Shockwaves of fear reverberated through her. What was happening?

She pulled on some thick flannel pyjamas and a dressing gown and ran out into the corridor and downstairs where, in her small entryway, she saw Lucas zipping Harry into his winter coat.

He looked up but said nothing. He didn't need to. His expression said it all.

He regretted his night with her.

She stumbled back a step, the humiliation hitting her like an avalanche of pain. She'd thought she'd moved on from her past. Learnt her lessons. Buried her shame and remorse at having been so unwittingly played. But she hadn't. She hadn't come even close. It had all been right there, just below the surface, waiting for her.

Something must've played across her features and spoken to Lucas, because out of the silence and through the roar of blood pounding through her head she could hear him muttering something about nursery, change of clothes, a bath…

They were all legitimate reasons to take his son home. Definitely. But before he'd even woken up? The poor little boy was leaning against his father, half asleep, as Lucas fitted on him first one boot and then another. The sweetest little pair of boots that until now Kiara hadn't realised she'd loved seeing lined up next to her bigger boots and, next to them, Lucas's even larger ones. It had made her little cottage look more like a home than a dream. A hope.

And that was when it really hit her. This beautiful cottage that she loved so much, that she'd lavished with Christmas decor and scented candles and cushions and more fairy lights than the rest of the homes in Cornwall put together… She could have given all the money directly to charity rather than spending it on blinging up her house on the premise of raising awareness. She'd been showboating after all. Advertising her hunger to be a part of something. Anything, really. And the mortification that she'd been so public about her loneliness threatened to crush her.

'I'll see you later at Carey House?'

She saw the comment form on his lips…was not even certain she'd heard it. He certainly didn't mean in a romantic context. They wouldn't be dipping into the supplies cupboard and having a quick snog. Not the way this was going.

'Sure,' she managed. 'Of course.'

'And are you all right if we…you know…keep last night between us?'

He had the grace to wince at his request, but there was no chance he could know just how much it hurt her.

She couldn't begrudge him his behaviour. Not on a logical front. He was a widower with a young son to think of. Harry's welfare was paramount, and dragging him round the village on one-night stands was definitely not how Lucas operated. Even through her pain she knew this to be true. He might not want her any more, but he wasn't a cruel man. And she couldn't hold him to ransom for being the same level of Machiavellian as her ex.

But it didn't make it hurt any less. Or ease the pain she felt. With an apologetic flick of his eyes, he lifted his son into his arms and opened the door… The cold air was a mirror of the cold blood running through her veins.

The moment the door closed behind them she let the truth settle into her bones.

She was going to be someone's dirty little secret again.

* * *

How she'd managed to get into work that morning was a complete mystery.

'Everything all right?'

She stopped in the entryway, turned and saw Hazel's expression laced with concern.

'Fine!' She forced herself to give a bright smile, then tapped her head. 'Just…you know…recovering from yesterday.'

'Too much mulled wine?' Hazel asked with a knowing grin.

Kiara smiled back. She'd seen Hazel make a couple of return trips to the punch bowl as well. But she'd also seen her drinking water, and excusing herself to get home for 'something sensible to eat' afterwards.

The fact she was here with a smile on her face indicated that Hazel knew when enough was enough. Something Kiara wished she knew about falling in love. Because that was what had been happening to her these past few heady days. She'd been falling in love with Lucas—and with Harry—even though there was a part of her that had known all along that she shouldn't.

They weren't hers to love. They were on their own journey. One that didn't include her. Not in public, anyway. Not for Lucas. And there was no way she wanted to be someone's dirty little secret again.

'I've got some paracetamol if you need any…' Hazel began to dig in the reception desk drawer.

'No, no…' Kiara took a couple of steps up the stairs towards the midwives' lounge but then, remembering her manners, turned to offer a smile of thanks. The kind of pain she was enduring wouldn't respond to any kind of medication.

At just that moment Lucas came through the front door.

She froze in panic.

'Good morning, Dr Wilde!' Hazel greeted him cheerily. 'And how are we this morning? Full of festive cheer?'

Kiara almost physically felt the flash of panic that crossed Lucas's face.

Oblivious, Hazel danced knowing looks between the pair of them.

As if he was literally drawing a line under the days they'd spent together, Lucas said, 'Oh, you know… That's more Harry's department. Christmas isn't really my thing.'

And there it was in a nutshell. The addition of the insult to the injury. He might as well have had the message printed on a banner and flown it across the sky for the impact it had. She'd been a fool to fall for him. He'd only done all this for his son's sake. Played along. The kiss and then the lovemaking had all been a mistake. *She'd* been a mistake.

And as the true impact of what she'd done hit her she turned and took the stairs two at a time, unwilling to let him see just how much the loss of him had devastated her.

CHAPTER TEN

'MAKE SURE YOU take them every day—all right, Mr Thomas?'

Lucas's patient screwed up his face as if he'd just spoken to him in Martian.

'He will. My poor man can't hear without his hearing aids, and he didn't want to wear them—what with the infection and all.' Mrs Thomas gave her husband's leg a pat and then shouted, 'You'll be taking your medicine every day!' She tapped the prescription Lucas had just handed them. 'Right up until Christmas Eve.' She turned to Lucas; her face suddenly stricken. 'Will that mean no Christmas cheer for him?'

Lucas made a remorseful expression. 'I'm afraid not. Not with antibiotics.'

'Oh, well!' Mrs Thomas turned to her husband again, turning her speaking volume up to eleven. 'It's a good thing we went out to Mistletoe Cottage for the mince pies and mulled wine—isn't it, love?'

Lucas rubbed his chin…hastily shaven and with a couple of nicks. Something he hadn't done in a long time. He didn't remember seeing the couple there. Which shouldn't come as a surprise to him. He'd only had eyes for Kiara.

The thought stung as an image of her face when she'd seen him this morning, a wretched mix of fear and sorrow, flashed across his mind's eye.

Mr Thomas grinned. 'It certainly is.' He patted his tummy. 'Those were the finest mince pies I've had in yonks. And imagine…eating them for charity!' A look of panic zapped across his face. 'I mean, they were the finest apart from *yours*, love. Obviously.' He leant across and gave his wife's sweet, dried apple face a kiss.

Mrs Thomas's features softened. She put her palm on her husband's cheek and then gave it a gentle pat before turning to Lucas with a happy smile. 'Forty-seven years of marriage and I've finally got him trained.'

Something in Lucas's heart twisted, unleashing the raft of feelings he'd been trying to keep at bay all day. The reaction went well beyond the parameters of witnessing a lovely moment. It was a combination of loss and hope. Loss that he'd never share that sort of exchange with Lily, and hope that—

He cut the thought off. He'd been an absolute idiot this morning. He'd seen Kiara plain as day in Reception, and when he'd had a chance to extend some sort of olive branch to her he'd stuck his foot in it.

Christmas isn't really my thing.

What had he been thinking?

No prizes for answering that. He hadn't. From the moment he'd woken up he'd stopped thinking, and his body had gone into the mode it had been in during Lily's final months: simply reacting.

Holding Kiara in his arms, smelling the soft perfume of her shampoo as her hair tickled his chin and his chest, feeling safe and warm and part of something bigger than himself—all that had awakened something in him he'd thought he'd left in the past. Happiness.

He'd felt happiness. Pure, wonderful, undiluted happiness. It hadn't been frantic, or wild, or just beyond his reach. It had been right there in his arms and it had smelt of cloves and cinnamon sugar and mint. And its name had been Kiara.

As soon as the sensation had registered, the guilt had poured in.

He'd never imagined himself feeling that way again. At peace with someone. As if he were part of a team. A future. And yet there he'd been, less than three years after his wife had died in his arms, holding another woman and never wanting the moment to come to an end.

The realisation had savaged him.

It was nothing to do with Kiara. Well… It was everything to do with Kiara. Or, more accurately, with his reaction to her. His feelings for her. The fact he'd wanted nothing more than to make love to her last night and had done so without a thought for how he might feel in the morning.

She was entirely faultless in this. It was one hundred percent him, and the fact that he'd never imagined caring for someone in that way ever again. He'd not known what to do with the new raft of feelings. Happiness. Contentment. Actual joy.

Feelings that had slammed up against his past so hard and fast he'd barely been able to breathe.

He'd had everything he'd ever wanted with Lily, and then she'd been taken away from him. In such a cruel way.

Harry hadn't been old enough to know the loss, but

now he was. He adored Kiara. Loved everything about her. When he was with her, he glowed with happiness. He couldn't risk his son experiencing the level of loss Lucas had when he'd lost Lily. Not that Kiara was sick—but you simply didn't know, did you? Anything could happen. Sickness. Car crashes. Freak weather events…

His mind had run wild with the thousands of reasons a man could end up standing at a graveside with nothing but a pathetic flower in his hand. A paltry show of feeling for a love that had been his life force. He didn't know how to love someone without loving them completely. With his whole being. Body. Heart. Soul.

Burying Lily had been like burying a part of himself. Even considering the possibility of experiencing that level of loss again was driving large wedges of ice straight into his heart. Fear. Panic. Confusion. Pain. Each one darker than the next to the point where he'd been completely and utterly panicked, convincing himself that his future had already been laid out for him.

He'd been so certain that his future was with Lily and life had showed him otherwise. He didn't know anything. He was destined to be alone. The perfection he'd shared with Kiara was not his to take. Not with what she'd already been through with her ex. What he'd been through with his wife. He was in no place to make promises for the future when he knew firsthand that the future was not in his control.

So he'd left. Convinced himself that he was doing it for Harry. That if, perchance, his son had found him with Kiara it would have confused things. And now here he was, face to face with a couple who, by the look of things, had enjoyed forty-seven years of marriage and were still smiling.

'What's your secret?' Lucas asked.

'For a good mince pie?' Mrs Thomas asked.

'What's that?' Mr Thomas leant in closer to his wife.

'He wants to know what my secret for a good mince pie is, Harold!'

They shared a look, then began to cackle. Low at first. Then building to a high fever-pitch of giggles.

'She buys them, lad! She buys 'em down the shops and pretends they're home-made.'

They laughed until they wiped tears away, and once again Lucas was struck by how wonderful their companionship seemed. Multifaceted, and at its very core a deep well of love.

'I meant the secret of your marriage,' Lucas persisted. He'd take any advice he could get. Living his life half in the past and half in the present wasn't working. He had to find a way to go forward—only he didn't know how. 'What's the secret to staying so happily married?'

'Agree with everything she says,' Mr Thomas said, still laughing, and then putting on a placating voice. 'Yes, dear. That's right, dear. Anything you say, dear…'

Mrs Thomas swatted at him. 'If only it was that easy.' She leant forward and said conspiratorially, 'You'll not even come close to guessing the tricks I'll have to play to get him through these antibiotics. He's stubborn as a mule, he is. I had to promise him a steak pie tonight just to get him to come and see you.'

'That's just because I wanted steak pie!' Mr Thomas gave his wife a little tickle, then sobered as he turned back to Lucas. 'The real reason I came is because I want to make sure I'm around as long as she is. Drives me bonkers with all her energy—but, by God, it doesn't half keep me going. Wouldn't have lived a day of my life without this woman. Worth her weight in gold, she is.' He leant forward and in a stage-whisper said, 'The real secret is making it clear to everyone around you that you won the lottery the day she agreed to marry you.'

The look Mrs Thomas gave her husband was so tender and full of love it nearly broke Lucas in two. He'd thought he was on track to have what they shared years back, when he'd asked Lily to marry him, but life had moved the goal posts for all of them. Lily, Harry and himself. And now, because of his poor behaviour this morning, for Kiara.

He had destroyed the very beginnings of something without even giving it a chance.

He had no idea how to shift the course of his own path to cross with Kiara's. Perhaps that had been the problem. Their fleeting connection had been a lesson to him to exercise more caution. Show more care. And never, ever again to hurt a woman who'd been so open, sharing with him her deepest humiliation only to feel it again by his own hand.

He owed her an apology. But words weren't going to be enough. The old saying was right. Actions did speak louder than words. And he had to make sure he was matching whatever apology he made to his intentions.

Until he knew what those were he was right back where he'd begun. Caught between his past and the present, not knowing which way to turn.

* * *

When Kiara opened the door for her next patient, Catrina, she was shocked to see Lucas, chatting away with her.

Not so much because it was weird for a GP to be speaking to a patient, but because it was weird for him to be outside a door he knew she'd be opening when he'd made it crystal-clear yesterday that he wanted nothing more to do with her.

She ran her thumb along the jagged remains of her festively decorated fingernails…all nibbled down yesterday.

He hadn't been *that* awful.

Despite her nerve-endings still burning like a bee sting, she had to concede that he hadn't cold-shouldered her or anything. He obviously just didn't want what had happened between them to happen again. Or, if he did, he wanted it to be between them. A secret. And if there was one thing she'd promised herself when she left London it was that she'd never again let someone treat her the way her ex had. As a secret.

'Hey, Kiara.' His grey eyes met hers. 'All right?'

'Fine, thanks,' she chirped, although the subtext was clear: *No thanks to you*. 'Catrina! So lovely to see you. Gosh… The twenty-eight-week appointment! If I didn't have it right here in black and white, I wouldn't have believed it from the size of you.'

'I know!' Catrina ran a hand over her neat bump then grinned, 'But look at me from the side!' She turned and jutted out her belly—which, to be fair, did look bigger from that angle.

Lucas hadn't moved a centimetre during this exchange and Kiara could feel him watching her. Was he inspecting her to see how she really was? Well, tough.

'Excellent.' She flicked her eyes to his and then to her patient's. 'Shall we get you out of the corridor and talk privately?'

It would be obvious that she didn't want him there, but she couldn't help it. Her response to Lucas was visceral. She wanted to touch him. Smell him. Taste him again. But wanting all those things rose like bile in her throat as she remembered his expression when he'd first laid eyes on her the morning after they'd had sex.

It might have been subconscious, but she'd seen the way he'd pulled Harry just that little bit closer to him, hunched his shoulders that extra centimetre lower… Small but unmistakeable visual cues that had told her he thought he'd made a mistake. That moment had shot her straight back to the day she'd cheerfully answered her phone and listened with dawning understanding as an unfamiliar female voice had informed her that her 'boyfriend' had a wife and children.

She'd never felt more humiliated and ashamed.

And that doubled the pain. Because she knew in her heart that Lucas wasn't anything like her ex.

Peter had been a self-serving, duplicitous married man with a God complex.

Lucas was a widower with the kindest, most gentle spirit. A protective father who'd taken his very first steps into having a relationship. Not to mention the best kisser she'd ever met.

She squashed the physical response that came with those memories and forced herself to be practical.

Deep down, she knew he wasn't the sort of man to go around kissing people willy-nilly. Or to blank them the next day. They'd had a connection. He'd acted on it. Then he'd realised he'd made a mistake.

Perhaps the simplest explanation as to how they'd ended up in bed the other night was that they'd both had too heavy a dose of Christmas magic. But that somehow made it hurt that much more. Being someone's mistake.

Catrina, who was standing and waiting to go into the room, but couldn't because Kiara still hadn't moved, gave her an inquisitive look. 'Everything all right?'

Kiara popped on a chirpy smile she knew didn't reach her eyes. With a level of defiance she knew would travel all the way to the tall, dark and handsome GP whose eyes were glued to her, she said, 'Fine. Never been better. Sorry… I should be asking you if you're all right. Okay, then…away we go.'

Kiara stood to one side to let Catrina enter the room and, despite trying not to, looked at Lucas as she pulled the door shut.

There was something in those grey eyes of his she couldn't read. Remorse? An apology? She didn't know. Whatever it was, she didn't want it anywhere near her. She couldn't go down that road again. No matter how much of her heart she'd already lost to him. She'd simply have to soldier on until she grew yet more scar tissue.

And with a simple click of the door she promised herself that that would be that.

But of course it wasn't.

A few hours later she was on the phone to both of her parents, in a video call so they could witness her ugly crying in High Definition. She told them everything. About Lucas and Harry and how she'd fallen for them both. About how much she'd enjoyed doing all the festive events with them. About how things had gone further with Lucas but that it had obviously been a step too far for him. Whether it was because he was a widower or because she just hadn't been a good fit, she didn't know, but it had brought up all sorts of feelings and memories, and she'd thought she should tell them everything.

They sat silently, compassionately, and listened as she told them about Peter. About how he'd courted her. Wined and dined her straight into her own bed. Occasionally a hotel bed. But never his. Until, three years later, she'd found out why.

Her parents were shocked, but not disappointed in her as she'd expected. They comforted her, and called him a scoundrel and a rake and a couple of other words she hadn't realised her parents knew, and eventually her tears began to dry.

'Would you like to come home for Christmas, love?' her mum asked.

She had to admit she was tempted. To have hot water bottles magically appear in her childhood bed each night. To have that wonderful mish-mash of Indian cuisine from her mother's childhood and English from her father's on the Christmas dinner table after hours of laughter and fun in the family kitchen. Board games. Sentimental films.

But the idea of leaving her cottage—her new home—made her feel worse. As if 'The Incident' with Lucas, as she was now calling it, was driving her out of the new life she'd carved out for herself here in Carey Cove. Leaving, she realised, would be the worst thing she could do.

'I think I'll stay here,' she said.

'We can always come down to you, you know.'

Her spirits brightened at that. And without her having to say a word, her parents began to plan. Her father pulled a notebook on to the kitchen table as her mother rattled off a long list of things they mustn't forget to bring.

Before she knew it, Kiara was laughing. 'They have shops here in Cornwall, you know, Mum.'

Her mother feigned shock, then laughed as well. 'You know, love, we're more than happy to come. We want to come. But if you happen to chat to your young man and…you know…decide you'd like to celebrate Christmas in a different way, we're happy to go with whatever decision you make.'

Kiara scrunched her nose, feeling the sting of tears surfacing again. 'Thanks, Mum. But I think it'll be just us Baxters opening presents around the Christmas tree this year.'

They chatted a bit more, then said their goodbyes. Wanting to recapture a bit of the Christmas magic she'd lost over the past twenty-four hours, she went and got her duvet and made a little nest for herself on the sofa. She put on a Christmas film—the kind where brand-new work colleagues turned out to be princes from far-off kingdoms—and snuggled in for the evening.

A bit of fiction never hurt a girl. Especially at this time of year.

'I can't get any of the candy canes to stick!' Harry dropped the red and white striped sweets onto the table and folded his arms across his chest in a disgruntled huff.

'Come on, Harry. You said you wanted to decorate a gingerbread house.'

Lucas picked up a candy cane, squirted some of the white icing onto it, as the woman leading the workshop had instructed, and then, lacking the will even to try, ate it in one go.

'Can I have one?' Harry said, his lower lip beginning to tremble.

'Sure.' Lucas took another candy cane out of its protective wrapping and handed it to him.

'No! With icing on it, like you had!'

Lucas didn't fight it. He did as his son instructed and together they sat, side by side, amidst tables full of happy families merrily constructing gingerbread houses out of every sweetie known to mankind.

Lucas watched as Harry chomped and then swallowed his minty treat without so much as a glimmer of a smile. It wasn't top parenting. It wasn't even top adulting. Lucas knew he sounded as dispirited as his son.

Harry looked up at him, his big grey eyes a reflection of his own, his blond curls an echo of his mother's. 'I thought Kiara was going to be here.'

Lucas had too. And to be honest he was doing a terrible job of keeping up his part of the bargain: playing along. 'C'mon, son. She can't be with us for all our outings.'

'Why not?'

There were myriad reasons she couldn't accompany them absolutely everywhere, but the number one reason she wasn't here right now was because of the way Lucas had behaved. He'd panicked, and it had come across as cruel. He'd dug a hole for himself he didn't know how to get out of—because the truth was he didn't have the answers. He'd never been a widower before. Never fallen for anyone other than Lily…

He closed his eyes and instantly saw Kiara's expression when she'd found him bundling up a half-asleep Harry and listened to him muttering nonsense about getting him home for uniform and the right socks. It had been ridiculous and she'd known it. Of course Harry had needed those things, but usually a good parent would wait until their child had had a full night's sleep before taking them out of their girlfriend's—

The thought caught him up. He'd been thinking a lot of things about Kiara over the past couple of days. Thousands of them. How kind she was. How generous. Thoughtful, beautiful, strong… The list went on. But he'd never once thought of her as his *girlfriend.*

Was that what she'd become to him? It wasn't as if he was a Jack the Lad, jumping into bed with every woman who took his fancy. He'd not actually been with or wanted to be with anyone until Kiara had lit up his life—*their* lives—both literally and figuratively.

'It's not as much fun without Kiara,' Harry said mournfully.

'You're right,' Lucas conceded. 'It's not.'

And he'd pulled the plug on the possibility of Kiara being with them ever again. The way he'd treated her, he deserved the icy glances she'd been sending his way. But he simply didn't know how to come back from that. Not after what she'd been through.

He forced himself to try and look enthused about the unadorned gingerbread house sitting in front of them. 'But she couldn't make it today, so what do you say we make the best of it, eh? How about these chocolate buttons? Should we try putting some on the roof?'

Harry looked at the buttons and then up at his father, tears welling in his eyes. 'Why didn't we go past Mistletoe Cottage today?'

Another good question with a host of bad answers.

'I—' Lucas began, and then, not knowing how to explain to his son how he was feeling torn between his past and a future that felt as if it would betray the past, he began eating the chocolate buttons that were meant to be tiling the gingerbread house neither of them had any interest in.

'Daddy?' Harry tugged his father's arm. 'I want to see Mistletoe Cottage.'

Lucas's heart felt punctured by the request, because he knew the subtext. Harry wanted to see Kiara. And so did he. The days weren't as nice without her. Not as bright. They were certainly bereft of any Christmas spirit. But if they went past the cottage there was every chance they would run into Kiara, and he simply didn't know how to put into words what he felt.

He dropped a kiss on top of his son's head and pulled him in for a hug. Sitting here being more miserable wasn't helping anyone. 'What do you say we go out to the harbour and see if we can get a glimpse of her house from there?'

It wasn't the perfect solution, but if they walked out on to the quay Lucas was pretty sure Kiara's spectacularly decorated house would be shining away, a beacon for all who could see it.

They bundled up, and after making their excuses to the woman hosting the gingerbread-house-making went down to the harbour.

'Daddy?' Harry gave Lucas's hand a tug.

'Yes, son?'

'Why did you tell the lady I wasn't feeling well?'

'Ah, well...' Crikey. Now he was going to have to explain about white lies. Tonight was going down as an epic fail in the parenting department.

'Is it because we don't feel like smiling when Kiara's not here?'

The question pierced straight through his heart. He stopped where they were and dropped down so that he was face to face with his son. 'Hey... Hey, bud. Do you feel that sad without her?'

Harry nodded. 'And you do, too, Daddy.'

Lucas frowned, humbled by his son's observation and how accurate it was. He didn't feel good without Kiara. In fact, he felt downright miserable.

A thought suddenly broke through the fug of gloom he'd been wandering around in for the past couple of days. Was he paying a penance for loss that he had never actually owed? Lily had been clear with him. He wasn't to hold back from life. Not for her. Or for Harry. More to the point, he was to live life to the fullest *for* Harry. Living life mired in the past was something she had never wanted for her son. Or for Lucas.

Harry took his index fingers and put each one on the edges of Lucas's lips, first pushing them up, then down, as he said, 'When we're with her we smile, and when we're not all we want to do is be with her.'

Lucas sat back on his heels and looked at his wise three-year-old. That was pretty much it in a nutshell.

'Do you—' he began, and then stopped as a swell of emotion hitched in his throat.

He was about to ask his son a big question, and putting it into words felt as powerful as pulling his own heart out of his chest and asking for advice on how to go forward. How to live their lives.

'Would it be all right if—' Again the question caught in his throat.

How did you ask your child if it was all right to date someone who might possibly never want to see him again? Particularly when that little boy had never really known his mother's love. Two women loved Harry. Only one of them was here, up in that thatched-roofed, ornament-laden, fairy-lit testament to joy.

This was the decision Lily had wanted him to make. Accepting the joy. Loving another woman wasn't about forgetting his past. It was being grateful for it and then, with care, being willing to open his heart to yet more love. More joy. More happiness.

He no longer battled the emotion bursting in his chest. 'You know your mummy loved you very much, don't you?' he said.

Harry nodded, then pointed at his heart. 'That's why she lives here.'

'Yes. Yes, that's right. And if I were to ask Kiara to spend a bit more time with us—'

Harry beamed and clapped his hands, 'You mean a *lot* more time with us?'

Lucas wiped away a couple tears of his own and said, 'Hopefully. If Daddy hasn't mucked it up.'

Harry's little eyebrows drew together and he asked, 'Did you tell Kiara we weren't feeling well, too?'

Lucas had to laugh. 'Something like that. And now we have to find a way to let her know we're feeling better and that we'd love to see her again.'

A fresh burst of energy sent an empowering charge

through his entire body. He rose and took his son's hand in his.

'C'mon, Harry. Daddy's got an idea. Shall we go and see if we can make it work?'

His son's cheers were all the encouragement he needed.

CHAPTER ELEVEN

KIARA'S NEWEST PATIENT and friend, Liane, was glowing with excitement. And it wasn't just her baby she was excited about. Kiara was about to unveil yet more decorations for her house, as it was now only forty more sleeps until Christmas.

Not that she was counting.

She was absolutely counting.

'Honestly,' Liane said to Kiara. 'This is the absolute best Christmas I've ever had. The whole of Carey Cove thinks so, if I'm honest. Will you be doing this every year?'

Kiara made an indeterminate gesture that she hoped said *Sure!* And also *There are no guarantees in life!* What she really wanted to say was *Absolutely, yes, but my heart's not in it nearly as much as it was back when Lucas and Harry were—*

She cut the thought short. Lucas and Harry weren't anything any more, apart from Lucas-and-Harry-shaped holes in her heart. As much as she wanted it to be otherwise, it simply wasn't to be.

She'd never been more grateful for a weekend in her life! It wasn't so much that she wanted to avoid Lucas… Well… She *did* want to avoid Lucas, because no matter how hard she tried she still couldn't shake the feeling that there was something unfinished between them. Just as there was that mysterious *something* missing from her home's over-the-top decorations which, like the final piece of a puzzle, would make it perfectly perfect.

'C'mon!' Liane rubbed her hands together, clearly beginning to feel the cold of the crisp, bright winter's day. 'I'm going to turn into an icicle if you don't choose soon.'

'I can't choose!'

Kiara's face stretched into a helpless expression. If this had been three days ago she knew who would be choosing. Harry. She swallowed back the lump of emotion and brightened her tone.

'You choose. Which one?' Kiara held up a star and then an angel.

'The angel, for sure.' Liane's grin widened. 'She looks just like you.'

'Ha!' Kiara smirked, holding up the blonde, blue-eyed archetypal angel and then giving her dark ponytail a flick. 'Maybe if I did this…' She lifted the angel above her head and struck a beatific pose, then, as she looked at her new friend, realised she was properly freezing. 'Wait there!'

She ran into the house and grabbed a cosy blanket off the back of the sofa, desperately trying not to remember the last time she'd been on it, her limbs tangled with a certain tall, dark and handsome GP.

She ran back, flicked the blanket out to its full length and wrapped it round Liane's shoulders. 'There you are. Got to keep you and your little one cosy.'

Liane laughed, said thank you, and then, as she

pulled the blanket close, her expression turned earnest. 'Seriously, Kiara. I mean it. I know you're my midwife, and all, and that we haven't known each other that long, but I hope you know I count you as a friend. I mean—you're amazing. You achieve big things in small amounts of time.'

Like falling in love with the one man she shouldn't? Yup. She'd certainly done that straight away. Tick! Done and dusted.

'Hardly,' she said, instead of pouring her heart out to her new friend and telling her about everything the way she'd done with her parents. With Lucas. The pain she had tried to keep at bay was threatening to burst through her mental blocks. This moment was proof that she didn't have to rely on Lucas for friendship.

Liane held her hands out wide. 'Look at what you've done in the last two weeks! I haven't managed to do anywhere near the same in ten years of living here! I hope you stay. I hope you stay for ever and we grow up to be old ladies in wheelchairs, admiring Carey Cove's famous Christmas lights at Mistletoe Cottage.'

Kiara pressed her hands to her heart, truly touched and then she said, more mischievously, 'When we're that old we'll have to hire some strapping young men to put up all the decorations!'

'Ooh…' Liane's eyes lit up. 'Why wait until we're old? We could hire some now.' She suddenly pulled a face. 'Do you think my husband would mind?' And then she burst out in hysterical laughter, pretending to be in a panic that he might have heard. 'Aw… Bless… He's the best-looking man in the village for me—and that's what counts, isn't it?'

Kiara nodded, absorbing the sight of her friend's

face turning soft with affection as she no doubt conjured an image of her husband wearing a tool belt or possibly nothing, while her own thoughts instantly pinged to the man she would happily have as her Mr January through to December if she could. But she couldn't.

'I guess we'll have to leave it until we're older, then, before getting some young men to put up the rooftop decorations.'

They both looked up to the roof, no doubt imagining entirely different men up there, doing alpha male things in various stages of undress.

'And I guess I'd better get back and make tonight's tea.' With a small, contented sigh, Liane began to fold up the blanket Kiara had handed her, and then she asked, more seriously, 'Do you have any more decorations you want putting in awkward places? I'm happy to ask Gavin if you need me to. He's not brilliant at DIY, but he is happy to give things a go.'

Kiara did want more decorations, but she just couldn't put her finger on what was missing. She looked up at Santa on the roof of the cottage. He was by the chimney, posed to look as if he was about to climb down with a big bag of presents. The orange and red glow of the sunset was disappearing in the sky, and the lights she had strung like rows of icing along the house were beginning to offer their warm glow to the fast-approaching darkness. She heard jingle bells and smiled. Christmas really had gone to her head!

'Did you hear that?' Liane asked, cocking her head to the side. 'Are those...*jingle* bells?'

Kiara started. So it hadn't just been her. She tilted her head to one side, as if that might be the best way to hear something better, and, yes… It was faint, but there was the unmistakably cheery sound of jingle bells rising up from the main road at the port. The way the road was angled made it possible to see whoever was coming once the vehicle came round the first bend.

'It must be someone with bells attached to their car,' Kiara said, feeling a shot of festive adrenaline spiking through her.

'No…' Liane's voice was awe-filled. 'It so much better than that.'

Kiara couldn't even speak and agree. Liane was right. It was a million times better than that.

It was Lucas. And Harry. On top of a flatbed truck that was somehow transporting the most beautiful sleigh with a full complement of reindeer hitched to the front.

How he'd found a sleigh—glittering and twinkling in the approaching darkness—let alone reindeer tame enough to be hitched to a sleigh with full swags of jingle bells was beyond her. She felt as if she was in the middle of a Christmas miracle.

She clearly wasn't alone. She could see front doors being flung open and children and adults alike running out into their gardens to cheer and sing snippets of Christmas songs as the enormous truck—bedecked in fairy lights, no less—slowly worked its way up the hill until, with a great sense of purpose, it came to a halt right in front of Mistletoe Cottage.

Lucas and Harry were in the driver's seat of the sleigh. Harry was bouncing all over the place, waving and pretending to steer the reindeer, and generally enjoying being the centre of attention, but it was Lucas

Kiara was watching… Because his eyes—his entire energy—was solely on her.

She felt his gaze as if it were a sparkling Christmas elixir…magic from a fairy godmother's wand. Only he was no godmother, and the look in those grey eyes of his would enchant her for ever. He cared for her. She could see it now. And, more importantly, she could feel it. For Lucas, a hugely private man who'd endured so much emotional turmoil over the past few years, to make such an enormous, public, *festive* show of affection meant only one thing: he was falling in love every bit as much as she was.

What they'd shared was now the opposite of a secret. It was out there for the whole of Carey Cove to see.

The only question was…could she trust it?

Before an ounce of doubt that the gesture was genuine could creep in, Harry was out of the sleigh and clambering down onto the flatbed, where an obliging neighbour swung him off as he cried, 'Kiara! Kiara!'

Her heart filled to bursting as he ran and leapt up into her arms as if they'd been parted for an eternity. She buried her head in his little-boy scent as he wrapped his arms round her neck. He smelt of Christmas trees and cloves and winter mint. He smelt of love.

Eventually, he pulled back and asked, 'Do you like it?'

'I love it,' she answered honestly, as the pair of them turned and looked up at the sleigh where Lucas, still aboard, was looking down at the pair of them.

As their eyes met, her heart near enough exploded. His expression was a charged mix of hope and concern. Affection and intent. She could tell he wanted to talk, and she did, too… But it appeared having a sleigh arrive in front of her house warranted action, not a quiet conversation by the fire with a cup of hot chocolate which was what she really wanted.

Lucas was charged for action…and yet standing up here on the flatbed, watching his son run into his girlfriend's arms—for that was what Kiara was to him if she'd forgive him—made him feel more complete than he'd felt in years.

Everything about this moment was unbelievably outside the box for him. Making a gesture so epic, not only to show Kiara he knew he'd made a mistake, but that he cared for her, was definitely not in the emotional toolbox he'd left home with when he'd set off for medical school all those years ago. Life had changed him. He now knew how precious it was. How foolish it was to let fear and pride make decisions for him when really, all along, he should have been listening to his heart.

He wanted to go to her, pull her into his arms and whisper apologies, tell her how much she'd changed his perspective on both life and love, but it seemed when you drove a sleigh and reindeer up to the home of the woman you hoped loved you as much as you loved her, you weren't the star attraction. The sleigh and the reindeer were.

The whole of Carey Cove appeared to have gathered outside Mistletoe Cottage and somehow, magically—Kiara would definitely have said magically—everything began to move into place as if the entire thing had been planned.

Kiara's little red car was relocated to a neighbour's drive. The snowmen were rearranged. The dancing penguins were put into action, wiggling their little animatronic bums as if they, too, had been waiting for the sleigh and reindeer to appear.

Davy Trewelyn, the publican, a tall, portly, white-bearded man, turned up with a 'Ho-ho-ho!' in a perfect Santa suit. And his wife, the rosy-cheeked and ever-smiling Darleen, showed up in a Mrs Claus outfit complete with a huge tray of gingerbread men.

The village's children were beside themselves, but between the schoolteachers, the firemen, the local bobby and, of course, the parents, who had all gathered to see Santa's sleigh and reindeer, a jolly kind of order was formed out of the chaos.

The sleigh and reindeer were unloaded and set up in Kiara's drive, flanked by a row of living Christmas trees, lined up in red pots and each decorated with a whorl of fairy lights and topped alternately with stars and angels. But there was only one true angel in his eyes: Kiara Baxter. The woman who had touched his life in a way he hadn't thought possible.

He kept trying to get to her, but across a fence of jumbo candy canes they shared a look of mutual understanding: their talk would have to wait.

Eventually, when the reindeer had had their fill of carrots and Mr and Mrs Claus needed to go back to their 'day jobs' at the pub, and the children's tummies began to grumble for their suppers, the crowd began to thin.

One of the mums from the local playgroup asked Lucas in a knowing tone if Harry would like to come to supper at theirs. 'It's spaghetti tonight, and bowls of vanilla ice cream for afters. Nothing fancy, but—'

'Spaghetti's great,' Lucas said, not even looking at her.

His eyes had been glued to Kiara all night and, as if they'd been sharing the same enriched pool of energy, hers had been locked on his. Except for this exact moment now, when his son was barrelling into her for another hug.

The look on their faces as they wrapped their arms around each other made him feel as if his thirst was being quenched with a life-affirming soul juice. As they waved goodbye to each other, and promised to see one another soon, it was as if a multicoloured aura surrounded them. One made up of hues of pure joy, contentment and peace. That Christmas song about peace on earth came to him, and in a moment's stillness he caught himself mouthing the words, about how the place love and harmony had to come from was within.

That was when he knew. Straight down to his marrow he knew he was in love with Kiara. And if she would have him, she was his future.

He reduced the space between them in a few long-legged strides and pulled her into his arms. She didn't push him away or demand an explanation. She just held him, and their bodies exchanged energy, heartbeats. When at long last, arms still wrapped round each other's waist, they pulled back to look at one another, Lucas knew she felt the same way, too.

Not even caring about the wolf whistles the few remaining Carey Covers were sending their way, he kissed her. By the time they parted there was no one else around. It was as if they'd been left in a snow globe entirely of Kiara's creation. And he loved being a part of it.

'Are the reindeer going to be all right?'

Lucas grinned, turning her so that his arms were still around her, but his chin was resting on her silky hair, her ponytail tickling his neck. They watched as the reindeer dug into the bags of hay they'd been left.

'The owner is coming to collect them soon. They'll be back with their manger tonight.'

Kiara twisted herself so that she could shoot him one of her trademark cheeky grins. 'Their manger, eh? I thought you were immune to Christmas magic.'

'Not with you in my life.'

She pulled back then, and asked the question he'd seen in her eyes all night. 'Am I in your life? Is that what you want?'

He nodded, and then gestured towards her cottage. 'Shall we go in? I can grovel inside so you don't freeze to death.'

She laughed and blew out a little cloud of mist, as if to affirm that inside would definitely be a better choice. Then she hesitated a moment. 'Grovelling won't be necessary, but…' her top tooth captured her lower lip for a moment as she sought and found the best word-choice '…honesty will. One hundred percent honesty, okay?'

He crossed his heart and held up his hand in a Boy Scout's salute. 'I promise nothing less.' He flattened his hand against his heart. 'I owe you nothing less.'

'You don't owe me anything, Lucas. That's the point.'

She didn't sound angry or vindictive. She sounded determined. Resolute. As if she was showing him where she'd set her moral compass and it was up to him if he was on the same trajectory as her.

He let her comment hit its mark and then settle as they went into the house. She excused herself to make some warm drinks, assigning him the task of lighting a fire. As he went about making a pile of kindling and putting the logs in just the right place, he realised she was absolutely right. A relationship wasn't about obligation. It was about choice. And he chose loving Kiara over not loving her.

When they were settled on the sofa, a fire crackling away in the fireplace and warm mugs of hot chocolate complete with marshmallows in their hands, he took a sip, then set down his mug and turned to her.

'First and foremost, I would like to offer you an apology for my behaviour the other day.'

Kiara nodded, neither refusing nor accepting his apology. She was waiting for the explanation.

'You're the first woman I've felt like this about since…'

'Since Lily,' she filled in for him. 'She's not a secret, Lucas. She's part of who you are. Part of who Harry is.'

It was a generous gesture. Openly acknowledging the woman he'd loved and then lost to a terrible disease. The woman who had given him Harry. A boy without whose energy and verve he might not have survived her loss as emotionally intact as he was.

'I thought I'd finished grieving for her.' He raked a hand through his hair and gave the back of his neck a rub. 'Meeting you taught me I still had another step to take.'

She nodded, openly and actively listening.

He gave a little laugh. 'I actually needed to take her

advice. She wanted this…' He moved his hand between the two of them. 'For me to fall in love again.'

Kiara's breath hitched in her throat. 'Is that what's happening?'

Lucas gave a proper laugh now. 'It's what's *happened*! I'm in love with you, Kiara Baxter.'

'But…?' She said it without malice, but she was still waiting for her explanation and she was right. He owed her the truth.

'At first I thought it was betraying Lily to love another woman the way I love you. But then…' His breath grew shaky as he rubbed his hand against the nape of his neck once more. 'The truth was I was scared. Loving someone—loving *you* the way I do… I can't do it half-heartedly and that frightened me. I didn't want to lose sight of myself the way I did before. But I realised fear and vulnerability are all part of loving someone. Love isn't about limits. It's about opening up. Expanding your heart, not blocking it off.'

He stroked the backs of his fingers along her cheek.

'It's about being brave with someone. Trusting someone enough to believe that whatever you do, no matter how frightening, it'll be so much better facing those things together. I want to be brave with you.' He pressed his hands to his heart. 'You've made me realise my heart has a much greater capacity for love and resilience than I thought. Harry adores you. I adore you. I mean…' He held his hands out wide. 'If you can get *me* to enjoy *Christmas* you're obviously a miracle-worker.'

Kiara was smiling now, and laughing, and crying, and moving across the sofa to climb onto his lap and receive the kisses he was so hungry to give her.

After a few moments she pulled back, and without

words began to trace her fingers along his face. His forehead, his cheekbones, his nose and chin. As if she were memorising him. As if she was finally believing that she didn't need permission to love him—she just needed to love him. And that was when it hit him. She had been every bit as frightened as he was.

'It takes courage, doesn't it?' he asked. 'To love after being so badly hurt.'

She nodded, and he saw a swell of emotion rushing through her eyes. 'It does.' She scrunched her nose and gave it a wriggle. 'I guess after you left I felt as if my future was destined to always be somebody's secret, and I didn't want that.'

'I hate it that I made you feel that way.'

Again, she scrunched her nose. 'The way you left did hurt me, but really I think I'm the one who made myself feel that way. I could've called you on it then and there. I knew in my heart you weren't a "love 'em and leave 'em" kind of guy, and that there had to be something else going on, but I let my past experience colour how I responded.'

'Hey…' He ran his fingers through a lock of her hair, then brushed her cheek with his fingers. 'I made a bad call. I was scared and I acted like an idiot, and that behaviour triggered the fears and hurt embedded in you. It was a not-so-perfect storm.'

'One that's blown over?'

'One that's definitely blown over,' he confirmed solidly.

'Should we seal that with a kiss?'

A smile teased at the corners of her lips, and then blossomed into a full-blown grin as he tugged her in close to him again.

'I think we should seal it with a thousand kisses. Maybe more?'

She giggled and asked, 'Just how long do you think it's going to take Harry to eat some spaghetti and a scoop of ice cream?'

'Long enough for me to do this...' Lucas said, scooping her up and laying her out on the sofa where, smiling and laughing, they tangled their limbs together and enjoyed a good old-fashioned kissing session...as if they were teenagers.

And that was how he felt. Young again. Unweighted by a past that he didn't know how to move on from. Stronger for having Kiara in his life. For accepting and giving her love. Their strength united in loving his son.

This, he realised as the twinkle of the star atop her tree caught his eye, was the true meaning of Christmas. And he was excited to be celebrating it with a full heart for the rest of his life.

EPILOGUE

'WHO WANTS TO put the star on the Christmas tree?'

'Which one?' Harry and Kiara asked in tandem, instantly dissolving into fits of giggles.

Lucas pretended to look confused, and then rotated in a slow circle to see where not one, nor two, but seven full-sized Christmas trees circled the front garden, with five more to come. They'd decided their famous decorations—famous for Cornwall, anyway—should come with a new twist this year.

The first tree was covered in ornamental partridges made of every material imaginable. Felt, papier mâché, glass, plastic, wood… They were all decorations that visitors had brought to be part of the Mistletoe Cottage Merry Christmas Fest. Some of the decorations had been handmade by people of all different ages. One artisan glass blower had even made the tree-topper for that one. A robust, but beautifully ornamental partridge that glowed in the wintry sunlight.

Today, of course, was swans, and the tree glowed with all of the offerings from both near and far.

While the stream of visitors was steady, it still felt very much as if this was the same small local project that Kiara had begun in the name of charity. The fact that she'd been able to give First Steps healthy donations every year for the last few years on behalf of the wider community was just the icing on the gingerbread man.

But, more than that, now that Harry and Lucas had moved in Kiara's house no longer felt like her little cottage—it felt like a home. A family home for her, and Lucas, and Harry—whom she'd now officially adopted—and their latest addition, a precocial curtain-climbing kitten called Holly.

'Oof!' Kiara's hands flew to her tummy, extended to accommodate a thirty-seven-week pregnancy.

Lucas was by her side in an instant, putting Harry in charge of holding the star. 'Everything all right, love? Is it time?'

Kiara shook her head, although she was uncertain if this was the real thing or not. 'You'd think with my experience I'd know!'

Lucas laughed and said, 'Remember Marnie? She said pretty much the same thing when her baby was due.'

Kiara nodded, breathing through a pain that was mixed with the pleasure of knowing their baby would be with them at Christmastime. She already had a list of Christmas-themed names she hoped Lucas would like. And Harry, of course.

He was hopping up and down, singing, 'Baby! Baby! I'm going to get a baby for Christmas!'

Lucas gave his son's head a playful rub and said, 'Yes, you are, son—but should we maybe get Kiara to the sofa, so she can have a rest before we figure out if we need to take her up to Carey House?'

Kiara grinned. 'I think the fact that we have a midwife "just popping in to see the decorations" on the hour every hour will probably stand us in good stead.'

'That's a good point. Do you want to ring Nya?'

They shared a smile. Nya was the one who'd had the very first inklings of their romance, and as such, when they'd found out Kiara was pregnant earlier this year, they'd thought it only fitting to ask if she'd be their midwife.

'I'll ring her when the next one— Oof!' Kiara flinched again.

Harry's eyes went wide. 'Daddy, quick! Get the sleigh to come! The one with the reindeer! Then we can *fly* Kiara to the hospital!'

Lucas gave him a hug, told him it was a great idea, and then pretended to think a minute before suggesting, 'Why don't you grab Kiara's bag and we'll go the normal way?'

'Walking?' Harry looked confused. 'Can she do that?'

'It's what every good midwife recommends,' Lucas said. 'I have that on good authority.' He tapped the side of his nose, then gave Kiara's cheek a kiss. 'Unless you want to kill me for saying as much and put you in the car like any normal panicked father?'

Kiara grinned, every bit as thrilled and panicked and having no more idea what to do than her 'men'.

'Walking's fine. It's a beautiful day.'

And it was. She gave her husband a kiss and then, because he looked as if he was feeling left out, dropped a kiss on Harry's forehead.

She loved being his parent, and a wife to his father. And she couldn't wait to have this baby so that they could all enjoy the Christmas season as one big happy family.

* * * * *

FESTIVE FLING TO FOREVER

KARIN BAINE

MILLS & BOON

For Josephine. Now reunited with Paddy. xx

CHAPTER ONE

THIS WAS AS adventurous as Sophie French liked to get. Actually, even being here on the jetty waving off Clem the boatman and Jack Matthews was a tad out of her comfort zone. Enys Island might only be across that stretch of water Jack was sailing over to get supplies but it wasn't Carey Cove and she didn't like to stray too far from home.

'See you later,' she called hopefully into the wind. It was Jack's pregnant wife she was here to see, otherwise she would never have ventured to somewhere so isolated in this weather. Her job as a midwife at Carey House meant she sometimes had to travel to the more remote areas around Cornwall to see her patients but putting herself in any jeopardy was not in her nature. If not for the sake of her patients she would happily stay put in her hometown for the rest of her days. Given the chance, she would have all of her pregnant ladies safe and sound in the maternity ward at their cottage hospital lest anything happened, but not everyone thought as she did. Some mothers-to-be preferred the idea of a home birth, praying they would have a perfect, natural delivery. There was no reason they shouldn't, but Sophie liked to be prepared for all emergencies.

She had always been a cautious child. Much to her parents' chagrin, she was sure, when they had the kind of adventurous spirit she'd never possessed. Whilst they had travelled the world on a shoestring budget, Sophie had been content to stay at home under the care of her grandmother. As a young girl, all she had craved was the security of four walls and familiar surroundings over snow-capped mountains and humid tropical forests. Things had not changed in her twenty-nine years. Especially when her fears had been proven tragically correct.

Only once, when she was ten years old, had she tried to convince everyone, including herself, that she was ready to travel with them. Only to get cold feet at the last minute and disappoint everyone. Her guilt was further compounded when they'd been killed in a mountaineering accident on that very trip.

Since then she had become what some people called overcautious, but she only wanted to keep herself and her patients safe. Her one nod to her parents' legacy was her chosen career. After discovering her mother had trained as a midwife herself before quitting to travel, Sophie had followed in her footsteps to nearby Carey House.

Now a midwife herself, Sophie went on the journey along with her pregnant patients. Including home visits to isolated islands in wintry weather.

She hoisted her bag onto her shoulder and pulled her scarf up around her nose before facing into the wind. It was a short walk to the cottage but the weather and rocky terrain would make it a challenge. The land was mostly used for grazing and it was not conducive for sightseeing or travelling medical professionals.

The warm glow in the window up ahead and the cosy prospect of a home fire burning spurred Sophie onwards. She would never have survived her parents' Bohemian lifestyle, not knowing where or when she would next find shelter or food. Sometimes she wondered if she had been swapped at birth when she was so different to the people she had been born to. Perhaps there was a quiet, unassuming family out there somewhere, struggling to relate to their free-spirited daughter, who did not fit into their world either.

Sophie rapped on the door out of courtesy, even though she knew it would be unlocked. There was no need to worry about anyone breaking in on the island when the majority of the inhabitants were livestock. The Matthews could see everyone who visited Enys from the window of their front room.

'Hey, Molly. It's Sophie, the midwife from Carey House.'

'Hi, Sophie, come on in. It'll take me ages to haul my backside up out of bed to let you in otherwise,' the voice shouted from upstairs.

Usually Molly was already up doing her chores when Sophie got here, even with only a matter of weeks left of her pregnancy. To find her apparently still in bed was not like her at all.

Sophie hustled upstairs to the bedroom where she had done Molly's previous pregnancy checks. The room was dark, the curtains unopened and Molly was lying flat on the bed. She hadn't even managed to sit up for her visitor.

'Do you mind if I open the curtains for some light so I can see what I'm doing?'

'Go ahead,' Molly replied, mid-yawn.

'How are you feeling today?' Even in the gloom of the afternoon Sophie could see how pale and weary she looked. Not at all her usual vibrant, blooming self.

'Exhausted. I think it's the time of year. The darker days and horrible weather always make me feel tired.'

'Well, I'll just do a few checks to make sure there's nothing else going on. I'll go and give my hands a wash first, if that's okay?'

'Sure.' Molly attempted to hoist herself up and Sophie hooked a hand under her arm to help her into a sitting position. She propped up the pillows for Molly before going to wash in the bathroom.

'Not long to go now,' Sophie commented on her return, the thought of bringing another life into the world putting a smile on her face.

'Thank goodness. At this rate I think I could pass as Father Christmas if you put me in a red suit and beard.'

Sophie chuckled. It was always the same when her patients were late into their third trimester. As much as they were looking forward to the arrival of their little bundles of joy, they were also glad to get back control of their bodies.

Sophie had not experienced pregnancy for herself—perhaps one day if she was lucky—but she had dealt with enough pregnant women to witness their frustration and some of the more challenging aspects of childbearing.

'At least the little one will be here in time for Christmas to make it extra special.' The picture of a happy family gathered together always brought a lump to her throat. It was something she had never really had with her parents. They'd usually spent the winter months in exotic climes, leaving her with her grandmother for

Christmas. As much as she had loved her gran, she'd longed to experience the kind of family get-togethers normal families had at that time of year. A quiet turkey dinner for two and the prospect of unwrapping a travel journal or some Peruvian panpipes did not hold the same excitement factor everyone else seemed to have leading up to the big day.

'Yes, I have all the present shopping done so I'm fully expecting not to leave the house once Jack brings the other supplies home. I will be happy with just the three of us cosied up in the cottage for Christmas.' There was a twinkle in Molly's eye as she said it. Highlighting to Sophie once more that the season was about being with family and loved ones, not token gifts or a desire to be somewhere warmer or more exciting than Carey Cove. That ache in her heart hurt a bit more.

'Sounds lovely.'

'Hopefully I'll be able to shake off this malaise or I won't be fit to even push this baby out when the time comes.'

'Don't worry. It will do you good to put your feet up for a while. I'm sure that lovely husband of yours will do anything you need.'

'Yes, I'm very lucky. He's been doing all the cooking. Not so good at the cleaning, but he's been a great help.'

'That's what I like to hear—a husband who isn't afraid to muck in when called upon. It makes life easier if there are two parents actively involved in the household. Now, I'm going to take a look at your blood pressure to make sure there's nothing else making you tired.' Sophie took out the cuff, wrapped it around Molly's arm and took the reading. Low blood pressure was common during pregnancy, but any significant drop could be a sign of something more serious, so it was necessary to keep a good record.

'Have you experienced any dizziness, blurred vision or excessive thirst?' The symptoms most associated with low blood pressure.

'No. As I said, I'm just sleepy today.'

'That all seems fine,' Sophie said, undoing the cuff again, satisfied there was not a problem to worry about where her blood pressure was concerned. 'Do you have a urine sample for me?'

'It's there on the dresser.' Molly pointed over at the plastic sample bottle propped up on the dressing table.

Using the test strips from her bag, Sophie noted the results. 'Absolutely perfect. While I'm here I'll check on baby's progress too. If you could shuffle back down the bed that would be great.'

With Sophie's assistance Molly was able to lie down in order for her examination.

'I'll try and warm my hands up first,' she said, rubbing her hands together as Molly lifted her nightdress up over her sizeable bump.

Applying firm pressure, Sophie felt around, trying to gauge the baby's position. With five weeks to go she would have expected the baby to be moving freely but it soon became apparent the head was already engaged in the pelvis.

It wasn't completely unheard of and didn't mean there would be a problem or even that Molly would go into labour immediately. However, the baby remained in the occipito-posterior position, facing towards the stomach instead of the back, spine parallel to the mother's. Most babies would spontaneously rotate to face the right direction before birth, but on those rare occasions when the baby did not rotate there could be a prolonged delivery and severe backache where an epidural was needed to alleviate the pain. It could mean a hospital stay and she would prefer a transfer to St Isolde's, the main hospital in the area which dealt with their high-risk pregnancies.

'Is something wrong?' Molly queried when Sophie took her time confirming what was happening.

'Nothing to worry about, but your little one is facing the wrong way at the minute. There's plenty of time for him or her to turn around. Sometimes it can happen right at the last minute. I know you want a home birth, but a hospital delivery is something we might have to think about if things don't change.'

She could see the news had made Molly more emotional than usual, her eyes welling up with tears. It was understandable. Sophie wanted all of her patients to experience the birth process whatever way they envisioned it, it being such a special time in a mother's life. However, she had to put their welfare first.

'I would want Jack with me.'

'Of course. We don't need to make any decisions yet, just keep an eye on baby's position.'

With that, the mobile phone sitting on the night stand began to buzz.

'Speak of the devil.' Molly smiled and stretched across to answer it.

Sophie watched her smile transform into a frown before she handed the phone over to her. 'Jack wants to speak to you.'

'Hello? This is Sophie.'

'Sophie, I was hoping you could break the news to Molly… I don't want her to panic.'

Sophie's stomach plummeted into her shoes, waiting for the bad news to follow. Whatever it was, on top what she had just told her it was liable to send Molly into a tailspin, and she didn't need any further upset.

'Uh-huh?' She tried not to worry Molly, who was listening intently to every word, her forehead lined with concern.

'There's a storm rolling in. The weather changed so quickly Clem doesn't think we're going to be able to get back tonight.'

Sophie was momentarily stunned into silence as she processed the implications of what he was saying. Not only did it mean she couldn't get Molly to hospital if needed, but she wouldn't be getting home either. They were stranded here for the night.

'Okay. Let me know when that changes.' She made the decision not to share her concerns about the baby's position with him. There was nothing to say Molly would go into labour tonight and they could deal with that tomorrow, getting her a referral to St Isolde's. As usual, she was probably being overcautious, but it was better to be safe than sorry.

For now, the best she could do was keep her patient calm and ride out the storm with her.

Sophie watched the ominous grey sky from the kitchen window as she tackled the mountain of dirty dishes in the sink. Molly's fatigue and Jack's inability to keep up with the household chores meant she had something to keep her busy, to stop her mind wandering into the worst-case scenario now they were completely cut off from the mainland. It would be scary enough for two women alone in the house with a storm raging outside and the possibility of losing power without her imagination making matters worse. Add a possible complicated birth into the mix and it was the stuff of nightmares. Sophie catastrophised most situations anyway so this one was in danger of making her brain explode.

A sudden crack of thunder sliced through her silent reverie to startle her, making the soapy plate in her hand slide quickly back into the suds. The sky lit up, lightning flashing behind the dark clouds, and her heart beat a little faster. She was not a fan of storms. Where some people were content to watch the drama unfold and marvel at the power of Mother Nature, Sophie could be found blocking plugholes, turning off electrical devices and unplugging everything in case lightning struck the house. Even a one in a million chance was enough for her to take precautions.

Goodness knew how Molly was sleeping through all of this, but she needed the rest. To her credit she had taken the news about Jack's delayed return better than expected. Sophie supposed the couple were used to their lives being dictated by the weather, living on this remote island. She, on the other hand, had her days carefully mapped out and preferred to stick to her schedule. Despite the circumstances being beyond her control, it did not sit well with her having to phone and rearrange her other appointments. She didn't like going into the unknown unprepared.

Another boom of thunder reverberated, closely followed by a flash of lightning illuminating the gloom. Sophie shuddered. If she had been at home she would be tucked up in bed with the curtains closed and the covers over her head so she couldn't see or hear what was going on outside.

The next rumble seemed closer, louder than the last. She could still hear it when the world outside lit up again. Then Sophie realised the noise was coming from upstairs. Molly.

She placed the last dish into the rack, leaving the soapy water to drain away, and went to dry her hands.

'I'm coming. Hold on, Molly.' A tall order, she knew, if the baby was determined to make an early entrance after all.

By the time she got upstairs Molly was standing at the window, doubled over in pain. The sight was sufficient to snap Sophie back into her professional frame of mind. Labour and babies she knew how to deal with. Even when there were a few curve balls thrown in along the way.

'Hold my hand and just breathe through the pain.'

'That's easier said than done,' Molly managed to pant out through gritted teeth, grabbing hold of Sophie at the same time.

'Is this your first contraction?'

Molly nodded.

'Okay. It should subside soon and we'll try and get you into bed before the next one comes.' Sophie coached her breathing until the contraction subsided, her hand squeezed so tight she thought her circulation had been cut off at one point.

As soon as Molly was able to move again she helped her back into bed.

'It's too early. I need Jack here.' For the first time since Sophie had arrived Molly had fear in her eyes.

No matter what happened, it was her job to keep her patient calm and reassured that everything was going to be all right. Regardless if she was having a wobble in confidence herself. Out here Sophie only had the contents of her medical bag to handle an emergency. There was not nearly enough equipment to cover all eventualities.

'He'll be here as soon as he can. In the meantime you've got me and I'm going to make sure you and the baby have the best care I can give you. Now, let's take a look and see how things are progressing.' It would be best for all concerned if Molly was simply experiencing Braxton Hicks contractions, practice for the real thing. The baby would have a better chance all round if Molly made it past the thirty-six-week mark.

Unfortunately, it soon became apparent that this was the real deal. 'Okay, Molly, you're four centimetres dilated. There's still a long way to go, but I would prefer to get you to a hospital as a precautionary measure since this is technically an early labour and because baby is facing the wrong way.'

The tears Molly had been so bravely trying to keep at bay now fell unchecked. She was afraid and, if Sophie was honest, she was too. They were so far out from the mainland that if there were any complications… Well, it didn't bear thinking about.

'But how? If there's a storm coming no one can get to us without risking their own lives.' Molly was scrambling to sit up again as panic took over, but Sophie needed her to remain calm if they were to have any hope of slowing this labour down.

'I'll put in a call for the emergency helicopter. I'm sure they can still get to us, and they'll have more equipment on board to monitor you and the baby until we can get you to the hospital.'

Flying in a helicopter in a storm wasn't something she would ever have contemplated if it weren't for the benefit of her patient. Her parents would be proud. It was the sort of thing they would have done without a second thought for their safety. Certainly not for the young daughter they had left behind. Thankfully she had learned from her parents' mistakes. If she had to get on that helicopter it would only be because it was a matter of her patient's survival.

'That's it, Molly. You're doing so well.' Sophie wrung out the wet flannel into the basin on the night stand and placed it across Molly's forehead.

'I want Jack,' she sobbed, understandably emotional as her labour progressed, undeterred by the less than desirable circumstances.

'I know, sweetheart. I'm sure you will see him soon. For now we have to concentrate on getting you through these contractions.' Labour had progressed quickly, and she was already six centimetres dilated. This baby was coming tonight, with or without outside assistance. For everyone's sake, Sophie hoped she would not have to deliver this baby alone. It was not that she couldn't do it, goodness knew she had delivered babies in all sorts of situations. Her training and experience had prepared her well, but with a premature birth there were more risks involved and she didn't want to leave anything to chance.

'This isn't how it was supposed to be,' Molly groaned as another contraction took hold.

'I know it's not the home birth you'd quite expected,

but what a story you'll have to tell. Choppered off the island to reunite with your husband is romantic in its own way.' As long as the baby didn't arrive before the helicopter and there were no life-threatening complications for mother or baby.

'Does Jack know the baby's coming?'

'The line wasn't great when I spoke to him again, but he knows and he's going to meet us at the hospital.' Only trouble being that she didn't know how long the helicopter would take to get here, if at all.

Molly's cries echoed through the cottage and there was nothing Sophie could give her to help her through the contractions. Even if she had been in hospital, her labour had advanced so rapidly there wouldn't have been time to give her an epidural if she had wanted one. This was the worst part for her and her patients, both powerless until nature had taken its course.

'This will all be worth it when you have that little baby in your arms,' she said, brushing Molly's damp hair away from her face. The stress, the pain and the whole labour often faded in the face of a brand-new life being brought into the world. For Sophie included.

Although she was still praying they would get to the hospital in time, it was looking more unlikely by the second with the closer contractions.

That didn't mean she wasn't relieved when she heard the noise of the helicopter over the house. Sophie couldn't leave Molly when she was in the last stages of her labour, but she did rush to open the bedroom curtains to see what was going on. It did nothing to allay her fears. The chopper was battling against the wind, struggling to land. A line was thrown out, it too swinging from side to side. A figure in bright orange risked life and limb to traverse it and Sophie's heart was in her mouth simply watching. At this stage she knew she was delivering this baby here and now and backup should have been a comfort. Instead, it gave her another life to fret over. In the end she turned away, unable to stomach witnessing the dangerous mission unfold.

It was only when she heard banging at the front door she was able to breathe again.

'The door's open. We're up here,' she shouted above the noise of the helicopter being buffeted about by the storm outside.

Whichever daredevil had been dispatched to assist her would have to do without a welcoming party as Molly panted frantically through her contractions.

'Okay. So where are we?' The heaven-sent paramedic had entered the room, but Sophie's relief was short-lived as she recognised the face as well as the voice. Roman Callahan, the man who had broken her heart and who all other men had failed to live up to since.

He was still as handsome as ever, his black hair tousled in that sexy devil-may-care way and with a lean, muscular body to remind her he was not a teenage boy any more. Sophie made the decision not to introduce herself. If he didn't recognise her she certainly wasn't going to remind him who she was and how they had parted over a decade ago. Although after being best friends for years it would be surprising if he didn't know her. That led her to conclude he was either trying to save her blushes or pretending not to know her to avoid rehashing the past. It was possible he also believed this birth was more important than their ancient history.

The last time she'd seen him was when they were eighteen, just before they'd gone their separate ways to university and she had made the impulsive decision to kiss him. That one rash decision to act on her teenage crush had ensured her best friend had walked out of her life ten years ago, never to be seen or heard from again. Until now.

Despite all the questions whirling around her mind about where he had been, what he had been doing and if he had ever thought about her, Sophie had to set her personal crisis aside to focus her attention on her patient. Since he hadn't chosen to acknowledge her in any other way than a professional capacity, she chose to do the same. For now. When this was all over she might have one or two things to say to him. All that was required of her now where Roman Callahan was concerned was to ignore her fast beating heart reacting to seeing him again. If she had a spare moment she would be completely humiliated to see him again.

'Ten centimetres dilated and the baby's head is crowning,' she told him after checking on Molly's progress.

'It looks as though you've managed on your own just fine, Soph. I don't think you needed me at all.' So he had recognised her after all. Even if it hadn't led to the tearful reunion she'd often dreamed about when she'd thought of running in to him again.

'Well, you're here now and Molly and the baby will still have to get to hospital.' Out of the corner of her eye she saw the flash of neon orange as her new colleague moved closer to the bed.

'Hello, Molly. I'm Roman and I will be your paramedic escort for the evening.' Apparently he was still the same flirt, the same joker he had always been. It might be reassuring for his patients, but not for an ex-friend who had spent the last ten years trying to get over him.

'Roman, could you get me some of those towels from the dresser?' If nothing else, he could make himself useful.

'Sure. I'm here at your disposal.' To his credit, he didn't immediately attempt to take over the situation, despite her call for help. He appeared to respect her position and experience as a midwife even if she had lost his friendship so long ago.

'When the next contraction comes, Molly, I need you to bear down and push this little one out. Okay?' It shouldn't be long now, and Sophie was reassured there was a chance of getting them to the hospital.

'You're doing really well.' Although Roman was looking at Molly as he passed over the towels, Sophie had a feeling he was talking to her. Perhaps it was her subconscious seeking reassurance but sometimes even a trained professional needed a confidence boost.

She spread a towel under Molly and could tell immediately when her body tensed up that the time had come. Whilst she got ready to catch the baby, Roman moved to the head of the bed.

'Time to push, Molly. I'm here and Roman's here and we are going to help you both through this.'

'Take my hand, swear at me, whatever it takes.' He took Molly's hand as she pushed through the contraction and Sophie watched Mother Nature take over, a new life slipping into her hands.

He was smaller than expected and Sophie moved quickly to cut and clamp the umbilical cord. She swaddled him in another of the towels and moved into the light where she could see him better.

'I want to hold my baby,' Molly cried, and Sophie had to ignore the swell of nausea in her stomach as she looked at the pale bundle in her arms. The baby still hadn't made a sound and had some staining on his skin, indicating that meconium was present. Sometimes baby could have a bowel movement and excrete the sticky green substance into the amniotic fluid. If inhaled, causing meconium aspiration syndrome, it could lead to severe lung problems.

She began rubbing his back, praying with every breath in her body that they would soon hear his cries.

'We just need to do some observation on the baby before you can hold him.' Roman was doing his best to placate Molly but it would soon become apparent all was not well.

'Come on, little one,' Sophie urged quietly, hoping she could somehow bring him back to life.

She felt Roman's presence beside her as she reached into the infant's mouth to clear anything which might be preventing him from breathing. They exchanged a concerned glance, sharing that overwhelming desire for a miracle. There was some meconium in the baby's mouth blocking his airway. Sophie took an aspirator from her bag and suctioned out the substance she could see.

'Do you want me to try?' Roman asked softly.

She was on the verge of agreeing and letting him take control, in the hope he could do what she could not, when there was a small ragged cry from the babe in her arms.

Their collective exhaled breath and the urge to weep signalled the relief that this might have a happy ending after all. When she looked into Roman's all too familiar eyes she could tell he was as moved as she by the moment.

'I think that's his way of saying he has had enough fussing,' she said, pulling herself together.

'I'll get him some oxygen to help with his breathing.' Roman turned away to get the mask and pump from his bag, but Sophie didn't miss the swipe of his hand across his eyes. It was typical of him to resist expressing his emotions. That at least hadn't changed. He had always been difficult to read. She blamed him for letting her make a fool of herself, believing he loved her as much as she did him. Only to find out too late it had all been one-sided.

'Is everything all right?' Molly enquired.

'Roman's just going to give the baby some oxygen to help him breathe. He had some fluid in his airway, but I've cleared it. The hospital will do some X-rays to make sure there's nothing left in his lungs and give him some antibiotics to prevent possible infection, but he looks fine.' Sophie handed the now very vocal tot to Roman so she could attend to Molly to deliver the placenta and make sure she was fine to transfer to the helicopter.

She cast a glance over at Roman, who looked unexpectedly confident and content cradling a baby in his arms. It did little to help control her emotions when she'd spent much of her teens imagining this moment. Only with Roman cooing over their own child.

* * *

Throughout all the drama Roman had kept in touch with the helicopter crew and it was a relief when his walkie-talkie crackled to life with news that they had managed to set down outside.

'That's us, folks. Time to get moving.' He was holding the baby in one arm whilst hoisting his medical bag onto his other shoulder.

'Will…er… I have to fly too?' She would do it if she had to but being in a tiny tin can being tossed around by a storm was not in keeping with her idea of playing it safe.

'Not this time, sweetheart. I'm afraid we just don't have room on board.' The term of endearment casually tossed into the air had no less effect on her now than it had when she'd been younger. As a teenager she would have done anything to have him call her that in anything other than his usual teasing manner. It was easy to see with hindsight how a lovestruck girl could have mistaken his friendship for something she really wanted.

'I'm sure you'll give Molly and the baby the best possible care in my absence,' she assured Molly, along with herself.

It was hard to hand over responsibility of one of her patients. He seemed a very competent paramedic, but she knew nothing about Roman Callahan any more. On the positive side, at least in the hospital they could give the baby any extra care he might need.

'I'll get Jack to bring you back as soon as the storm dies down.' Molly eased herself up from the bed and Sophie helped her get dressed to protect her from the elements. Ideally, she would have some time to rest and recover so quickly after the birth but, as any mother, she was willing to set aside her discomfort for the sake of her newborn.

'Don't worry about me. It'll be nice to have some time on my own here and I'll get in touch with Clem in the morning. There's plenty of cleaning-up to do. I'll be fine.' The lie would be worth it to prevent Molly from fretting any further.

She thought she caught a flicker of something in Roman's eyes challenging her. It was possible he remembered her fear of the dark. A minor inconvenience in comparison to the things people like Roman, who put their lives on the line every day, did in the line of duty. At her age she really ought to have got over her childhood hang-ups, but that meant facing them head-on and she was the queen of procrastination when it came to dealing with her emotional baggage. Tonight, on her own on an island in a storm was going to be a real test of strength for her.

They transferred their patients into the waiting helicopter, ducking below the rotating blades. Once she was satisfied Molly and her son were secured by the crew, Sophie stepped back. Her hair whipped about her face when the helicopter began to lift up off the ground. It was already getting dark but the lights from the chopper lit up everything on the ground below as it took off, catching her in its spotlight.

Perhaps that was what prompted Roman to lean out for one last goodbye.

'It was good to see you again, Sophie,' he said, before the world around her was suddenly plunged back into darkness. Leaving her all alone for the second time in her life.

CHAPTER TWO

ROMAN COULDN'T GET Sophie out of his head. Of course he had known he would probably run into her again after moving back to the area. It was possible that had prompted his decision to return in the first place. After every breakup, amicable or otherwise, it always made him think about Sophie and how she was doing. If she was happily settled down with someone else or what could have happened between them if he'd stayed and let something develop between them. Without doubt, his relationship with his parents would have been strained if not non-existent, as it was today.

When it came to Sophie though, there were still unresolved issues. His last partner, Lena, had asked him why he was so afraid to commit, and Sophie had been the first thing which came to mind, his thoughts turning to how he hadn't been able to give himself to her when she was the only person he had really loved, so how could he possibly settle for anyone else?

It had been pointed out to him in the midst of the breakup that he wasn't getting any younger and he would end up a sad, lonely man. The words had haunted him because it was probably true. He didn't want a wife and kids now, but what if he realised too late that he did but he was too set in his ways to share his life with someone else?

When the temporary position had come up in his home town he had believed it was the chance for him to get some closure. He knew he would run into Sophie at some stage and be confronted by his past but apparently he hadn't been prepared for the impact that would have upon him. Or was that the reason he hadn't actively sought her out? Deep down, had he known that seeing her again would make him question why he had left her in the first place?

They hadn't parted on the best of terms. One kiss between them had changed their relationship, and brought everything into sharp focus for him. He'd known he was in love with her, but a romance would never have worked between them. They were too different, and he knew he could never bring her the happiness she deserved. She was someone who needed stability and security, where he couldn't wait to break free from the shackles his parents had imposed upon him.

He didn't regret the decision to leave, especially when he'd seen first-hand how capable and confident she was in her job. In leaving his old life behind, he'd had the opportunity to experience much more than he ever would have staying in one place. He was always moving around, taking temporary placements where he could so life never got boring.

Sophie had never needed him, but he did miss her friendship. She was the only one he had ever been able to confide in, who'd understood him when his family never had.

He had left soon after their ill-fated kiss, going to medical school against his parents' wishes. Now he was back, and in some ways it felt as though he had never left.

Sophie was the same natural beauty she had always been. Her wavy dark brown hair was longer, her curves more pronounced, and now she had a confidence she had lacked in her adolescence. In short, she was breathtaking.

Roman was glad she had emerged from the dark shadow of her parents' death. She had always seemed to judge herself by their standards and zest for life, believing she was in some way lacking for not being like them.

Though never in his eyes. Their friendship had blossomed during her grief. He had noticed her retreat from the world and recognised that loneliness. Even though he had family at home, he'd never felt as though he belonged there when his parents had always wanted more from him than he was prepared to give. They had pushed him to join the family business in land and property management, but he'd had dreams of his own to go into medicine which were not in keeping with their ingrained traditions. His older brothers had fallen in line, rendering him the black sheep of the family.

As it was the end of his shift he wasn't likely to see Sophie today and catch up on her life since they had parted all those years ago.

'Hey, Roman. Good to see you.' Theo Turner, an obstetrician at the hospital, crossed the corridor to speak to him.

'You too.' Roman shook his hand, genuinely pleased to see him. They had been introduced during his first day on the job and instantly seemed to hit it off. Although they didn't hang out after work, their schedules often clashing, Theo had been nothing but kind and supportive, asking how he was doing any time they ran into each other. Everyone seemed to respect him, and he came across as a genuine, compassionate soul who cared a lot for his patients and colleagues. The sort of man Roman wished he'd had as a father, as a male role model, growing up. Instead of an overcritical, controlling figure who had cast a dark shadow over his entire life.

'Another rescue mission? You've had quite a few recently.'

'Yeah, I think it has a lot to do with the time of year and the weather. People are more prone to accidents or can find it difficult to access medical help in some of the more isolated areas around here.' In the summer, his colleagues told him, they dealt with more beach rescues with swimmers in difficulty or those stranded out walking on clifftops. The winter brought dangerous icy roads, inhibiting patients and emergency services alike.

'We would all be lost without you.' Theo clapped him on the back. He had that unique ability to make everyone feel at ease, and Roman particularly. As though he was part of the team here. It was nice to be appreciated and have his work validated. He didn't let praise go to his head, but it did always serve to remind him he had taken the right path after all.

'That's very kind of you, but we just do the picking up and dropping off. As a matter of fact, I've just transferred a new patient.'

'We both know your job entails a lot more than being an air taxi. You've saved countless lives where we couldn't get access to patients in jeopardy. Case in point being Molly Matthews and her baby. They're doing well now, but goodness knows what would have happened if you hadn't been able to get out to the island.'

'Now, I can't take credit for that one. Sophie had everything in hand by the time we got there. I'm sure she could have managed until the storm was over.' Although he hadn't stopped thinking about leaving her behind on her own. She didn't fool him. Despite the bravado, he knew she'd had no desire to set foot on that helicopter or be left in the dark. She might be all grown up, but he was sure there was some of the Sophie he'd known still in there. He had seen the fear in her eyes when the helicopter had lifted off, leaving her alone in the dark, but he also knew she would never have accepted him staying behind to look after her rather than their patients. She was too professional and proud to do that.

'Sophie French—the midwife from Carey House? Yes, she's great. We work a lot with the midwives there.'

'You know her well, then?' This could be a way to satisfy his curiosity without venturing into old territory to do so. He had a feeling that once he did he would be opening up a can of worms.

Theo smirked. 'Ah, has our young midwife caught your eye? It's not surprising, I suppose, when you find a beautiful young woman who is also smart and good at her job. The whole package.' There was a wistful look in his eyes that knocked the wind out of Roman. He had no claim over Sophie. Not since he had abandoned her. Yet, even after all these years, his first reaction to the possibility of another man taking an interest in her was to be jealous, possessive even. Sophie would have found that ironic.

'Are the two of you…together?' The word almost choked him, and it was then he realised that Sophie was part of the reason he had returned. Even if he had not known it until this moment, he had never really got over her. Now it appeared he was too late to do anything about it.

Theo chuckled and gave him another hearty slap on the back. 'Goodness, no. I'm still smarting from my divorce. Don't worry, as far as I'm aware she's unattached.'

Although relieved to find his new friend wasn't involved with his first love, Roman didn't want to risk gossip around the hospital before he had a chance to reconnect with Sophie properly. He wasn't sure what he expected if he saw her again, but he was sure she wouldn't appreciate being the subject of false rumours involving him. Although she hadn't challenged him about the past, it was probably only because they'd had other things to deal with at the time. Without a patient in premature labour taking priority, she might not be so amenable towards him.

'It's nothing like that. We grew up together in Carey Cove. I haven't seen her since we left school and I was simply curious about what she's been up to since.' He played down their past relationship since there was nothing to tell. They had looked out for one another as kids, but he had realised in the nick of time that Sophie could do better than him. Before he admitted he had feelings for her too and potentially ruined her life and disappointed her, the way he had his family.

'I didn't know you were a local.' Theo shook his head, clearly bemused by the information.

It wasn't something Roman had purposely kept secret, but he hadn't been back long enough to be comfortable sharing personal details about his life.

'Carey Cove born and bred, but I flew the coop a long time ago.'

'And now you're back. Were you homesick?' Theo teased, not completely off the mark.

'Something like that.' Growing up, it hadn't been the eight-bedroom, four-bathroom mansion which had been his sanctuary. It had been Sophie. She'd been home to him and Roman was feeling decidedly nostalgic.

By getting closure on their past, he wondered if it might help him to settle down in the future.

'Are you sure you want to take this on all on your own today? It's your day off. Wouldn't you rather take some time out for yourself? You've had a rough couple of days.' Kiara, one of the newer members of staff, was peering at Sophie as though she were one of their pregnant ladies needing a little coddling.

Sophie dumped another box on top of the pile already taking up residence in the hallway of Carey House.

'That's exactly why I need to keep busy. Too much time on my own lately. Besides, it's Christmas and it's about time it looked like it around here.' She had survived her night on the island, physically at least. Mentally, it hadn't been so easy, and it wasn't merely her fear of the dark keeping her awake. The shadows of the past had spooked her too.

That blasted Roman Callahan, dropping into her life like some kind of superhero, had totally rocked her usually ordered world. It didn't help that he had disappeared equally as quickly, leaving her with more questions than ever. Like what would have happened if he had reciprocated her feelings and they had stayed together?

These past years she had played it safe, whilst it seemed Roman had continued to live on the wild side. Taking risks and living life to the full. Her parents would have loved him. She didn't think they could ever have been compatible as a couple, but she would never find out. Her overactive mind, however, didn't stop conjuring up images of them being together and what it might have been like sharing her life with him over these past years instead of being on her own for most of the time.

Sophie unboxed one of the many Christmas trees they decorated the building with and began to unfurl the rustling plastic branches. Even though everything was fake, designed to give the impression of real snow-dusted fir trees, there was a real scent of cinnamon and citrus emanating from the packaging.

Once she had put the layered Christmas tree together she found a scattering of real pine cones lying in the box. Lifting one to inhale the scent, it became apparent the smell had not been a result of her overactive imagination after all.

'I'd forgotten about those. I made them with the local kids at the Christmas Fayre last year. I got roped in by Marnie to represent Carey House with a craft stall,' she explained to Kiara, who was watching her with the hint of a smile on her lips.

'What?' she asked, wondering if she was covered in as much glitter and fake snow as the pine cones.

'You are very distracted today. Not your usual focused self.'

Sophie knew it was not an insult, her colleague would never intend to hurt her feelings, but the comment stung nonetheless. She hated anyone thinking she wasn't giving her job one hundred percent, even on her day off.

Deciding it was best to be honest about what was going on rather than have someone think the worst about her, Sophie sighed. 'A blast from the past literally dropped in on me and it has kind of thrown me.'

'Oh?' Kiara, who had been on her way out of the door, now took a seat on one of the sturdy boxes, ready to hear the full story. The novelty of Sophie sharing any personal info apparently drew a captive audience. Nothing out of the ordinary normally happened to her and she was happy that way.

Of course she'd had a boyfriend or two over the years but those relationships had occurred organically, developing between her and men she generally got to know through work. Delivery drivers, their postman, even a male receptionist from St Isolde's for a while. None of those relationships had raised an eyebrow from her colleagues and, if she was honest, they had not excited her much either. She had chosen men she deemed safe and reliable, who wouldn't go off her and hurt her, as Roman had. The problem with that being that they lacked the excitement and skipping pulse which he'd brought. Something which had not changed, judging by their most recent encounter.

'The paramedic who attended Molly Matthews's birth, Roman Callahan. We…er…grew up together.'

'Ooh! Childhood sweethearts? Tell me more.' Kiara rested her head dreamily on her hand, waiting to hear the next great love story. As someone who had recently fallen head over heels, she thought everyone must be walking around with those same heart-shaped eyes. Sophie, however, remained sceptical about ever finding 'the one'.

Once upon a time she had believed that was Roman, later to be proved tragically mistaken. Since then it had been more of a case of 'this one will do', without anyone ever really rocking her world again. Something she had sworn until recently she did not need. Now she was curious about what that would be like, even for a little while. A bit of excitement to shake up her staid life might put some pep in her step.

When she was young and naïve she'd thought she could have it all—romance, a career and a family of her own. Experience had made her more jaded about that being possible. Sometimes her ideas had clashed with those of her partner, the last one expecting her to give up work if they were going to start a family, something she wasn't prepared to do for anyone. If she became a parent, yes, she would give it her all, but not at the expense of her career. Her own mother had done that, and she believed that was partly what had caused her restlessness. Not that she'd been the most attentive mum either, which might have been born of resentment when having Sophie had changed her life.

Sophie did not want the same for her or any future children.

'Not really. Certainly not on his part, at least. I

haven't seen him in over ten years and the unexpected reunion brought up a lot of old memories.'

'Roman Callahan... I think he's the guy who played Father Christmas. You know, the one who abseiled down from the helicopter at the fair?'

'That doesn't surprise me,' Sophie muttered. The sight of someone dressed in a fat suit and bushy white beard risking his life to deliver some presents had caused her to look away at the time, afraid one wrong move would end in tragedy and trauma for all those watching. It made sense that daredevil was Roman. Someone who had never prioritised his personal safety over a thrill.

'No offence, but I wouldn't have thought he was your type. He's so daring and charismatic I can see the attraction though.'

'Roman Callahan is the reason I don't take risks when it comes to dating.' That wasn't strictly true. Her parents had a lot to do with that too. After all, they had repeatedly abandoned her long before Roman, in favour of seeking thrills. Until they had left her for ever. With Roman going off to uni, it had simply compounded the idea that playing it safe was the only way to protect the broken fragments left of her heart. Now he was back she was not sure how to react. The fact that he had been home for a while and had not made any attempt to contact her said he hadn't missed her. Yet that didn't prevent her from constantly thinking about him and the one kiss they had shared.

Kiara stood up and brushed the dust and fake snow from her uniform. 'Maybe you should start. You certainly haven't been happy playing things safe. If I see him I'll put in a good word for you.'

'Don't bother—' Sophie began to say, but Kiara simply winked and hurried away down the front steps, leaving her to wonder if she had heard her or chosen to ignore her instruction. Either way, the prospect of seeing Roman again caused a tingle of anticipation to ripple along Sophie's spine. Her feelings hadn't disappeared just because he had.

Carey Cove hadn't changed much in the years since Roman had left. Walking through it was akin to time travelling back to his childhood, each building bringing long-forgotten memories flooding back into his mind. That was part of the reason he had yet to venture near his family home. Apart from delaying another inevitable confrontation about his life choices, he couldn't face the ghost of past arguments once he set foot on the property.

So he found himself heading towards the beach, which he associated with happier times. With Sophie. Thinking of her yet again, it made sense that when Carey House came into view, overlooking the rest of the main village, he should instead decide to veer up that way to make sure she was all right after the events on the island. They had literally stranded her there and though she projected that tough exterior, he knew better than most how easily it could shatter.

He had never paid much attention to the old stone building when he was younger, but now he could see it for the wonder it was in an area where the population had grown and needed extra medical facilities. The house had been converted into a hospital in 1900 to provide maternity services for the more rural areas and now, with expansion, provided GP access to the local community. There was even a field out the back for the helicopter to land, should they ever need it for emergencies.

'Hi. I was hoping to speak to one of the midwives today. Sophie French?' As he approached, a woman was leaving the building with her medical bag in hand.

'Are you one of our expectant fathers?'

'No, I…er…work with the air ambulance service. I wanted to make sure she was all right after the recent drama on the island. Roman Callahan.' He held out his hand and gave her his best disarming smile in the hope she would trust him enough to divulge Sophie's address.

It was rare for him to have time off and rarer still that he should spend it in Carey Cove. If he didn't follow this up now there was the possibility their paths might never cross again, and that was suddenly an unimaginable thought.

The midwife's frown faded as she shook his hand. 'Nya.'

'Ah, Theo over at the hospital mentioned you the other day. He said to give you his best wishes if I should run into you.' Unfortunately the message only served to make her frown again, indicating that there was a history between them too.

'How is Theo? He hasn't come to Carey Cove for quite a while.'

Although Roman was not privy to Theo's private life, it certainly seemed that during their recent interactions he did appear more downbeat than usual. Perhaps it had something to do with his divorce, or not seeing his children as much as he would like.

'He always appears to be working any time I've

been at the hospital. I'm not sure he's had much time off at all recently.' The news, though it explained Theo's absence, did nothing to placate Nya's concern. She merely nodded.

'Could you tell me where I could find Sophie? I'm not sure when I'll get over this way again. No rest for the wicked, eh?' Another smile and attempt to convince her he was not a stalker who couldn't be trusted with the knowledge of her colleague's whereabouts.

'She's probably at home, Christmas-ifying her house after going to town here.' Nya raised an eyebrow at the red and silver tinsel wrapped around the hand rail outside. It was then he noticed Sophie's signature decorate-everything-in-sight-with-twinkling lights-and-sparkle design. She loved to go over the top at Christmas. He figured it was her way of compensating for the family Christmases she never got to have.

His house had never been a bundle of laughs on the big day either. Although his parents had always spent a fortune on big, extravagant gifts, it was never on things he had wanted or had any interest in.

He and Sophie had enjoyed their own Christmas of sorts. Meeting up at some point, stealing away from their fake happiness to exchange silly handmade gifts that had meant more to him than anything his parents had ever splurged on.

'I don't know the address, sorry.' He should have kept in touch but after the way they had parted he had thought it best. By severing all contact he would not be tempted to do something stupid, such as kissing her again, or worse.

Now that they had reconnected he was sorry he no longer knew anything about her. For all he knew, she could have married, had children and a life which had nothing to do with him. In hindsight, it might not be a good idea to turn up unannounced. As usual he had been thinking only of himself and what he wanted.

Roman was ready to concede it was not meant to be and walk away when Nya stopped him.

'She's still at her grandmother's place. Sophie inherited the cottage when she passed away a few years ago.'

'Oh.' That one word couldn't possibly convey how hard those words had hit him. Sophie was all alone. She had lost the only family she'd had left and he had not been there for her. He knew how close she'd been to her grandmother, and he'd had a soft spot for the old lady too. She'd often brought him in and treated him as her surrogate grandson, fussing over him and making him feel wanted and welcome in their home.

In that moment Sophie's grief became his. That ache in the pit of his stomach told the tale of his loss and empathy for Sophie. Now he had to find her and apologise. He'd never meant to leave her here all alone.

'You didn't know?'

'No.'

The look on Nya's face at his admission said he couldn't possibly be a friend of Sophie's to have missed that traumatic event in her life. No one could have been sorrier than him about that.

'Perhaps I should phone and let her know you're coming…'

'Please don't. I want it to be a surprise,' he said, already making his way towards the cottage. He didn't want to give her the chance to avoid him when he had so much making up to do.

* * *

The scene as he crested the hill was as Christmassy as he could ever hope to set his eyes upon. Sophie, donned in a fluffy red jumper, was hanging fairy lights around the cottage door. All that was needed was a dusting of snow and perhaps a sprig of mistletoe to help break the ice. Without a medical emergency requiring their immediate attention, he couldn't predict how this meeting would go.

Roman was almost reluctant to interrupt her enthusiastic carol singing. She clearly hadn't heard him approach and he cleared his throat to alert her to his presence.

The singing abruptly ended as she spun around, pulling the string of fairy lights down around her. Leaving her trussed up like a Christmas tree.

'Sorry. I didn't mean to startle you.'

'You didn't,' she insisted, disentangling herself from the string of flashing lights.

He knew better than to argue with her when she was on the defensive. When she felt threatened, or on the back foot, she retreated into her spiky shell, fists figuratively raised and ready to fight. He shouldn't have expected anything less. Regardless of her happy, sequin-robin-embellished appearance.

'I wanted to see how you were. Nya told me where to find you.'

'I'm fine.' She turned back and began to reattach her decorations.

'Can I give you a hand with that?' He didn't wait for the inevitable 'no' or he would never get to say what he wanted.

With his extra height advantage he was able to hang the lights on the door lintel with ease.

'Thanks,' she muttered with noticeable reluctance.

At least with the sparkling garland hung, there was no reason for her to ignore him.

'I didn't know about your grandmother. I'm so sorry I wasn't here for you.'

She shrugged, pretending it was not the big deal he knew it to be, her eyes already brimming with liquid emotion. 'I wouldn't have expected you to come.'

Her dismissive tone at his genuine remorse was a blow. Not only because she didn't believe his sincerity, but because it highlighted the distance which had developed between them. The old Sophie would have cried in his arms and let him comfort her. He missed that emotional connection they had once shared. Something he had never come close to having with anyone else since.

In his daydream he had imagined by turning up here they would have a big heart-to-heart and she would forgive him, relieving him from his burden of guilt. It was asking a lot after the way he had left her. Which she had clearly not forgiven him for, but Roman wondered if she still thought of the kiss they had shared too. He had certainly never forgotten it. So much had happened in the interim and he wanted to explain why he had run out on her, but it wouldn't achieve anything. Telling her he'd thought he wasn't good enough for her wasn't going to change events. It could simply leave them both asking 'What if?'. Sure, they were bound to be different people after all this time apart, but something familiar remained between them that he wasn't ready to let go of again.

A fat drop of rain landed on his forehead, bringing him back to the present, followed by another and another. Sophie opened the front door. 'I suppose you had better come in.'

It wasn't the effusive invitation he wanted but he supposed she was right to be wary. Molly and the baby were fine, so he had no real pretext for being here other than their personal connection. No one could blame her if she was unwilling to cover old ground when it must have hurt her as much as it had him.

'Thanks.' He wiped his boots on the 'Merry Christmas' doormat before stepping into the cottage and he was immediately transported back to their schooldays. When he'd hung out here rather than going home to more arguments with his parents.

With the warmth of the fire in the front room, the smell of baking emanating from the kitchen and the quaint, old-fashioned décor, he half-expected Sophie's grandmother to pop her head around the door to say hello. It must have been tremendously difficult for her living here with the loss. They had been so close Roman envied their relationship, never experiencing that close bond with anyone in his family. By spending time here he had experienced that level of unconditional love second-hand at least.

'Why are you here, Roman?' She had politely brought him into the living room and invited him to take a seat, but he could tell by the defensive arm folding she didn't want him here.

'I was at the hospital and Theo said Molly and the baby are doing really well.'

'I know that. As her midwife it's my duty to know how she is keeping.'

'I also wanted to check in with you to see how you were after all the drama on Enys.'

'I'm fine. Clem picked me up in the boat the next morning.'

'Good. I'm sorry I didn't come to see you sooner, Sophie,' he blurted out his regret, which was even greater now with her giving him the cold shoulder.

'There's no need. We were both doing our jobs. I'm quite capable of surviving alone for one night. I've been doing it for years.'

'I'm not talking about just the other night.'

'I know. My answer still stands.' Sophie's unrelenting spikiness made Roman think he was fighting a losing battle in trying to make amends. They were very different people now and too much time had passed. He should have realised he couldn't simply walk back into her life and pick up their friendship again. That easy rapport they'd once had was gone, replaced by this awkward, uneasy tension.

'I should go…'

'Have you seen your parents yet?'

His decision to leave was postponed by the change in conversation. Not one he was particularly keen to pursue, but at least she was giving him some air time.

'I haven't been home. I'm renting a place close to the hospital. To be honest, I haven't spoken to my parents since I came back.'

'Don't you think you should? They might be miffed to find out you've been here all this time and haven't bothered to get in touch.' Sophie thawed enough to sit down instead of hovering, waiting for him to leave. Roman wondered if her concern towards his mother and father related to her own emotions surrounding his return.

'It's more complicated than you know, Soph. I've barely spoken to them since I left for university. Just dropping back into someone's life isn't easy, you know.'

She cocked an eyebrow.

'I don't know how they'll react any more than I knew how you'd feel about seeing me again.'

'It was a lot,' she admitted, though he had known by her expression at the point of recognition on the island. He had chosen not to enter into a dialogue about their past relationship during the emergency, not only because it wasn't the time or the place but also because he hadn't been prepared either. Not that he was readier today, despite walking here with the sole intention of seeing her.

'I should have come to see you before now. I didn't know if you would want to have anything to do with me again.' The thought of Sophie hating him and experiencing it first-hand had been too much to bear. It had been easier to keep thoughts of her at bay. The same way he had got through the rest of his life without her.

'If we're going to go there I think I'll need a drink. I have some mulled wine on the stove if you'd like some?'

Roman was glad of the offer to fortify himself. He had an inkling that the honest conversation they needed to have was going to be a tough one.

CHAPTER THREE

'IT SMELLS DELICIOUS.' Roman had followed Sophie into the kitchen and as she stirred the saucepan the heady smell of cloves, cinnamon and orange was already intoxicating.

Hearing his uncertainty about coming to see her lessened Sophie's ire towards him. He had thought about her at least and not simply swaggered in, expecting to pick up where they had left off, feigning ignorance over the hurt he had caused her.

It had caught her off-guard and with her defences lowered there was a chance those old feelings she harboured for him would come rushing back. Especially when he seemed keen to make amends by seeking her out in this manner.

'You can't have Christmas without mulled wine.' And memories, she added silently. Her gran had always made the drink specially at this time of year. Non-alcoholic, of course, but Sophie made a more adult version these days. A real winter warmer from the inside out.

She poured the hot liquid carefully into two glasses and handed one to Roman.

'Cheers.' She clinked her glass to his and took a hearty sip of the spiced goodness.

'Mmm… Just how I remember it. Although I think yours has more of a kick to it.' He smacked his lips in appreciation.

'We're both over eighteen so I think we're allowed to have a little tipple now.'

'I don't suppose you have any shortbread to go with it?' Roman grinned.

Gran had always made a tray of shortbread to serve with her mulled wine, and he hadn't forgotten. Sophie was glad she still stuck to family tradition, even though she usually had to bring it in to Carey House so she didn't eat it all herself.

She reached for the old biscuit tin on top of the fridge and pulled off the lid to reveal the sweet treats within.

Roman looked at her imploringly with his big brown eyes and she was thankful it was the only thing he was asking from her. One glance into those peepers and she'd be hypnotised into doing anything he wanted.

'Go on, help yourself.' To the biscuits only. Everything else would have to be negotiated. If he was even interested. After all, he hadn't gone out of his way to contact her in all these years.

Roman selected a sugar-dusted star-shaped piece of shortbread and bit into it. He closed his eyes and sighed in ecstasy. That was when Sophie knew she was in real trouble, her body quivering with that same giddy excitement that used to overtake her when they were together as teenagers. All that past hurt, the years apart, dissipated as her body reawakened to the sights and sounds of her old crush.

'Just like Gran used to make.' He opened his eyes and smiled, which didn't help her to keep hating him.

'Years of practice. She wasn't able to make them for quite some time because of the arthritis in her hands in her later years, so I took over.'

'That's too bad. I'm sorry. She was a wonderful woman. I remember the two of us scoffing a whole tin of shortbread between us when she wasn't looking.'

'I think that was your idea and you ate most of it,' Sophie reminded him.

'We both got a scolding from your gran, but she never told my parents. I had a soft spot for her and, if I'm honest, I was envious of the bond you two had.' Roman finished his biscuit in two bites, his appetite as hearty as ever.

'I think she saw you as another waif and stray to look after.' Her gran had enough love to go around for everyone. Sophie didn't know why her mum hadn't inherited the same warm maternal instinct, but she was lucky enough to have had at least one nurturing relative growing up.

'I was grateful to have somewhere to come to, where I was welcome. I had a closer relationship with you and your gran than I had with my own family. We didn't spend a lot of time together. It only led to arguments.'

Back then Sophie hadn't given much thought to Roman being at her house all the time, glad to just have a friend for company. Looking back, she had never had the pleasure of staying at the big house on the edge of town where most people would have been content to live.

She had clearly been mistaken in her later years, when she had believed she was the attraction, but now she was more curious than ever. 'I would have thought your house had more to offer than this cottage.'

The same reasoning could be applied now. All she could give him was wine and shortbread, when he had a whole lifetime to catch up on with his parents.

'I had a complicated relationship with my family. I was more comfortable here with you.'

'You make me sound like some ratty old security blanket,' she complained. 'Comfortable' was worse than 'nice'. It implied she was as exciting as a worn-out pair of slippers.

'Trust me, you were everything I needed.' The words, the sincerity and the intensity with which he was looking at her sent shivers dancing across her skin. If only it were true. Her mind took her by the hand and led her back to that scene when she had kissed him and he had rejected her, to remind her not to get carried away. The consequences were far too painful to make that mistake a second time.

'Whatever happened between you and your parents, I'm sure you can work it out. Perhaps this is the time to check in with them.' It would focus his interest on something other than her, and give her some breathing space.

'Do you know how they are? Have you seen them?'

'Sorry, I don't know them very well and I don't think they mix in the village that much.'

'That would be right. They probably order everything in from London rather than mingle with the great unwashed.' Despite Roman's eye-rolling, Sophie didn't believe him to be joking about their snobbery. It would explain how she didn't know them even after growing up in the same village.

'At least you still have family.' Only someone who had lost everyone close to them could see how utterly futile in-fighting was in a family. It was a waste of precious time together and it made her blood boil when she didn't have that chance. She would have given anything to have one more day with hers. Even her parents, who she had never bonded properly with the way she had with her gran. She didn't think there was anything that couldn't be resolved with time and the reminder that you only got to have one family.

'I didn't mean to be insensitive. Sorry, Soph. It's just that my happiest memories are of being with you here.'

'Yeah. Gran knew how to make everyone feel safe and loved.' She hadn't understood how important that had been to Roman as much as her until today.

'I'm not talking about your gran, Sophie. I don't know what I would have done without you back then.'

Sophie's skin prickled as Roman set his glass down and moved closer. A sense of panic gripped her, knowing she was already lost to him again. If he wanted to renew their acquaintance, she knew she would jump at the chance. Regardless of the risks.

'You could have fooled me. From what I recall, you couldn't wait to get away from me.' She tossed back the rest of the wine, letting it burn her throat, bringing the pain of the memory to life.

They had been celebrating the end of their high school days, partying at a schoolmate's house with the rest of their year. Whilst everyone had been getting drunk and pairing off, they had spent the night cosied up discussing their future plans. They were going to spend the summer together before university and had talked about going travelling. It had given

Sophie hope that there was more than unrequited love between them.

Over the years she had watched Roman flirt with and date every other girl he came across, all the while yearning for him to see her in the same light. She had dated but no one made her feel the way Roman did. From the time he had reached out to her when her parents had died, she'd harboured a crush which only got stronger the more time they spent together. He'd been different with her than he was in school, where he was a Jack-the-Lad daredevil. She got to be with the more caring Roman, who had always been there as a shoulder to cry on.

The fact that he had chosen to sit with her rather than show off at the party, the way he usually did, gave her reason to believe he had some feelings for her. She even believed they were having a moment when they stopped talking and he was looking at her the way she had longed for him to do for so long. That was the only reason she had moved in for the kiss. If one of them hadn't made the move, she thought she was going to be friend-zoned for ever and with them planning on going to different universities Sophie was afraid she would lose him if she didn't show him how she felt.

She'd lost him anyway.

'I wasn't rejecting you, Sophie, but my life here. I needed to start over and at that point in time I thought you did too.'

It was a twist on everything she had ever believed about the situation. Not once had she considered that Roman hadn't kissed her back because he was thinking about her future. Suddenly it opened her mind to what could have been and everything they had possibly missed out on together. It was one thing if it had been a mutual attraction Roman had decided not to follow up. Quite another if the pain resulting from their lack of communication had dictated the safe, boring nature of her subsequent relationships. That need to protect her heart had controlled her love life and now she was discovering it had all been for nothing. Sophie was feeling very hard done by, to say the least.

'We were friends, Roman. You didn't even try to contact me. Do you know how much that devastated me?' Not only had she lost her best friend of eight years, her constant companion through grief and school and all other teen dramas, but she had lost the love of her life. He'd cast her aside so easily it had been a brutal blow to her poor fragile heart.

Roman sighed and at least hung his head in shame when reminded about his behaviour. 'I did think about it, Soph, believe me. I had feelings for you, but it wouldn't have been fair to either of us to act on them.'

'You…you had feelings for me?' The knowledge that it hadn't been a one-sided affair after all justified her actions that night and she could at least stop blaming herself for driving him away. However, his admission still left a lot of unanswered questions. The most pressing one being why he hadn't returned her kiss that night.

'Of course I did. I wouldn't have spent all my time with you if I hadn't thought so much of you. I was afraid of ruining everything between us by making a move. You know I didn't stay with a girl very long before moving on to the next.' He smirked at that but Sophie wasn't finding anything amusing about the situation. By keeping her in the dark all this time he had made her doubt herself and everyone else who subsequently came into her life.

'You never thought about how much it hurt me to see you with a string of other girls?' He must have known how she'd thought of him by then and his colourful dating history seemed to be rubbing her nose in the fact she couldn't hold his attention. It had made her feel as though she wasn't pretty or interesting enough for him to be with on a romantic level. It had crushed her self-confidence as well as her heart.

'I'm sorry, Soph. I don't know what to say, other than I was a teenage boy who didn't know how to deal with his emotions. I thought I could ignore them but then things came to a head that night…'

'Why…how could you reject me like that, Roman?' She was dismayed by the tell-tale hitch in her voice as she regressed to that spurned girl, so lost and alone when he had walked away.

Roman got up out of his seat and walked over to her, the close proximity and the intensity of his gaze upon her making Sophie shift uncomfortably in her chair when she was vulnerable and exposed.

He took her hands in his as he sat on the settee beside her. 'I never meant to cause you pain, Soph. Believe it or not, I thought I was doing the opposite and saving you from getting hurt. I loved you, I wanted you, but I couldn't see us together.'

'I wish you had told me that,' she muttered, wanting to weep for that young girl who had been mortified when he had pushed her away and left the next day without as much as a goodbye. If he had only explained his motives and told her he was leaving, it might have relieved some of the sorrow.

'What good would that have done? We never had a future together, both going in opposite directions with our lives. You would never leave Carey Cove, I knew that, and I was restless, desperate to get away. I didn't want to give either of us false hope.'

He had never given her a chance to explore the idea of moving away, but he was probably right. She had too many memories here—the only real connection to her family were the graves at the cemetery. This house, where she had lived with her grandmother for so long, was the one place she truly felt safe. She hadn't even redecorated so she could keep that feeling of familiarity and security, even without her beloved guardian's presence. Still, he should have at least attempted a conversation about his decision when it had directly impacted on her. If she had been given a say in what happened next her life could have turned out very differently. That loss of control, that sense of being abandoned was the same as when her parents had died and she had spent the intervening years avoiding that same hurt.

'I thought it was me. That I was the reason you left so suddenly, and I'd messed everything up because you didn't think of me the same way I thought of you.'

He tilted her chin up, forcing her to engage in eye contact and making her pulse skip. 'Hey, I was showing a lot of restraint, trust me.'

This time she knew she wasn't imagining the spark reigniting between them. Older and with more experience, Sophie knew the signs when a man was interested. Roman's darkening pupils and husky voice were strong indications that he saw her now as more than a childhood friend.

It was electrifying and her heart was beating so

quickly with anticipation of what might happen she was afraid she might pass out and miss it.

Roman was everything her life was lacking—he was excitement and danger personified. They were too different to have any sort of future together, that certainly hadn't changed, but for a short while Roman might just be what she needed to shake things up around here.

'Don't you wonder what could have happened between us if we had acted on that kiss?' Now it was all she could think about. All those fevered fantasies she'd had about the two of them were now allowed to play out uninhibited in her head.

If they did give into temptation just once, now that they had cleared the air, it would give her closure on that part of her life. It would also validate her actions and feelings way back then, which was important to her when she had been blaming herself for so long for Roman leaving. Plus, it had been an age since she'd shared a bed with anyone, and she just knew he would absolutely rock her world.

She had been brave once, in showing him how she felt, and this time they were older and wiser, no longer two naïve kids who couldn't express themselves adequately. They were adults and she definitely wasn't the same Sophie who'd believed in happy-ever-afters. All she wanted tonight was validation that she was as good as any other girl Roman had been with.

'Of course I thought about it, but the timing was all wrong.' There was nothing he had wanted more than to take Sophie into his arms and his bed, but that was the one time he had decided to play it safe. She wasn't the kind of girl to sleep with on a whim. He had known it would have been a big decision for both of them and had been afraid it would change his mind about leaving.

That didn't mean he hadn't lain awake at night imagining what it would have been like.

'And now?' Sophie cocked her head to one side, a slow smile spreading across her mouth. It was difficult to tell if she was teasing him or attempting to flirt. In which case she really was different from the shy Sophie he'd had to coax out of her shell when they were kids.

'What are you saying, Sophie?' It had been a while since he'd had any sort of relationship. He didn't tend to stick around in one place for too long. There was less chance of him disappointing anyone else that way. Although he had already done that with Sophie, so he had nothing to lose.

She reached up and popped open the top button of his shirt. 'I'm saying we could make up for lost time and opportunities.'

Roman could hear the blood pounding in his ears as she made a start on the second button. He grabbed her hand to halt her progress.

'That would be playing with fire, Sophie.' He couldn't promise her anything more now than he could then, and she still deserved more than him.

'I'm single and I presume you are too. Maybe we could both do with things heating up around here.'

Roman's heart rate was rising as rapidly as his libido. 'We might burn ourselves out.'

'It's a risk I'm willing to take.'

'Sophie, I'm only in town for a while. On a temporary placement. I can't make any commitment to you.' He didn't want to deceive her. If they were finally going to give in to those urges they'd apparently felt towards one another, he needed her to know it would be a one-time deal before he moved on.

'Perfect. I don't want one.'

Roman was mesmerised by Sophie's parted lips and the mischievous twinkle in her blue eyes. If this was her way of getting back at him for leaving her he was going to call her bluff. One hot and heavy kiss and she would realise how dangerous this idea could be. Sophie French would never be someone to willingly court danger. He, however, embraced it with open arms.

He placed the hand still held in his around his neck and pulled her closer to him. Roman intended the kiss to be punishing, his mouth hard on hers to make her see this would be a mistake. Except having Sophie in his arms was everything he wanted. No woman had ever matched up to her. He had never had the same connection or the shared history which had made them so good together.

Sophie had been his first love, his only true love, and the one he had let slip away. Now she was kissing him back, giving him a second chance to undo that mistake, he couldn't remember why he was fighting against the idea.

She was moaning softly against him, draped sensually along his body, breaking through the pretence that this was nothing more than working through unresolved issues. Now it was about expressing his regret, how much he had missed her and how much she still turned him on.

That hard, unyielding lesson in doing the right thing was now a tender kiss full of yearning and passion. This time he was being honest about his feelings instead of hiding from them, instead of trying to convince Sophie they were different.

'You know where my bedroom is,' she whispered in between greedy kisses.

Heaven help him, she wasn't doing anything to help convince him this was wrong. Just like last time, it was going to be down to him to end things and keep Sophie protected. Except he wasn't sure that had been the right move after all. If it had been, then why were they right back here ten years later? Still wanting each other and no one else.

Perhaps if they had given in to those urges that came with the first flush of young love, the shine would have eventually worn off. After being denied the pleasure of one another too long, that wanting had flared back to life with a vengeance.

'Sophie, is this really what you want? I can't promise you anything more than today.'

She took him by the hand and faced him with a determination he didn't ever remember seeing in her before. 'It's only sex, isn't it? Who says I want or need anything more than that?'

It was all the confirmation Roman needed to finally give in to that fantasy he'd had about her since they were teenagers. However, as he followed her to the bedroom he had a feeling they were both trying to fool themselves that this wasn't going to change things for ever.

Sophie's bravado was fuelled by lust alone. She knew if she didn't take this opportunity she would never take that walk on the wild side she had always dreamed about. With him only in town for a short time there was less chance of her getting her heart broken again. There wouldn't be time for her to fall for him all over again and invest in a future that was never going to happen.

Now she would find out if being with Roman was all hype conjured up in her mind over the years or if he was just like anyone else who had shared her bed. If that was the case there was no need to get her knickers in a twist over it. To her, sex had never been particularly mind-blowing and she would admit to being curious about whether it might be different with Roman.

The concept of what she was getting into made her legs tremble as she pushed open her bedroom door and led Roman inside.

'It's exactly how I remember it,' Roman commented with a smile.

Sophie never took much notice of her surroundings when they were so familiar to her. Looking at it through Roman's eyes made her cringe. It was the same frothy pink room they'd hung out in as teens. He would think she hadn't moved on at all from that naïve girl he had left on the beach a decade ago.

'If it ain't broke don't fix it…' She shrugged, wishing she had at least unpinned the photographs of her and Roman on her noticeboard. At least the *Mrs Sophie Callahan* and *Sophie + Roman = 4 ever* doodles had been consigned to the back of old school notebooks and were not in plain sight.

'No… I just thought…you didn't move into your gran's bedroom.'

It had never occurred to Sophie to take over the main bedroom. She might be the new owner and sole occupant of the house but in her head it would always be her gran's.

'It would seem disrespectful to take anyone in there.' What with all the sex she had not been having.

She swore she saw Roman flinch at the mention of other men, and it went a long way to restoring her confidence. Perhaps there was a tiny bit of him which thought of her as his.

'Now, where were we?' She popped open some more of his shirt buttons so they could refocus on what they'd been doing previously.

'I think you were telling me you only wanted me for my body.'

'Is that so difficult to believe?' Sophie yanked open his shirt, uncaring as the last couple of buttons pinged across the floor. She needed to convince him she was not a naïve spinster who couldn't handle the idea of a sex-only liaison. Only time would tell if that was true, but she wanted to try.

Peeling his shirt off, revealing the manly chest nestled within was a feast for the eyes. The rounded biceps, the solid pecs and rippled abs were clearly the result of his physical adventures. Along with the light dusting of hair, his body was telling her he was no longer his scrawny teenage self either. He was all man, and she wasn't sure she knew what to do with him.

She'd had lovers but within the parameters of a safe relationship. A love by numbers playbook where there were no nasty surprises. Or excitement, if she was honest. This burning need inside for Roman was new to her. At least on this adult level.

It's just sex, she repeated in her head, reaching for the fly on his trousers and unzipping him.

'Hey, just because this is on a physical only basis, it doesn't mean we have to rush things.' Roman tilted her chin up so she was looking into his eyes instead of focusing on undressing him, making her melt all over again.

He bowed his head to capture her mouth, Sophie's eyes fluttering shut as he did so. The soft pressure of his lips took her back to that day when she had last thrown caution to the wind. Before everything was ruined. This time they were literally going along for the ride.

The feel of Roman's hand sliding under her jumper was unexpected, but his warmth was a welcome salve against the goosebumps on her skin. Sophie let him set the pace, happy to follow his lead. After all, he was the one known for taking risks and he had survived this far.

He stood back and whipped off her jumper before expertly unhooking her bra. Sophie gulped, a rush of arousal encompassing her body as he devoured her with his gaze. There was no doubt he wanted her, answering the one question which had plagued her all these years.

He came for her mouth again, this time the tender connection a passionate yearning she shared. While his lips and tongue were causing havoc upon hers, his hand was caressing her breast, his thumb teasing her nipple to attention. Making out like this was something they should have done as teenagers—the sort of after-school activity which could have got her into serious trouble. Second base only made her eager to hit that home run.

Roman left her gasping when his mouth fastened around her nipple, sucking and licking until she was fit to burst from sheer ecstasy. She could hear her heavy breathing, responding to Roman's groans of pleasure as he tasted her sensitive peaks of flesh. He was taking her to places she had only visited briefly before, and that had been on her own when her partner had failed to satisfy her. It was all she could do not to jump his bones like an eager to learn, born again virgin. Then she really would be showing her naivety when it came to the sort of sexy flings Roman was obviously used to.

He was kissing his way down her belly now, causing her to suck in a shaky breath as he came to the waistband of her reindeer-print leggings. With his hands on her hips, he slowly eased them down, dipping his tongue down further with every exposed inch of skin.

Her breath was coming in short, shallow bursts to match the frantic beat of her pulse. Could he feel what he was doing to her? She couldn't help but wonder if it was like this for him every time—exciting, breath-stealing…intoxicating. Indeed, was he even enjoying this as much as she was? When he pulled away her underwear and thrust his tongue into that most intimate place she could no longer think about his pleasure when she was completely focused on her own.

Roman buried his head between Sophie's thighs to taste the sweetness of her arousal. If this was the only chance they had to be together he wanted them both to remember it with a smile on their face. He took his time, savouring every moment of passion and each drop of Sophie's arousal. She came quickly, as though she had been waiting for him to touch her and trigger this release of teenage hormones he had fought so hard against.

He could see why. This was playing with fire. Sophie had insisted that she was not expecting more than one night but, as before, Roman couldn't be sure it would prove enough for him. He still wasn't the right person for her long-term, always moving around, never staying in one place too long, while Sophie was content living the life she always had. The fact she was even giving him a chance to redeem himself was a miracle in itself and that was what he intended to do. For one night he could make her happy and help them both move on from the past. Hopefully without losing his heart or mind in the process.

Sophie's panting breaths and quivering legs drew his attention back to the present. He feverishly kissed his way back up her body, doing his best to memorise every bit of her so he could finally stop wondering about what he had walked away from in the past. Although her magnificent naked body once seen would not be easily forgotten. He doubted the wanting would ever stop. All he could do was be thankful he had this time with her.

Sophie wrapped her arms around his neck as he kissed her heartily on the mouth. He grabbed her legs and hoisted her up around his waist to carry her over to the bed. She clung to him as he stripped away his own clothes, before tumbling onto the bed together. With the condom he had taken from his pocket he made sure they were safe from creating any unwanted complications before he joined their bodies together.

He had not been a virgin for a very long time, but it somehow felt like his first time when he slid into Sophie's wet warmth. Excited as a schoolboy, he couldn't get enough of her. Natural instinct took over, dictating the frantic pace. So much for taking things slowly, but they had waited a long time for this. Besides, Sophie was crying out for more with every hard thrust inside her, clearly enjoying losing control with him.

Sophie captured his face in her hands, forcing him to look into her eyes and see the undisguised passion for him burning bright. He kissed her again, expressing that longing, his desire and admiration for her from the very depths of his soul.

When she tightened around him, her throaty cries becoming high-pitched, Roman knew she was close to orgasm again already. How quickly he was getting used to knowing her body. With time he was certain they could be phenomenal together, but the future was an option they didn't have. For the moment they had to simply revel in the ecstasy they were creating here and now.

Making love to Sophie was something he had only dreamed of, and it was fulfilling his every fantasy. She was so responsive and unexpectedly vocal it was an ego boost for the man who had let her down once too often.

He anchored one of her legs to his hip so he could plunge deeper inside, eliciting a sharp intake of breath from her.

'Are you okay?' He slowed down, not wanting to hurt her, regardless of the blood pounding in his head making him unable to think straight.

'Don't stop,' she gasped, biting playfully at his neck and tearing through the remnants of his restraint.

He held onto the headboard of the bed for support and thrust; that sensation pulling him in deeper, tighter was something he could easily become addicted to.

Relentlessly chasing that ultimate release left him dizzy and Roman climaxed harder than he ever had before. Years of holding back from this exact moment. Utter bliss.

'Wow.' He had no other words to describe what had

just happened, even if he had enough breath left in his lungs to speak.

'Uh-huh,' Sophie concurred, apparently suffering from the same affliction.

They took some time out, lying side by side staring at the ceiling until they recovered. Eventually Roman was able to speak again.

'Are you okay? Was that okay?' He was uncharacteristically concerned about his performance. Not that he didn't usually care about his partner but he was confident in bed. It was different with Sophie. Tonight could be their one and only time together. If she hadn't enjoyed it as much as he had she might come to regret it. It would also ruin the chance of a repeat performance, should the occasion present itself again. After what he'd experienced he wouldn't say no.

Sophie rolled over onto her side, pulling the mussed bed sheets up to cover her nakedness. She stared up at him, a wry grin crossing her kiss-swollen lips.

'More than okay. We must do this again some time.' Although she was teasing him, Roman was struggling not to get his hopes up.

Sophie held her smile in place, waiting for Roman's reaction. If he rejected the idea she could laugh it off as a joke. Regardless that inside she would crumble if he said no to her indecent proposal. He had unlocked a whole new world for her, shown her what she'd been missing, and she wanted to enjoy it a little longer. It would be cruel to make her inner sex goddess a prisoner again after her liberation.

Roman was not a safe option. He had already broken her heart once. However, he was definitely the best lover she had ever had to date. Perhaps it was because they knew each other so well, or it could be down to the fact that they were complete opposites. Whatever it was which caused the explosive chemistry between them, she wouldn't be human if she didn't want to test it again. And again.

If she could remember this time around that Roman wasn't the one, simply a fantastic time, there was no reason they couldn't have an adult fling with no expectations other than making each other feel good.

She'd managed to get Roman's attention.

'Sophie, as much as I would love to, I'm not looking for anything serious. You know that. I don't do long-term. With anyone.'

'If I wanted anything serious I wouldn't be here with you.' She was trying to be flippant when he had made it clear he didn't want anything requiring a commitment, but she saw him flinch. Apparently he had feelings to hurt, regardless of his cavalier attitude towards relationships.

Given his long-standing feud with his parents, it wasn't clear if Roman would even be staying long and she was counting on that to avoid falling for someone so unsuitable again. She could enjoy being with him while it lasted, armed with the knowledge it wouldn't be a long-term arrangement. Once he was gone she could return to her safe old life, no longer having to wonder about what could have been.

Sophie could enjoy that walk on the wild side with Roman that she had been so fearful of and have the memories to last a lifetime. Hopefully minus any more scars.

Roman sat up. 'You would really be all right about keeping this a strictly sex thing?'

It was impossible to read his face but there was a flare of something in his eyes that suggested he might be excited by the prospect. She knew this was all he was offering and to read anything more into it would be foolish. Why shouldn't she have fun for once?

'I'm a grown woman, Roman, not a naïve teenage girl. I no longer believe in happy-ever-afters.'

'That's a shame. You deserve one.' He traced a finger along the curve of her shoulder, bringing goosebumps to the surface of her skin at the slight touch.

'I'll settle for a happy-for-now,' she insisted, dismissing the notion he should feel sorry for her. Until he had shown up again she'd been content with her lot, unaware that anything was missing from her life. Now she feared she would get too used to this post-sex bliss and confuse it with true happiness, something she wasn't convinced she had experienced, without another trauma stealing the moment from her. This time around she was calling the shots and attempting to get control of her emotions.

'So…this isn't a one-off?' He let his wandering hand slip down to the indent of her waist and the curve of her buttocks before drawing her possessively close. Inwardly, Sophie was squealing with delight but remained cool on the outside, as though this casual attitude was the norm for her.

'Not if you don't want it to be.'

'That sounds like an offer I don't want to refuse.' Roman rolled over on top of her, kissing his way along her neck and setting off fireworks throughout all of her erogenous zones.

To make this work they would have to set down ground rules, boundaries that would keep her heart from disintegrating when it came to an end.

At this moment all she cared about was prolonging this euphoria Roman was causing throughout her entire being.

CHAPTER FOUR

'HAVE YOU DONE something different with your hair today?' Nya Ademi, their head midwife, asked Sophie as she gathered her notes and bag to begin her rounds.

'No, I just wash and go, as always.'

'Hmm. Maybe it's your make-up. You've definitely got a glow going on,' Kiara offered, peering closely at her.

Heat suffused her cheeks at being studied so intently. 'I haven't done anything different. Now, if you don't mind, I have pregnant women to attend to.'

'Well, whatever you're doing, you're out-glowing every one of our mothers-to-be. You're not expecting, are you? We've got a temporary replacement starting at the beginning of December while Marnie's on maternity leave, but it'll be tough going if we lose you too.' Nya was teasing and even though they had taken precautions Sophie's hesitation to consider the possibility handed her colleagues all the ammunition they needed. It was the astonished gasps which prompted her into a response.

'I am not pregnant.'

'But you're seeing someone?' It was clear Kiara had kept the secret about Roman to herself, not sharing even with their superior. They were not a gossipy group and Sophie thanked her lucky stars she worked with such lovely people.

With anyone else this wouldn't have been headline news but because it was Sophie, someone who kept herself to herself and only dated people she got to know first, it was apparently the lead story. They crowded around her, waiting for the big reveal. Sophie knew they only wanted to be happy for her but she wasn't ready to share the details of the arrangement between her and Roman. In the cold light of day it might sound seedy.

It had been different lying naked in bed with him, agreeing to a casual fling. Continuing a strictly physical relationship was the most she could hope for with Roman. Not least because he would be moving on again. By his own admission he was only here as a stopgap. Goodness knew what had brought him back in the first place, it certainly wasn't his family, but Sophie was glad he was here even temporarily. In fact it was probably better for her, so she wouldn't have a chance to get too attached to him again. This was likely her one chance to be with Roman and she had grabbed it greedily with both hands. A short-lived fling with Roman was possibly the only way she would survive being with him, knowing from the outset that it wasn't for ever.

However, admitting that was all it was to her friends would make her sound sad and desperate for accepting those terms. In the end she decided to keep the details private.

'I am seeing someone but it's early days.'

'Aw, I'm glad you've met someone.'

'I'm so happy for you.' Kiara sounded relieved she could actually talk about it freely now.

The strong hugs and excited squeals which followed her news were heart-warming but also a tad disconcerting. She was touched that her friends were excited for her, but at the same time it said a lot about how boring her stale life had become to cause such hysteria with a romantic interest on the horizon.

'Thanks. It's nothing serious,' she reiterated.

'Anyone we know?'

'Er...' It was a tricky one. Sophie didn't want to lie but also didn't relish her fling with Roman being common knowledge, making it into something it wasn't—a relationship.

'Just one of the paramedics from St Isolde's.' It was partly true but if she had mentioned he was on the helicopter crew they would have known exactly who she was talking about. It wouldn't have taken people long to uncover their history and she and Roman were trying to put the past behind them.

'I hope everything works out for you, love.' Nya gave her another hug, satisfied with that small amount of information.

The others wished her well too before setting off for their working day.

Sophie was still smiling as she climbed into her car. Catching sight of herself in the mirror, she could understand why her colleagues had quizzed her. She was positively radiant. As though that warm satisfaction Roman had brought her had spread from the inside out.

Even thinking about their night together gave her the same sort of head rush she got when she stood up too quickly. Was this the same adrenaline buzz he got from all of his crazy adventures? In which case she could see why he was always seeking the next one. At least great sex wasn't as life-endangering as climbing mountains or dangling from helicopters if she became hooked on this feeling.

It was provident that she had work today or they might have worn each other out completely in bed. The lack of sleep wasn't something she could sustain long-term, even if their nocturnal activities had been oh-so-pleasurable.

This was her reality. Sleeping with Roman was merely a romantic fantasy which would probably be over all too soon, but she would enjoy it whilst she could. Before feelings and expectations barged in to ruin the illusion.

'Hi, Nina. How are you this morning?' Sophie wiped her feet on the doormat before entering her heavily pregnant patient's home.

'Exhausted. As you can see, I haven't even had time to get dressed this morning.' She pulled at her shapeless, food-encrusted nightdress.

'Rough night?' Sophie closed the door behind her and followed Nina into the kitchen, where her toddler was playing in a bowl of cereal in her highchair.

'This one was up half the night teething. Not that I could sleep anyway when my heartburn was so bad.'

At this late stage of pregnancy it wasn't an uncommon complaint, with the baby pressing against most of the vital organs. It could be an uncomfortable time for a lot of Sophie's patients.

'Can your husband help you out a bit more at night?' With a toddler to take care of and a baby on the way,

Nina was going to have to learn to delegate some of the responsibility elsewhere or she would burn herself out.

'Dean was working away from home last night. His last overnight shift before the baby arrives. He'll be back later to take over.' Nina leaned back, manoeuvring herself onto the sofa in the living room, not bothering to stop the little one from splashing any more milk onto the floor.

'That's good. I tell you what, I have some time before my next appointment. Why don't I look after little Amy and let you go have a soak in the bath?'

Nina's eyes lit up at the suggestion. 'Are you sure?'

'Of course. It will be better to take your blood pressure after you've had a nice relaxing bath.' For Sophie, part of her duty to her patients was looking after their mental health too. It wasn't the first time she had done a spot of babysitting to give one of her mums a well-deserved break. She didn't mind. With no other family, she had never had the chance to coo over babies at family gatherings and she did enjoy the opportunity when it arose.

She had always pictured herself settling down with a husband and family. Creating the scene she had never had for herself in Carey Cove. However, as time had gone on and her relationships had failed one after the other, she had begun to think that having a baby of her own was never going to happen. She didn't want to bring another child into the world without the love and stability of two parents. So far there hadn't been anyone in her life who saw themselves being with her for ever. Sophie was beginning to think she was completely unlovable, so Roman had come at just the right time to give her an ego boost. Even if it wouldn't have the final outcome she had always hoped was possible.

'I was about to wash and change her.' Nina pointed to the changing mat and basin of water sitting on the table.

'That's fine. I'm sure I can manage,' Sophie assured her with a smile. It was enough to get Nina back on her feet, the lines of tension across her forehead already evening out.

'Well, Miss Amy, it looks like it's just you and me.' Complete with sound-effects, Sophie aeroplaned the rest of the baby's breakfast into her mouth. Amy babbled contentedly as her new babysitter cleaned up the mess on her highchair tray and made no complaint when she was lifted out.

Sophie stripped off the milk-sodden sleepsuit and nappy to wash her all over with a flannel. She couldn't get enough of those baby giggles when she tickled her tummy or the little hands grasping for hers. Being broody was part of the job. Yes, she saw the less glamorous ailments which came for pregnant women, but she also saw the rewards in the form of gorgeous, happy bundles of fun like Amy.

It increased her yearning for a family of her own, to have chubby babies and do all the things she'd never got to do with her own parents. Baking cookies, teaching them to ride a bike or tie their shoelaces, going to nativity plays and doing the school run. All normal things people took for granted and did out of love, not obligation. Her grandmother had been a substitute for Sophie's parents but, as much as she'd loved her, she had often wished to have her parents there on special occasions. She vowed if she ever did become a mother her children would never feel abandoned or a burden.

That was why she could never pin her future on a man such as Roman, someone who couldn't be relied upon to be a constant source of support. It was the reason she had settled for 'safe' in her relationships to date. Unfortunately, it wasn't possible to have both and though she was enjoying wild passion with Roman it would be fleeting. Eventually she would come to her senses and remember to put her hopes and dreams above her libido. With Roman, the only future she was facing was one with a broken heart and that was a poor choice against the possibility of a stable relationship and a family of her own.

If only she could find a man who excited her as much as he did, minus the commitment-phobia, she might actually have that happy ending everyone else seemed to get.

Roman should have headed back to his place to sleep after the day he'd had. Being on scene at two major RTAs had been stressful, even if the casualties were on their way to recovery.

Except he'd been looking forward to the end of his shift so he could see Sophie again. They hadn't made plans per se, it wasn't easy with their hectic schedules, but he hadn't been able to stop thinking about last night. If he was honest with himself she'd been on his mind since his last breakup.

Lena had flung a few home truths at him when he had called things off between them before he'd come back to Carey Cove. Comments which had made him take a good hard look at the life he had created for himself. She had accused him of being afraid to put down roots and terrified of getting close to anyone. That he used his career and his 'flighty playboy image' as an excuse to avoid commitment.

Roman had never considered himself to be a coward in his entire life, always one to face a challenge or accept a dare. Where relationships were concerned, though, he began to realise she'd been right. His issues had started with his parents and ended with Sophie French. A mother and father who were so disappointed in him had led him to believe he wasn't good enough for Sophie and even though he had loved her he had sacrificed a future with her to save them both. Staying for her would have meant remaining tied to his family but, more importantly, he would have ended up hurting her, something he would never have intentionally done. Everything he'd done since then had been his attempt to avoid conflict. He wasn't so sure that had been so successful in any capacity.

When the job had come up in Carey Cove he'd imagined it was fate, a chance to see he had done the right thing all those years ago. Except he had been afraid to go and see Sophie and find she had moved on after all, when it seemed he couldn't.

Roman wasn't sure sleeping together was going to do much to help them put the past behind them, but Sophie had seemed so sure that was what she wanted. That giving into their libidos for a short time, ignoring any residual emotions from their teenage years, was exactly what they needed. Well, he wasn't made of stone.

Waking up in her bed for an encore performance had been a bonus, even if he'd had to leave early for work.

Now, instead of returning to his rented, cheerless

accommodation, he found himself on the road to Sophie's cottage, the rainbow lights welcoming him in the darkness. He rang the bell and waited, his breath hovering in the frosty air as he listened for the sound of footsteps to confirm she was at home.

'Roman? What are you doing here?' She answered the door swamped in an oversized cardigan and wearing fluffy pink slipper boots, clearly not expecting company tonight.

'I...er...' It didn't seem in keeping with their casual agreement to admit he couldn't wait to see her again. 'Just thought I'd swing by on my way home.'

'Uh-huh. Is this what a booty call looks like?' she asked, arms folded, eyebrow raised, and her mouth curved up into a smirk.

As much as he wanted to say yes and cart her back off to bed, she still deserved more than that. The truth was he simply wanted to spend more time with her. If this was the last time he came back to Carey Cove or their final chance to be together, he wanted to get to know her again. For however short a time they had.

'I thought you might like to go out somewhere.' He leaned casually against the doorframe so it didn't seem like a big deal for him to be here.

'A date?'

'Yes. No. I don't know. We can stay in if you prefer?' He waggled his eyebrows in such an overtly suggestive manner it made her laugh.

'It depends on what else is on offer.'

He had to think quickly and free his mind of all thoughts involving Sophie naked, lying beneath him.

'I don't think anything's going to top that, but if

we're talking outdoor pursuits, I thought we could pay a visit to the Christmas market over in Hodden. We could get some mulled wine, buy some handmade tacky decorations and sit on Santa's lap.'

'How could I refuse an offer like that?' She reached for her coat hanging in the hall and replaced her slippers with a sturdy pair of boots. With a swirl of her scarf around her neck, she closed the door, ready to follow him. He was grateful she didn't want to play games with him and was quite happy to go along with him. Any other woman he had spurned in the past might have sought payback or played hard to get. Sophie was still the same honest person she had always been when it came to her feelings. He was the one who had issues in that department.

They walked the short distance towards the nearby village, the festive hub glowing in the darkness of the winter evening. Even in the icy air there was an undercurrent of heat between them, as if the small talk about their working day and this trip out was the foreplay before another amazing night in bed. He certainly hoped so, although he was content merely to be in her company.

Since coming back he'd had to start over making friends and getting to know his colleagues. With Sophie it was so easy to be himself. She was familiar and welcoming. Everything coming home should have felt like to him. Now they had reconnected as adults she was even sexier and more fun than he remembered. It almost made him regret walking away all those years ago, though he had done it for all the right reasons and made a life for himself away from the disapproving stares of his parents. Even if he was starting to see that it was not as fulfilling as he had once thought. If he had been truly happy jumping from one job and relationship to another he would never have felt the pull back here, to Sophie.

She pulled her scarf up further until only her eyes were visible behind the shield of forest-green wool. As tempted as he was to pull her close and share his body heat with her, it might have been a bit presumptuous. She might not want their temporary relationship status to be public knowledge. He was sure she wouldn't want to start explaining it or their history to her friends and patients.

Roman played it safe and led her over to one of the log cabin-style stalls selling hot beverages.

'Hot chocolate, spiced cider or mulled wine?' he asked, scanning the menu.

'Ooh, a spiced cider, I think.'

He decided on the same and handed a cup to Sophie. With her hands wrapped around the cup she closed her eyes and breathed in the rising steam. 'It smells like Christmas.'

'Tastes like it too,' he added after taking a sip.

'This whole place looks like the cover of a Christmas novel.'

'Haven't you been here before? I thought this would have been your idea of heaven.' As a child Sophie had been almost obsessive about the season, whereas he could have happily let Christmas pass by without a celebration. It had only brought more arguments in his household, his brothers getting the better presents and Roman deemed ungrateful for the gifts they'd thought he should want.

They strolled past the stalls selling hotdogs and cupcakes, the savoury and sweet aromas making him hungry.

'I'm usually too tired after work and Christmas hasn't really been the same for me since Gran died. I go through the motions but it's like I'm trying to force it these days.'

It would be a shame for Sophie to be as miserable as he usually was at this time of year and Roman was determined to give her a good night out.

'Tonight we are going to reawaken your Christmas spirit. So drink up and get your Christmas jingle on, Sophie French.' At least she had kept up with the Christmas decorating and baking and he was sure she simply needed a nudge to truly rediscover her love of the season. To get back to the Sophie he used to know.

'Oh, yeah? How do you reckon you're going to do that, Roman Callahan?' She nudged him with her elbow as he was knocking back the rest of his cider so it dribbled down his chin and splashed onto his coat.

'I'm so sorry.' She pulled off her glove and began to pat at his chest. That slight touch was enough to spark vivid memories of last night, sending heat coursing through Roman's entire being.

'It's fine. I'm sure we can put our heads together and come up with something to make you feel warm and cosy.' He held Sophie's gaze and saw the flash of desire, matching his own. It would be the most natural thing in the world to take her in his arms and kiss her senseless, and that was exactly what he wanted to do. Except he couldn't be certain that Sophie would be pleased about doing that in front of the rest of the village. Instead, he took a step back and brushed himself down, composing himself to get rid of that husky hunger in his voice.

'There's an ice rink. What better way to get us in the Christmas mood?'

'Sliding about on the ice, falling on my backside and potentially having my fingers amputated by a sharp blade when someone skates over my hand? Sure, it screams Christmas.' She rolled her eyes at him, the heat of the moment cooled by her cynicism.

'Come on. It'll be fun.' Plus they would be in a crowd so there was less chance of him succumbing to his desire to kiss her until they were somewhere more private.

'There's a very good reason I've never had broken bones or stitches. I avoid activities where there's a chance I'll get hurt.'

Yet she had entered into this arrangement with him. Roman thought it was time for Sophie to explore a little further beyond her comfort zone. Then when he inevitably moved on she would be ready to do the same. For as long as he had known her, Sophie had played it safe. All the more remarkable that she had suggested a no-strings fling with him. She knew he was anything but the reliable option. If she had any misconceived notion that they had a long-term future ahead she was sure to come back down to earth with a bump when she remembered who she was dealing with. Roman Callahan always disappointed those close to him. That was why he didn't stay in one place for too long. Whether that was so he didn't witness the fallout or to pre-empt it he couldn't be certain.

Perhaps he should never have come back. It had been a reckless idea to seek Sophie out and definitely a bang-his-head-off-the-wall mistake to sleep with her. However, the deed was done and never to be forgotten. If anything, he wanted to repeat the mistake over and over again. The best he could hope for was damage control and that started with helping Sophie take baby steps onto the ice.

'Don't you trust me, Sophie?' Roman held out his hand, waiting for her to accompany him to the rink.

She knew it was a dare, a test to determine if she trusted him not to hurt her. No. Not when it came to matters of the heart, but she was trying to play it cool and pretend that casual hook-ups were nothing more to her than convenient.

Sophie slapped her hand in his, accepting the challenge. It wasn't as though she had gone into this with her eyes closed. She knew the score and was prepared to take the risk to reap the reward. The same could be applied here when it meant spending more time with Roman.

'If I lose a limb I'm blaming you.'

'Don't worry, I know first aid and a very good surgeon.'

'You're so reassuring,' she muttered as he got their skates from the booth at the side of the rink.

'I promise I'll be with you all the way,' Roman told her as they laced up their skates.

Sophie had no control over the extra beat her heart gave, deliberately misinterpreting his meaning. If only that entailed longer than it would take them to lap the ice she wouldn't be wishing for insurance to cover future heartache.

She stood up on her blades and wobbled. Roman reached out and grabbed her.

'Great. I'm not even on the ice yet and I'm a liability.'

'I've got you.' He took her by the hand and helped her teeter over to the edge of the rink without as much as a waver in his gait.

'Let me know which bit of this is supposed to be fun.' Other than Roman having his arm around her, she didn't see what there was to be gained from this.

He laughed, not put off in the slightest by her blatant cynicism and determination not to enjoy this.

'Just put one foot in front of the other and keep moving,' he helpfully suggested as her foot met the ice and immediately slid from beneath her.

'Maybe I should get one of those penguin helpers.' She saw the other newbie ice skaters pushing around solid fibreglass penguin figures, relying on them for stability. It didn't matter it was mostly under-tens using them, it had to be more dignified than being held up by another adult.

'You'll be flying around the ice in no time. Relax. Focus on moving forward instead of what your feet are, or aren't, doing.' He put his hands on her hips and pushed her forward so she was gliding across the ice.

'How are you such an expert?' It was infuriating that they were not both starting out at the same level. She was at a distinct disadvantage already, seeing he could move with more grace than her baby deer learning to walk impression.

'I've dated a lot, and you know ice-skating at Christmas is romantic. I've seduced a woman or two with my fancy footwork.' He skated around her, then spun around on the spot before coming back to keep her upright.

Sophie knew he was teasing her but she could hear the truth in his words. It wasn't a surprise to find there had been other women. It was the fact that she wasn't special that called to that emptiness inside her. This was Roman's *modus operandi* when it came to casual relationships. It somewhat dimmed the romantic glow of the evening. Regardless that he was doing this for her benefit, to make her think there was more to this than a tumble in bed.

'You don't need to impress me, Roman. I'm a sure thing. We don't have to go along with this farce, and I certainly don't have to humiliate myself in the process.' While he was boasting about past lovers she was trying not to fall on her backside in front of tiny tots and gangly teens. None of this was bringing her joy, only misery burning the back of her eyeballs.

Roman swung around and took her face in his hands. 'Hey. No tears. I just wanted to spend time with you tonight and I thought ice-skating was one thing we could do together. If you're really hating it that much we can do something else. I think there's a bucking bronco dressed as a reindeer if you'd rather do that?'

That made her smile, albeit a quivery one. Deep down she knew he cared, and that had to be enough because it was never going to be any more than that.

She sucked up her self-pity and got her flirty alter-ego back on. 'Now that is a ride I'd rather do in the privacy of my own home.'

The concern etched on Roman's face slowly changed into a much sexier grin. Deciding to capitalise on the moment, Sophie gave him a quick peck on the lips.

She could tell she had caught him by surprise by the shocked expression he wore but if his reaction was to be believed he wasn't averse to her spontaneity.

He came back for more, returning her brief kiss with a leisurely, full-lipped experience. Not only was it hot enough to melt her and the ice she was balancing on, it drew a few whistles and a comment from one not so impressed skater.

'Not the time or the place,' she sniffed as she jostled them on her way past, knocking the couple off-balance. Roman fought valiantly to stay standing, refusing to let go of Sophie.

She was tempted to shout, *Save yourself*, as her skates slid back and forth, failing to find traction, but the hard fall on her backside knocked the words out of her. Roman swore before tumbling down beside her.

After the initial pain and shock of her ungraceful landing, Sophie saw the funny side of them sprawled on the ice and began to giggle. It was apparently contagious as Roman joined in.

'Hey, you two. Get a room. It'll be much warmer than lying down there.' Kiara Baxter from Carey House was looking down at her with a knowing smile.

Before Sophie managed to formulate a retort her colleague was skating away hand in hand with Lucas, her other half.

Seeing her embarrassment catching up with her, Roman got to his feet and helped her to do the same. 'Do you want to get out of here?'

Sophie looked around, saw other couples hand in hand and tottering their way around. So she had fallen and survived, her colleague had seen and the world hadn't ended. She had a bruised backside and her clothes were wet through. It seemed silly not to stick around for the rewards of her efforts when she had already endured her worst fears.

'We've already paid for the session.' She took his hand. 'I might even be having fun.'

'Yes!' he exclaimed a little too loudly and punched the air. It was true, he did know how to show her a good time in and out of bed.

With renewed determination to conquer the ice and her irrational fear, Sophie followed Roman's tutelage until she was able to take a few steps on her own. Even if she did throw herself back into his arms after her initial solo success, it gained her a touching kiss on the top of her head and a cuddle, making it all worth it.

When their time was up she had mastered a wobbly solo skate and was glowing. As indicated by her red nose and rosy cheeks, which she caught sight of in the funhouse mirrors nearby. She was also cold and hungry.

'Hot dog?' Roman asked as they passed the stall, reading her mind.

They sat down to eat at a nearby table, where they were able to watch the ice-skaters and market-goers. Seeing families enjoying the evening together inevitably made her think not only about her parents but Roman's too.

'Would you ever think about reaching out to your family? They must be keen to find out how you are.'

'You'd think so,' he scoffed.

'Whatever happened, surely you can work it out? You could get to spend time with them. Not all of us are that blessed.' Although Sophie's outlook was vastly different to that of her mother and father, she would give anything to have family around her again, especially at this time of year. She couldn't fathom what could have happened for Roman to completely divorce himself from his.

'That's the reason I never told you the way things were at home for me. I knew it wouldn't be fair to complain when you had lost your own parents. Perhaps if I had explained what was going on it would have helped you understand why I had to leave and why I never intended to come back.'

Sophie suddenly lost her appetite, tossing the remnants of her hot dog back in the mustard-covered cardboard tray on the table. It was true they'd never talked about Roman's home life, and she had assumed it was because he lived the perfect childhood there in the grand house, wanting for nothing. She had been too caught up in her own grief, too self-centred to even think there was something wrong at home. If she had stopped to think she might have realised all was not well. Clearly, Roman had also thought she had no interest in his problems or he would have shared them with her. They had been close but obviously not as much as she had imagined if he couldn't confide in her.

'I'm sorry you didn't think you could talk to me.'

'It's not your fault, Soph. I was a privileged teen, you were an orphan. I didn't think I had any right to be unhappy.'

'I'm listening now. What was so bad you thought you had to leave for ever?' At the time she had believed she would never see him again and she was the cause. With neither assumption true, she wanted to know the real reason Roman had been driven away and what, if anything, she could do to help. If it was something which could be resolved it might make him reconsider staying. For his own peace of mind. It certainly wouldn't make her life any easier if he hung around longer than their fling lasted.

Roman sighed, though he had managed to finish his snack. He scrunched up his rubbish and tossed it into the nearby bin. 'They wanted me to follow them into the family business, I wanted to go to medical school.'

'Surely that's all in the past though? You made the right choice and you have a good, admirable career.' Sophie could see how that might have transpired into a battle of wills at the time, but with so much time passed his parents should have got over the decision he'd made. They might not have thought of him as an adult at the time, capable of making his own life choices, but he was now. Plus, whatever they role they had envisaged him taking in the company would have been filled long ago. She saw no reason for any lingering resentment to prevent a reunion, merely stubborn pride on both sides.

'You would think so, but they made it clear they thought they knew best. Anything less than taking the reins in the company wasn't worthy of the family name. My brothers are both heading up international branches of the company and, though we do occasionally keep in contact, I haven't seen them in years.' Even talking about his family was clearly making his blood pressure rise, the colour in his cheeks coming from more than the cold weather.

'This was the argument you had before going to medical school, but you hinted at some ongoing problems.' It was important for her to dig deeper to find out what had had such an effect on him. To better understand Roman and their relationship. She owed him, and herself, that much.

'Nothing I did was ever good enough for them. I wasn't the son they wanted. My brothers conformed to the ideals they had, and they couldn't understand why I wouldn't. I insisted on being my own person. As you know.' The nod to his exploits growing up, including dangerous stunts he'd undertaken to get a rise out of her and whatever audience he had around him at the time, at least brought a smile to his face again.

'I may not have always agreed with or liked the things you did, but I learned to accept that you doing crazy stuff was part of our friendship. It was who you were and I lo… I loved that you were your own person.' A slip of the tongue almost gave away her true feelings and if Roman was afraid of anything it was expressing real emotions. Nothing would put him off the idea of this convenient dalliance more than knowing she had real feelings for him. Something she was desperately trying to ignore herself.

'Me being me was not acceptable to them and they let me know it at every opportunity.' The memories of which were setting his jaw to stone as he ground his teeth together. Sophie wondered if it was time for a change in topic to prevent him from getting stuck in the darkness of his childhood.

'I'm so sorry, Roman. You were so outgoing and confident I never considered you had so many issues at home. I always wondered why you took an interest in me, the quiet wallflower.'

'We might have had very different circumstances, but I think I recognised that same sadness and isolation in you when you lost your parents.'

'I always thought it was pity for the poor orphan. Thank you, I needed someone, other than my gran, of course, to remind me there was life outside of my grief. Even if you did worry me half to death with some of your stunts.' Her fingernails had been bitten down to the quick watching him jump off the school roof or diving from the cliffs into the sea, whatever needlessly dangerous dare he undertook because he felt like it.

'Sorry. I didn't do those things solely to annoy you. I knew I could do them and it gave me a sense of achievement. Praise from my peers was intoxicating when it was something I didn't get at home.'

Sophie found it difficult to have any empathy for his parents, even though they had all lost Roman ten years ago. She knew better than anyone that a person couldn't be forced to become someone else simply because it suited another person's agenda. They had pushed him away, and if they weren't remorseful in the slightest about their actions they could lose him for ever.

'I just worried about you. I'd lost my parents to all of their crazy risk-taking. They abandoned me to pursue that lifestyle, didn't give a thought to the daughter left behind. I think that's why I went the opposite route, to keep myself safe. The one time I did take a risk and kissed you, you abandoned me too. I wasn't enough for my parents or you. My broken heart taught me I'd been right all along to protect myself.'

Roman hung his head. 'I'm sorry if I made you feel like I didn't want you. Believe it or not, I was trying to do the right thing. I knew I would only let you down the way I'd been letting my parents down my whole life. It was never about not wanting you, Sophie.' He reached out and brushed a strand of hair away from her face.

'And now?' It took all her strength to ask, putting her heart on the line for a second time and tempting another rejection, but she needed to know once and for all.

Roman arched an eyebrow before taking both of her hands in his. 'I still want you, Sophie French.'

Okay, it was not a declaration of undying love, but it still made her squeal inside. It was the most she could hope for when they had spent so much time apart. Who knew, maybe that physical need might transform into something more. Did she want that? Probably. Was it asking for trouble? Definitely. The trick was to not let Roman think that she was conning him into something more than he had agreed to.

She stood up and held out her hand. 'In that case, what are we doing wasting time out here in the cold when I have a lovely warm bed for you at home?'

CHAPTER FIVE

'HEY, SOPH. HOW'S THINGS?'

Roman's voice on the hands-free speaker filled Sophie's car, making her day a little brighter.

'Hi. I'm just on my way to see a patient. Is something wrong?' It wasn't long since they'd parted and usually he texted her during the day, knowing she was often too busy to take a call. Lucky for both of them, she was visiting one of their mums-to-be who lived a little way out of civilisation, giving her more driving time and an opportunity to speak to Roman.

Hearing him made it feel as though he were more present, so she didn't have time to miss him. Goodness, she had it bad. She had tried to fool herself that she could be with him and not lose her head or her heart, but the reality was quite different. Sleeping with Roman only gave her more reason to love him, when she knew it was a wasted emotion. He'd only gone along with this because she had promised it would mean nothing to her and he could move on soon with a clear conscience. It wasn't his fault he had made her fall for him even deeper, and he didn't ever have to know. She didn't want this to end now they had finally acknowledged there was something more between them than teenage crushes and friendly banter. They might only have a limited time together, but she wanted to explore their relationship further. As far as Roman would allow.

His chuckle echoed around her, reaching right into her chest to give her heart a little squeeze. 'You know me too well. I'm afraid I have some bad news. I'll have to cancel our dinner date tonight.'

Sophie's good mood evaporated. The thought of him cooking the famous Spaghetti Bolognese he had boasted about for her and taking her into his bed later that night had been fuelling her day so far. For every backache and urine infection she had dealt with today, she had envisaged pasta and a naked Roman waiting for her to get her through. It was unnerving how quickly he had become such a huge part of her life again.

'Why?' She tried not to whine like a spoiled child upset at not getting her way, even though that was exactly who she was in that moment.

'I'm afraid the flat isn't fit for company. The pipes have burst and flooded the place. I'm here now, paddling in my kitchen. I think because I haven't been home much and haven't had the heating on the pipes froze. I'm sorry, babe.'

It was a horrible thought to imagine his belongings ruined like that and Sophie cursed herself for being so selfish when Roman was having a difficult time.

'Do you need me to come over after work and help clean up? I could bring a takeaway with me if you'd like?'

'No, it's okay, but thanks for the offer. I'm clearing up now. I've turned the water off at the mains, but the plumber can't get here until tomorrow. I'll have to pack a few things and find somewhere to stay for the night.'

'Why don't you stay over at mine?' The words were out and Sophie couldn't take them back, despite cringing into the driving seat once she'd said them, afraid of coming across as too keen and needy. The opposite of how she should play this if she had a chance of convincing Roman she was the sort of woman he was used to being with. One who wouldn't weep and wail when he had gone.

The tell-tale silence made her want to disappear through the floor of the car. When Roman's voice eventually crackled to life again with the stuttering familiarity of a lost connection, for once Sophie was glad the wilds of Cornwall had bad reception.

'Sorry, Roman, I didn't get that. I don't think the signal is great out here.'

'Can you hear me now?'

Once she confirmed she could hear him loud and clear again, his response finally reached her. 'I was just asking if you were sure that was all right.'

She thought about it. What could possibly be bad about offering him a place to stay for one night? The only thing that came to mind was the possibility it could seem a bit too much like having a relationship, but if it was okay with Roman…

'Of course. There's no point in paying for a hotel room when you will likely be staying over at mine anyway.' The offer was not entirely altruistic when she was making sure he would be warming her bed tonight.

'Thanks. I probably will when I can't stop thinking about you and all the things we should be doing to each other right now.' His voice dipped, reaching that part of her aching to have him tonight and every night after.

'When can you come?' She was breathy now with the anticipation of another evening with their naked bodies entwined in her sheets.

'I'll be over as soon as I can. I promise not to bring my pipe and slippers with me, although I will need my toothbrush.' He was teasing her about things becoming too complacent between them already, but Sophie doubted she would ever take him for granted when the nature of their relationship was so precarious. She wouldn't dream of expecting him to move in long-term when that was the one thing she could be sure would never happen. Tonight was an emergency situation and it was convenient for both of them. Much like their current arrangement.

'Yeah, I don't want your dragon breath in the morning,' she replied, keeping things light. This was no big deal. Just Roman Callahan moving into her cottage for an adult sleepover.

Roman's day had been a washout. He'd spent it dealing with his landlord, the insurance company and the plumber. Thankfully, there was only superficial damage to the furniture and his personal possessions had been largely unaffected by the indoor deluge of his apartment. However, it had been a headache he could have done without. Now he was looking forward to being with Sophie and forgetting, even for a few hours, that it had ever happened.

Now he was on his way, though, with his overnight bag packed, he was beginning to wonder if things weren't a little too cosy. She had been his first call after dealing with the emergency, relying on her counsel and support to help him through something he would usually have sorted without a second thought. It was as though he was using any excuse to spend time with her, to the extent he was already moving in. Albeit temporarily.

With any new partner it usually took him a while before he even spent the night, never mind bring his belongings with him. He didn't want to give anyone the wrong idea about the possibility of a future relationship and be tied down. Both parties maintained their own space, then there was no chance of any confusion.

Of course these were extraordinary circumstances, with the problem at his apartment and knowing Sophie for so long, but it still rang alarm bells that he was doing this already. That he was looking forward to making himself at home in the cottage. He could see why she had been reluctant to change anything there since her grandmother had died when it was just as comforting as ever to him too being somewhere so familiar and safe. A dangerous position for someone like him to be in.

Once the initial euphoria of great sex wore off he might need a little space from her, just so he could get his head straight. Start relying on his common sense rather than his libido to guide him through the minefield of a casual relationship with his childhood sweetheart.

After tonight, of course. He'd been looking forward to sharing dinner and bed with Sophie too much to deny himself the pleasure at the last minute. He wasn't a masochist.

Sophie had the door open before he had even

stopped the car. Simply seeing her face was a reward after a fraught day. She calmed him and reminded him that life didn't always have to be lived at full pelt. He was beginning to enjoy the simple pleasures everyone else took for granted. Before his return to Carey Cove, Roman hadn't seen the appeal in rushing home after work just to sit around watching TV when there were so many more activities available out there to try. He filled his spare time with outdoor leisure pursuits or planning his next adventure holiday. Now, there was nothing he wanted more than to chill out with his feet up, simply enjoying Sophie's company.

'Hey, you.' He kissed her on the cheek and set his bag down in the hall. It had all the markings of the very domestic scene he'd been avoiding his entire life. The only thing worse than finding himself in the middle of it was the fact he liked it. Perhaps that was what he feared more than commitment itself. That if he did find himself settling down with someone he would be leaving himself open to the same criticisms he'd faced at home, breaking his spirit and expecting him to be someone he wasn't. He couldn't go through all of that again, more so with Sophie. It was probably better that they did leave this as a no-strings fling and remember it as a happy memory than to end up resenting each other, the way he and his parents had.

'Rough day?' Sophie took his jacket and hung it in the hall. He followed her into the kitchen, where the table was set for two with soft music playing in the background.

Roman sighed out his frustrations at the devastation caused in his apartment, glad he had someone to vent to. 'A lot of hassle I could have done without, but hopefully it will all be done by tomorrow. I might have to do a spot of redecorating but at least I caught it before it was a complete washout. Now, what smells so good in here, apart from you?'

He grabbed Sophie for a quick cuddle and buried his nose in her hair to inhale that sweet scent of vanilla and strawberries which had come to smell like home to him.

'I thought I'd cook since you had a good excuse to get out of it tonight.'

She handed him a glass of wine and pulled out a chair for him to sit down.

'I could get used to being spoiled like this,' he said, giving her a soft kiss on the mouth to thank her for all of her effort. He had forgotten what it was like to have someone looking out for him, to be there when he needed them, making things right when everything seemed to be going wrong. Just like when they were kids and he'd turned to Sophie after clashing with his parents and needing a place of refuge. She was still his sanctuary.

'Oh, this isn't for your benefit. I was just really in the mood for some Spag Bol,' Sophie teased as she dished up the home-cooked meal he hadn't been expecting tonight.

'And how was your day, dear?' he asked with a hint of sarcasm as he tucked into his pasta, slipping into the role of the nineteen-fifties husband this domestic scene seemed to require of him.

Sophie grinned. 'I started with the walk-in clinic for mums-to-be at Carey House, did my rounds in the car, weighed some babies and came home to make dinner in time for my man coming over.'

Roman knew she was kidding around but the more this began to look and feel like a comfy relationship, the more uncomfortable he was becoming. Yes, they were joking around about the situation they had found themselves in tonight, but the ease with which he was accepting the situation was what made it unpalatable. A fling should not include too many prearranged overnight stays nor cosy homemade dinners for two. When he thought about it, his motivations were all wrong. This thing between them was only supposed to have been about sex, not some fake marriage situation.

He dropped the forkful of food he was no longer hungry for. 'What are we doing, Sophie?'

She frowned, then smiled before answering what should have been a rhetorical question. He knew exactly what they were doing and why they shouldn't be doing it.

'Er…we're having dinner. Did the water short-circuit your brain today?'

'No, I mean this.' He gestured to the lit candle in the middle of the table and to his bag, sitting in the hallway waiting to be unpacked.

Now Sophie abandoned her meal and pushed her plate away. 'Look, Roman, you needed somewhere to stay and I offered you a bed for the night. I was cooking dinner anyway and I knew you'd had a rough day. There was no great plot to trap you into a life of domesticity.' She was ticked off at him and rightly so, when all she had done was be there for him. Roman was the one with the problem, he knew that. Commitment and intimacy issues ensured that the second he had anything resembling happiness in his life, he had to question it.

'I just don't want you thinking that this is anything other than a fling or that tonight is more than a favour.'

'Oh, get over yourself, Roman Callahan. What makes you think that you're such a great catch I would want to give up my independence and become the little housewife, waiting for you to come home from work to give my life meaning? I've been looking after myself for a long time. If you don't want to stay the night, fine. We'll screw and you can book yourself into a hotel room for the night if you'd prefer.' The pink spots in her cheeks were glowing brighter with every harsh word she threw at him. He hadn't been prepared for her reaction to be so, well, visceral. Roman couldn't be sure if it was that display of undisguised passionate anger or her denial that she needed any form of relationship with him outside the bedroom, but he wanted her right now.

'Maybe I would.' He stood up and leaned across the table. Sophie mirrored him, then all at once they were kissing, mouths and tongues clashing as they gave in to the electricity arcing between them and causing this sudden power surge.

Head buzzing with thoughts only of having her, he cleared the table with one swipe of his arm, dishes and pasta sauce spilling everywhere.

'I'll replace it,' he told her as the smashed crockery hit the tiled floor.

'It doesn't matter,' she gasped, crawling across the table so they could reach each other more easily.

Roman knew this was about asserting the nature of their 'fling', for both of them, but he was still hot for her after the way she had spoken to him so vehemently and honestly. Sophie wasn't afraid of saying what she thought and she didn't play games. She was exactly who he needed.

Sophie's heart was fit to burst it was pumping so hard and fast against her ribcage. For a moment she'd thought Roman was going to end things there and then, simply because she had cooked him a meal. Now raw passion had turned her kitchen into a den of iniquity, and she didn't care. Yes, her outburst had been prompted by fear of losing him and that desperate need to convince him she wasn't going to get clingy, but now it was all about the sex. Just the way he wanted and what she had agreed to.

She was sitting on the edge of the table now, Roman pushing her dress up her thighs and pulling off her panties. When she'd been standing making dinner she would never have guessed it would have led to something so wild and erotic. She didn't let her lips leave his as they both worked to push his trousers and boxers out of the way, but there was one thing they had to be mindful of.

'Condom,' she gasped, aching to have him inside her but also fearful of the consequences if they weren't careful. A pregnancy was the one thing guaranteed to see him running for the hills.

Once contraception was taken care of, Roman pushed her gently back onto the table and pulled her along the table towards him so he was standing between her legs. She was ready for him, aroused by the sheer notion of what they were about to do on her kitchen table.

He filled her with one flex of his hips and Sophie stretched out, hands above her head, surrendering her body to his will. His grunts of effort and satisfaction as he pushed into her matched Sophie's. It was bliss every time they joined together. Here, she was content. There was no pressure to mind what she was saying in case she scared him off when she knew he was every bit as happy to be doing this.

With every thrust they rose and clung together, driving towards their mutual goal, their bodies in tune even if their minds remained on different things. They fitted perfectly together, snug and right. Some day Roman might come to see that.

Despite their short-lived tiff over their arrangement and insistence they were only together for sex, Roman had spent every night since in Sophie's bed. Minus the luggage which had made him question their status in the first place.

He knew they were veering into dangerous territory, and it disturbed him more than his usual adrenaline-fuelled exploits. It was making him question his true feelings as much as Sophie's. He was becoming too used to climbing into her bed at the end of a shift and waking up beside her in the morning. There was nothing like winding down from a stress-filled day and coming home to make love to her. When he was with Sophie he didn't need to be searching for the next daredevil stunt. He was content in her company, and he was sure she felt the same. Except when they were having sex, when 'content' turned to 'mind-blowing'.

The revelations about Sophie's teenage mindset had weighed on his mind since the night they had gone ice-skating. If he was guilty of taking too many risks, she had taken the opposite path, afraid of taking any. He hadn't realised the lasting impact the loss of her parents had had on her, or how much it would shape her life. If he had, he might have handled their separation with more care. His intention had never been for her to feel abandoned or unwanted, he had experienced enough of that himself to ever inflict it on anyone else. Now that he knew the truth, he had a duty to rectify his mistakes and undo the belief Sophie had harboured for so long which prevented her from living her life to the fullest.

They had grown closer since that night when they had opened up about their families and the issues which had crept into their relationship. While he was enjoying it, it was important for them both to remember this thing between them was not for ever. He hadn't changed from who he was, and Sophie would be disappointed if she believed otherwise. This time, when they parted ways, he wanted to make sure it was a mutual, pain-free exercise. He hoped that if he was able to help her move further out of her comfort zone she would realise she didn't need him or anyone else to validate her.

Although she'd been resistant even to the idea of ice-skating, it had not taken much to coax her into participating and eventually enjoying it. He intended to get her more involved in the sort of activities he did outside of work, to get her blood pumping and remind her she was alive. That she had not died along with her parents or her grandmother.

Today he was making another surprise Santa visit at the local village fair and Sophie was waiting for him on the ground below with the rest of the crowd. Abseiling down from a helicopter was part of his job and not something which made him nervous at all. However, he knew she would be watching and worrying, and he wanted to prove to her it wasn't necessary. That she could enjoy the spectacle without anticipating the worst might happen.

'Ready when you are.' He signalled to the pilot before donning his long white curly beard and red felt hat.

He leaned out and waved to the crowd below, the cheers drowned out by the sound of the helicopter blades above his head. After making sure his safety harness was secure, he grabbed hold of his sack of toys and leaned back. He tried not to think too much about Sophie, whose heart would be in her mouth, watching his descent, focusing instead on lowering out of the helicopter. They were hovering above the middle of the village green, the families below spreading outwards to leave a wide circle for him to drop into.

He hit the ground and quickly disentangled the safety rope. 'Ho, ho, ho.'

A round of applause erupted around him, giving Roman that sense of satisfaction that he had achieved something. People were happy to see him, even if it was because they were expecting a gift and a promise that he would bring more on Christmas Eve.

As he shook hands and said hello on his way over to the grotto they had set up in the community centre, he was scanning the assembled throng for Sophie. He spotted her standing on her own, her hood pulled up to protect her from the elements and giving him the thumbs-up with a grin on her face. It was a start and a relief to see her as pleased as the rest of the crowd welcoming his safe arrival. Fingers crossed, she would be equally happy when they went their separate ways because she still needed someone who could give her more than he ever could.

'Are you in the queue?' a mother holding a baby in her arms and a toddler by the hand asked Sophie inside the community centre.

'No, sorry. Go on ahead.' She'd been daydreaming about Roman and inadvertently got caught up in the rush of children hoping to see Santa. Moving from the hallway to the main hall gave her more breathing space, as well as the chance to see him up close.

This past week with him had been glorious and eye-opening. Not only were they having the most amazing sex, but they were really getting to know each other on a deeper level than ever before. She was learning something new about him every day. And herself. With the confidence he had in his abilities, she'd had to trust he knew what he was doing by dropping in today by helicopter. That fear for him would probably never leave her, but Roman always landed on his feet. Today she'd had to ignore that urge to look away and simply appreciate the joy he was bringing to the children with his unusual arrival.

'He's great with the kids, isn't he?' Nya, dressed in a festive Mrs Claus outfit, walked up beside her.

'He is. Everyone is leaving with a smile on their face.' She watched the families troop out of the grotto with the children clutching their presents and chattering excitedly about the time they'd got to spend with Father Christmas.

'How are things going between you two?'

'Good.' She didn't have to say any more than that, sure the smile on her face said it all.

'So you wouldn't mind working together?'

Nya's question drew Sophie's gaze away from Roman and added a frown. 'What do you mean? If it involves jumping out of helicopters, it's a definite no.'

'Don't worry, it's nothing medical-related or airborne. Unless the helicopter crew come back with an emergency. No, we need someone to take the pictures. Our photographer is a little under the weather and wants a break.'

'I'm not an expert by any means. Isn't there someone else who could stand in?' Sophie didn't want the responsibility of potentially ruining the memory of someone's visit with a blurry snap.

'Don't worry, it's an instant camera. All you have to do is snap away. I'd do it myself, but I have to organise the queue and keep the kiddies happy. You know it's all about the present anyway.' Nya laughed and led Sophie over to the grotto without giving her the opportunity to say no.

Considering the lack of budget and space, those who had built Santa's toy room had done a good job. An archway cobbled together with plywood and covered with red tissue paper and a layer of cotton wool gave the illusion of a little house. Roman sat on a huge chair inside, surrounded by colourfully wrapped gifts, with a little boy sitting on his lap.

Nya handed her the camera. 'Point and click. Good luck.'

'Thanks,' Sophie mumbled to her back as she had already exited the small space.

Roman, who was listening to the seemingly never-ending Christmas list of his little visitor, raised his eyebrows when he saw Sophie coming to join him.

She held up the camera and shrugged.

'I will see what I can do for you, Matthew. Now, here's your present and if you look into the camera Miss French will take a photo for you to keep too.'

'Say "Christmas",' Sophie encouraged to get a smile from the child and once she was sure she had both of them looking straight at the camera she pressed the button.

Matthew's mother came to collect him and marvel at the car set he had enthusiastically unwrapped the second he had bounced off Santa's knee.

'Don't forget your photograph.' Sophie handed over the now developed pic, which had caught the subjects perfectly. She was pleased to have been part of the moment.

Once the couple had moved on, Roman stood up and came over to her. 'What on earth are you doing here? Not that I'm complaining. I just didn't expect to see you until later.'

'Nya strong-armed me into filling in for your photographer. Apparently he wasn't feeling very well.'

'It might be the heat, with so many people packed in here. I know I'm melting under this fat suit.' Roman patted his fake belly. He looked cute, regardless of the extra weight he was carrying and the big beard hiding his handsome face.

'Come here.' Sophie fished a handkerchief out of her bag and dabbed at the beads of sweat on his brow.

The costume and the crowd outside the grotto no longer existed as she looked into his eyes. He too appeared to have forgotten where he was as he leaned towards her, his gaze trained on her mouth.

She put a finger to his lips. 'I think it might cause a scandal if Father Christmas is seen kissing one of his helpers.'

'Later?' It sounded like more of a promise than a question and only made Sophie wish more than ever that they were alone.

'Later.' She gave him a wink, suggesting they would be doing more than kissing.

He went back to his chair in time for Nya to chaperone another young visitor into the grotto.

'This is Alice, Santa, she's a little bit shy.' Nya held hands with the child, who was reluctant to get any closer to Roman.

'Hi, Alice. What can I do for you today?' He knelt down on the floor beside the little girl, his voice soft and unthreatening.

Alice turned and buried her head in Nya's skirts, the experience clearly too much for her.

'There's no need to be frightened. Father Christmas only wants to give you a present,' Nya coaxed to no avail.

Roman held his hand up. 'It's okay. I'm not going to force her to talk to me, but I don't know how we're going to find out what she wants as a gift…'

He gave an exaggerated sigh and reached for some of the wrapped parcels. 'I wonder if she would like a toy car? A skipping rope? Maybe a teddy bear?'

The last option managed to turn the little girl's head.

'Would you like a Christmas teddy bear, Amy?' Roman held out the small parcel, still kneeling on the ground and putting no pressure on her to follow the usual protocol when visiting Santa.

It was enough to tempt Amy into reaching out to accept the gift. When the glimmer of a smile crossed her lips, Sophie immediately caught the moment on film. It wasn't the traditional Santa picture but as she watched it develop before her eyes she knew it was every bit as precious as all the other memories which had been captured tonight. As confirmed by the parents who rushed up afterwards to commend them for their efforts with their daughter.

'Thank you for being so patient with her. She's shy but we're encouraging her to mix a bit more before she goes to school. We were pleased when she took Mrs Claus's hand, but the fact she actually interacted with Santa is just wonderful and we have a photograph to remember the moment.' Amy's mother clutched the snap to her chest whilst her little girl was happily showing off her newly unwrapped teddy to her father in the background.

'You're very welcome.' Sophie accepted the praise on behalf of them all and promised to pass on the compliment.

She had been impressed by Roman's interaction with the child too. For someone who seemed to rush at life headlong he had taken his time with Amy, patient until she'd felt comfortable with him. It set Sophie's mind to wondering what he would be like as a father. Compassionate and kind, yet the adventurous sort of parent who would take his kids camping and open their minds to the whole world around them. The only flaw being he might not stick around long-term.

Just like her parents. Personally, she would never willingly subject another child to a life of uncertainty.

Only then did she realise she was adding herself into that picture of Roman's potential future family. He had never even said he loved her. Not when they were teenagers and certainly not recently. Although she had never spoken the words aloud, her love for him had been there in her thoughts and actions. Even now, despite her attempts not to admit it to herself, she knew that love for Roman Callahan was burning bright.

If only he was the sort of man who wanted to settle down and have a family she might have been truly happy. Then again, she'd been with men who wanted that, who'd offered her stability and safety and it hadn't satisfied her. Perhaps she would only ever love risk-takers who went against every instinct in protecting her heart. It was possible Roman Callahan was the only man she would ever love. Either way, she knew she was doomed to have her heart broken again. The most she could wish for was more time with him, all the while pretending that it could last for ever.

Once all the gifts had been distributed and the children had gone, Roman was keen to change out of his costume. And get to kiss Sophie without the fear of traumatising the local children.

'Thanks for stepping in. Maybe next time we can talk you into sky-diving, dressed as Rudolph.'

'Don't push it, Santa.' Sophie tugged gently on his beard, and he could tell she was as keen as he was for him to get disrobed.

'I'm just going to change into something more comfortable. I won't be long.' He set off, waving goodbye to everyone, careful not to let anyone see him disappear into the changing rooms so he could take off the outfit and not spoil the illusion for anyone.

He was used to doing these events, but he knew Sophie didn't engage in a lot of community activities outside of work. It had taken him by surprise to see her happily snapping away and helping him wrangle some of the more restless toddlers into sitting for their photographs. She had shared with him her reasons for holding back a huge part of herself, but with a little nudge she could be encouraged to step into the unknown. Taking photographs in a Christmas grotto wasn't physically dangerous—unless you counted the couple of badly behaved children who had kicked him in the shins—but it all went to prove she didn't have to live for ever in that protective bubble she had created around herself. Doing something spontaneous caused her anxiety, but he had seen how much she'd enjoyed it tonight and when they had gone ice-skating. Not to mention their reckless non-relationship. At heart, Sophie was an adventurous spirit too. She just didn't know it yet.

'Are you ready to go?' When he walked back into the main hall the stallholders were packing up what was left of their stock. Sophie had apparently been buying in his absence, carrying a bag he hadn't noticed before.

'Ready when you are.' She took a grey chunky knit scarf out from the bag and tied it around his neck.

'For me?'

'Yeah, I know it's a cop-out since I didn't make it myself, but I thought we should keep the tradition going.' She was talking about the home-made gifts they used to exchange at Christmas. His had tended to be something to make her laugh, while Sophie had always put a lot of thought into making something special. He still had one or two.

'Christmas is weeks away yet.'

'I know, but we might not be together by then.'

He was about to ask why when he remembered the deal they had made. Time had got away from him since he and Sophie had hooked up and for once he wasn't looking for an escape route.

'It's the nature of my work, I'm afraid.'

'I know, there's always something more exciting around the corner.'

'Exactly.'

Sophie had hit the nail on the head, but he could see she wasn't thrilled about it. With his medical training, there were always new opportunities available to him. He'd worked as ambulance crew before, an exciting, unpredictable job which he had enjoyed. However, the chance of jumping out of helicopters for a living had been too perfect to walk away from. He didn't know what the future held for him, but he knew Carey Cove wasn't part of it. There were too many memories here for him. Especially the more recent ones he had made with Sophie.

He would never find anyone like her again, but settling down wasn't on the cards for him. Seeing her interact with the children tonight, it was easy to see she wanted to be part of one of those happy families who had come through the door. Roman couldn't imagine being a parent or a husband, having to change who he was to fit into either role. His mother and father had shown him that anything less than what people expected from him was unacceptable. Sophie needed someone safe, and that definitely wasn't Roman. If she didn't ask him for more than he could give her they could keep pretending otherwise for a little while longer.

They walked towards Sophie's place in silence. The earlier frisson between them had dissipated and she had become withdrawn. He knew it was because of what he had said about looking for the next thing to claim his attention. That wasn't directed at her, but she was going to have to get used to the idea of him moving on. It was in the terms and conditions of their agreement.

Sophie suddenly called out and she gripped hold of Roman's arm. 'Whoa. The ground's starting to get icy. I should have worn my skates to get home.'

Roman grabbed her tight and ushered her away from the icy pavement. 'We should walk on the grass. Less chance of breaking a leg.'

As he had done on the ice rink, he held her hand as they picked their steps carefully, ready to catch her if she fell.

'You couldn't have got us a ride home in the helicopter?' she joked as her foot slipped on a patch of crispy white grass and she lost her balance.

He jerked her back and wrapped an arm around her waist to keep her anchored. 'If I thought for one second you would have got on board I would have.'

'Excuses, excuses.'

Roman knew she was still prickly about his earlier comment and he was glad they had this time walking home for him to try and win her over. He wanted them to enjoy whatever time they did have together.

'If you're keen, I'll put in a word and see if I can get

you in for some training.' He called her bluff, knowing she would never agree to it.

'Okay, then.'

'Fine,' he retorted, convinced it was only irritation spurring her bravado.

As they lapsed back into a painful silence, with only the sound of the grass crunching beneath their feet, a car came skidding around the bend, headlights blindingly bright.

'Look out!' Desperate to keep Sophie out of the path of the vehicle now sliding across the road and onto the grass verge where they were walking, he pushed her away. If these were his last moments on earth, he wanted to do something to show her how much he cared for her.

It took a moment for Sophie to realise what had happened. The last thing she'd seen were car headlights, followed by the frantic sound of a horn and brakes screeching. She was sore, cold and lying in a ditch, but she was alive. Roman had pushed her out of the way. Roman! He was nowhere to be seen.

Her head was spinning, her stomach lurching at the thought of what could have happened to him.

'Roman!'

'Sophie? Where are you?' The sound of his voice made her want to cry with blessed relief that she hadn't lost him.

'Here!' She waved her hands over her head, hoping he could see above the ditch she had apparently rolled down.

Roman appeared above her and held out his hand towards her. 'Thank goodness you're all right. I'm sorry if I was too rough, but all I could think about was getting you away from danger.'

He helped her up the steep bank and Sophie climbed it in a zombie-like state. She was trying to process what had happened, including that his first thought had been for her. Either of them could have been seriously injured or killed, through no fault of their own. They had been walking on the grass to prevent an accident, and it brought it home to her that, no matter the steps she took to stay safe, there were always outside factors she had no control over. She could wrap herself in cotton wool for the rest of her life, but ultimately she had no real control over her own fate. It made her wonder how much she had been denying herself unnecessarily over the years. Especially when taking a risk had led to so much pleasure with Roman these past days. Although she was never going to be a daredevil like him, perhaps she should start living the life her mother and father had never got to have.

'I'm so glad you're okay.' When she reached the top of the grassy slope she threw her arms around Roman and hugged him tight, afraid to ever let go. She knew in that moment it would break her heart to lose him a second time. As much as she'd tried not to, she could no longer continue to deny that she was in love with Roman as much as ever.

He was in her every waking thought, as well as the raunchier ones she had in her sleep. She'd felt more alive in the few days she'd had with him than this past decade without him. They were still good together, making each other laugh and enjoying one another's company, but now as adults there was so much more to their relationship. Even if they were both afraid to call it such. The passion which flared to life every time they came into contact was like nothing else she had ever experienced before and, overall, having Roman back in her life again made it so much more fulfilling. She didn't want to lose him tonight, or ever. With only a limited time together, Sophie wondered how she could convince him to take the ultimate risk and stay indefinitely in Carey Cove. Give them a chance to explore their relationship further.

'I'm fine, but the driver's hurt. We need to help him.'

Despite her need to cling to Roman a while longer, she heard the urgency and concern for the driver in his voice and let go.

'What happened?'

'I think he skidded on the black ice and lost control of the car. It crashed into the trees back there.' Roman led her back to the scene of the accident and she realised just how far she had rolled. Thanks to him, she'd been kept out of harm's way, and thankfully he had too. She didn't know what she would have done if anything had happened to him. The young driver hadn't been so lucky. The front of the car was practically wrapped around the trunk of the tree, clearly having hit it at speed. The blinking headlights and ticking engine made the otherwise quiet scene foreboding.

While Roman wrenched the car door open to assess the driver's injuries he was able to tell her that the young man was unconscious and unresponsive but still breathing. Sophie made the call for an ambulance, despite her own shaken nerves. Once she had passed on the details of the accident and the driver's non-responsive state, she went to assist Roman. It was then she saw the smashed windscreen, streaked with blood, and the large gash on the young man's forehead.

'Should we move him?' Although he had been wearing his seatbelt, with a head or neck injury it would be risky to move the patient in case of exacerbating the injury.

'Normally I would wait for the emergency services to get here but there's smoke coming from the engine. I'm concerned in case the car catches fire, and in this case I think it's more important to get him to safety.'

'Whatever you think is best.' Since Roman had more experience dealing with road traffic accidents, she was happy to follow his lead. She trusted he knew what he was doing, just as he had trusted her judgement when it came to her patient's unexpected premature labour.

He managed to get the driver out and dragged him to a safe distance away from the car.

'He's not breathing. I think he's swallowed his tongue,' Roman told her, kneeling beside the unconscious man.

Sophie immediately took up position on the other side of the prostrate body to help. Although actually swallowing your tongue was impossible, it was the term used when the relaxed tongue muscle fell back to close the airway. Not unusual in circumstances where the patient was unconscious due to a blow to the head.

Roman supported the man's head and gently raised his jaw to open the airway, the movement forcing the tongue forward to unblock the airway. He listened for signs of breathing and checked his pulse. When Sophie saw the relief on his face she felt it too, knowing he had saved another life.

'He's breathing but we need to get him into the recovery position.'

Sophie extended the man's arm at a right angle to his body with the palm of his hand facing upward. She reached across for his other arm and brought it over, so the back of his hand was resting on the cheek closest to her. Roman set the man's knee at a right angle and rolled him over towards Sophie, his head supported by his bent arm. Roman tilted the chin up and made sure his airways remained clear and Sophie covered him with her coat to keep him warm. It was only then she and Roman were able to sit back and ruminate over what had happened. She didn't care that her backside was cold on the hard icy ground because she knew her shaky legs wouldn't hold her up.

'Thanks for saving me, Roman. I'm sure he'll thank you too when he's able to.' It was a feeble attempt at humour, but it did raise a smile from her companion.

'It was pure instinct. I just knew I had to get you somewhere safe.'

There was nothing she could say to that which wouldn't make her cry, so she simply shuffled over to sit beside him. Roman took his jacket off and wrapped it around their shoulders. Sophie tucked her head under his arm and cuddled into his warmth. It was all she needed to make her feel safe again, and that was the way the paramedics found them a few minutes later.

By the time they made it back to the cottage they were so cold and weary Roman insisted on heating some more mulled wine for them as a nightcap.

'To prevent shock,' he insisted.

It did go some way to warming her up again, but

exhaustion had set into her very bones as they made their way to bed.

'I'm so tired I can't even be bothered to undress,' she said with a yawn, sitting on the end of the bed.

'That's because you've just been involved in a traumatic accident.' He came to kneel at her feet and began to undo her boots for her.

'So have you.' He'd been much closer to the accident and saved a life so she shouldn't really be the one complaining.

'Yeah, but I deal with these things a lot more often than you do. I can't say it doesn't affect me, but it will have been a bigger shock to your system than mine. Now lie back.'

'Sorry, I'm too tired, Roman.' As much as the wanting him never left her, she simply didn't have the energy for their enthusiastic lovemaking after everything they had gone through tonight.

He tutted. 'I wasn't talking about that. I'm trying to take care of you. Now, lie back.'

She did as she was told this time and lay there, half dreaming, she thought, as he stripped off her clothes, leaving her in just her underwear. He pulled back the covers and climbed into bed beside her, apparently having undressed without her witnessing it.

'So tired,' she mumbled, her eyes already closing.

'Go to sleep. I'll keep you safe.' They were the last words she heard, secure in Roman's warm embrace as sleep finally claimed her.

CHAPTER SIX

LAST NIGHT HAD been unsettling for Roman in so many ways. The car accident in itself had been traumatic, but so had that split-second of seeing the car hurtling towards Sophie. He had always been the one taking risks, much to her annoyance, and he'd recently been encouraging her to do the same. However, that near miss made him want to envelop her in protective bubble wrap for the rest of her life. An impossible task, literally and figuratively. Due to the unfortunate loss of her parents, Sophie had apparently lived her entire life keeping 'safe'. Yet she had still been in the path of that vehicle travelling at high speed. If he hadn't been there… Roman shuddered. Now they had reconnected he couldn't imagine not having her in his life. A problem in itself.

Despite not having his eye on more thrilling job opportunities, Roman feared it would soon be time to move on. Two things were inevitable about his return here and they would make a permanent stay impossible. He was bound to see his parents, whether through accident or choice, and it was sure to end in a row to sever their relationship once and for all. There was no chance they had changed their opinion of him in all this time, when they hadn't made any attempt to make amends and he had lived quite happily without their constant disdain in the meantime. The other factor was Sophie. This had to end between them, but it wasn't something he was looking forward to. He also knew he couldn't keep seeing her after the split. The temptation would be too great to make it into something more, when they both knew they weren't compatible. They would only end up hurting each other. Though he wasn't in a hurry to leave just yet…

She was curled up into him now, trusting him to keep her safe as he had promised. The words had slipped involuntarily out of his mouth, a natural reaction to almost losing her. Sophie needed him tonight and he wanted to be with her, but it was a promise he couldn't keep for ever.

'I can hear the cogs whirring in your head,' she mumbled. Roman had been so caught up in his thoughts he hadn't noticed the change in her breathing, signalling her return to consciousness.

'A lot happened last night. I keep going over it in my head. I mean, I didn't expect to have you turn up as one of Santa's helpers. If I had known I would have given you some pointy ears and stripy stockings.' It was much easier to joke about the events before the accident than tell Sophie what was really on his mind.

She playfully tweaked his nipple and though the slight, brief pain was unexpected, he was not averse to it. 'The idea of that would give anyone reason to be awake at this time of the morning.'

He kissed the top of her head. 'Even when you save a life it doesn't stop you going over what happened. I'm sure you know that.'

Although they were in different areas of medicine, Sophie was bound to have experienced her fair share of death and tragedy. Last night notwithstanding. It had the effect of making you evaluate your own life. He was certainly contemplating his future and how difficult it was going to be without Sophie in it. Yet the alternative seemed a step too far, even for a risk-taker like him.

She sat up. 'Usually I would be awake all night, overthinking what happened, or could have happened, or what I should have done differently. I think I was too exhausted last night. It was nice having someone here to take my mind off things. For once, I wasn't going through it alone.'

Her words ought to have been enough to see him scrambling to get away and make the break. Instead, they simply made him want to cuddle her closer and lie here for ever if it brought her some peace. He owed her that much after years of her believing he had rejected her, that she was the one with the personality flaws instead of him. The idea of spending a day or more in bed with her was also appealing on a base level. Not only did it mean they wouldn't have to face reality for a while longer, but they could take their time getting to know each other's bodies all over again.

'I'm glad you're okay.' He dipped his head and kissed her.

'Thank you for saving me.' Sophie kissed him back.

'Any time.'

She snuggled back down against his chest. 'Do you…do you think we could keep this thing going for a while? I mean, we haven't killed each other yet and as far as I can tell we're enjoying each other's company…'

Roman's heart just about stopped. This was it. The

moment when she had to go and spoil things by expecting too much from him. He closed his eyes and braced himself for the breakup speech he hadn't had the courage to say the last time he'd left her.

'Soph—'

'We may as well see Christmas through together. There's no point in both being alone on the day. No pressure, but we could have Christmas dinner here if neither of us are working. You'll want to go to the Guise Festival too. Everyone wears masks and costumes and there's a dance on the village green…' She was rambling, a habit she had when she was nervous, and he supposed it was because the idea was breaking all the rules of their arrangement. It made little difference when they'd already strayed away from the bedroom into almost dating territory, ice-skating and visiting the local fairs together.

He let out a heavy breath, thankful this didn't have to come to an end just yet. There was nothing appealing about spending the nights alone in his rented flat, never mind spending Christmas there too. At least there was a final date, so they knew the time frame they had to stick to—a Christmas Countdown he was both looking forward to and dreading at the same time.

'Is that what you want?'

'If that's what you want?'

They dodged around making the commitment, which was sufficient evidence for him to believe they could indulge themselves over the season without causing serious harm. This was simply a time extension to make the most of this thing between them before they went their separate ways.

'Just for Christmas?'

'Well, just for the sex,' she teased, running a fingertip across his chest.

'In that case, what are we doing wasting time talking?' He rolled Sophie over onto her back, her squeal of surprise soon turning to moans of pleasure as he stripped away her underwear and used his mouth to tend to all of her erogenous zones, worshipping her naked body with his searching lips and teasing tongue.

As long as he and Sophie both knew where they stood, Roman saw no reason why they couldn't continue their fling for now. They both deserved to have a little fun and lay a few ghosts to rest in the process. It was closure, not the start of something new and dangerous. He hoped.

Sophie had finished her last appointment of the day with her patient in Hodden village. Driving home, the sight of the Callahans' grand house on the hill caught her eye. She drove past it several times a week and never gave it a second thought. Despite it being Roman's childhood home, she didn't associate him with the place, probably because he had never really talked about it until the other night. Now all she could think about was how unhappy he must have been there, and how he was still avoiding the place.

When she came to the junction in the road where she should have turned off to head back to the cottage, she found herself driving into the large winding road up to the house instead.

She and Roman had had a breakthrough last night. Not only had he admitted how afraid he had been of losing her, to her surprise he had agreed to move the deadline of their liaison until after Christmas. With every moment she got to spend with him, she found herself wanting more. They were good together and, unless something drastic happened to change that, she wanted Roman in her life for as long as possible. Not only were they having the most incredible time in bed together, but he was broadening her horizons elsewhere too. She was beginning to see she couldn't keep herself locked away for ever. There was a world out there to explore, which didn't necessarily mean dangling on the end of a rope or jumping out of a helicopter. It simply meant putting herself out there, and she had certainly done that by asking him to stick around for a while longer.

There was one cloud on the horizon which might force him to leave again, and Sophie wanted to take steps to prevent that from happening. If they had a chance as a couple she didn't want his parents spoiling things a second time. A truce with his parents might encourage him to stay longer and think of a future with her.

She drew up to the house and managed to slip through the electric gates slowly closing after the car in front. Roman's parents, she presumed, seeing the family resemblance as they got out of their vehicle to glare at her. Although their features were sharper, and their mouths already tight with disapproval at her.

'Can we help you?' Mr Callahan asked, his gruff demeanour already making her regret her decision to try and act as mediator between them and their son.

'I'm not sure if you remember me, Mr and Mrs Callahan. My name is Sophie French, I'm a friend of your son, Roman.' They would have no reason to know her since they had never been introduced, but she was counting on Roman having mentioned her at some point when they were growing up.

'Wait. Are you the girl he used to spend so much time with when he was young?' Mrs Callahan enquired, recognition clearly sparked by the mention of her name. Roman must have talked about her at home and the thought gave her a warm feeling inside, which was much needed at present.

'Roman and I were friends, yes.' They had gone long past that now, but these people didn't need to know that, even if she'd thought they had the slightest interest in their relationship.

'Well, we don't know where he is. He left here ten years ago in a fit of pique and we haven't heard from him since.' Mrs Callahan tilted her fine tapered nose into the air, clearly claiming the upper hand in the matter.

'I think it was more than a fit of pique,' she muttered, aware of how great the decision to go must have been for Roman. He hadn't left behind everything he knew because he was having a teenage tantrum. It had been brave of him to follow his dream against his parents' wishes.

'Whatever it is you want from us, we can't help you.' Mrs Callahan locked the car and turned to go into the house, taking her husband's arm and leading him away too. Conversation over as far as they were concerned, but Sophie wasn't going without saying her piece. She owed it to Roman to try and get his family back for him before it was too late. Thinking about how lonely it must be for him, not having loved ones around, was too much for her to bear.

She had to move quickly to catch up with them before they disappeared inside the grand entrance.

'You misunderstand. I don't want anything from you. I simply wanted to let you know he's back, in Carey Cove. There might be a chance of reconciling if you could just sit down and talk with him.'

Mr and Mrs Callahan slowly turned to look at her. 'He's here?'

Sophie nodded. 'It was a surprise to me too, but he's doing really well. He's a paramedic with the emergency helicopter crew. You've probably seen it about. He's very brave, rescuing those in need of emergency medical help nearby.'

While she was singing Roman's praises Mrs Callahan was rolling her icy blue eyes. 'Still messing about and not taking life seriously, you mean. That boy will never grow up.'

Sophie couldn't understand what she was hearing. They had a virtual stranger telling them their son put his life in jeopardy every day to rescue those in distress and they were accusing him of acting the fool. If these had been her parents she would have been keen to walk away from the toxic atmosphere herself.

'I don't think you understand—'

'No, I don't think *you* understand, Ms French. We offered our son an enviable, lucrative position in our company. He would have been set for life, but he threw it back in our faces and went back to school rather than grow up and face his responsibilities.' Mr Callahan was becoming agitated now as he vented his disappointment in his son's choices, a bizarre reaction to a man who only wanted to help people. A concept, Sophie assumed, his family couldn't comprehend against their own selfish wants.

She thought she would take one last shot to get them to see what a wonderful man Roman was before they, and she, lost him for good. 'Roman is a good man. He cares deeply for other people and he has saved countless lives over the years. You should be proud of him. I think if you would sit down and talk with him you would realise you were wrong about him.'

Mr Callahan's face was as dark and foreboding as thunder. 'Please do not presume to know anything about us or our family. Roman chose to walk away from his family and good career prospects and you think you can come here and tell us we were the ones in the wrong? We have nothing to say to you or Roman. Come along, Penny. We don't have to listen to this.'

'Roman is a good man,' she insisted as they turned their backs on her again, refusing to hear it. They walked inside and slammed the door on her.

Sophie shuddered and pulled her cardigan closer around her shoulders. She had come uninvited, but in her opinion they were the ones being rude when they wouldn't even invite her inside to hear what she had to say. It was no wonder Roman thought he had no other choice but to walk away, and why he refused to even see them. She could only imagine the way they'd talked to him when they had been so rude to her, a stranger on their doorstep.

All of a sudden she was infused with rage on his behalf. They had no right to look down their noses at her or Roman simply because they had more money and didn't appreciate or respect the medical profession as much as they should. Normally she wouldn't interfere in anyone's personal matters but Roman was different. She couldn't bear to hear his own parents make disparaging remarks about their wonderful son.

Without taking time to take a deep breath and count to ten, Sophie marched straight up to the door and banged on it. Roman deserved more from his family and if he wouldn't say it, she would.

There was no answer from inside, but she wasn't about to walk away without saying her piece. She kept hammering on the door until it was wrenched open again and she was faced with the red-faced Mr Callahan.

'We have said all we are going to say on the subject of our son.' It was plain to see nothing Roman did would ever be enough in their eyes unless he submitted to their wishes and joined the family business. Controlling, manipulative behaviour which no longer had a hold on Roman, and that was probably what drove them mad.

'Well, I haven't.' She wedged her foot in the door, holding it open until she said what she had come here to say. Okay, so it wasn't going to end up in a tearful family reunion after all, but they would hear her out.

'Your egos might not let you be proud of your son but, let me tell you, he is the most courageous man I have ever met. He puts his own life on the line day in and day out to help others in need. To me that means so much more about a man who could have happily sat behind a desk and accepted a big, fat pay cheque at the end of every month. It was his dream to make a difference to other people's lives, not just his own. You don't know what you have missed out on with your petty grievance that he wouldn't fall into line and join the family business. He has his own mind and, yes, he takes more risks than most sane people, but that is what makes Roman the man he is.' It was on the tip of her tongue to say he was the man she loved, but that was probably obvious without saying the words. Why else would she be here defending him to his parents?

The effort of trying to get them to open their hearts and minds to the wonderful man he was, and getting no response, brought tears to her eyes and with a grunt of frustration she had to admit defeat. Sophie withdrew her foot from the doorjamb and made her way back to the car. She didn't know how Roman would react to the news that she had come here, or that it had been entirely futile. Indeed, it remained to be seen if she would even tell him. He might not be best pleased that she had done so without consulting him first.

The visit did settle one question in her mind though: they would never reconcile with Roman. It was obvious nothing he said or did would ever be enough for them to let him back into their lives, even if he wanted that. The fact that they wouldn't even listen to anything good she had to say about him was proof of their continued—and, in her opinion, misdirected—disdain. Whether Roman would appreciate her attempt to end their estrangement or treat her involvement in the matter as brusquely as his parents remained to be seen.

In future she wouldn't interfere in Roman's issues with his parents or judge him for wanting to keep his distance from them. At least her family had loved her, even if her parents had spent most of their lives chasing adventure. Just like Roman. They might not have been in her life as much as she'd wanted but they had never bullied her into doing what they'd wanted. She had put the pressure on herself to be more like them, believing she had to change to suit them. Deep down, she knew they'd loved her, even if it had been from a distance at times. They'd never come home without a present for her and tales to tell her at bedtime. She couldn't recreate that kind of parental love for herself or Roman, no matter how hard she tried.

It was difficult to comprehend how the Callahans couldn't love their own son when she couldn't stop herself falling deeper for him every day. They had agreed to keep their casual arrangement going until Christmas, but in her heart she knew that would never be enough for her. After meeting Roman's parents it didn't seem fair to keep him here solely for her benefit, where he was reminded of the pain of his childhood every day.

As she drove home her heart was heavy with the knowledge that the fantasy was coming to an end. For the second time, Roman would be leaving her and there was nothing she could do about it.

Regardless of how weary he was, Roman couldn't wait to get back and see Sophie. They both had very demanding jobs, but they had fallen into an after-work routine of dinner together and chilling out in front of the television for a few hours before going to bed. Other than collecting clean clothes and showering, he had spent little time in his own apartment since meeting Sophie again two weeks ago. He was getting too comfortable with the situation, but he couldn't find it in him to disrupt what they had together. It was a long time since he had felt so enamoured by someone and cherished in return. An intoxicating state of affairs for someone who was not used to the comfort of a loving home to come back to. If he had been the settling-down type he would have happily moved in with Sophie if she'd asked him but, as it was, he was content to take things day by day. The alternative was to move on, and he wasn't ready to do that just yet.

He was almost sprinting up to her front door in his haste to see her. As he made his way up the path she threw open the door, as though she had been waiting for him with equal impatience. Roman launched himself at her and Sophie flung her arms around his neck. They were a hot tangle of mouths and limbs as he backed her into the hallway.

He wondered if it would always be like this or if the novelty would eventually wear off. It was hard to believe he would ever tire of the taste of Sophie on his lips, or the feel of her in his arms. Certainly his body reacted to her as if he was seeing her for the first time whenever they met up at the end of the working day.

'Hello to you too,' Sophie panted when they eventually came up for air between kisses.

'I missed you,' he admitted, even though it would have been obvious from his enthusiastic greeting.

'You only saw me this morning,' she said, laughing, though she was clinging to him as though they'd been parted for months too.

'It's been a long day.' One shift including a woman who had come off her horse and broken her back and a climber who had fallen and knocked himself unconscious had made the day seem never-ending. The thought of being here with Sophie was the thing that had got him through the danger and drama.

'Speaking of which… I have something to tell you—'

'Later. Right now, all I want is to take you to bed and

forget everything else that happened today.' He wanted to lose himself with her, in her, and ignore the warnings his inner voice was shouting at him that he was getting too involved with Sophie. That she was such a big part of his life again that walking away was going to be as painful as it had been first time around. If not more. Even if he didn't leave now, he was sure the urge to keep moving would come eventually. That was who he was, a nomad who did better on his own than he ever did with anyone else. He was sure this contentment he had with Sophie could only ever be fleeting. That panic would inevitably set in when sharing his life with someone made him feel trapped, as though he was compromising who he was for their happiness. He much preferred dancing to the beat of his own drum. Usually. For now he was having way too much fun with Sophie to worry about the future.

'But—' She made a half-hearted attempt to put the brakes on as he backed her towards the bedroom, but Roman had no desire to talk about work or anything else which might bring reality in to spoil everything.

'But what? Is there something else you'd rather be doing than this?' He kissed her neck at the spot he knew made her go weak at the knees and began unbuttoning her tunic.

'N-no,' she gasped. He could feel the frantic beat of her pulse under his lips and knew she needed this as much as he did.

'Right answer.' He slipped her clothes off and divested himself of his own, leaving a trail down the hall towards the bedroom. This was only supposed to be about sex and if they kept it that way, free of emotions and feelings, they could keep seeing each other without fear of repercussions.

Sophie knew she was being a coward. She needed to tell Roman everything that had happened today, but admitting she had gone to his parents behind his back was sure to anger him. Perhaps it was selfish of her to go along with this, knowing it was likely for the last time, but she needed it—she needed Roman.

He was making it impossible for her to think or even begin to recount the events of the day anyway when he was so clearly intent on seducing her. With his hands, his mouth, his tongue…

Sophie didn't know how she came to be on the bed, so lost to the sensations he was creating within her. They were both naked, Roman's body a perfect study of masculinity in the moonlight. The silver glow of the night highlighted every curve of muscle and delineated plane of his torso. She smoothed her hand over his rippled abdomen, marvelling at his beauty and hoping to capture the sight and feel of him in her mind for ever.

His kisses were passionate, but for her they held a certain pathos because she knew this was all going to end too soon. Their lovemaking was slow and intense, like a lingering last goodbye. Her climax came with a cry of anguish mixed in with the temporary euphoria, knowing she would never have this again. No one else could ever make her feel the way Roman did.

Before they could even catch their breath properly, the guilt poured out of her about what she had done.

'I have something to tell you, Roman.'

He rolled over onto his side, head propped on his bent arm, listening intently to what she had to say.

Sophie gulped. She tried to think of a way to ease gently towards recounting the events but there were no words to soften the harsh reality of what had happened.

'I hope you're not about to tell me you're married and I'm going to have your estranged husband after me.' The shine of his smile in the darkness melted her heart, no less because she knew it would soon disappear.

'No, I'm not married. I… I went to see your parents today.'

She braced herself for fireworks, but the ensuing silence was somehow even worse.

'Did you hear me, Roman? I spoke to your mum and dad.'

'I heard you. I'm trying to figure out why you would do that.'

Sophie sat up, clutching the sheets to her like a security blanket as she replayed the whole terrible scene in her mind. 'I thought if I could get them to talk to you there might be a chance you would stay for good.'

'That wasn't the deal.' The scowl didn't have as much aesthetic appeal as the short-lived smile.

'I know… I just… I thought since they were the reason you left the last time, if you could patch things up we might have the chance of a future together.' She was taking the biggest risk of her life by admitting that was what she wanted when Roman had told her that was not possible, but she was going to lose him anyway if they kept to their Christmas schedule. When there was a tiny chance of him wanting the same thing, Sophie was willing to take the gamble.

'And? What did they have to say?'

This was the hard part. Once she told him that she had resolved nothing, probably only made matters worse, there would be no reason for him to want to stick around, but she owed it to him to tell the truth.

'They didn't want to talk about you or listen to anything I had to say.' The cruelty of it made her want to weep for the young Roman, who'd had to live with that vitriol his whole life. Ten minutes in their company had been sufficient to understand what a toxic home environment he had grown up in and why he'd spent so much time with her and her gran.

Roman's mirthless laugh sent chills across her skin. 'Don't say I didn't warn you.'

'I know.' She'd spent the rest of the afternoon and evening unsuccessfully trying to come up with an explanation for Roman which would not paint her as the interfering busybody she was.

He scrubbed his hands over his face and scalp, almost tearing his hair out at her actions, and Sophie was chastised all over again.

'I'm sorry. I was trying to help.'

'No, you were trying to manipulate things to suit you, Sophie. I told you I didn't want to speak to them. Warned you that I'm not relationship material, yet you believe you can change the way I think. That's the type of behaviour I really cannot live with. It's why I left in the first place.' He climbed out of bed and began pulling on his clothes with a different urgency than when he'd torn them off. Now he couldn't wait to get away from her.

'Is it so wrong of me to want more time with you?'

'Yes. Everybody wants something more from me, then they're disappointed when I'm found wanting. You knew who I was when you agreed to this. It's not fair to expect me to fit into the mould of the man you should be with. That's not me, Sophie.'

But she wanted it to be and that was the whole problem.

'So you're leaving me?'

Just like her mum and dad and her gran. She wasn't enough to keep Roman with her here either.

'That was always the plan. It wasn't me who changed it. I'm sorry, Sophie, but this is going to have to be the end.'

'It doesn't have to be. I messed up. I'm sorry. Don't let one mistake ruin what we could have here.'

Roman pulled his sweater over his head and perched on the side of the bed. 'It's not just about you going to see my parents, don't you see? Your reason for doing so was because you thought it would change my mind about what I want. Who I am. It's simply opened my eyes to our differences. You need someone who wants to settle down, who will give you the security you crave. We both know that's not me. I made that clear from the start.'

'I know, but—'

'No buts, no exceptions. There's no point delaying the inevitable when it'll just cause more hurt.'

Too late, she thought. Her heart was breaking, slowly and painfully, with his every word. If she thought it would make any difference she would drop to her knees and beg him to stay, but he had that same look on his face as he had the last time he'd walked away from her. His mind was made up and she had no say in the matter.

'You're leaving me.' It was a statement of fact in her attempt to believe it was actually happening. Her life had been so full these past weeks, so consumed was she with Roman and being with him. Now she didn't know how she was going to carry on without him. How could she possibly go back to her old life when she'd had a taste of a better one with Roman in it?

'I was always going to. I thought you understood that.'

She nodded. He was right, of course. She had agreed to this fling on the basis that it would never be anything serious. That hadn't stopped her yearning for more. It was her own fault she was hurting so much now. Roman didn't owe her anything. He simply didn't love her as much as she loved him and never had.

She was totally exposed, physically and emotionally, and when he moved towards the door she didn't follow. There was no certainty her legs would carry her when her whole body had gone into shock at her loss. Even the tears wouldn't come, though they were there hiding and waiting until she accepted it was over for ever.

'Goodbye, Sophie, and thank you for everything.' He hesitated for a moment in the doorway, perhaps waiting for her to repeat the sentiment and provide him with a guilt-free getaway. She couldn't bring herself to do it. To make it final.

When she was not forthcoming with the response he desired, Roman gave her a half smile she liked to imagine was full of regret for everything he was throwing away, turned and walked away.

She watched him until he had disappeared out of her sight and her life, not knowing how she was going to recover a second time from a broken heart.

CHAPTER SEVEN

SOPHIE LAY IN the dark for some time, replaying everything that had happened between her and Roman, the good and the bad, until she could bear the memories no longer. It was late but she knew sleep would not be forthcoming and needed something to take her mind off her loss. She left her discarded clothes lying on the floor, the memory of Roman taking them off in a frenzy of desire too much for her to face.

A run, that was what she needed. She donned her running gear and added a few extra layers to protect her from the cold. Scarf, gloves and trainers on, she was ready to escape the ghost of Roman, trapped for ever in the cottage with her.

It was pitch-black outside, save for the stars and moon shining above, and she could see her puffs of breath hanging in the air as she ran but the conditions didn't faze her. The cold would revive her flagging spirit; the dark would hide the tears sure to fall. She hadn't run the whole time she and Roman had been together, preferring to get her exercise in the bedroom. Now she had no choice.

Sophie ran along the coast road, the thunder of the sea doing little to block out the voice in her head grieving the death of her relationship with Roman, even if it had been all in her head.

She pounded the tarmac until her lungs were burning and her legs were jelly. Curse Roman Callahan for coming back here and stirring up her feelings, only to run out on her again. She could happily have spent the rest of her life in ignorance of the fantastic sex life she could have or how much more her very existence would be with Roman in it. Now she would spend the rest of her days mourning it all.

Eventually she had to stop for a break, bending over double and gasping for air. It was then she noticed the safety barrier which ran alongside the road was damaged. Something had crashed straight through it, leaving bits of glass and debris glinting on the ground.

Sophie peered over the edge of the cliff, the long way down and the vicious waves crashing below making her dizzy.

'Hello! Is there anyone down there?' she shouted into the night. It was difficult to see anything, but she thought she saw a wisp of smoke and the flash of something on the ledge halfway down.

A faint, 'Help!' drifted up to her on the wind.

Sophie's heart was hammering with fear and trepidation. Someone was down there, and she was the only one around to provide assistance. She remembered her phone and pulled it out of her pocket, hoping the light would help her spot whoever it was in trouble. As she squinted into the shaft of light she could just make out the car which had thankfully landed right side up, but was now resting precariously on a rocky shelf halfway down the cliffside. The small yellow hatchback was instantly recognisable to her and it made her stomach tighten into a knot of anxiety. It belonged to one of her patients.

'Kirstie? Is that you?'

The small figure bent over at the side of the car straightened up and waved. 'Yes. Can you send help?'

'It's Sophie French. Are you hurt?' She wanted to know what she was dealing with so she could pass it on to the emergency services and better prepare them for her rescue.

'Just a bit shaken… Argh!' Kirstie's assurance that she was fine was belied by the loud groan which followed.

'Kirstie?'

The groaning went on for a few more seconds and Sophie grew concerned that she had hurt herself and was no longer able to communicate. She dialled for the emergency services, knowing that there was only one team who could possibly get down there to help her.

'I'm having contractions and I think my waters broke.' The voice came from the darkness just as Sophie was relaying directions to the operator, making the rescue more urgent than ever.

'Oh, and please get here as soon as possible. The lady is in labour.'

'Roman?'

'Hello, Mother.'

Roman was almost as shocked as she was to find him pitched up on the doorstep of the family home. It was the argument with Sophie which had finally prompted him to confront them. He'd burned his bridges where she was concerned so he might as well raze the whole of Carey Cove to the ground while he was here. There was no way he could ever come back now. Without Sophie, there was nothing for him here. They'd had closure of a kind, even if he had so much more to regret when he thought of her. So many more memories to torture him at night when he was in bed alone, because if he couldn't make it work with the only woman he'd ever loved he couldn't make it work with anyone else. Now it was time to get closure on the rest of his life at Carey Cove.

He'd been avoiding this confrontation for too long, afraid of what they would say and of how they might make him feel, but nothing could make him feel any worse about himself today.

'Can I come in?' She hadn't slammed the door shut in his face already, which he was taking as a good sign and pushed a little more.

Although his mother didn't make a formal invitation, she did step aside to allow him entrance.

'Your father is in the lounge.' It was difficult to tell if it was an instruction or warning but that was where he headed, his heart pumping in time with his fast steps. This conversation was long overdue, though the thought of saying what he needed to remained a daunting prospect.

'What are you doing here?' The first unwelcoming words out of his father's mouth were not surprising but they were still capable of wounding, with the suggestion he didn't belong in the family home. Roman had never expected a happy reunion but there was a part of him hoping his parents might have mellowed over the years.

With Sophie having interfered, they at least knew he was in town and he would have expected it to prompt a conversation between his parents at least. If there had been one, obviously they hadn't revised their opinion of him.

What was he doing here? What had he hoped to achieve by coming here, other than another argument? Deep down he knew it wouldn't change anything, but Sophie had braved their wrath to say her piece and now it was his turn. He hadn't appreciated her trying to manipulate the situation to get him to stay but he did admire her courage in coming to speak to his parents when he had chickened out of doing it until now. They had both found courage in each other to brave the things they feared the most.

'I've been working locally and I thought it was about time I paid a visit.' Although neither of his parents had invited him to take a seat, Roman plonked himself down into an armchair.

His father, who had been sitting with his feet up, was now standing, no doubt readying himself for a fight. His mother was hovering in the doorway, apparently reluctant to be in the midst of the imminent fray.

'It took you long enough.'

Roman knew his father wasn't claiming they would have expected him to come earlier but seizing the opportunity, as always, to have a dig at him. A good son—either of his brothers—would have made home their first stop. It didn't matter that they hadn't contacted him over the years, it was another chance to highlight Roman's many failings. Not that they needed to. His breakup with Sophie, his inability to commit to the woman he loved, already proved what a disappointment he was to everyone.

Nevertheless, Roman tried to ignore the jibe so he didn't get distracted from what he had come here to say.

'Well, I'm here now. Although not for long. I'm only on a temporary contract.'

'Yes, your friend Sophie mentioned you were working on a helicopter or something,' his mother butted in then to acknowledge their other unexpected visitor, who likely hadn't had a better reception than he had.

'I'm a paramedic on board the helicopter for medical emergencies.' Roman wanted them to know he wasn't simply messing about in the skies for fun, that his was a noble profession, even if it wasn't the one they had chosen for him.

'It's only temporary, though? Don't you think it's about time you got a proper job?' Now it was his mother's turn to disparage his accomplishments. He'd forgotten how they liked to tag team with their criticism. Although it was possible the comments were stinging so much more because there was some truth in what they were saying. He couldn't go on moving from one place to another for ever, never setting down roots. It was about time he found himself a permanent position and, though he enjoyed the work he was doing here, his wreck of a personal life made it impossible for him to stay. He was going to have to put more effort into finding a permanent position and finally settle somewhere. Once he had said his piece and probably seen his parents for the last time, he was hoping it would close the chapter of his life in Carey Cove for good and let him move on.

'I save lives every day. I wouldn't have thought there was a job much more admirable than that.' There was no point being coy about it when he was being forced to defend his job as a key health worker. Any normal family would be proud of him.

'There was a place right here at home for you,' his father grumbled, remaining unimpressed by his achievements.

'I know that, Dad. It's not like you didn't tell me every day of my damn life.' It was impossible not to bite back after years of repressing the hurt they had caused him. The best kind of therapy was probably to get it off his chest once and for all about the damage they had caused him growing up.

Except, before he had time to elaborate, his father had crossed the room to stand in front of him, red in the face and pointing a finger at him. 'We gave you everything and you threw it back in our faces.'

'Why can't you see it wasn't about you? It was about me.'

'You always made everything about you, Roman. You couldn't just fall into line like your brothers, it was one drama and tantrum after another.' Spittle was forming in the corners of his father's mouth as he let rip at Roman, but he had enough anger of his own to fuel retaliation.

'That's it, isn't it? You couldn't control me the way you do everyone else, so you made my life hell when I was growing up.'

'Roman! We only ever wanted the best for you,' his mother interjected as she came to join them in the room.

'No, you wanted what was best for you. Another slave with no will of his own who you could manipulate at will. You should have been proud you had a son who knew his own mind. What was so wrong about wanting to help sick people, for goodness' sake?'

'I worked my backside off to build my business, to give you kids a secure future, and you just threw it back in my face.' His father was so focused on the snub to his legacy that he wasn't listening to what Roman was saying.

'You have to see how it looked to us, Roman. Everything we gave you, everything we had planned for you just wasn't enough. Your brothers are happy in the family business and you, who wanted to go your own way, are still moving from one job to another. That doesn't sound like someone who is content with their choice. The two of you are both too stubborn to admit when you're wrong.' It was his mother who was trying to find some common ground between them but Roman knew she was fighting a lost cause when his father was waving a hand at her, dismissing everything she had to say.

'You never asked me what I wanted and if I dared to tell you I was shot down. You had no interest. I was supposed to shut up and do as I was told. I wasn't ungrateful, I was unhappy. Why do you think I spent so much time at Sophie's house when we were kids?'

'What went on in this house was none of anybody else's business.'

'Dad, you're focusing on the wrong details. Oh, this is pointless.' Admitting defeat, Roman got to his feet and prepared to leave. 'I just came to tell you what I was doing. I didn't expect you to approve, but don't worry, I won't be coming back any time soon.'

'Good. All you've succeeded in doing is upsetting

your mother and me,' his father shouted at Roman's back, since he was already on his way out to the door.

Roman spun around with one last thing to get off his chest. 'Do you know why I don't stay in one place for too long, why I haven't settled down with a wife and kids? Because you made me feel as though I wasn't good enough for anyone. Perhaps if you had shown one iota of love towards me as a child things would have been different and I wouldn't be walking out on Sophie again.'

He hadn't meant to let that last comment slip out but in the heat of the moment it was her face which had flashed before his eyes. She was the biggest loss in his life, and he knew if he hadn't been so damaged by his relationship with his parents he would have been trying to fix things. He wouldn't have interpreted her attempt to talk to them as manipulative if he hadn't spent his whole life with his parents trying to control him.

'You never did take responsibility for anything, Roman. Was it any wonder we tried to give you a secure future when you seemed so determined to mess your life up? Don't blame your mother and me for your failed relationships. I'm sure you managed to mess those up all on your own, son.' Apparently having finished what he had to say, Roman's father went to sit in a chair but suddenly clutched his left arm and collapsed onto the floor.

His mother let out a scream.

'Dad?' Despite the bad blood between them, Roman immediately rushed to assist him.

The look of fear in his father's wide eyes was something he had never witnessed before and never wanted to see again. His skin was pale and clammy as Roman undid the top buttons of his shirt to loosen the fabric and help him breathe a bit easier.

'Dad? Can you hear me?'

He was unresponsive, his breathing and pulse weak.

'I think you're going into cardiac arrest but it's okay, I'm here. Mum, go and phone an ambulance.'

'Is he going to be okay, Roman?' his mother asked, already in tears.

'We need to get help as soon as possible. Now, please, do as I say.'

She rushed off, leaving Roman to apply chest compressions to try and keep the blood pumping around his father's body. Kneeling by his side, Roman leaned over and, with arms straight, fingers interlocked, he began pushing down onto his chest.

'The ambulance is on its way.' His mother came back into the room with the news he needed to hear.

'Come on, Dad. I know you're a stubborn so-and-so. Come back.' He was doing all he could for now, but Roman still felt helpless as they waited for the paramedics to arrive. Despite everything which had taken place tonight, he knew if anything happened to his father he would never forgive himself. Just because they didn't see eye to eye, it didn't mean he didn't love him.

If his father didn't make it through this and they hadn't resolved their ill feeling, Roman knew it would haunt him for the rest of his days. He would agree to disagree with his parents on the subject of his choice of career if they could simply let him live his life without constant criticism.

Thankfully the ambulance turned up within minutes before guilt got the better of him that he had caused his father's heart attack by turning up here and he did something stupid like agree to work in the family firm after all.

Roman gave the paramedics the lowdown on what had happened. There was still no sign of life from his father, but he continued with CPR until they cut his clothes for the defibrillator they had brought with them.

They attached the pads and relieved him of his duty as the defibrillator took over. It delivered the first shock to try and get his heart back to a normal rhythm. When it was unsuccessful, the paramedic delivered some more chest compressions. After another shock his father opened his eyes and attempted to talk.

'Don't try to speak, Dad. You need all your strength. Let the paramedics look after you.' Roman took his father's hand and tried not to get in the way as the medics got ready to transfer him to the ambulance. His legs were so wobbly he was in danger of collapsing himself after the drama and subsequent relief of averting disaster.

'Thank goodness. I thought I'd lost you, Edward.' His mother was weeping beside him and he let go of his father's hand so she could take his place. Roman was sure he would prefer to see her face than his during his near-death experience.

They walked the stretcher out to the ambulance and his mother climbed into the back of the vehicle. Before he could follow, he was buzzed for a medical emergency. Checking his messages, he felt his mouth go dry and his stomach roll as he saw the details of a road traffic incident involving a midwife.

'Is that work?' his mother asked.

Roman nodded. 'It might be Sophie. We…er…had a row and there's been an accident…'

There was no way of knowing for sure if it was her but he couldn't take the chance in case something had happened to her. Except his father was on the way to the hospital after a heart attack too. He was torn about whether or not to get into the ambulance.

'Then go. You saved your father's life and if Sophie's in trouble she needs you.' With a quick and unexpected hug, his mother gave him her blessing. His throat constricted against the emotions bubbling up inside him at that simple sign of affection denied him so long. It was the acknowledgement he had waited for from his parents all of his life, that he had finally done something right and worthwhile.

It was the sort of pivotal moment he would have been running to Sophie to share. He could only hope he wasn't too late and there was still time to salvage a relationship with her as well.

'I'll be down to see you as soon as I can.' Roman closed one of the ambulance doors, with his father still in his line of sight. Lying on the stretcher, as pale as the white cotton sheet draped over him and attached to the machines monitoring his heart, he no longer looked like the intimidating adult who had cowed him throughout his childhood. Here, he was simply a frail old man fighting for his life and Roman actually felt sorry for him. It was a start to any idea of reconciliation that his emotions extended beyond anger and fear and he hoped, if his father's condition improved, they could find some way to mend bridges.

Just as he was closing the other door, his father sat up and pulled off his oxygen mask.

'Thanks, son,' he managed before he collapsed back down again.

This time Roman couldn't stop the sob which erupted from his throat. He had actually done something to make his parents appreciate the road he had taken. Perhaps he wasn't a waste of space after all and there might be something to stick around for, as long as Sophie was okay and was willing to forgive him.

Roman didn't know what could travel quicker than a helicopter but he wished he was in it. Considering the weather and time of year, road traffic accidents were unfortunately all too common. The location would make it tricky, but nothing they hadn't dealt with before. It was the possibility of Sophie being involved which terrified him. He knew he'd upset Sophie, yet he'd left her alone and now she might be lying hurt somewhere.

It had only been a matter of hours, but he already knew he'd made the biggest mistake of his life in leaving her again. She had been naked in bed and asking him to stay. Would it really have been so wrong to try and make things work? Yes, he'd let her down in the past, but she'd been willing to give him a second chance. And he'd been afraid of opening up his heart and sharing his life with anyone when he'd been so independent for so long. Sophie loved him, it showed in her every action and, though it scared the life out of him, Roman knew he loved her too. Now it might be too late to do anything about it.

'Are we nearly there?' he asked into his headset, poised to lower himself down the second they spotted whoever it was in trouble out there. If it was Sophie he would put his life on the line without a second thought to save her.

'You in a hurry to be somewhere else tonight, Callahan?'

'He must have a hot date.'

The other guys on the crew teased him with their usual banter. This was just another call to them and to deal with the stress and horror of the job they often used humour to defuse the tension. They weren't to know how shaken Roman was about this one, or how he might be personally involved. If they had they probably wouldn't have allowed him to go out on the call. Exactly why he hadn't informed them of a potential connection to the injured party. No matter how experienced the rest of the team was, he wasn't going to put Sophie's life in anyone's hands but his. That was where she belonged and the next time he had her there he wouldn't let her go. He prayed nothing had happened to her.

'I can see someone on top of the cliff.' A figure in a reflective top lit up under the helicopter's spotlights. As they came closer he could see it was Sophie and he almost collapsed with relief. Then he remembered there was still someone in trouble down there and steeled himself once more to run into the fray.

The reason he had taken this job was for this kind of adrenaline-pumping, life or death scenario that would never be boring. Although tonight he was regretting ever leaving Sophie's bed. He'd been stupid to think that would never be enough to satisfy them both when they had been perfectly happy these past days. Using the excuse that Sophie had been trying to manipulate him the way his parents had was nonsense and he knew it. It was a knee-jerk reaction to what she'd done. Going to talk to his parents, trying to reason with them so he would have reason to stay was something done out of love, and that was what had terrified him. Sophie was the only person who had ever loved him for who he was, way back when he was a wayward kid and again now, as an adult still scarred by his childhood.

'We'll put down in the field over there,' the pilot informed him, crushing any idea he had of abseiling down and grabbing hold of her for a windswept kiss. The job had to come first.

The second the chopper set down in the field Roman grabbed his medical equipment and climbing equipment for getting down to the patient and he and his colleague, Griff, ran towards where he had seen Sophie on the clifftop.

'Roman?' She seemed surprised to see him, but he was sure he could also see relief in her eyes. Or was that wishful thinking on his part?

'Hey, can you tell me what happened?' He had to resist getting personal for now and keep his focus on getting down that cliffside without injuring himself or anyone else.

'I didn't see, but the car went through the barrier and came to rest on the ledge down there. I know the driver, Kirstie. I don't think she's injured but she is in labour. How on earth are you going to get her up here if she's about to give birth?'

'One step at a time. I need to get down to her and then we'll see how best to proceed.'

Sophie digested the information then stood a little

straighter, her chin tilted up with a determination he knew too well. 'I'm coming down with you.'

It took a moment for Roman to realise what she was saying. 'No way. I don't have time to coax you down there and I'm not having you risking your life. I'll do this on my own.'

'It's not up for discussion. Kirstie is in labour. She's my patient and she needs me. Now, show me what I have to do.' Sophie asserted her position, regardless that this expedition went against every notion of keeping herself safe.

'She's right, Roman. If there are any complications you're going to need a qualified midwife down there. I'm sure the two of us can coach Sophie through everything she needs to know to get down there.' Griff offered his opinion, though Roman already knew what needed to be done. He simply wasn't happy about it.

Sophie was putting her patient first and facing all of her fears to do so. It only made Roman love her even more.

So many emotions were flowing around Sophie's body they were in danger of making her dizzy. Not a good omen if she was about to chuck herself over a cliff. She was afraid for Kirstie and the baby, for Roman and for herself. Seeing him again had brought a surge of relief tinged with sadness that he would never be hers again. As ever, it was the priority of her patient which won out.

'If you're sure, we'll get you kitted out with all the necessary safety equipment.' Roman waited, probably giving her a chance to change her mind when he knew how scared this sort of thing made her.

'I'm sure.' She trusted him to get her down safely, just as Kirstie would have faith in her doing her job and delivering her baby, regardless of the circumstances. They might still have time to get her to the hospital before the birth but at least if Sophie was there it might put Kirstie's mind at ease.

Roman and his colleague got her rigged out before he kitted himself out with the climbing gear. All the while he was shouting down to Kirstie, letting her know what was happening and that help was on the way. Sophie could only pray that she didn't get tangled, lose her nerve or plummet to the bottom of the cliff and end up needing to be rescued herself.

Roman tugged at her straps to make sure everything was secure and checked her safety helmet was on tight, even after Griff had already carried out the checks. 'Are you ready to do this?'

She gulped and nodded, though her very soul was shouting, *No!* There was never going to be a time when she was ready to launch herself off a cliff.

'Okay, you need to go to the edge and lean back.' He walked back with her to the end of the clifftop.

Apparently there was something more terrifying than mountain-climbing and that was doing it backwards in the dark. Although they had torches on their helmets and Griff was shining a light source down the cliff side, she really was going into the unknown, not able to see anything other than that directly in front of her. Perhaps that was a good thing when she could hear the wind whistling around her and the sea crashing down below. One wrong move and she could be plummeting to her death, just like her parents.

'I won't die, will I?' Roman had promised her once

he would keep her safe and she needed that reassurance more than ever, regardless if he wanted her or not.

'Not if I can help it.' With the solid set of his jaw, Sophie was inclined to believe him and took a deep breath, preparing to take the biggest risk of her life.

'Just keep talking to me so I know I'm not doing this alone.' With Roman by her side she might be more inclined to think she could actually do this. It was hard to believe he did this on a regular basis as a job and she had nothing but admiration for him, even if she did think he was crazy. The world needed more crazy people to do jobs like this, risking their lives daily to save others.

'No problem. I'm here for you. Now, ease yourself over the edge and just walk back, feet against the cliff.'

It sounded so simple until she thought about something going wrong and instead of walking down the drop her feet might refuse to move and she'd go head first. Roman disappeared over the cliff but she knew he was waiting for her to follow. She didn't have time to overthink and panic when Kirstie was down below, in labour.

A few more deep breaths and she followed her companion, clinging tight to the rope she was dangling from.

'We can take this slow. Gently bounce against the cliff as you make your way down, feeding the guide rope through your hands.' Roman demonstrated a couple of steps, basically walking down the cliff at almost a ninety-degree angle, not bothered that there was only a rope stopping him from tumbling to his death.

Sophie concentrated her thoughts on her patient and the baby about to make its way into the world, both of whom needed her to do this. She pushed off, landing back gently further down.

'Good. Just keep going like that,' Roman encouraged from beside her with no trace of impatience, only praise.

It convinced her she could do this, taking bigger and bigger steps, confident her feet would find the rock face again each time. Seeing her progress spurred Roman to carry on down at his own pace and she wanted to keep up so she wouldn't become a hindrance to the rescue. With renewed bravado she went to push off again, but her foot slipped, her body slammed into the cliff, the jagged edges tearing at her skin and clothes. The shock caused her to let go of the rope and suddenly she was free falling, with nothing to cling to.

'Grab the rope, put the safety clip on, Sophie, before you hit the ground!' Roman was yelling from in the darkness. He didn't sound that far away and she knew she had little time to react before she slammed into the ground below.

She had several attempts to right herself before she managed to get the safety clip on and halt her rapid descent. For a while she dangled in mid-air, her rapid breath clouding the air around her.

'You're almost there. Just take it easy. I'll guide you down.' Roman was there as always, encouraging her and convincing her she could do this.

Sophie put her hand out and felt for the solid wall before pulling herself in towards it. She rested her head against the cool surface for a moment while she gathered herself together again before making the final descent.

After a couple of steps she felt a hand at her back

and Roman guided her back down onto solid ground. Her hands were shaking as she undid her harness and practically threw herself at him when she was free. It didn't matter that he had effectively dumped her only hours earlier, she needed him to hold her.

'You made it. I'm proud of you, Soph,' he mumbled into her hair, his arms wrapped around her waist and hugging her as though he didn't ever want to let go. She wished he didn't have to but there was one person who needed him more than she did.

'I did.' And she couldn't have done it without Roman's help.

Reluctantly, Sophie let go of her anchor and looked around the ledge for the person she had put her life on the line for. 'Kirstie? We're here.'

'I'm in the car!' she shouted before another pained cry pierced the night.

Using their head torches, Sophie and Roman picked their steps carefully over to the car. With the back door open, they found Kirstie lying across the back seat.

'I need to make sure the car is safe for her to be in before we do anything else.' Roman went to secure the vehicle, leaving Sophie to check on her patient.

'How are we doing, Kirstie?' she said, leaning into the car to check for any injuries.

The car interior light was dim but along with her head torch she was able to see the dirt and blood marring the young woman's face.

'I feel like I need to push,' she managed to get out through panting breaths.

'Okay, I'll take a look and see where we are.' From her preliminary observation it was mostly superficial injuries leaving Kirstie scratched and bruised. However, her body would have taken quite a battering before the vehicle had come to rest on this ledge, and possibly the baby too.

At that moment Roman came back to update her. 'We're far enough from the ledge for the car to remain stable and I've disconnected the battery to prevent the possibility of an electrical fire. I've radioed so hopefully the helicopter will be here soon to transfer the patient to the hospital.'

'Hmm. It might be too late for that. I'm just going to look and see how far along the labour is now.'

Kirstie let out another yell, the contractions coming fast.

'If you can just draw up your knees, Kirstie, I'm going to check your progress.'

Roman opened up the medical bag he'd carried down on his shoulder and Sophie took out a pair of surgical gloves. These weren't ideal sanitary conditions, but she would do the best she could to keep things sterile to prevent mother and baby contracting infection.

'Okay, you're fully dilated, Kirstie. Baby won't be long now. Roman, you'll have to tell the crew to hold off for a while. We're not going anywhere until this baby gets here.' While Roman went to radio in the latest update, Sophie hunkered down and prepared to deliver in one of her most unusual births to date.

'But how are we going to get out of here?' Kirstie was half crying as she tried to control her breathing. Now wasn't the time to tell her that, along with her newborn, she would have to be winched up into a helicopter. There was no need to further stress a woman in labour when she had other things to worry about.

'You leave that down to us.' Roman was back, adjusting the front seats to give Sophie more room to work in the back of the car. He was always thinking ahead. Something which was great for the work he did but not so good for anyone wishing to have a relationship with him.

'My labour bag is in the boot of the car,' Kirstie suddenly remembered and Roman immediately went to retrieve it.

'That's very organised of you, or were you already in labour when you set out this evening?' Kirstie was on her own, her boyfriend not prepared to settle down into family life, so she'd had to do everything alone so far during the pregnancy. Sophie supposed she should think herself lucky she hadn't been in a similar situation when Roman had decided he didn't want to be with her long-term. Although the thought of having his baby did appeal…

'I have one at work and one in the hallway at home too. I didn't want to get caught unaware.' Her laugh was interrupted by another contraction, but Sophie was glad of her overanxious mothering instincts. The bag, retrieved by Roman, contained clean towels, which she was able to spread down under Kirstie. There were nappies, baby blankets, toiletries and a change of clothes for mother and baby. Even the snacks would come in handy between now and the transfer to the hospital. Everything needed to make the pair comfortable and warm after the birth. All Sophie had to do was make sure it all went smoothly. No pressure at all.

She thought of the journey she had just been on, of Roman who was by her side, and knew they would get through this.

'Okay, Kirstie, I can see the baby's head. With the

next contraction I need you to push. That's it.' The miracle of birth would never cease to amaze Sophie as she watched the baby emerge with Kirstie's efforts, her screams echoing in the air.

'I know you're exhausted, honey, but we just need that last effort to get baby here.'

Kirstie let out an almighty roar as she pushed, and the baby slipped out into Sophie's arms. She quickly clamped the cord and wrapped the little girl in one of the blankets.

'Congratulations, Mum. You have a daughter.' Sophie had tears in her eyes too as Kirstie burst into happy, relieved sobs.

'I'll take her and get her cleaned up.' Roman had some cotton wool and a bottle of water ready as he took the crying infant from her arms. There was something poignant in that moment between them as they looked at the baby and at each other. A reminder of everything they could have had together if the past hadn't scarred them both so deeply.

It was bittersweet to see him cradling a baby so gently, being so caring and compassionate to that tiny stranger when he couldn't do the same for her, or himself. Her heart was broken all over again, watching a scene which would never be in their future. Fate was stabbing her with one last dagger to the soul.

'Can I hold her?' The mother's plea halted Sophie's self-pity and prompted her back to her midwifery skills.

'As soon as we finish here. I just need to deliver the placenta and make sure you're ready to be transferred to the hospital.'

Once all necessary examinations had been completed, Roman handed the baby over so mother and daughter could have some skin-to-skin contact.

'We don't need anyone else, do we, sweetheart?' Kirstie murmured to the little bundle curled contentedly on her chest.

Sophie envied that bond she would likely never have with another human being. Unconditional love. Even Roman had come with strings attached—don't fall in love, don't ask him to stay and definitely don't go and see his parents behind his back to try and reconcile them. She was doomed to be on her own for the rest of her life. Kirstie didn't realise how lucky she was to have someone, to have a family.

'If we're ready I'll radio in for transfer. We don't want anyone out in the cold for too long.' Roman reminded them that this was no warm, cosy delivery suite but the edge of a cliff face at the very end of November. Kirstie and the little one were vulnerable and needed to get somewhere safe as soon as possible.

They all set to work getting mother and baby dressed and ready to be transported. Sophie was trying not to think about how she was going to get back onto solid ground in case her look of panic set Kirstie off too. The idea of winching a newborn up into a helicopter wasn't for the faint-hearted.

She couldn't believe any of this was happening as the helicopter came into view above them, lights shining, blades whirring and the wind whipping around them. It was all the drama she'd never wanted in her life but it had come to her unbidden and she had got through it. The baby certainly hadn't asked to be brought into this world in this manner. Fate, it seemed, paid no mind to plans and precautions.

Roman's colleagues took over responsibility for her patients from the moment they lowered themselves down on ropes from the helicopter, lifting mother and baby to relative safety. It was only when the crew flew off into the night, plunging Sophie and Roman back into relative darkness, that the implications of her position became apparent. Stranded on a ledge with her ex at night.

'Er…how are we supposed to get back?' There was a lot of other deeply personal stuff she wanted to say to him but probably not here where she couldn't get away from him when he said something she didn't want to hear. She was already tired and emotional without being reminded of her failings as a potential partner.

He handed her the climbing gear she'd hoped to have seen for the last time when she had taken it off earlier. 'What comes down must go up again.'

'I don't think that's a thing. Tell me you're kidding me, right?' Sophie glanced up at the sheer face of the cliff as far as the eye and head torch could reach. The top seemed even further away from this angle.

'Nope. They don't have the time or resources to come back out just for us. Someone will come and pick us up at the top in a support vehicle. You've done it already. There's nothing to it. You'll just have to follow my path and footholds on the way.' He made it sound as though they were going picking wildflowers, not climbing rocks in the dark.

'Easy-peasy,' she said with a shrug, hoping he could see her eyes rolling at him in the light of his torch.

'I know you can do it, Soph. I've just seen you abseil down a cliff and deliver a baby in the back seat of a car. You're a real-life superwoman.'

But still not enough to convince Roman that he wanted to be with her.

'Yeah? In that case could you tell the powers that be I'd really appreciate a pair of wings or a flying cape to get me to the top?' It wasn't as if she had any choice but to start climbing or she would be stuck down here all night and she really wanted to get home to her bed. Even if it would be on her own for the first time in weeks.

'You've done the hard part. Come on, I'll give you a leg up.' Once Roman had given her all the necessary safety checks and brief instructions on how to make her ascent, Sophie knew there were no more excuses.

She gripped onto the rocks and found her first foothold before Roman gave her a boost up off the ground. It wasn't an easy climb and took twice as long as her earlier descent. The fine rain falling and misting everything in its path didn't help, making the surface slippery under her feet. A few times she lost her footing, her knees and shins taking a battering in the process. But Roman was there for her every step of the way, encouraging and pushing her, sometimes literally, to get her to the finish line. By the time she reached the top every part of her was shaking from the cold and exertion of getting there.

Roman took off his safety gear and came to her, wrapping her in his arms and instantly providing some heat. Everything seemed to hit her at once. The drama of the birth, the adrenaline of her climb and the sheer heartbreak of being with Roman and knowing it could be the last time. She broke down and sobbed into his chest.

'You did so well, Soph. I'm really proud of you.' He

was making this so much harder for her with his kind words and hugs and, really, he was lucky she didn't push him back over that cliff.

When the support car came to collect them and caught their embrace in its headlights she quickly let go. It was bad enough Roman had witnessed her breakdown and total inability to accept their situation without anyone else seeing it. They got into the car and both were swathed in emergency foil blankets to keep them warm.

'I suppose you'll want to get home to bed after all that excitement.' Roman was trying to make small talk with her in the back of the car.

She thought about the dark empty cottage and the ghosts waiting for her there. 'No, I want to be dropped off at the hospital to see how Kirstie and the baby are doing.'

'I thought you might.' He grinned but it irked her that he knew her better than she knew herself.

'There's no need for you to attend. She's my patient. Feel free to get dropped off at your place first.' Sophie was not putting him under any obligation to spend any more time with her. He must be desperate to make an escape after tonight's unexpected turn. It was always awkward when you dumped someone then had to spend the rest of the night together on an emergency medical call out delivering a baby on a cliff edge.

'No, I want to go. I prefer to see my patients right through their transfer, so I know everything was done properly.'

Sophie wasn't going to argue with him. If he was trying to make a point he could make it and then go home, and she could start getting used to the idea that he would no longer be in her life.

As the car jostled along the coast road Sophie rested her head against the window, watching the distant waves continuing to crash as though nothing had happened tonight. As her eyes began to flutter closed she wondered if she could ever be as unaffected by the world around her as the sea.

CHAPTER EIGHT

ROMAN WATCHED SOPHIE SLEEP. He didn't rouse her even though he had so much he needed to say. She deserved her rest when he knew what the past few hours had taken out of her, and not just physically. She had faced her fears head-on, tackled them mostly without complaint. Her bravery put him to shame when he had run away from his rather than risk getting hurt. Despite him ending their relationship earlier in the evening, she had set aside her own personal issues to work alongside him, doing whatever it took to keep her patient safe. Including risking her life, a feat he was sure she didn't undertake lightly, given the fears which had plagued her since her parents' death.

Working with an ex, abseiling down a cliff in the dark and delivering a baby in a car…and he couldn't even tell a woman he loved her. Afraid of committing in case he wasn't enough for her and somewhere along the line she told him so. Roman wasn't the daredevil everyone believed him to be. He was a coward.

When they reached the hospital he was forced to wake her, giving her a gentle shake. 'Sophie? We're here. Are you sure you wouldn't rather go home to bed? I can call in and let you know how they're doing later if you've changed your mind.'

At the very suggestion she bolted upright, defying that she was in any way tired. 'No. I won't sleep until I know they're doing okay.'

After watching her fall into such a deep sleep so quickly he doubted it. She was clearly exhausted. But Roman didn't wish to cause her any embarrassment or cause a row between them. Regardless of everything, he didn't wish them to part on bad terms.

He opened the car door for her and she did accept his hand when he offered to help her out. Mostly, he suspected, because her legs were a little wobbly after the night's events.

'When you get home you should make yourself a stiff drink and run a bath to ease those muscles.'

'I know how to look after myself, thank you.'

He regretted attempting to tell her what to do when she snatched her hand away again. She marched up to the reception desk, back ramrod-straight, giving nothing away about how weary she must be, and enquired about her patient.

'Oh, you're the pair who rescued her? You're a couple of heroes around here.' The young receptionist stood up, drawing attention to them from the few people in the waiting room.

'Just doing our jobs. Now, if we could see her...' Sophie batted away the praise as easily as she had deflected Roman's concerns. He could see her defences already rebuilding brick by brick and it was sad to see when she had been so open with him. His fault for letting her believe they could have a future together and leaving it too late to tell her otherwise. Of course it had always been on the cards, he'd been foolish to think otherwise. Sophie wasn't one to hold back her emotions the way he did, but he had selfishly not wanted to end things when he'd enjoyed being with her so much.

His life was spent hopping from one job, one town, one short-lived relationship to the next and he had never been as truly happy as he had with Sophie. Whatever time they had together surely was better than the nomadic life he'd been leading since the day he'd left home? But as she marched ahead with no desire to wait for him Roman wondered if he had left it too late to fix his mistake.

He decided to give her some space before he attempted a grovelling apology and took the elevator to the cardiac care unit to see his father.

'Hello, Roman.' His mother was sitting by his father's bedside, holding his hand.

'I thought I would call in and see how you were feeling, Dad.'

'Sore,' he managed to get out from behind his oxygen mask.

'I'm sure you are. Sorry if I was too heavy-handed.' Bruised or even cracked ribs were often the result of chest compressions, even though it was necessary to press down hard to keep the blood pumping around the body.

'You did what you had to, to save your father, and we're both very grateful.' The crack in his mother's voice and her usual composure said how thankful she was to still have her husband here, no matter how poorly he remained.

'Just doing my job,' he said, hoping they realised

now how important it was to have medical professionals like him in an emergency.

'What about Sophie? Is she all right? She's such a lovely woman. Give her our apologies for the way we may have spoken to her.' Despite his mother saying all the right things about Sophie, Roman was stuck on the last part of the comment. She hadn't mentioned getting a bad reception as such, but he could imagine the disdain with which she might have been treated. Sophie didn't deserve any ill treatment when she had gone there to try and smooth things over between them. Yet again she had been the innocent victim in the fallout of his disastrous personal life.

'Sophie's fine. It was one of her patients who was in trouble. What did you say to her?'

'You know your father. He wasn't in the best of moods and he doesn't like being told what to do.' His mother tried to excuse her husband's behaviour and not for the first time. Too often she had been complicit in his berating of Roman too, sometimes joining in, giving opinions he wasn't sure were hers or his father's. Still, neither of them had gone out of their way to stop him leaving home a decade ago.

'That's not a reason to be rude to the woman I love. I don't care what you think about me, but please, never speak to Sophie the way you ever did to me.' Roman was aware he had used the 'L' word and said it to the wrong person. It was wasted on his parents, and it was Sophie who deserved to hear it from him first. Even if she rejected it and him.

'We are sorry, son,' his mother reiterated, uncharacteristically contrite. Perhaps his father's near-death experience had made them reconsider the way they conducted themselves.

'You were outstanding tonight and the staff have been telling us about some of the other emergencies you've been involved in. It appears you're very popular around here.' Despite his obvious discomfort, his father was doing his best to make amends.

In all the scenarios which had played out in his head of meeting his parents, he had never imagined it like this. They seemed almost…human.

'And respected,' his mother added, nudging his father.

'You should rest, Dad. This can wait for another day.' Roman didn't want him to waste his energy. He'd waited a lifetime for this conversation so he was sure another few days wouldn't hurt. Except his father was waving away his concerns as per usual, stubbornly determined to have his say no matter what.

'I know we've never seen eye to eye—'

He snort-laughed at his father's understatement of the millennium.

'We will probably never agree on a number of things, but on this occasion I think we can say we were wrong.'

Edward Callahan's almost-apology was supported by a nod from his wife. Roman could only listen on in incredulous silence.

'We would have preferred you had gone into the family business like your brothers, but you've done us proud in your chosen career nonetheless.'

He was sure there was a residual barb in his father's words, but it wouldn't take away from the gesture. It was an olive branch. More than had been offered in over a decade and more than he had ever expected from them. If not for Sophie, he would never have followed up on a visit to his parents. His dad's heart attack had been the catalyst for ultimately getting them all to see sense, but it was only because of her efforts that they had even had a conversation.

As Roman had learned through many of the tragedies he saw in the nature of his work, life was short and should not be lived in bitterness, or alone.

'For the record, I think Sophie is a fantastic match for you. She's as passionate and headstrong as you always were, but her heart is in the right place.'

'Thanks. I think.' Roman's mind was whirling with the implications of this moment with his parents. Did this mean he hadn't disappointed them after all? That he was not the useless son he had been told his entire life but 'passionate and headstrong', qualities which they had struggled to accept? It didn't change who he was but perhaps the way he perceived himself when he had been so afraid of having the same toxic relationship with someone else. Now they were accepting they were to blame at the same time he had been considering making a commitment to the only woman he had ever loved. His parents seemed to have a high opinion of Sophie too, not that it mattered to him, but it took someone extra special to get their approval.

'I hope we'll get to meet her again soon. Perhaps both of you might come to dinner one night when your father is feeling better?' his mother suggested, trying again to build a bridge across the years spent apart. It could prove to be too little too late, old quarrels might raise their head again, but Roman had spent too long on his own, anticipating the very worst that could happen in any of his relationships. Sophie had shown him that sometimes you simply had to get on with things, no matter how afraid you were, and hope for the best.

'We'll see. I'll have to talk to Sophie first.' He had a lot to say to her, if she even wanted to hear it. She was more than capable of continuing her life without him in it, as she had proven time and time again.

'We just wanted to say we're sorry, son, and we're proud of you.' Roman knew exactly what it would have taken for his father to admit to being wrong. That praise was something he had wanted for his entire life but tonight it fell flat as he realised he had made mistakes too where Sophie was concerned. She was more important than celebrating a win over his parents.

'Thanks, I appreciate it. Now, you rest up. I'll call in again later, but I should go and check on Sophie.' Roman didn't know if he was going to be around for much longer to build on their budding relationship. It all depended on Sophie and whether or not she would forgive him for letting her down after all.

'Hey. How are you two doing?' Sophie poked her head around the cubicle curtain to see Kirstie sitting up in bed with her daughter cradled in her arms. There was nothing in her smile to suggest the birth had been traumatic, despite the circumstances. Sophie hoped they had managed to minimise her distress as much as possible.

'We're doing great. Thanks to you and your colleague.'

'Roman.'

'Is he here with you?'

'He was…' She'd expected him to have caught up

with her now. Perhaps he had decided to wait until she had gone before visiting Kirstie to avoid any further awkwardness between them. After all, it was only a few hours ago that he had told her he didn't want to be with her any more. She should be glad he was avoiding her—except in emergency labour situations—it might make it easier for her, not seeing him and being reminded of how much she loved him.

It hurt. If she had fallen off that cliff, bounced the whole way down head first into the sea, she didn't think she would be in as much pain as she was now. Working beside him had merely reminded her of all the reasons she did love him. His support and patience getting her down the cliff, the tenderness with which he'd held the baby and the courage which he showed every day in his work. The only thing lacking in her perfect man was love for her. Something kind of important when considering a relationship. Which, clearly, he never had.

'Oh. Maybe I'll see him later. I just wanted to say thanks again to both of you. I dread to think what would have happened if you two hadn't gone out of your way to get to me.' Kirstie hugged her baby a little tighter.

'I'm sure you would have managed. You did so well out there on your own. I hope the circumstances didn't spoil the experience for you.' Sometimes a difficult birth put women off having any more children or made it hard for them to bond with their child. Although Kirstie looked totally smitten with her little girl.

'Not at all. If anything, it's made me believe we can do anything. She's a survivor like me.'

'I'm sure you'll make a great team.' Sophie loved to see parent and child bonding, but it did make her think about Roman holding the baby. Her idea of a perfect family, but one she could never hope to have.

She was about to excuse herself before she made a scene when the baby began to grizzle.

'I think someone's hungry.'

'I was going to go and let you settle anyway, Kirstie. I'll put you on my schedule for a home visit when you're ready. Goodnight.' Sophie stumbled back out into the hallway before the tears of self-pity began to fall.

'Soph?'

It was just her luck having Roman walk up to her in that moment and witness her emotional breakdown after managing to stay so strong all night. Well, most of the night, if she erased the memory of collapsing into his arms after climbing back up the cliff.

'Kirstie's just in there feeding the baby at the minute. I'm going to head home.' She put her head down, hoping he hadn't seen her crying, and hurried past him.

'Wait.' Insisting on prolonging her humiliation, Roman jogged down the corridor after her.

After deeming it too childish to ignore him and keep walking, she let out an exasperated, 'What?'

'We need to talk.'

'What else could there possibly be to say, Roman? You don't want to be with me. Fine. Let's not pretend there's anything more to it than that.'

'Don't be like that, Soph.'

'I'm not being like anything, Roman. We're not together. We never really were. You've made that abundantly clear.' There was no point in stringing this out or continuing to pretend to herself they'd had anything other than a fling. Which was exactly what she had signed up for, so it was entirely her fault she was hurting, but still, she was feeling sorry for herself and was entitled to be a little spiky in lieu of ice cream and chocolate to console herself after their breakup.

'Will you please stop stomping off and talk to me?' Roman grabbed her and dragged her into the nearest empty cubicle.

'You know, they probably need this for a patient. I don't know why—'

'I went to see my parents earlier.'

'How did that go?' Curiosity apparently had overtaken her rage as she waited for him to share the details of the encounter.

'Not so good. My father had a heart attack.'

'Oh, Roman. I'm so sorry.'

'It's okay, he's here in the hospital. I managed to bring him back.'

'I'm sure they were glad to have you there, but I'm sorry you had to go through that.'

'Yeah, well, it put a lot of things into perspective and we're back on speaking terms at least. By the way, they said to say sorry for the way they treated you and…' he took a deep breath '…told me they were proud of me.'

Her eyes must have shown her incredulity that they had expressed any positive emotion towards anyone, but especially him, after the terse conversation she'd had with them.

'I know. I think my father's brush with mortality might have made him think about his life choices. Perhaps my mother realised if she lost him she doesn't have anyone else around her.' He shrugged. 'I don't know what brought it on, but they did seem to be making an effort. Although he's that woozy from the medication I'm not sure he'll remember.'

'Your mother will remind him if it comes to it. I'm glad you finally got some acknowledgement of your accomplishments.' Sophie was happy that something good had come out of this mess after all, but it didn't change anything for her. Even if he did decide to move back permanently and make reparations with his parents, he wouldn't be doing it for her. She hadn't been enough reason for him to stay.

'People make mistakes…say things they don't mean.'

'It doesn't make the words any less painful.'

'No, but an apology and a second chance can make all the difference to both parties.'

'I guess.' She didn't know why he was saying these things to her. It was none of her business what happened between him and his parents, as he'd told her earlier.

'I want to apologise too. For what I said and for not being honest with you. I'm sorry I was too afraid of being a failure in your eyes to think we could have a future.'

'And now? What are you saying, Roman?' None of this made sense to her. Talking about his parents and apologising was all taking time away from drowning her sorrows in calories and alcohol, unless he had something better to offer her.

He made a strangled groaning noise and ran his fingers through his hair, leaving it in soft waves behind his ears. 'You'll have to excuse me. I'm not used to asking anyone to take me back or telling them I love them.'

Sophie's heart pumped a little faster, though she did appear to have stopped breathing. 'You haven't. You didn't ask me to take you back or tell me you love me.

I would have noticed when they're the words I've been waiting to hear from you for a lifetime.'

If he was really going to lay out all of his emotions in this cubicle, she would do the same. Although her revelation might not come as much of a shock as Roman's. Could it really be true? She didn't dare hope, through fear of being the victim of a cruel joke.

Roman took her hands in his and fixed her under his brown-eyed gaze to ensure she wasn't going anywhere. 'I love you. Will you take me back?'

'Not that I want to ruin the moment, but why? Only a few hours ago you were telling me the exact opposite and now I'm supposed to believe this is what you really want? What happened for you to change your mind about staying with me? Apart from a near-death experience on a cliff.' Perhaps Roman was going through the same thing as his father, thinking about his own mortality and deciding he didn't want to be alone. Whilst she wanted Roman to be in her life, she wouldn't accept anything less than real love and commitment this time. Her poor heart couldn't take any more false promises.

'It's not about what happened out there tonight. Well, I suppose it is, in a way. It just reminded me of what an amazing woman you are. I never changed my mind about the rest. I've always loved you and always wanted to be with you, but I was afraid of letting you down. I didn't want to see the same look of disappointment in your eyes that I saw in my parents' every day, when you realised I couldn't live up to your ideals.'

'But I never—'

'You never asked anything of me, I know. But in my heart I felt the weight of expectation to be everything to you your parents hadn't been. I know I've been an idiot, but if you can find it in you to forgive me maybe we could try again?'

'You're making me dizzy with the sudden turnaround, Roman.' It was difficult to accept what he was telling her now as the truth when she was still hurting from his earlier rejection. Even if he was giving her his best puppy impression.

'I always wanted to be with you, but what we've had together has been so good it terrified me. It made me think we couldn't possibly sustain it past Christmas. That I couldn't be the person you need to make you happy. I'm truly sorry for hurting you and I understand if you don't ever want to see me again. All I want is for you to be happy and in my twisted logic it made sense that I left and let you move on.'

Now that Roman had explained his behaviour there was a bud of hope blossoming in Sophie's soul that all wasn't lost after all. Her heart had been broken when she'd thought she would have to face life without Roman again and though things weren't perfect and they had a lot to learn about communicating their emotions, working through their problems was preferable to another separation.

'Haven't you learned anything? It's never better for me when you leave.' She slid her arms around Roman's waist, wanting to hold him close and remind them both of what they had together.

'Nor me. Perhaps it's time I stopped thinking about the worst that could happen, to concentrate on the here and now.' The look of love was there in Roman's eyes as he gazed down at her, in the warmth and strength of his embrace as he held her, and for once he was recognising it. There was only one thing left for him to do if they were going to have a future and that was to make a commitment. Something he had been running from for over ten years.

'Never mind doing what you think is right for others, what is it you want, Roman?'

'You.'

'Right answer,' she said, making them both smile.

'Apparently you meet with my parents' approval too.'

'I'm so glad.' There was more than a hint of sarcasm in her voice.

'It's got me thinking that maybe I could be a good long-term partner for you too, if you would give me the chance? What do you say about getting hitched, Soph?' he asked with a lopsided smile that made her question if he was being totally serious.

'As much as I've longed for this moment to happen some day, I didn't anticipate such a casual proposal.' Sophie was trying, and failing, to control her haywire pulse, unable to believe that this was happening. Afraid to buy into it too quickly, only to crash back down to earth when it turned out not to be her fairy tale ending.

Roman frowned, marking the end of the so-called happy occasion. 'Is that a no?'

'Roman, I don't want you to ask me because you think it's what I want or what your parents want. It has to be something that comes from your heart. I can't risk you changing your mind and abandoning me somewhere down the line. I would rather be on my own than be with you if you didn't love me. I need to know you're serious.'

'I'm completely serious. I've told you I love you. I always have and always will, Sophie. I was ready to make a commitment to you before we even went down that cliff because I missed you so much. And seeing you face your fears so bravely only strengthened my resolve to do the same. None of my decisions were ever about not wanting to be with you but because I was afraid of ruining things between us. Meeting my parents tonight, hearing them say they were proud of me was simply the icing on an already special night. I just wanted to make things official so we can stop questioning if we have a future together. We can wait as long as you like, or we don't have to get engaged now if I need to prove my commitment to you first. I simply need you to know I'm yours for keeps.'

She knew the gesture was so much more than a spur-of-the-moment decision when he was telling her everything she had ever wanted. Roman had never promised her anything more than he was willing to give, and she was aware how significant a lifetime commitment was for him. Now it was her turn to be brave and believe they could finally have a future together instead of hiding away from the world for the rest of her life. It was time for her to start living without fear.

'You don't need to prove anything more to me, Roman. I trust you.'

'In that case, Sophie French, will you do me the honour of becoming my wife?' Roman got down on one knee and, despite the sterile environment around them and the smell of disinfectant, Sophie thought it the most romantic moment of her entire life.

'Yes, Roman Callahan, I will marry you.' Being with him had taught her to take a few risks now and then and she thought this was one worth taking.

Everything they had gone through together had been

leading to this moment, making every second of their separation and her heartache worth it for them to realise how much they needed each other. It was perfect. All of it.

EPILOGUE

Three years later

SOPHIE EASED HERSELF into the front seat of the car and waved to Penelope and Edward until they disappeared back inside their house. ‘Phew, I’m glad that’s over. No offence, Roman, but I can only take your family in small doses. Especially on Christmas Day. I just want to get home to our own place and veg out in front of the TV for a while.’

Roman finished clipping Freddie into his car seat in the back before getting into the driving seat. ‘Me too. Now you know why I preferred being at the cottage with you and your gran when I was younger.’

She understood very well now that she had experience of being in the company of Roman’s family. Deep down, Sophie knew they were good people, but neither she nor Roman were able to fully relax around them. He and his dad always clashed over something, today over letting Freddie open his presents before they went to church. The Callahan family tradition of unwrapping gifts apparently meant he should have waited until after the service. However, Roman had been quick to point out *their* new family tradition was completely different. They weren't going to stifle Freddie's joy on Christmas morning. If they were honest, she was sure she and Roman had been equally excited to see him open his presents under the tree, even if at eighteen months old he wasn't entirely aware of what was going on.

Nonetheless, they were family and they loved Freddie. A mutual feeling when he showered them often with wet kisses and they didn't even complain when he put his sticky hands on their expensive clothes.

'Boys will be boys,' was often the response, which always made Roman roll his eyes. Although he was happy they were making better grandparents than parents, for his son's sake. Sophie was on tenterhooks on their visits, unused to such grandeur and with a toddler let loose in the vast space she was always worried he would cause some catastrophe. Roman, as always, was the one to calm her down and reassure her their son was simply exploring and couldn't be wrapped in cotton wool for ever.

For sure, they were all happiest at home in the cottage. Which, though often messy and chaotic, was full of love.

'Are you sure you don't mind if I go on this hiking holiday without you next week? I can cancel if you would prefer for me to be at home in the New Year?'

'It's fine. As long as you're careful.' She would always worry when Roman went off on his adventures, but she had accepted that his love of life was who he was and she couldn't take that away from him. Besides, he always made it up to her by taking her on a lovely, relaxing holiday in the sun. After their wedding two and a half years ago they had spent a particularly luxurious fortnight in the Bahamas, during which he had persuaded her to do some scuba diving.

'I will be careful. I've got too much to lose.' He lifted her hand and kissed it.

'I'd go with you but you know—' She nodded towards the bump, which was becoming noticeably bigger these days. Even her fingers were getting fatter, and she'd had to take off her wedding and engagement rings, something she hated having to do when they held such sentimental attachment for both of them.

The engagement ring was a family tradition Roman's mother had saved especially for him. The exquisite diamond had been his grandmother's and Penny Callahan had reserved it for her youngest son, in the hope he would eventually come back into the family fold. The significance had not been lost on either of them. Sophie treasured it, along with the wedding ring she had picked out with Roman on a romantic trip to Paris he'd surprised her with to celebrate their engagement. Until her body was hers again, Sophie would have to hold onto the memories alone.

'Maybe next year we'll think about having Christmas dinner at home. You know, start a new Callahan tradition.' It was his excuse for doing things his parents didn't approve of and seemed to be working fine so far. His parents could see what a great father he was and had no reason to criticise him in that area at least.

'I like the sound of that. Especially when we'll have two small children to handle.' She liked the idea of the cottage on Christmas morning, full of toys and chaos and a family happy to be spending time together. Just as she had always imagined it.

* * * * *

MILLS & BOON®

Coming next month

RESISTING THE SINGLE DAD NEXT DOOR
Louisa George

'Carly.'

She turned to face him, her belly dancing with lightness. 'Yes?'

'Thanks again.' He leaned in and pressed a friendly kiss to her cheek.

She closed her eyes as the touch of his skin sent thrills of desire rippling through her. She pulled back, looked at him and caught the heat in his gaze, the need.

She should have turned then and climbed into her truck. She should have driven away into the darkness. But she was transfixed by the way he was looking at her, as if she was...everything.

His previous words about not being distracted seemed to melt from her brain and all she could focus on was his face, his heated eyes, his delicious mouth. So tantalisingly close.

Later, when she thought back to this moment—and she thought back to this moment a lot—she wasn't sure how it had happened. One minute they were looking at each other, the next moment they were kissing. Hot, hard and greedy. Desperate. Frantic. Out of control.

The heat of his mouth made her moan and stoked the burning in her belly. She spiked her fingers into his hair and pressed her lips against his, her body hard against his. The outline of his muscled chest pressed against her and, lower, she could feel just how much he was enjoying this. How much he wanted her.

'God, Carly…' His hands cupped her face and held her in place as he captured her bottom lip in his teeth, then took her mouth fully again and kissed her, kissed her and kissed her.

He tasted of hot chocolate and a warm, delicious spice that she couldn't get enough of. He smelt of the smoky fire. He tasted of coming home and of somewhere new, exotic and enticing. Exciting.

It was too much and not enough all at the same time. She didn't want it to end, this night, this kiss lasting for…

Someone committed to staying around.

His words came back to her in a hard jolt of reality. She had an interested buyer visiting tomorrow. A plan to be gone as soon as feasibly possible. So kissing Owen was an impossible and ridiculous idea and a sure-fire way of ruining the fledgling friendship they'd grown.

What on earth was she doing?

'Sorry. I've got to…' She took two shaky steps away from him, jumped into her car and got the hell away.